SHE BACKED AWAY A FEW STEPS.

"The nickname...silver squire...is it because of how you look?" Emma blurted out chattily.

"How do I look?" Richard echoed with a smile.

"Your blond hair and gray eyes..."
She rattled off her observation so fast and quietly, she hoped he would dismiss it and change the subject, but his amusement increased.

He teased her very gently.
"You've looked at me long enough to notice I have gray eyes. I'm amazed!"

Emma flushed in earnest.
All she'd intended was a little civil dialogue!

D0708697

Mary Brendan was born in north London and lived there for nineteen years before marrying and migrating north into Hertfordshire. Always a keen reader of historical romances, she decided to try her hand at writing a Regency novel during her youngest son's afternoon naps. What began as a lazy lunchtime indulgence soon developed into a highly enjoyable occupation. Presently working part-time in a local library, she dedicates hard-won leisure moments to antique browsing, keeping up with two lively sons and visiting the local Tandoori for a prawn damask and a glass or two of red wine....

THE SILVER SQUIRE
MARY BRENDAN

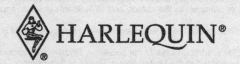

TORONTO • NEW YORK • LONDON
AMSTERDAM • PARIS • SYDNEY • HAMBURG
STOCKHOLM • ATHENS • TOKYO • MILAN • MADRID
PRAGUE • WARSAW • BUDAPEST • AUCKLAND

ISBN 0-373-51166-3

THE SILVER SQUIRE

First North American Publication 2001.

Chapter One

'You little fool! You *will* speak to Mr Dashwood and what's more you'll show gratitude and a little grace in your address when you accept!'

Margaret Worthington's thin fingers locked with surprising strength onto an elbow that was ceaselessly jerking to free itself.

'You are wasting your time, Mama, and that of our...*guest.*'' The epithet was spat through gritted white teeth. 'I will not marry him, nor will I even deign to sit in the same room as that despicable roué.' Emma Worthington picked at her mother's clawed digits. The restraint was soon reapplied and Emma wearily sighed. 'Please let go of my arm.'

'I shall not! If you do not enter the drawing room of your own volition, you will enter from mine, or your papa's...or perhaps even Mr Dashwood's. He demands a biddable wife and one of unimpeachable virtue. Well, the latter condition you honestly meet, the former I own I've embellished upon. He might have to encourage that quality... And I'm sure he will now he's laid down two thousand pounds on your father's account.'

'Two thousand pounds?' The fury and disbelief in Emma's tone rendered her voice little more than an outraged squeak. 'You have allowed that...that vile man to purchase me for two thousand of his disgusting, blood-stained pounds?'

'Don't be so ridiculously melodramatic, Emma,' Margaret Worthington hissed. 'Besides, there should be another sixteen thousand of those disgusting notes to follow, when you are wed, and that should just about set your papa's finances to rights. How can you be so stubborn and selfish? Are you so determined to rip a modest comfort from your doting parents in their twilight years? I tell you, it's not to be borne!'

Taking abrupt advantage of her daughter's momentary daze, Margaret managed to swing open the drawing-room door with one determined hand whilst the other propelled Emma, with an ungentle shove, into the room. Margaret reclined daintily against the mahogany panels; a sturdy, unseen hand was planted at her daughter's back, preventing her retreat. It prodded her forward.

Emma tilted her chin, endeavoured to separate her grinding teeth and walked purposefully towards the gentleman who had gained his expensively shod feet at their ungainly arrival.

Tawny eyes of the most exquisite shade and oval shape met the dark gaze watching her. She politely extended pale, slender fingers to him and bobbed a curtsey. 'I'm so sorry to have kept you waiting, Mr Dashwood. Unfortunately, there appears to have been a misunderstanding between myself and my parents on the matter of your marriage proposal. I can only apologise to you for the confusion and beg you forgive us for detaining you.'

Emma just caught her mother's shocked gasp from behind but she kept her sooty-fringed amber eyes on the gentleman balancing the tapered tips of her ivory fingers on the swarthy blunt pads of his. His dark head angled out of his courteous bow a little and assessing olive eyes arrowed sideways at her.

Something in that low-lidded gaze slew her attention to where they held bodily contact. She curbed a shudder as she noted a few wiry hairs sprouting from sturdy knuckles. Jerkily, her hand recoiled to the folds of her skirt.

Jarrett Dashwood gave a low, unamused chuckle as he straightened into stiff-backed stillness. A piercing glance sliced over the top of Emma's honey-brown head to her mother's stricken countenance. 'I appear to be missing something here, Mrs Worthington,' he began, so smoothly amused, it almost belied the fierce glint in his eyes. 'On meeting with you and your husband earlier this week, I could have sworn you both gave me to believe your daughter was not only agreeable to my offer but ''happy and honoured' was, I recall, the phrase you used…? Perhaps you have another daughter? One who more resembles your description of a shy spinster of advanced years with an amenable nature…ah, yes, and a fondness for reading frivolous romantic fancies penned by Jane Austen.' Barely pausing for breath, he drawled, 'Well, to bastardise that good lady's wise words: it is a truth universally acknowledged that a single man with a good fortune must be in want of a wife: most assuredly so once a little of said fortune has been transferred to his insolvent prospective in-laws.' With the same oiled ease, yet through lips that seemed motionless, came, 'Where is your husband? Fetch him, if you please.'

'My husband is unwell, sir.' The words were faint and breathy. 'I beg you will excuse him this afternoon. I beg, too, you will allow me a few moments alone with my daughter. She, too, I believe must be suffering the same malaise: confusion…muddled thoughts…'

'Your husband's usual complaint, then, Mrs Worthington? Your daughter, on the other hand, seems remarkably sober.' Jarrett Dashwood's silky sarcasm had Margaret squirming and blushing, then his disdainful olive gaze pointedly turned on Emma's dowdy appearance.

Despite her resolution that she would not, Emma also flinched beneath his distaste. She snapped her face up, unwilling to be intimidated, even by a man whose reputation as a black-hearted roué was unsurpassed. Their eyes clashed before his heavy lids drooped lower and an insolent look slid over her thin frame.

Emma bridled, clenching her hands at her sides. Let him check her over. He was sure to shortly be congratulating himself on a lucky escape!

She had never been praised as a beauty, even in her heyday nine years ago. When launched into society at eighteen she had found the superficial friendships and earnest rivalry between debutantes competing for male attention degrading and boring. She had never preened and primped at her appearance as other young ladies did, curling and rougeing and poring over the latest Paris fashions, even when her mother fair frothed at the mouth insisting that she did.

With her unusual fawn hair and eyes, creamy complexion and sculpted elfin features, she was never going to be a 'rage'. There was nothing extreme enough in her looks and colouring. She was only fair to middling in every way, as her mother had dispiritedly pointed out on numerous occasions. If only, her mother sighed, she were a petite, pink-cheeked blonde like Rosalie Travis who had had slavish gentlemen trailing in her wake for some twelve months before she'd settled on a Marquis; or she resembled Jane Sweetman, a tall, porcelain-complexioned redhead, who attracted beaus as bees to acacia. For her own part, Emma praised the raven-haired, grey-eyed perfection of her dearest friend, Victoria Hardinge.

Victoria was now Viscountess Courtenay, married to a man of her choosing, a man she loved, a man who adored her in return. And that was what Emma wanted. She was determined to settle for nothing less. And since the only man she had ever wanted to beguile had been totally impoverished, totally unsuitable and totally obsessed with someone else she had become reconciled to her quiet life in Cheapside, socialising on the fringes of polite society with a few sedate friends of similar tastes and circumstances. And she had believed that her parents had reconciled themselves to allowing her that simple, unassuming existence.

For affection and romance, Emma fantasised of fictional heroes: they were so much more reliable in providing her requisite perfectly happy ending.

Aware of Jarrett Dashwood jerking her a wooden bow, she returned a cursory bob, then he strode past and was speaking in a driven undertone to her mother by the door. Emma spun on her heel to watch. Her stomach tumbled as her mother's heightened colour seeped away, leaving her pasty-faced. The woman gestured in feeble apology, looking close to tears, and Emma's eyes closed in consternation.

She must not be browbeaten! she exhorted herself. She deserved better! Marriage to a man such as this would destroy her. The very idea was galling when she knew she could have attracted a worthier gentleman had she, in her prime, taken pains to court attention and flirt as other debutantes did. She had rebuffed several adequate suitors because she felt incapable of loving them. With arrogant idealism, she had determined to settle for nothing less than absolute bliss.

A few paying court had been pleasant enough and would have shown her kindness and respect. A sharp stab of guilt and regret...and ultimate understanding...pierced her. She now knew why her mother had ceaselessly nagged about security and status and marriage. It had been to protect her only child from a time such as this, when the only thing of value her irresponsible husband had left was his daughter.

Emma's tawny gaze raked over the side of the dark profile presented to her. Oh, Jarrett Dashwood was handsome enough in his way, if rather swarthy of countenance. His black hair was glossy and neatly styled. He was of medium height and a little stocky but his shoulder breadth was derived from muscular strength rather than portliness. His nose was a little sharp and hooked and his mouth too sensually fleshy, but overall he held the appearance of a dignified gentleman in his thirties. No stranger would have guessed that his wealth had come from plantation crops produced with barbaric slaving or that nearer to home he had a reputation as an insatiable lecher whom, gossip had it, beat inept mistresses. Even within the small, staid circle in which she socialised, Dashwood's meanness, his ruthlessness, his wealth were discussed with terrified curiosity and censure.

She had been reared with the consequences of her father's drunken antics, listening to her mother's sibilant stricture as yet another pile of merchants' bills went unpaid. Yet always they had survived. A business deal came good, a wager turned up trumps, a sympathetic friend loaned money at a good rate. Teetering on the brink of disaster, they had always managed to sidestep the abyss and find solid ground again.

To her shame, she realised she, too, had become complacent. When recent arguments between her parents had become exceptionally heated, she had simply retreated to the sanctuary of her room and a book. When meals had become meagre, she'd eaten less. When her maid had been dispensed with last month she had sadly bidden Rosie farewell with a small gift and tended to her own needs. Part of her had known disaster was again threatening but subconsciously she had trusted fate would again make it right.

Two nights ago when her parents had sent for her to join them in the parlour, she'd realised Lady Luck had finally deserted them. Her papa would not meet her eyes. Her mother had fidgeted ceaselessly on the chair-edge, and their unease had chilled her skin. Yet never had she imagined they would sacrifice her so callously in a bid to buy her father's extravagance another reprieve.

A marriage must be made, her mother had firmly decreed,

while her papa had mumbled incoherent assent and blotted at his face with his handkerchief. Nothing Emma had suggested about further economies or a little time to think had made the slightest difference. And now she knew why: the marriage contract was already sealed and money had changed hands.

The sound of the door cracking closed as Jarrett Dashwood left started Emma from her miserable memories.

'Well, miss, you've done your work well!' was hissed shrilly at her. 'Do you know what awaits us all now? Your spurned suitor has just promised your father an indefinite sojourn in the Fleet...and for us an indefinite sojourn in the nearest gutter. We are ruined...finished!'

'Mama, how could you consider turning me over to such an odious individual?' was Emma's broken, soft rejoinder. 'A marriage I would have agreed to. But you must allow me a man of my own choosing: someone I can at least respect, if not love. You know of Dashwood's reputation...assuredly better than I. He is reviled as a slave-master...and a whore-master. Yet you would force me to live my remaining years with him?'

'Some of the noblest, richest families in the land are built out of Jamaica, and have philanderers at their head. Are you to find fault with all of those too?' her mother impatiently snapped. 'You quibble unnecessarily, Emma!'

Margaret's tone honeyed persuasively. 'As his wife you would enjoy a life of pampered luxury. He would treat you well: after all, we all know how greatly he believes he has appearances to keep. Why do you think such a man would settle on purchasing himself a sedate spinster? He wants her virtue and gentility and the assurance she is never likely to humiliate him by shamelessly gadding about. Once you had provided his required heir or two, what more use would he make of *you*? A man so rich has his pick of beautiful courtesans to quench his lust.' A derisive, summarising stare preceded, 'You are fortunate to get any offers when you have so little to recommend you. You're too thin, you're too old—despite the fact you look like a gauche adolescent with your scrubbed complexion and buttoned-up gown. Even your hair has lost its rich hue as you've aged...your eyes too. I swear you're now all tea when once you were chocolate. Your musical accomplishments, I suppose, are adequate...' she allowed on a sniff.

'I hardly think Jarrett Dashwood is to be swayed to stay home by cosy musical evenings about the pianoforte, Mama,' Emma mentioned on a sour laugh.

'How fortunate for you! In his absence, you could nestle into domesticity with a child on your lap and one of those soppy romantic novels in your hand.'

An impatient sigh escaped Emma at the ridiculously whole-some imagery. 'It might not be all so bleak for us, Mama,' she cajoled. 'You are right—Mr Dashwood does covet status and respectability. He will never sue Papa for fraud. Papa is known to be ailing. Dashwood would hate being seen as vindictive enough to dun a sick man without conceding him time to make amends. He will allow us a while to repay him...you'll see.' Warming to her theme, she enthused, 'I can work. I am educated well enough to be a governess...or a companion to a wealthy lady...or a housekeeper...'

'Housekeeper?' her mother choked, outraged. 'You have been gently reared! The success of your twenty-fourth-birthday ball was the talk of the *ton* for months afterwards. Had you deported yourself more...more becomingly to the gentlemen present that evening, you would have been wed these past three years or more and no longer draining us with the expense of your keep.'

As though unable to contain her fury or bitterness, Margaret's lips and eyes narrowed in exasperation. She approached her daughter on wobbly, stiff legs in the manner of a mechanised rickety toy. As she passed a side-table something caught a glaring eye and she grabbed up the leather-bound volume and looked at it with intense loathing. 'All this ridiculous daydreaming you do of love and heroes and happy endings...it is a shameful indul-gence and not to be borne, Emma.' She snorted a sour laugh. 'It is a truth universally acknowledged,' she parodied in a shaking voice, 'that a wilful, selfish daughter of seven and twenty will prove to be a tiresome burden on her parents. Her presence should no longer be tolerated!' The volume of Jane Austen's work was skimmed abruptly towards her, and with chance ac-curacy smacked a hefty blow on a slender shoulder.

With a moan of recalled pain, Emma Worthington pushed her-self upright in bed, her breathing fast and erratic and a pale hand instinctively seeking the tender bruise below her collarbone. Her head drooped forward, thick tan hair coating the sides of her face, as she waited for the pounding of her heart to steady and the vividness of the dream to recede a little.

A hand fumbled out to the unfamiliar table at the side of the alien bed and sought the candle, drawing it close to gain its weak, guttering light. She held it aloft in an unsteady hand. As she shook back tresses from her blanching face, wide, darting eyes surveyed the moon-striped tavern chamber, every gloomy nook scoured for spooks and intruders. But she knew it was nothing other than inner demons that had startled her awake.

The dream had so sharply, so accurately retraced events of two days ago that she might have been back in the drawing room of Rosemary House, facing her mother's spite and Jarrett Dashwood's menacing presence.

She drew her knees up close to her body, her slender arms hugged about them for warmth and comfort and she laid a cold shivering cheek atop them. A bar of silver light bathed her bent head as the moon again escaped scudding cloud. It shifted to incorporate her entwined fingers and she stretched them towards the pearlescence. Replacing the candle on the table, she quit the hard bed and padded softly over cold wood to the small leaded window.

A velvet night sky was visible through a net of shimmering nimbus. Her gaze swept the courtyard below. Immediately she shrank back. Her eyes had, by chance, located a courting couple by an outbuilding, their faces and bodies fused together. Compelled by an uncontrollable fascination, Emma slipped back, seeking again the shadowy outline of a tall man and a woman wedged between his sturdy body and the stable brickwork. She whirled away, her face stinging with hot self-disgust, and scrambled back into bed.

Shifting backwards against the crude wooden headboard, she distractedly picked up her book with one hand and the candle with the other. After a few minutes of mindless reading, she accepted that balancing the thin candle-flame this way and that to try and illuminate the pages was a pointless task. Her eyes were strained from deciphering print which seemed to merge into shapes like entwining lovers. Abruptly, she replaced the book and candle on the table and slowly sank down into the bed with a weary sigh.

Turning on her side, she stared wide-eyed and sightless at the perfect full moon as it emerged from cloud. She thought of Matthew and wistfully smiled as she wondered how he would react to her unexpected arrival; after all, they had seen nothing of each other for two years and she was still awaiting a reply to the last letter she had sent to him some six months ago now.

Perhaps it had been undelivered... 'Please God, don't let him have moved away,' she whispered at the silver orb. Doubt and guilt trembled through her as she thought of her parents in Cheapside. Were they anxious? Furious? Remorseful? She should have left a proper note...not just a few lines that begged them not to worry...or to try and find her.

She twisted restlessly on the soft mattress, frowning at shadows on the ceiling, while thinking of unrequited love and a man who had buried his heart with his first wife and of whether she would ever come to love step-children.

'Not been bit by the bed bugs, I 'opes,' the young man said. 'I seen folks wi' legs swole up an' as red as can be from the nasty blighters...'

'No, I'm quite well, thank you. Just a little tired still.' Emma responded to his query as to whether she had slept well. 'You seem very busy today.' A look through the window indicated the bustling courtyard.

The young potman inclined his dark head to conspiratorially impart, 'Quality wi' a queer name turned up late last night. His nibs be travelling on early wiv 'is family to Bath, so I 'eard. Get you anythin' else from the kitchens?' he offered cheerily, stacking Emma's plate and mug neatly together.

Emma returned him a smiling shake of the head. He swaggered off with a lewd wink for a girl sluicing tankards, and it was then that Emma, with pinking cheeks, recognised the young couple she had seen through her window.

Just as the sun was gilding the horizon, she had given up hope of sleep and made her way downstairs and into a small taproom. The cheerful landlady had served up tea and buttered crumpets, refusing to take payment, while patting at Emma's hand in such a knowing, sympathetic way, Emma had swallowed her protestations and pocketed her coins. She had savoured the delicious crumpets as she viewed unfamiliar sun-dappled countryside through dusty square panes, and pondered the woman's unexpected generosity. Was her unfortunate predicament so obvious? Was there something about her demeanour which branded her an impecunious spinster absconding from mercenary parents and a detested suitor? Or was the landlady simply a kind soul and, having been in the company of very few of those lately, she'd become cynical?

Collecting her carpet bag from beneath the rustic oak table, she made her way out into the fresh September morning to await the arrival of the coach and newly shod horses. She hoped the poor beast that had forced them to overnight at the Fallow Buck would be allowed to rest—one of its front legs had looked badly swollen as though more than just a blacksmith's skills might be needed for it to continue pulling the cumbersome coach.

She was now keen to be travelling on. Even if her mother had at first dismissed her absence at mealtimes as a fit of sulks in her room, she surely would, by now, have found the brief note she had left on her dresser.

She doubted they would search for her. They had neither the resources nor, she imagined, the inclination to send investigators after her. She was, after all, a spinster of twenty-seven, not a child in need of protection. Besides, her mother had declared her presence was no longer to be borne. Far from arousing anxieties, the reverse might be true, and her removal from Rosemary House deemed a relief. How they dealt with the odious Mr Dashwood and his recompense was their own concern. She would not dwell on it...nor feel guilty! The predicament was not of her making!

September morning mist was wreathed about the low brick and wood stables of the Fallow Buck posting house and with quiet appreciation she lingered to watch a spider, stealthy on the edge of its dew-beaded gossamer web.

As she strolled to the perimeter of the dusty gravel courtyard, her wide golden gaze roamed the recently harvested cornfields. Even denuded, they had a spare barren beauty to her unaccustomed town eye. She breathed deeply of the cool morning air, now mingling with a warm aroma of baking bread wafting from the kitchens, feeling unaccountably optimistic and uplifted. Sighing contentedly, she turned from the fresh, sun-dappled vista back towards the tavern.

Her confident step forward faltered, ground into gravel, halting her so abruptly she stumbled. Yet her eyes never relinquished the man. Something in his height, his breadth of shoulder and confident stature was unnervingly familiar, yet, try as she might, in those few, breathless seconds, she couldn't recall why. But whatever association it was produced an odd, terrified exhilaration that knotted her stomach and started her heart hammering.

Her eyes flicked over immaculate dark clothes to a silver-blond head, so unusual a shade that it ought, immediately, to have solved the mystery.

He was a wealthy, influential gentleman; that much was apparent from his attire and bearing. She was watching, analysing him with such rapt attention that she hadn't immediately noticed the child approaching. The boy clung to long, charcoal-grey legs and was immediately swung into his arms. She had sight of his profile now. His cheekbone and jaw were lean and angular and deeply tanned...an exotic contrast with his lengthy white-blond hair. He laughed at the boy in his arms, turning with him towards her...

Emma instinctively dipped her head and tilted her bonnet over her face before swivelling towards the fields she had recently admired.

Don't be so idiotic! she silently berated herself as she tried to steady the frantic pulse leaping in her throat. He was a stranger...probably a foreigner, judging by his sun-bronzed appearance. She immediately recalled the potman telling her of a nobleman with a queer name who had arrived late last night and was travelling with his family to Bath.

He was a French count, she dreamily decided. And the fact he seemed familiar was no doubt due to him resembling some romantic character in a novel she had read. Cocking her head to one side, she crossed her arms about her middle and sifted through plots and people, searching for a tall blond hero of devastating good looks. Possibly he was the villain, she mused, recalling how oddly apprehensive the sight of him had made her feel.

* * *

Long oval fingernails scored deep ridges vertically, horizontally, into bronzed skin and, with an impatient grunt, the man rolled them both sideways plunging hard and fast, at the same time unlocking gripping, silky legs from about his muscular brown thighs.

He ignored her frustrated squeal as she tried to drag his hips back to hers with her calves and make him shed his seed within her. With an easy shove he tipped her away onto her back and within seconds was seating himself on the edge of the tumbled bed. Tanned fingers swept across his shoulder and came away red and sticky. He looked dispassionately at the blood. 'Trim those talons, sweet...' he ordered with very little inflexion, yet the quiet, casual words brought her blonde head up off the pillow and she caught her full lower lip between small teeth.

Yvette Dubois narrowed blue eyes on angry weals tracking skin that looked like cold bronze and felt like warm satin. 'I can't 'elp it, *chéri*,' she purred breathlessly. 'You excite the wildcat in me, you know that. 'Ow can I be thinking and *sensible* at such a time?' She pouted at his broad shoulders, trailed a moist, apologetic kiss across the welts and then, still ignored, she huffed and flung herself back onto the sheets.

He picked up a tumbler, downing the few remaining inches of cognac in a swallow. 'A wildcat with sheathed claws is fine,' he commented drily, collecting his breeches from the floor in a fluid movement as he stood.

'Why won't you give me all of you?' she husked at him, casually lowering the sheet seductively away from her breasts as he finally turned to look at her. She peeked up through dusky lashes into cool silver eyes and knew he understood her perfectly.

'A swollen belly and sagging breasts?' he mused with ironic deliberation. 'I think I prefer you this way, Yvette.' His grey gaze swept down her curvaceous figure to where the sheet just exposed a tantalising rosy nipple.

Aware of his observation, she stretched sinuously, arms raised above her head. Small fingers clenched on the bedhead, making the thrusting perfection of her full, firm breasts impossible to ignore and openly available to him.

A tanned hand came out, fondling first one then the other until she was arching and moaning, her hands clenching rigidly on the brass bedstead. He choked a laugh, stepped into his breeches and was buttoning them by the time he reached the window and stood staring out.

'Richard!' Yvette furiously screeched from the bed. ''Ow can you go now? I want you...'

'Cut your nails...' he mentioned impartially as he drew a cheroot from his pocket, lit it, and stood staring absently into the dusk. He sensed he was irritated and that irritated him further for there was no reason to be.

It was nothing to do with Yvette Dubois or her savage passion or her transparently mercenary desire to make him impregnate her so she'd have a lasting role in his life. She was wasting her time on all counts: he had no desire for an enduring liaison or for children. He slanted a glance at her, a quirk of a smile softening his finely chiselled narrow mouth as he noticed how she immediately perked up with his attention.

A long blonde ringlet was slowly worked about a small finger and she rolled onto her back, impatiently kicking away the tangling sheet from her shapely long legs so the dark blonde curls between her thighs were displayed.

She was very good, very adept: the pulse in his loins was picking up tempo already, just as she was calculating it would. He drew deeply on the cheroot and reached for his shirt on the chair. If he hadn't promised to return to Silverdale in time for supper with his visiting relations, he probably would have stayed longer and let her earn her keep.

The irritation niggling at him intensified with that callous thought and he raked five brown fingers absently through his thick white-blond hair, unwilling to actually acknowledge that something so insignificant...so idiotic could disturb him so.

His mind returned to the Fallow Buck posting house and the image of a dowdily dressed woman standing with her back to him. There was nothing about her that could have possibly interested him. On first glance he would have guessed her to be perhaps a high-ranking servant—a governess or housekeeper travelling alone on business. What irked him was the unshakeable notion that, despite seeing nothing of her apart from an unattractive bonnet and dismal brown travelling cloak, he felt he knew her.

He was certain she had concealed her face just as he'd turned towards her, and that compounded the mystery. He'd been curious enough at the time to start walking towards her but had managed only a pace or two when his brother had distracted him to settle the landlord's bill. On returning to the courtyard, the Bath post was just pulling out into the road and he'd just known the woman was on it. He'd shrugged and walked away and forgotten it...for all of a few hours. Now, for some insane reason, not having crossed to the fields to look at her was a major aggravation and the sheer farce of it was killing him.

'I don't want you to go yet. You leave me too much...too soon. It's not fair...' was called softly from behind, breaking into his reverie.

Even white teeth clenched on the cheroot and he drew on it steadily, but he turned towards her with a smile. 'So what do you intend to do about that?'

Yvette swung long legs off the bed and posed with deliberate provocation on the edge. Her throat curved archly, her blonde head tilted as she viewed him between barely parted porcelain lids. Pushing herself slowly upright, she undulated towards him, each sinuous step swaying her pouting breasts. 'I think I shall make you change your mind about leaving...about a lot of things...' she purred as she came right up against him and grazed her naked belly against the hard proof of his full attention. A long fingernail trailed up his thigh, scoring into fine cloth as it neared his groin.

He caught at her hand inches from its target, brought her palm to his lips and dropped a brief kiss on it. Turning her away, he gave her a gentle push towards the bed. 'I have to go...'

'Business...business...all the time business,' she flung at him, whirling back in a cloud of shining blonde hair. 'I am sick with this business all of the while,' she complained, her accent thickening in her rage. 'I am alone too much. I need some company...I need you...'

'You can't have me, Yvette. Understand that,' he said with slow deliberation so that she digested all his meaning, then endorsed it with a smile that didn't warm his metallic eyes. 'If you're lonely, get yourself a companion,' he added carelessly as he moved past her and towards the door.

'*What...?*' she screeched. 'How shall I? A friend just drops from the sky?'

'Advertise in the *Herald*...' he suggested with an infuriating smile as he closed the door behind him.

Chapter Two

With a deep, inspiriting breath, Emma took another determined peek around the hazel hedge.

The dilapidated exterior of weatherbeaten boarding and slipping roof tiles had her optimism again ebbing. The cottage looked deserted. Perhaps he *had* moved away. Please no, don't let that be! she silently prayed. The London post was already lost to view as the road dipped below the shadow-racing field, and would be well on the way to Bath, some two miles further on.

She had been dropped in the village of Oakdene and had wandered the narrow, rut-scored lanes looking for Nonsuch Cottage with many a villager's curious stare following her. A bramble embedding in her skirt had quite literally brought her stumbling upon what she sought: it was an aptly named little place, she smilingly realised as her honey gaze weaved past the crude wooden name-plate on the gate, through foxgloves and scarlet roses entwined with bellbind and cow parsley, and on to the crooked door.

Gently reared behind the graceful brick façade of Rosemary House in Cheapside, she had hardly realised that such ramshackle-looking dwellings existed, let alone expected ever to enter one. As for gardening, nurturing delicate hothouse blooms had been her only experience of the demands of horticulture. The association of a conservatory and exotic plants and happier days with friends evoked a flash of memory, puzzling and niggling at the periphery of her consciousness. She gave it barely a further moment's concentration before again focussing on the grimy whitewash of the cottage.

On closer inspection it seemed structurally sound. In fact, she decided, it held a definite rustic charm. The interior of the building might be quite neat and tidy; one couldn't expect a widowed gentleman of straitened means to bother about weeds when he had to attend to the needs of his small children. Curtains were visible at dusty windows high under the eaves, she gladly noted, yet it was so quiet it could have been deserted.

As though to settle that anxiety a female voice shrieked out something unintelligible; there followed a child's thin wailing. So the property was inhabited, and by a Billingsgate fishwife by the sound of it! A sudden awful suspicion stopped her heart, and she wondered why it had never occurred to her earlier: had Matthew not replied to her letter of six months ago because he had remarried? Before she could torture herself further on the subject, the white-boarded cottage door was flung open. A small mongrel dog hurtled, whining, close to Emma's skirts then scampered out into the lane.

'Blasted cur!' the young woman barked, and was about to slam the door shut when she noticed Emma. Slack-mouthed surprise was soon replaced by a stony expression. 'Whatever you be sellin', we don't want none. Be off with you. We've got Bibles aplenty 'n sermons 'n pills 'n potions...'

Emma wasn't sure whether to laugh or display outrage that this young woman's first impression of her was as some sort of pedlar! Was her appearance really so drab that she was deemed to be touting from door to door? Her own impression now of this young woman was that she wasn't Matthew's wife but his housekeeper, a judgement backed by her rough local dialect and faded black uniform.

Aware of the woman still staring aggressively, Emma finally detached herself from the bramble with a tear to her skirt, a prick to her finger and a spattering of mauve berry juice to her palm. Drawing herself up to her full height, her slender shoulders back, and topaz eyes glass-cool, she haughtily informed the woman, 'I have just alighted from the London stage and would like to speak to Mr Cavendish. Is he at home?'

Emma's unexpectedly refined accent had the woman's jaw

dropping again and a keen-eyed scrutiny slipping over her from serviceable tan bonnet to dusty, sturdy shoes.

'Close that blasted door, will you, Maisie? The draught is taking these papers all over the desk...' was bellowed from within.

'Matthew...' Emma whispered to herself at the sound of that well-modulated, if deeply irritated tone. But the relief she was sure would drench her at the first sight or sound of him was slow in coming. 'I should like to speak to Mr Cavendish,' she repeated firmly, with a nod at the door.

'Wait there,' the woman snapped discourteously, dark eyes skimming over Emma's modest attire, then the door was shut in her face. Within what seemed a mere second a tall man was stepping over the threshhold onto the grass-sprouting cobbled pathway. A hand was wiped about his bristly chin and across his eyes as though he was fatigued.

'Emma...?' Matthew Cavendish murmured disbelievingly as his fingers pushed a tangle of brown hair back from his brow for a better view of her. A white grin split his shady jaw and, with a cursory straightening of his shirt-cuffs and waistcoat, he was rushing towards her.

'Emma! How wonderful to see you!' He gripped her by the shoulders and warm hazel eyes smiled down into her upturned, uncertain face. 'Why didn't you send word you were coming? Oh, I'm so sorry...come inside...please. What an oaf you must think me, leaving you planted amongst the weeds! As you can see,' he added ruefully, gesturing at snaggled greenery, 'tending the roses isn't a fond pastime.' After drawing one of her arms through his they proceeded out of breezy late summer sunlight into the cool, dim interior of the cottage.

'Maisie will fetch some tea,' he directed at the woman while helping Emma to slip out of her cumbersome cloak.

Emma's eyes flicked to the small brunette and noted an odd insubordinate stare arrow from servant to master. Then, with a twitch of her faded black serge, Maisie was gone.

After a brief pause during which only polite smiles passed between them, there was,

'I must apologise...'

'I should explain...'

They had spoken together and simultaneously laughed, embarrassed, too.

'You first,' Matthew invited, ushering Emma towards a comfortable-looking chintz-covered fireside chair and pressing her into it. As he leaned towards her and gripped her hands, displaying his pleasure at seeing her, a recognisable sweetish aroma assailed her nostrils. She had too often been about her intoxicated papa not to instantly recognise the smell of strong alcohol about someone's person. There was a hint of red rimming his eyes too, she noted, with a hesitant smile up into Matthew's undoubtedly hung-over face.

'I was about to say, Matthew, I must apologise for visiting you without proper warning. But I had no time to write, or wait for your reply.' She gave him a wry look. 'After all, it has been six months since last I wrote and still, daily, I expect your letter...'

Throughout the uncomfortably sultry atmosphere in the coach jolting its way to this village, all that had dominated her mind was Matthew: how she longed to unburden herself to him, beg him to reinstate his marriage proposal of five years ago. Now, oddly, the desperation had evaporated. What remained was simple relief that she had distanced herself from Jarrett Dashwood.

'You must rest awhile after your journey, then dine with us,' Matthew said with an emphatic squeeze at her small hands within his.

Emma smiled her thanks; she was hungry; she was also grateful that Matthew was exercising tactful restraint. He had obviously sensed she needed a little time to compose herself before revealing the catastrophe that had forced her to break all codes of etiquette and arrive uninvited and unchaperoned at the home of an unwed man. Acknowledging that impropriety brought another to her attention: remaining with Matthew overnight as his guest, even if he had a female servant and children, was completely out of the question. She would need to find lodgings.

Emma glided small, unobtrusive glances at him as she looked about the untidy small parlour. Oh, he still appealed to her. He hadn't aged. But his unruly hair was tangled, his skin tone unhealthy and his attire dishevelled.

'I'll apologise for my appearance.' He shrewdly anticipated the reason for her eyes lingering on his unshaven jaw. A sheepish smile preceded, 'I attended a debate at the village hall last night. It was after midnight when I found my bed.' He made a determined effort to neaten his hair and clothes with slightly vibrating hands.

'Was it a literary debate?' Emma asked quite interestedly.

'Er...no,' Matthew laughed. 'Nothing quite so highbrow, I'm afraid, my blue-stocking Emma. It concerned the siting of a new water pump in the village and how division of the cost is to be made between tenants. Of course, once universal agreement was reached, we had to drink to it...'

'Of course,' Emma smiled, pleased and relieved that such an amusingly improbable incident was responsible for his hangover. 'And as the pump is not yet operative you were forced to settle for whisky rather than water.'

Matthew laughed. 'That's my Emma,' he said, with a gentle touch at her face. 'Actually, the toast was with ill-gotten geneva,' he revealed, sliding a finger to cover her lips.

Emma sensed her heartbeat quickening as their eyes held. She smiled against the light caress, then asked quickly, 'And how are your children? I believe I've already had a quick brush with your little dog.'

'Ah, Trixie...' Matthew muttered with a laugh. 'I heard Maisie chiding Rachel for allowing the dog back onto her bed. She's a rapscallion...'

'Your dog, your daughter, or your servant?' Emma asked with a laugh.

'All three at times...but thankfully not usually together,' he answered, with a rueful shake of the head.

Their tea arrived and Maisie poured and distributed it all the while sending brooding glances at them both. Reproof, almost warning was apparent in Matthew's glassy hazel eyes as he and Maisie exchanged a look before she quit the parlour.

'My apologies for Maisie keeping you on the path,' Matthew smoothly said. 'She is a little wary of strangers. But she's a good girl...'

Emma's tawny head turned, alert to a muffled noise...a snort of humour or anger from the hallway. Matthew gave no sign he'd heard yet, passing idly by the door, he pressed it firmly shut.

'Well, Emma,' Matthew said with a distracting smile. 'Drink up your tea for there are things to be taken care of: the children above stairs, the dinner, but most importantly, you...'

* * *

'Well, do you think Rachel and Toby much grown?'

'Indeed. I should never have recognised either of them,' Emma truthfully admitted. Then, finding nothing positive to add, fell silent again. She gathered her cloak about her as the breeze stiffened and turned her head to gaze out over darkening hedgerows and fields.

The dogcart shuddered and swayed over potholes as they travelled on towards Bath, and her evening's lodgings. Matthew had not quibbled when, over dinner, she'd informed him that she must seek a place to stay. He had simply asked, quite gravely, whether she had the means to pay for her board. Learning that she did had seemed to relieve him.

Mrs Keene's rooms in Lower Place, on the outskirts of Bath, were the most fitting place for a gentlewoman to overnight, he had then decisively informed her. But now, as they journeyed on in amicable quiet, she knew Matthew was hoping for some complimentary comment about Rachel and Toby. Yet, on meeting the children again today, Emma had been surprised and disappointed.

Rachel was now nine years old and Toby seven and they no longer bore any resemblance to the bonny children she recalled meeting two years ago.

One mild autumn afternoon the Cavendish family had joined her in Hyde Park for a last stroll together before they quit London for Bath. She and Matthew had exchanged good wishes, reluctant farewells and promises to write, while two fair-haired children, neatly dressed in navy blue clothes, had refused to scrunch through the glorious red-gold carpet underfoot as others were, and stood quiet and solemn. On cue, they had politely shaken her hand before their father led them away.

Today, she had uneasily watched Matthew half-heartedly chiding two grubby-faced urchins for failing to wash or neaten their attire before they sat down to dine with their guest. Reluctantly, almost surlily, they had stamped away to be returned by Maisie some few minutes later in a slightly improved state.

Emma had freshened herself for dinner in a small upstairs chamber, thanking Maisie for the washing water and cloth and receiving little more than a terse grunt for her courtesy.

The meal, prepared by Matthew's cook—an elderly widow who lived but a few yards along the lane, he had conversationally told her as they ate—had been plentiful and delicious. Roast mutton and veal and a boiled chicken had joined dishes of steaming vegetables and sweet blackcurrant tarts on the dining table. Wine had been set out and although Matthew had poured a glass for both Emma and himself, his own goblet had remained virtually untouched—something Emma had found inordinately reassuring.

Despite Emma's attempts to talk to the children they'd seemed reluctant to cease chewing for the few moments a response would take. On asking about their lessons, Rachel had informed her with a grimace that Miss Peters at the Vicarage tutored them. As for a friendly enquiry on special aptitudes, neither had given the matter much thought before admitting to knowing of none.

Their fond father had then deemed them too modest and defended their ignorance with recalled good marks in English or arithmetic. But with lowered heads they'd simply set enthusiastically about their meals with an air of concentration that precluded further questions or table manners.

The elderly dun mare pulling Matthew's dogcart stumbled into a rut, throwing them together. Matthew steadied Emma with a sturdy hand, then raised her slender fingers, touching his lips briefly to them. 'It's so good to see you,' he said softly.

It was his tactful way of saying that an explanation for her presence was long overdue, she realised. 'I have quit London to avoid being married to a detestable man,' she informed him simply, gazing over a flat, dusky vista. Instinctively her fingers tightened about his, at the oblique reference to Jarrett Dashwood, as though drawing from his strength.

'I guessed it to be something like that,' Matthew said softly, reining back so that the mare slowed its steady trot.

Emma looked at her fragile hand resting in his large fingers. 'My parents have arranged for me to wed someone in the hope he will set to right my father's debts. The man is a notorious blackguard.' Her voice shook with strengthening outrage. 'I had never believed they would act so brutally. The matter was concluded before I had even a hint of it. I will have none of their plots. They have treated me shabbily…abominably…'

'They must be in grave trouble to do so, Emma, I'm sure.' His thumb smoothed gently at her wrist. 'I'm very happy and flattered that you felt you could turn to me for support.' His voice became husky. 'Does this mean that you would now reconsider *my* offer of marriage?'

The air between them seemed to solidify. It was what she wanted, wasn't it? She had fled Rosemary House late at night instinctively to seek him and these were the words she had prayed he would utter. She heard herself say, 'I need time to think, Matthew. I'm confused...plagued by ambivalence. I feel guilty for abandoning my parents, yet, at times, I'm sure I despise them almost as much as Jarrett Dashwood.' Even with the lowering dusk, Emma could discern Matthew's abrupt pallor. The cart jolted as he reflexively tightened his grip on the reins and the mare pranced.

'*Dashwood? Dashwood* wants to marry you?'

The disbelief was plain and made Emma smile a trifle wryly. 'He has expressed a desire for a sedate, mature spinster to wed. She must be biddable and, I've no doubt, so grateful to attain the marital state, she will not challenge him about any of his disgusting goings-on. I imagine he has no more use for her than as a brood mare.'

Matthew gave her an ironic, sideways smile. 'Biddable? *You*, Emma?'

'Exactly,' Emma agreed, matching his rueful tone. 'My mother has a persuasive way with my attributes when she scents a bachelor...whatever his character.' She sobered and gazed into the distance. 'Thank you for your proposal, Matthew. I will give it very serious thought in the next few days. And thank you for your kind hospitality and for bringing me to my lodgings tonight. I was so relieved on finding you still resided at Nonsuch Cottage and were not now...remarried.' An amber glance arrowed at his profile. 'I know you were keen for your children to have a mother's care and as I had not heard from you for so long...'

'I'm sorry not to have replied to your letter. I seem to find so little free time. A pathetic excuse, I know,' he admitted on a shake of the head. 'And there has never been anyone else that I've met who would suit the children so well as you. You're so kind and dependable. You're a genteel lady and educated to such a degree you could tutor them yourself,' he enthused.

'And what of you? Do I suit you so very well?' Emma asked softly, sadly.

'But of course! That goes without saying, Emma.'

* * *

'This is a respectable house and we keep reg'lar hours. No gentlemen allowed in the parlour after nine o' the clock. No gentlemen allowed in the upper chambers at any time. Breakfast afore eight or none. Dinner in the parlour if you wants at a shillin' for a plate o' hot ordinary.'

'Yes, I understand,' Emma told Mrs Keene wearily as she glanced about the spartan room. But at least it looked clean and the bedlinen fresh.

'So wot's a nice young lady like yourself doin' alone in Bath?' the woman asked with friendly inquisitiveness, now she had laid down the rules of the house. 'Kin in the area, have you, wot won't board you?' The plump woman shelved her crossed arms on her ample bosom. A knowing nod preceded, 'I gets plenty o' such spinsters. Poor relations an' all they'll get off them wot's better sitchwated is mutton 'n porter once or twice a week an' a faded gown or two. Not that it's none of my concern, 'o course, or I'm complainin', like...for it suits me...' She wagged an emphasising finger.

'I'm seeking employment. I have no local family. Just a friend.' What had she said? Seeking employment? Why had she said that? Why not? echoed back. The logical answer to every pressing problem had helpfully presented itself. She had very little cash; she needed some time to think while she mulled over Matthew's proposal and meanwhile she needed somewhere to stay. There was little doubt in her mind that Mrs Keene would show her the cobbles as soon as she showed Mrs Keene an I O U.

Her landlady sucked at her few yellowing teeth. 'Seekin' employment, are you, miss? Well, not that it's none of my concern, o' course, but I'll keep me eyes and ears open for you. I'm known to run a respectable lodgin's for genteel ladies wot's on 'ard times, and it's not unknown for those as wants to take on to come to me first for their quality staff. No agency fees, you see. 'Course I accepts a small consideration—'

'Thank you...I should be grateful for help...' Emma cut the woman off. Undoing the ribbons of her bonnet, she dropped the dusty tan-coloured article onto the bed. She shook free her thick fawn hair, raking it back from her creamy brow, aware of the woman's gimlet eyes on her. Opening her carpet bag, she studiedly hinted, 'I'm a little tired...'

'O' course you are, miss. Will you be wantin' any supper?'

'No, thank you. I've already dined.'

'Tomorrow will you be wantin' any supper?'

'Yes, thank you.'

'Seven o' the clock in the downstairs parlour. Tomorrow's bacon 'n carrots. That'll be a shillin' an' you pay afore you eat.' With a gap-toothed smile at Emma, Mrs Keene was closing the door.

'You're late!'

'I'm here, aren't I?'

'Richard, you are becoming quite a trial to your mother,' Miriam Du Quesne stiffly informed her eldest son.

He seemed unmoved by her complaint and gave her an impenitent smile as he made for the stairs and took them two at a time.

'Come back! We have guests!' was hissed in a furious undertone at his broad, dark-jacketed back.

'And you're a wonderful hostess, my dear,' trailed back, bored, over his shoulder as he neared the top of the graceful sweep of mahogany bannisters.

'If you're not down these stairs and in the drawing room in ten...fifteen minutes,' she generously amended, in an enraged choke, 'well, I shall...I shall just...'

Sir Richard Du Quesne sauntered back to the top of the curving stairwell and looked past the priceless Austrian crystal chandelier, suspended low, at the top of his mother's elegant coiffure. 'You shall what?' he jibed fondly. 'Beat me? Shut me in my room? Make me go without my supper?'

'Richard! This is no joke!' his mother screeched, small fists scrunching her elegant lavender skirts in her rage. Aware that she was creasing the satin, she flung it away and tried desperately to smooth it. She resorted to stamping a small foot instead, while almost jigging on the creamy marble in exasperation. Abruptly changing tack, she stilled, gave him a bright smile and wheedled, 'Please, dear, don't keep us all waiting longer. Dinner has been on the warm since eight o'clock. It is now nine-thirty and we are all quite ravenous.' A tinkly laugh preceded, 'I'm quite wore out with finding conversation to amuse us all. Besides,' gritted out through pearly teeth, 'nothing much is audible over the growling of empty stomachs.'

Her son gave her a conciliatory smile. 'I'll be but a few minutes. I'll just freshen up...'

'Oh, you look well enough,' she said irritably, gesturing him down the stairs. He did too, she realised as her blue eyes lingered on her tall, handsome son's appearance. His sun-streaked blond hair was too long, but suited him that way, she grudgingly allowed. His charcoal-grey clothes were expensive and well-styled; nothing she said or slipped to his valet seemed to make him dress in brighter colours. The bronzed skin tone he had acquired abroad had at first horrified her but, she had to admit, gave him a wickedly foreign air, and those cool grey eyes... A delicious shiver raced through her for they so reminded her of her darling John.

Miriam focussed her far-away gaze back on the top of the stairs to note that, while daydreaming of her late husband, their son had disappeared. She pouted, flounced about and stalked back towards the drawing room with the welcome tidings for their graces the Duke and Duchess of Winstanley and their daughter, Lady Penelope, that dinner was now, indeed, very nearly served.

'I know where you've been, you lucky, randy dog.'

Richard dried his face with the towel, lobbed it carelessly towards the grand four-poster on a raised dais and glanced at Stephen. 'Where have I been?' he asked as he fastened his diamond shirt studs and walked to the mirror to inspect his appearance.

'Come on, this is your dribbling sibling you're talking to. She must have a *jolie amie* for your best brother. Preferably blonde but I ain't fussy.'

'You're married.'

'I'm bored.'

Richard's icy grey eyes swerved to the reflection of his younger brother's shrewd, smiling face. 'You're married. You've got a lovely wife and two beautiful children. What more do you want, for God's sake?'

Stephen Du Quesne shrugged himself irritably to the window and gazed into the dusk. The fluttering silver-leaved whitebeams that lined the mile-long drive to Silverdale swayed like sinuous, ghostly dancers in the light evening breeze. 'A little excitement...that's what I want. A little of what you've got...that's what I want. You get risqué women and I get responsibility. It ain't fair, I tell you. You're seven years older than me.'

'No one forced you to propose to Amelia when you were twenty-one. As I recall you wanted her and nothing was going to stand in your way. Not even her constant rebuffs. You finally won her over and the proof that you were lucky to get it so right is just along the corridor, asleep in the nursery. Grow up.'

'That's rich coming from you,' Stephen moaned as he stalked his elder brother to the head of the stairs. 'You're thirty-three and still gadding around as though you've dropped a decade somewhere. Even that reprobate of a best friend of yours has been wed these past three years and is now as dangerous as a pussy-cat by all accounts.'

Richard turned a smile on him, knowing immediately to whom he referred. 'That's love for you, Stephen,' he said. 'It can creep up on you when you're least expecting it...even when you're twenty-one and nowhere near ready. There's no shame in giving in to it.'

'Such an eloquent expert on finer feelings, aren't you?' Stephen ribbed him with a grin. 'Hard to believe most of your intercourse with the fairer sex is so basic and carried out while you're horizontal.'

'Shut up, Stephen, you are drooling,' Richard said, with a clap on the back for his sulking brother.

As they hit the marble-flagged hallway, Richard swung his brother about by the shoulder and studied him gravely. 'Look, if you're desperate for a little illicit entertainment, go ahead. But don't expect me to arrange it for you, or clear up the mess when it all goes horribly wrong. Amelia might just decide that what's sauce for the gander...' He trailed off with an explicit raising of dark brows.

'She wouldn't dare!' Stephen exploded, his face draining of colour. 'Besides,' he blustered as his older brother choked a laugh at the terror on his face, 'she'd never know...I'd be discreet.'

'Of course she'd know, you fool,' Richard scoffed. 'There'd be plenty of concerned ladies just itching to break the news. For her own good, of course. If you want a mistress, go and stand in the Upper Assembly rooms and look available. In five minutes you'll be knee-deep in frustrated wives, impoverished widows...' His long fingers tightened emphatically on his brother's shoulder. 'You're both envied, you know. You've a good marriage: you love your wife and she adores you and that's not easily found. It makes for a lot of green eyes and spiteful intentions. If you want to know the truth, *I* envy you.'

'Good,' Stephen said with slightly malicious relish. 'I think our dear mama is under the impression it's definitely time you were jealous no more.'

Sir Richard Du Quesne stopped dead and spun on his heel. 'God, she's not matchmaking again! Who's here? Not the Petershams?'

Stephen swayed his fair head, blue eyes alight with merriment. 'But of course not. We're aiming so much higher, dear one, now you're so much richer. Now you've added another million to the Du Quesne coffers, dear Mama scents a ducal connection...and as they were visiting in the neighbourhood...'

Stephen's drawling teasing came to an abrupt halt and the laughter in his eyes was replaced by horrified entreaty. For no more than a second he watched his brother striding towards the double oaken doorway, an exceedingly loud and awful curse flying in his wake.

Scooting after him, Stephen grabbed at his elbow and started dragging him backwards. 'If you disappear, so do I. I'll go and stand in the Upper Assembly rooms; you see if I don't. Mother will kill me if I let you escape!'

'*I* will kill you if you do not let go of my arm,' his brother sweetly informed him.

Stephen removed his hand and made a show of straightening the crumpled charcoal material of Richard's sleeve. 'Come on, Dickie,' he wheedled. 'Just smile and make them swoon a little.' Richard's grim countenance was unaltered. 'Well, just tell them about your money; that'll make them swoon a little.'

Richard tried to suppress a smile. He gazed at the rust watered-silk wall then back at his brother's anxious face. 'If I wasn't so damned hungry, I'd be out of here.' A tanned hand settled amicably on Stephen's shoulder as they turned towards the dining room. 'I suppose I should suck up a bit to his grace: I want the old bastard to grant me a lease on the land just east of the Tamar. There's a fortune in that clay-slate; I'll stake my life on it.'

'Better suck up to his daughter, then. You know the way to a fond father's heart is through his darling spinster offspring. And she is sweet on you, you know. You also know the old goat's concerned for his pheasants and won't let you disturb them with your noisy mining.'

'There's a fortune in copper there and I will have it some day. But don't tell Ross,' Richard laughed. 'He's convinced it's on the Cornish side in granite. Fool! Sometimes he lets his Celtic pride get in the way of his common sense.'

'Rival adventurers!' Stephen proclaimed. 'You'll bring him in on the deal, in any case. Me too, I hope! I've a growing family to support.'

'Make sure it's just the one legitimate family to support,' Richard told his brother, 'and perhaps I'll do that.'

Richard scowled at the ceiling. It was time he thought of marrying and producing an heir. A duke's daughter was soft on him. She was attractive enough to bed. The fact that she irritated the hell out of him with her vanity and her vacuous giggling was of little consequence: once she was breeding they need have little to do with one another other than on formal family occasions. Apart from exercising a little more subtlety, his licentious lifestyle need not alter. If Penelope found herself a beau it would not unduly worry him so long as she was reciprocally discreet. He could afford to be generous: her father was sitting, he was sure, on one of the richest copper lodes ever. And he was determined to mine the area.

The two brothers exchanged a rueful grimace before fixing smiles and entering the dining room. Richard's grin sugared for his mother as he saw her glower at him. Then he looked at the brunette, her face coyly concealed behind a fluttering fan. Brown eyes peeked at him over the top of ivory sticks. His teeth met but he bowed gallantly.

Damn you, David! he inwardly groaned as he thought of his best friend and his wedded bliss. He'd set a vexing precedent by marrying for love and being so nauseatingly happy and faithful. And he and David were too close...too alike...always had been since childhood.

Richard knew that aching void deep within David that only

Victoria could fill sometimes yawned wide in him too. And the restlessness, the emptiness just wouldn't go away no matter how hard it was ignored or crammed full of commerce or self-indulgent lust.

Think of the copper...and beating Ross to it, he encouraged himself as he proceeded into the room, with a wry, private smile. He pulled a chair close and sat beside his grace the Duke of Winstanley. 'How are the pheasants?' he asked gravely.

Chapter Three

'What is for dinner today, Mrs Keene? Not bacon and carrots again, surely?' Emma frowned and sniffed delicately at the wafting salty aroma.

'Not at all, my dear.' Her landlady shuffled into her room, apparently unruffled by this aspersion on her unvarying menus.

Emma's tawny eyes brightened and she let her novel drop. She had been perched on the window seat for the past hour, hoping that perhaps Matthew might call again today to take her for a walk or a drive into the countryside. But it was nearly six o'clock and unlikely he would come now.

'What *is* for dinner, then, Mrs Keene?' Emma asked, her mouth watering in anticipation of some tempting mutton later.

'Er...it's hashed pork, my dearie. With a little herb and stock 'n so on.'

'Is it cured pork, Mrs Keene?' Emma asked on a sigh.

'I believe it is at that, Miss Worthington,' Mrs Keene admitted with a jovial smile. 'Now, I've got some good news. An' I expect, 'cos it is such a piece o' luck for you that a busy soul like meself's managed to put herself out on account of a nice young lady, that you'll be insistin' on showing me a small consideration for me pains. Now, not that it's none o' my concern, o' course, but I know for a fact you've been scourin' that *Gazette* for a position as would suit. Well, now—' chubby hands were planted on fat hips '—what did I hear today from a friend wot's been

speakin' to a lady's maid?' She inclined forward from the waist
and beady eyes rolled between fleshy folds.

After a silent moment when Emma realised either she guessed,
enquired, or never learned, she obligingly said, 'I've no idea,
Mrs Keene. What did you hear?'

With a flourish, a scrap of paper materialised from a greasy
pocket. 'My dear young lady, the good news is that a gentlewoman in Bath is seekin' a genteel and modest companion. She
is a pampered lady and bored...' Mrs Keene acted the part,
shielding a yawn with a fat hand then simpering behind it. 'Soon
as I heard I put meself out to speak to me friend and sing your
very praises. She in turn spoke to the maid who had words with
her *madame*. The lady has sent you this little note with her address. Now, what do you say to that good luck and good friends
like meself?'

Emma's small white teeth caught at her full lower lip. What
did she say to that, indeed? She had been at Mrs Keene's lodging
house for a few days and had certainly been curiously flicking
through the *Gazette* for local positions.

But it had been a half-hearted investigation: she had little idea
where to start, or if indeed she wanted to start at all. She *had*
been gently reared and nothing in that refinement had prepared
her for at some time toiling for a living. She balked at the idea
of being an assistant to a mantua-maker or a haberdasher and she
had seen little else advertised.

Stung by her boarder's lack of effusive thanks and enthusiasm,
Mrs Keene huffed, 'Well, if it don't interest, I'll give this appointment to the new lady as arrived yesterday. She's fair desperate for a position and workin' for a foreign *madame* in quite
the best part of Bath will probably seem like heaven dropped in
her lap.'

'It's very good of you to remember me, Mrs Keene. I am very
grateful.' Emma gave the woman a conciliatory smile as she held
out a slender hand for the note. Interview details were written in
an elaborate script. 'I *shall* attend and if it seems the position
will not suit I can try elsewhere...'

'O' course...but I reckon it will suit, an' I reckon you'll always
remember wot good friend managed to winkle it out for you.'
Mrs Keene nodded good-naturedly at the subdued young woman
smiling vaguely back at her. Sharp eyes dissected her waif-like

appearance: a slender body that looked too delicate to tempt a man but such rich caramel hair and liquid honey eyes set in a complexion that was pure peaches and cream. Not that it was none of her concern, o' course, but it was puzzling for a body to decide if she was a raving beauty or plain as a pike-staff. Pike-staff, she plumped for; the pretty foreign *madame* wouldn't like a rival.

'Do you know what you're doing, Emma?' Matthew demanded shortly.

'No,' Emma admitted with a nervous smile as she straightened her bonnet and pulled on her gloves.

Matthew had called earlier that morning and on hearing she had an interview for employment looked startled and then disapproving. But he had offered to convey her in his little trap to South Parade on the opposite side of Bath to where Mrs Keene's lodging house was situated.

On now alighting at the top of a quiet, elegant crescent, Emma squeezed Matthew's fingers in thanks and affection. 'I need a little income while I decide what I must do.' She slid a glance at his tense profile and again lightly pressed his hand. 'And seeking employment doesn't mean that I am rejecting your proposal. Please understand that I need more time...'

With a slightly martyred air he offered, 'Shall I wait?'

Emma shook her head. 'I shall hail a ride. I've no idea how long I might be—perhaps only a few minutes, if Madame hates me on sight.' She sighed. 'Perhaps an hour or two if Madame tests my good nature with a protracted wait while she prepares to interrogate me.'

She had been jesting when she'd told Matthew she might be kept waiting. Emma raised her wide golden gaze to the sonorously chiming clock as it marked the half-hour she had been seated in a cool hallway on a hard-backed chair. It was now after three-thirty in the afternoon and she was becoming increasingly disillusioned and restless. She peered about for the dour-faced butler who had allowed her into the house. Madame Dubois was expecting her, he had intoned as he'd shown her to a seat, and had then disappeared with a stiff-legged gait.

Emma abruptly stood up and flexed her shoulders. She took a few tentative steps and peeked along the hall. When all remained still and silent, she meandered, admiring the tasteful decor, to the huge gilt scrolled mirror and studied her appearance. She straightened her bonnet this way and that, then glanced down at her fingertips trailing a glossy satinwood star inlaid into a rich rosewood console table. Swishing around with an impatient sigh, she returned to her chair. She would tarry just another few minutes then depart. A person inconsiderate enough to leave her totally ignored for so long would not make a good employer in any case, she impressed upon herself. She was on the point of reseating herself when a door along the corridor opened.

The figure that emerged was male and tall and very blond and had her gawping idiotically at his handsome profile. She had very recently seen those chiselled bronze features just visible beneath a fall of lengthy sun-bleached hair: it was the foreign count she recalled had been travelling on to Bath from the Fallow Buck posting house.

She quickly sat and folded her hands neatly on her lap, her thoughts racing. Of course! She had never made the connection that the *madame* in question might be this French nobleman's wife. The memory of the small blond boy he had lifted in his arms had her frowning at her hands. Would she be expected to nursemaid children? She had no experience of young people...but she could no doubt tutor, if need be...

Firm footsteps echoing against polished mahogany had her attention with the man approaching although her eyes stayed with her entwined fingers. His pace slowed and she knew he'd noticed her.

She glanced up demurely, politely, from beneath the shielding brim of her bonnet. Her face swayed back at once and she felt as though ice had frozen her solid to the chair. Her ivory lids drooped slowly in horrified, disbelieving recognition. French count! Her fingers spasmed as she sensed a hysterical laugh bubbling. No wonder he had seemed familiar! No wonder she had thought she knew him! She did!

But he had changed. It wasn't surprising she had not immediately been able to place him. His hair was no longer fair and stylishly short but long and white-blond, his complexion no longer city-pale but a deep golden-bronze.

An ostler at a rustic tavern had described him as Quality with a queer name…well, it had been perfectly correct. It was her whimsical romantic imagination that had concluded he must be a French nobleman instead of an English one.

On a misty September morning four days ago she had sensed meeting him somewhere before and fancied it to be in fiction rather than fact. Oh, how she wished that were so! For she had indeed seen him before. And on each occasion she had made it her business to insult him. Now she found herself sitting meekly in his house, hoping to be taken on. The sheer farce of it had the back of a hand pressing to her mouth to stifle a horrified choke.

She was aware of impeccably styled black hessian boots drawing into her line of vision. Please don't let him recognise me, she silently prayed, casually swivelling sideways on her seat, away from him.

He changed direction, veering off to the console table she had recently admired. From beneath the brim of her bonnet she watched long buff-coloured legs turn, the toes of his boots point towards her again and knew he was studying her.

It's been three years! she exhorted herself while an unsteady hand shielded her face by tidying stray tendrils of light tan hair into her dark tan bonnet. He'll never recognise you. Or if he does…he'll pretend he doesn't. They weren't married! This jolted into her consciousness at the same time. The woman's name was French-sounding, too, but not the same as his! God in heaven, she was auditioning as a companion to one of his…his women! Perhaps also as tutor to one of his bastards!

She sensed a writhing, seething indignation mounting. Three years ago when they had come together in London as social equals he had managed to instil in her just the same angry emotion. The fact that he had always been perfectly civil whilst with her, never meriting her hostility and sarcasm, had always flustered and shamed her. She could neither justify her aggression to him, when he'd casually enquired why she liked to insult him, nor to herself, nor to her best friend, Victoria.

She explained it away easily to herself now: it had been simple disgust at his hypocrisy and his condescension. Suavely charming he might have been to such homely spinsters as she, who he no doubt believed secretly swooned at the memory of his smile, but she knew him for a lecherous degenerate and had not been too coy to hint as much. She would have told him outright, in no uncertain terms, had the opportunity ever arisen.

Much to her mother's delight, he had seemed to show a friendly interest in her, but Emma knew it was all designing and insincere. For at that time his friend, Viscount Courtenay, had been laying siege to her own dear friend, Victoria Hart, and David had wanted Emma occupied so he could trap Victoria alone.

Despite the two men having infamously shocking reputations, they had been polite society's most popular bachelors, keeping the *ton* in a constant state of fascinated curiosity as to their philandering and drunken brawling. No scandal had seemed base enough to deter top society hostesses from fawning over them and sniping at each other to secure their coveted presence at balls and soirées. Once they were lured across the threshold, no freshly circulating gossip regarding that week's carousing had deterred ambitious mamas or their debutante daughters from beelining towards them with seriously immodest intent.

Emma felt her face stinging with heat on recalling how, at her twenty-fourth-birthday ball, her own mother had gladly foisted her upon this man as though she had been so much unsaleable baggage. Yet even now, despite that mortifying memory...or perhaps because of it...she could feel again the aggravating need to throw back her head and antagonise him. Perhaps acidly comment that it was obvious his morals hadn't improved along with his looks since last they'd met. What? What concern or consequence were his looks?

Her lids pressed closed again as the still silence throbbed with more intensity than the cased clock in the corner. Why won't he go? Why won't he say something? I know he's staring, she fretted.

'Are you waiting for Madame Dubois?'

His low, level tone was exactly the same; still it resulted in a jump and fluttering stomach. Her bonnet nodded at him. 'Yes, sir,' was stiltedly muttered in a voice even she didn't recognise. He remained quiet on learning that. Relief sang through her. Had he remembered her he would surely have mentioned the fact or swiftly removed himself.

Dainty footsteps tripped along the corridor and Emma managed to face the woman approaching without once revealing her face to the man standing opposite.

'So sorry to 'ave kept you waiting, *mademoiselle*... Are you still 'ere, *chéri*?' The woman interrupted her address to Emma on noticing the man, her voice taking on a completely different, husky inflection. The hem of a rose-pink gown was immediately sweeping away again as, ignoring Emma's presence, Yvette Dubois diverted her attention to him.

Involuntarily, Emma's head raised a little to watch them. She stared at the blonde woman's pretty profile, a delicate, pleased flush on a softly rounded cheek as she talked in a quiet, pouty way to her lover. An arch smile, then Yvette was onto tiptoe to whisper in his ear while a small finger trailed his dark sleeve.

Richard Du Quesne frowned at his mistress as though this untimely display of intimacy irritated him, then an icy grey glance shifted sideways. Emma was too late to avert her face and their eyes met and held.

He didn't know her! There was nothing at all in his expression that showed the least interest or recognition. The release was enervating, as was the desperation to be away from this house, these people. She glanced at her nervous hands on her lap, wondering how on earth she could extricate herself.

Yvette realised straight away that she had failed to lure Richard's eyes from the mouse-like creature seated on the hall chair. She was incessantly alert to a possible rival deposing her. Within a second a very female assessment had raked her prospective employee from head to toe. With intense satisfaction she concluded that the woman was as drab as she could possibly have wished, and no threat whatsoever.

A tilted blonde head draped ringlets over a pretty pink shoulder and a tight, malicious smile formed a rosebud of pink lips. Richard was unused to being in the company of such dowdy women and probably feeling some curiosity and sympathy for the thin little thing. *La pauvre* looked as though a nourishing meal would go down well, Yvette spitefully noted as her blue eyes narrowed on those fragile white wrists resting neatly on the girl's dun-coloured lap. It made her happily examine her own plump, bejewelled hands as she said sweetly, 'I must apologise for the delay, *ma'mselle*, and for 'aving forgotten your name. A moment ago I 'ad it and yet now...it is gone.' She gave a careless, continental shrug. 'Miss Woodman, is it, per'aps?' she guessed a trifle impatiently when Emma didn't immediately offer up her identity.

'Yes,' Emma confirmed after a further silent second. 'Miss Eleanor Woodman,' she quietly, firmly lied, and raised her face to them both.

The doorbell clattered shrilly, making Emma start and the butler appear from nowhere. He opened the door and received the post.

An enticing glimpse of sun and sky and a rattling coach drew Emma to her feet and towards freedom. 'I'm sorry, I have another appointment and am already a little overdue. If you will excuse me...' The words tumbled out breathlessly, for she was obliquely aware of the butler starting to push shut the large white door, cutting off her escape route. She also glimpsed Madame Dubois's pout slackening as she realised she had been summarily rejected. But it was Richard Du Quesne's pitiless grey gaze following her that hastened her nimble dodge through the shrinking aperture.

Once in the air, she sped down the elegant steps and, skirts in trembling fists, was running without thought for direction. What halted her several streets away was the need to gasp in more breath to put further distance between herself and those narrowed silver eyes. She backed against a wall and wrapped herself concealingly into her cloak as though still afraid she might be exposed as an impostor. A trembling hand went to the coldness on her face and came away wet. She angrily scrubbed away the bitter tears and slowly, sedately walked towards an area of railed park she could see in the distance.

She had no idea where she was but had a depressing, sinking feeling that Mrs Keene's boarding house in Lower Place was some considerable way away and probably in the opposite direction. As she took a second slow turn around the small recreation area, she slipped unobtrusive glances at fashionable people promenading; nurses tending their young charges, while taking the late afternoon air. Most were now making for the exit, mentioning teatime or the need to be home now the air was cooling.

Emma scoured the skyline for a familiar spire or rooftop that would point her home. She sighed on finding nothing but lowering storm clouds in the west. She should really ask someone for directions but was loath to bring herself to anyone's attention. She approached a small wooden bench as a young couple vacated it and strolled away arm in arm. Seating herself, she drew her cloak tight about her. The sun was setting behind that purply-grey nimbus, spearing golden rays into the chilling atmosphere. She'd obviously been lost for some while. She should have accepted Matthew's offer to wait and deliver her home, she inwardly chided herself. She would, by now, have been back at Mrs Keene's with the prospect of eating soon.

Thinking of food made her stomach grumble. The exertion of sprinting so fast and so far had sapped her energy and left her quite light-headed. She would be late and miss her dinner...and she had already paid her shilling for it. Well, it *would* be salt bacon again, she wryly consoled herself.

She searched in her pocket and drew out her small pouch. Tipping the coins into her palm, she carefully counted, wondering whether she could afford to purchase something to eat on the trek home. The idea of something tasty and different made her stomach roll hollowly again, yet even that consuming thought couldn't completely drag part of her mind out of that opulent, cool hallway and away from a man with piercing metallic eyes.

The shock and humiliation at meeting him again under such degrading circumstances were receding, allowing another worry to compete for notice. If Richard Du Quesne *had* recognised her but had been unwilling to embarrass himself in front of his mistress by saying so, he might not display such reticence in London on his return there.

He owned a smart residence in Mayfair; she knew that. Should he soon go to London and mention he'd seen her in Bath and Jarrett Dashwood came to hear of it... She recalled dark olive eyes sliding over her body with sly, nauseating inspection. That blackguard would make a vicious and vengeful enemy; of that she was absolutely sure. She swallowed a bitter lump in her throat, pocketed her coins and fairly bolted up from the seat as though the vile man might even now be on his way to fetch her. She would forgo food this evening and use her money for the safety of a carriage ride home, she decided.

'Miss Worthington?'

She stopped dead, her complexion paling in terror as she slowly turned.

Richard Du Quesne walked the path towards her and, as she instinctively stepped back, he gestured appealingly.

'Please, don't run away again...' he said, with a flash of a rueful white smile. 'It's taken me hours to find you as it is.'

Emma swallowed, still slowly retreating, even though her eyes had swept past him, taken in the plush phaeton visible beyond the railings that bordered the small park and digested the fact that it was, of course, his.

'I've no intention of running, Mr Du Quesne,' she lied quietly, while silently vowing that should the opportunity arise she would flee him with her last breath. 'How are you? Well, I trust? I'm sorry but I have no time to chat today, sir,' she fluently apologised, without waiting to discover how he did. 'I have to be going now. I have an appointment and am a little late.' She sketched a curtsey then spoiled all her confident ease by dithering over whether to walk back past him or turn and make for the opposite end of the empty park and thus enter yet more unknown territory. She settled for the unknown, whirled about and walked away.

A firm hand on her arm halted her and gently turned her about. 'Aren't you going to now allow me the courtesy of enquiring how you do?'

'Why? You know I don't associate you with civilised behaviour. I'm sure you're little interested in how I do...as, truthfully, I'm little interested in how you do.' She swallowed, bit her unsteady lower lip, ashamed of her unnecessary rudeness. All she had needed to say was that she did tolerably well, thank you.

She watched his light eyes darken behind lengthy, dusky lashes, then he laughed. 'For a while, I just couldn't conceive it to be you, Miss Worthington. Now I'm convinced it is. In three years you've not changed a bit.'

'Oh, but I have, Mr Du Quesne,' she said heartbreakingly huskily yet with a bright, courageous smile. 'I really have changed so much.' She felt a horrible, hot stinging behind her eyes. Please don't let him reminisce, she silently entreated; don't let him talk of their dear mutual friends, David and Victoria Hardinge; don't let him mention her darling goddaughter, Lucy, or any of those things that always brought a poignant mingling of gladness and envy to torture her.

Distraction came in the shape of a raucous cry that minutes before would have drawn her towards it. Her soulful amber eyes followed the progress of a woman hawking Sally Lunn's teacakes, a sweetish aroma strengthening tormentingly in the stirring evening air.

'Are you hungry?' Richard asked quietly, noting her exquisite eyes were fixed on the pedlar.

Emma shook her head and looked away immediately. 'The light's fading. I want to be home. I will be missed,' she lied again. She almost laughed. Who on earth was there here to miss her?

'I take it your mother is with you in Bath. Where are you staying? Why are you seeking employment?' His staccato questions were fired at her.

She avoided his eye. 'I...I'm not seeking work, sir,' she said slowly, while her mind raced ahead for plausible explanations. 'I must beg you to convey my apologies to your...friend. It was just a wager...a joke in very bad taste. Some acquaintances laid a bet that I should never have the audacity to seek a position or attend an interview. It was a stupid, inconsiderate thing to do. I bitterly regret getting involved at all.' She gained little solace from that small truth after such fluent lies and felt her face flame betrayingly.

When he remained silent, and all she was conscious of was his muscular height and the moonlight sheen of his hair in the enclosing dusk, she began backing away again. 'Good evening to you, sir,' she tossed back at him as she twisted around and hurried on.

He didn't touch her this time, merely strolled unconcernedly behind her. It was as good as any physical restraint. Emma swirled about, continued backwards for a few paces then halted. 'Go away!' she snapped furiously yet with a hint of pleading.

'No,' he said easily. He passed her, circled her, examining her minutely then hovered close, like a patient predator awaiting the right moment to close in for the kill. 'Tell me where you're staying. What you're doing here in Bath.'

'It's none of your concern! Leave me be!' she raged in a hoarse whisper, yet with a lowered face as she sensed her exhaustion, her hunger, her fear of not getting back to her lodgings before it was really dark undermining her composure.

'Of course it's my concern,' he drily contradicted her. 'You know how upset Victoria will be if she hears I've neglected your welfare whilst you were with me. And when Victoria's upset David's unbearable...which upsets me.'

'I am not with you!' Emma flung at him desperately. 'Besides, they won't ever know. No one must ever know.' She looked up slowly, realising she had just, stupidly, given him all the information he needed.

'You're here alone...and in trouble.' The words emerged quietly, as though he couldn't quite believe it himself.

As the hawker retraced her noisy way along the street, still loudly advertising her wares, Emma's frantic tiger eyes flicked to Richard. If she could just get him to go away for a moment...all she needed was an unguarded moment. 'I am hungry,' she stated breathily. 'And feeling a little faint.'

He held an arm out to her. 'Come...' he urged gently. 'We'll find somewhere to dine, on the one condition,' he mock-threatened, 'that you tell me what problems bring you here, so they can be dealt with.'

'That's very good of you, sir,' she meekly thanked him. 'But I'm a little giddy and nauseated. Perhaps a quick bite of something now and a short rest on this bench...' Emma approached the seat and sank gratefully, gracefully onto it, her elfin features drooping into supporting hands.

Richard glanced at the vendor almost opposite them now on the other side of black iron railings. Then he arrowed a shrewd look at Emma. Either she was a consummate actress or she really was famished. The vision of a thin, pale young woman sitting in the hallway of his town house haunted him. He certainly didn't want her passing out on him.

A large hand rested solicitously on one of her shoulders, an instinctively cautious caress skimming over fragile shoulder bones beneath the enveloping cloak. Resisting the urge to simply swing her up in his arms and carry her to his phaeton, which he knew with a wry inner smile would no doubt earn him a slap for his pains, he said, 'I'll be but a moment. I'll fetch you a bun and a flask of brandy from my carriage.'

From beneath the brim of her bonnet, Emma slanted feline eyes at his powerful, retreating figure. He wasn't fooled at all, she realised. He turned, vigilantly, several times, walked backwards, giving himself the chance to return to her in a second. Her heart squeezed, lead settling in the empty pit of her stomach as she noted his crisp, athletic step. Should she not time it exactly right, she knew he'd catch her before she'd managed a few yards.

Apparently satisfied, finally, with her air of slumped-shouldered debility, Richard swung away towards the gate. As soon as the railing was between them and he was heading in the direction of his phaeton, she rose stealthily and, with never a backward glance, sped off into shadowy trees bordering the lawns.

'Ah, Frederick, so you are up and about today. How very nice to see you at last. How long has it been now?' Jarrett Dashwood mimed concerned thoughtfulness. 'A sennight, perhaps, since last we had dealings together?' The darkly suave man sauntered further into the drawing room of Rosemary House. Without waiting for an invitation, he flicked back his coat-tails and seated himself on a gilt-framed chair.

Margaret Worthington looked at her husband, looked at their tormentor and closed her eyes. 'Do have some tea, Mr Dashwood,' she urged in a thin, trembling voice, while thin, trembling fingers fumbled at the silver pot on the tray. 'It is freshly made in readiness for your arrival.'

'More tea, Mrs Worthington? I believe I am awash with your tea, dear lady.' His wide, sensual mouth smiled at her, his olive eyes did not. 'Now were you today to offer me, say, two thousand pounds, or a private interview with that intriguing daughter of yours, I would certainly be tempted to partake. As it is, I am heartily tired of trailing here each afternoon to meet with her only to be fobbed off with tea and excuses.' Leaning back into the chair, he stretched out his legs, crossing them at the ankles. 'Where is your daughter? The longer we are apart, the more desperate I am for some time alone with her. It is said, is it not, that absence makes the heart grow fonder?'

Margaret and Frederick Worthington exchanged nervous glances.

'She is visiting her aunt...'

'She is ailing in her room...'

The couple glared, horrified, at each other at these conflicting versions of Emma's lengthy absence, each sure that they had voiced the correct one for today. Both shifted uneasily back into their chairs and, apeing their sinister guest's lead, examined their manicures.

Jarrett Dashwood used a fleshy thumb to shine a perfectly trimmed set of fingernails. 'Well, what's it to be? Is she visiting? Lying abed with her smelling salts or Miss Austen's romances? Shall I go above stairs and discover for myself how my poor, ailing fiancée fares?'

'Please, sir, do not term her so,' Margaret forced out in a high, wheedling tone. 'She refuses you; you know that. You have our sincerest apologies.' Margaret looked at Frederick, hoping for a modicum of assistance in dealing with this frightening man. Her perspiring husband simply gazed glassily into space. 'There is nothing to be done, Mr Dashwood.' Margaret emphasised her despair by crushing her handkerchief to her mouth. 'We cannot force her to wed against her inclination. Everything in our power...my power,' she gritted through the muffling linen, stabbing a glance at her florid husband, 'has been done to make the selfish ingrate see sense. But she is a woman grown and so stubborn she will take no heed of her fond parents' good advice.'

'Perhaps she will then take heed of me, madam,' Jarrett Dashwood smoothly said. 'Perhaps you both will do likewise. For this whole matter has now the stench of premeditated fraud about it. I have been fleeced, I believe, of my two thousand pounds, not only by you, good sir,' he mocked Frederick with a bow of his raven head, 'but also by you, madam, and your daughter. How many fiancés have you accepted for the chit in return for a little aid with pressing debts, only to find that she's turned coy afore the altar?'

Margaret's handkerchief dropped to her lap, her chalky complexion adopted a greyish-green tinge and her mouth worked like that of a beached fish. 'I beg of you, Mr Dashwood, never think it!' finally exploded from her. 'My daughter has received no other firm offers at all. She is accomplished at deflecting any gentleman's attention far sooner than that. It would be heaven indeed should she encourage just the one to come a-courting.'

'But I'm not convinced,' Jarrett Dashwood said easily, with a final lingering look at his flexing fingers. 'It is a truth universally acknowledged...' He laughed lightly. 'There...you see how the dear girl has affected me. I find I can continually bring to mind passages from her favourite books... Now, where was I? Ah, yes, with odd truths. Indeed, it is strange that the more one is denied something, the further it seems from one's grasp, the sweeter finally possessing it becomes. I believe I am developing a *tendresse* for your daughter which makes the money quite irrelevant. Even were you in a position to repay it, I would not accept. I want that spirited hussy as my wife. The documents pertaining to the marriage contract are signed and sealed. The marriage must go ahead.'

Finally bored with this polite charade, he said in a guttural voice, 'Find out to wherever it is she has absconded and furnish me with the news; I'm sure *I* can make her see sense. If you do not....' He smiled grimly at Margaret '...I understand that the Fleet is able to accommodate families...'

Chapter Four

'This is a respectable house, is it not, Mrs Keene?'

'Indeed it is, Miss Worthington. Oh, yes, indeed it is.'

'And no gentleman is allowed within it after nine of the clock, you said, did you not? So you will insist this gentleman immediately removes himself,' Emma prompted in a low, trembling rush.

Mrs Keene asserted nothing, simply gawked at the man to whom her lodger referred as though he were an apparition. Recovering her senses, she rolled her eyes at Emma, mouthing something completely unintelligible, before bobbing her mob cap and herself up and down as though in the throes of some palsy.

Emma watched her landlady's ridiculously obsequious display for no more than a second. Her furious glare turned on the blond man, lounging by the mantel in Mrs Keene's small parlour.

He looked right back. He couldn't take his eyes off her.

Sir Richard Du Quesne's jaw clenched…ached as he fought to keep his eyes from slowly stripping that virginal white nightgown from her slender body. Silver eyes returned sharply to her face and his angry attention had her valiantly, proudly tilting her chin. If it hadn't been for small, pearly teeth sinking steadyingly into her full lower lip he might have been fooled into thinking she was perfectly composed. He read her next move as it occurred to her and artlessly showed in those lucid golden eyes. Shifting away from the fire, he made for the parlour door.

A slow pulse throbbed low in his belly, spreading to tighten his groin, and he cursed at his feet in irritated frustration. He couldn't recall ever seeing a woman so simply attired—certainly none whose keep he was paying for and whose bed he shared. The women of his acquaintance, whether family or fancy, trailed about in lace with their hair in curls when ready to retire.

With a subtle air of disinterest he glanced at luxuriant, glossy fawn hair spilling over pristine, modestly embroidered cotton, tendrils curving into a gracefully narrow back. If her hair and eyes didn't resemble fine cognac she might not tempt him so much, he savagely mocked himself, shoving aside any ludicrous idea that she could join those whose bed he shared.

Emma turned warily on her heel as he passed, keeping him at the corner of a watchful tawny eye. His casual entrapment complete, he halted a few paces behind, forcing her to twist about to face him. Her eyes blazed copper beneath his silver stare until she abruptly looked away.

Mrs Keene's face was diplomatically lowered but her beady eyes were busy batting between the hostile couple. 'Ah, but that's no gentleman, you know, miss,' finally worked out of one corner of her mouth at Emma, while her eyes slid in the opposite direction.

A slender white hand flew to smother a hysterical laugh. Emma agreed through her quivering fingers, 'Yes, I *do* know that, Mrs Keene.' Very graciously she added, 'Nevertheless, on this occasion I think we shall allow him the sobriquet and insist on his immediate removal from the premises.'

'I can't do that, miss!' Mrs Keene whispered, horrified at the very idea. Her eyes slid to the tall blond man, who in turn had his sardonic mercurial gaze turned on her lodger.

'And why ever not?' Emma bit out, wrapping her slender arms about her night-robed body to warm it and conceal its quaking.

'It's the silver squire,' Mrs Keene spluttered out, so low and fast it merely emerged as a sibilant hiss and Emma could decipher none of it.

'What?' she queried on a frown.

'She said I'm the silver squire,' Sir Richard Du Quesne told her evenly. 'Lightly translated, that means I own the freehold of this house and the rest of the street together with quite an amount of the city of Bath.'

After a stunned moment, digesting the awful news that she

was actually attempting to eject him from one of his own properties, she fumed. 'And you think that gives you the right to come here and harass me, I suppose?'

'Your continual deceit earlier today gives me the right to come here and question you. So does a sense of duty to a close friend who cares about your welfare.' As though just noticing the goggling, hovering landlady, an explicit flick of a bronzed hand signalled her to remove herself.

'Don't you dare go!' Emma cried at the woman's back, noting she had immediately turned to do his bidding.

Richard shrugged easily. 'Please be seated, then, Mrs Keene, while Miss Worthington explains to me certain inconsistencies in her behaviour.'

'I am under no obligation to account to you for one thing, sir!'

Emma's thin hands tightened into fists behind her back. She could not believe herself to have been so stupid as to immediately race downstairs five minutes ago, on gleaning from Mrs Keene's garbled croak that a gentleman awaited her company in the parlour. Before she could interrogate the woman further her mobcapped head had disappeared from around her chamber door.

Pulling on her heavy cotton wrap, Emma had simply bolted after her, wondering how Matthew had managed to bribe her landlady to allow him entrance at this time of the night; wondering, too, why on earth he had not waited until the morning to enquire how she'd done with her interview. Then it had occurred to her, with a scattering of icy needles about her body, that it might be something more serious than the success of her jobseeking that had brought him here so late. Perhaps something pertaining to her flight from London...and Jarrett Dashwood... And she'd fair flown below.

Not once had she dreamed that Richard Du Quesne might be irked enough by her escape to bother discovering where she lodged and immediately track her. But then the novelty of being shunned by a woman, even a modest spinster such as she, had probably been enough to inflame a need for immediate retaliation.

'Did you walk back here?'

She glared at him, about to spit that he could mind his own business and go fly to the devil. A movement at one corner of a sensual, narrow mouth told her he was reading her mind.

'I hailed a cab,' she stiffly informed him.

'Why did you run away?'

'I was hungry,' she returned flippantly, gazing insolently past him, 'and couldn't wait longer for you to return with a measly bun. I decided to make my way home for one of Mrs Keene's delicious dinners before I faded dead away.'

He smiled at her churlishness, and at her long, slender fingers ceaselessly entwining then jerking apart.

'Are you going to tell me why you're here in Bath, unchaperoned?' he asked quietly so Mrs Keene was excluded from his dialogue.

'No,' Emma simply said, and disdainfully flicked away her tawny head.

'Very well. I'll send an express to your parents tomorrow and thus find out.' He was reaching for the door handle when she stopped him.

'Don't do that...please...' was forced out as her eyes squeezed shut.

He walked back, straight past her, seating himself in a chair by the small hearth. A movement of his long, dark fingers this time had Mrs Keene beetling for the door and Emma enviously watching her.

She didn't dare follow her landlady out, although he was taunting her with the opportunity. He had her exactly where he wanted her, she realised with impotent fury. Her face flung around, and she glowered her loathing.

He responded by smiling and settling back leisurely into the battered wing-chair, propping a booted foot on his knee. One dark hand was splayed idly against polished leather, the other against his face.

Emma sensed her teeth grinding, her fists curling. He was deliberately impressing on her just how easily he could keep her here, and that he was exercising patience in waiting for her to obediently disclose all to him. Her nails stabbed her palms as she suppressed a terrifying need to bound across the few feet that separated them and hit him.

'Do your parents know where you are?'

'My whereabouts are of no interest to them,' she snapped back. 'Why should they be? I am a spinster of twenty-seven and perfectly able to live alone.'

'I know how old you are, Emma,' he said softly. 'I attended your twenty-fourth-birthday celebration...remember?'

'Not by my invitation...' she sniped, then twisted away and closed her eyes. Do not antagonise him, she severely, calmingly chided herself. He is of no importance whatsoever. Just use half-truths and guile. It will satisfy his base curiosity, thus enabling you to rid yourself of his damnable presence...then all will again be well. He is simply a hedonistic fool ruled by lust and alcohol... She hesitated in her unspoken censure, recalling that there had been less of an inebriated haze about this man than about Matthew on their reunion in Oakdene this week...and several times since.

'Well?' His mild impatience shattered the tension after several silent minutes. When she steadfastly refused to look at him or speak because she still hadn't quite worked out which lies would serve her best, he added, 'Have you nothing at all to say?'

'Yes, I have something to say,' she announced, honey-voiced, as feral eyes pounced on him. 'And I do not think you will want to contact my parents to relay this. If you do not remove yourself this instant I shall scream and weep loud enough to wake the street and charge you with...'

'With...?' he prompted mildly through long, dark fingers curled against his sensual mouth, watching her from beneath heavy lids.

'With attempting to force your vile attentions on me...with molesting me. Now what do *you* say, Mr Du Quesne?' she flung at him, inclining slightly towards him in triumph.

He was out of the chair in a lithe second, making her jerk back and whirl away so fast, treacle hair flowed out thickly towards him.

'I'd say you're a little early with that complaint, Miss Worthington,' he purred as he walked right up to her. Smoky silver eyes eventually reached her white face, having leisurely mounted her body.

He watched real fear dilate her pupils. He also saw that she was still itching to slap him. His teeth met, shifting his jaw aslant, as he finally accepted that he wanted it too. He was just longing for her to touch him...in any way...in that way.

He forced himself away from her, cutting off her escape route, for she was now liable to flee and damn the consequences, then he still wouldn't know what the hell was going on. He stood with his back to her yet with her colouring, her sharp, sculpted little features imprinted on his mind. He laughed, low and private, in a way that had Emma swinging about, eyes raking the breadth of his shoulders to try and discover the reason for it.

Richard raised his sardonic dark face to the ceiling. So Yvette deemed herself a wildcat, did she? he mused ironically. Yvette was nothing more than a spiteful harlot...and spiteful in a manner that had little to do with how she liked to brand him as hers in a way easily recognisable to other women.

This was a wildcat, he realised ruefully...the genuine, un-adorned article. She even looked the part with her spare, graceful body and tawny colouring: like a small woodland creature...too beautiful to touch...too beautiful not to. And he felt a sudden drenching disgust at having resorted to subduing her with the threat of violation.

He'd never in his life done that...never needed to. Women, and plenty of them, came to him very willingly. Yet what tormented him most was, now he'd acknowledged the desire, self-discipline seemed to mock him. Angry frustration culminated in a dark fist cracking savagely against the door as he moved abruptly past it.

Emma jumped and stifled a small scream; so did Mrs Keene on the other side of the door, with one pudgy hand clamped to her mouth and the other to her battered, ringing ear.

Giddy with fatigue and hunger, Emma leaned against the wall to steady herself. She had eaten nothing since her meagre breakfast and was now ravenous. Her stomach endorsed its need for attention by growling loudly.

Richard arrowed a look at her as she instinctively pressed both hands to her flat abdomen, bending over a little as though to hide the offending noise.

'You've still not eaten, have you?'

'No.' There was no point in lying about something this trivial and obvious, she thought wryly. Deceit would be better employed on major issues.

'Mrs Keene...?' Richard said quite normally.

After a momentary scuffling sound, the woman was in the doorway, her apron polishing at the brass knob as though she intended shining it away.

'Just afinishin' off me chores, sir,' she explained gruffly, still managing to bob her head at him as she toiled.

'Quite...' he said very drily. 'I take it you have something appetising to eat about the place?'

Emma choked a spontaneous laugh, making Mrs Keene look nervously at her and Richard arrow her a speculative look. Now why had that not occurred to her? she thought hysterically. Had she offered him one of Mrs Keene's delicious dinners, no doubt he would even now be halfway home.

'Why, o' course, your lordship. I'd be happy to fetch it direct,' Mrs Keene hastily offered, elevating Richard's rank in her enthusiasm. 'La, miss, you missed out on your supper, didn't you now? You should've said for it slipped me busy mind. Now, there be beef silverside and vegetables roastin'. Or mutton hotpot on the hob...an' a dumplin'...'

Richard looked at Emma questioningly for a choice but she simply held onto her newly gurgling stomach and stared at Mrs Keene in amazement. Beef? Mutton? Dumplings? Where was salt bacon and carrots?

'Now, not that it be none o' my concern, o' course, as to what you choose, but the beef do look a treat an' fit for a conasewer o' fine fare...'

'Fetch two plates of the beef and hurry, if you please,' Richard clipped across Mrs Keene's recommendations, making the choice for them both.

Mrs Keene was like a whirlwind. Within a few minutes of her leaving them alone, she was back, accompanied by the young girl who helped in the kitchens. Cutlery, bread, butter, pickles, wine and beer all decked the small parlour table while Emma watched. Then, just as she was about to get a grip on her pride and her senses, and tell him he could dine here alone for she wanted none of it, the steaming plates appeared and she was lost. The beef certainly looked and smelled as good as her landlady had lauded.

Mrs Keene hovered in the doorway with her knees bent and a piece of her skirt held daintily out at an angle in thumb and forefinger.

'Thank you, Mrs Keene,' Richard said graciously. 'And your chores for the day are finished now, are they not?'

'Yes, sir, indeed they are, sir,' she emphatically declared, and at his peremptory nod she was gone.

Emma remained by the wall, her eyes on the table, still striving for the courage to reject it...and him. Just a chunk of that aromatic bread would suffice, she realised, if she could snatch it on the way to the door.

'Sit down.' His order sliced evenly through her half-hearted abstemiousness and for some reason she immediately obeyed. Approaching the table, she sank into the chair he had pulled out. Seating himself opposite, he pushed one laden plate of beef and vegetables towards her, lavishly buttered a chunk of springy warm bread and, unperturbed, started eating.

After a silent moment when Emma simply stared hatefully at the tempting savoury repast as though wishing it all to be stringy, salty bacon and carrots boiled to a mash, she picked up her knife and fork.

They ate in silence yet Emma refused to meekly avoid his eyes. From time to time, she forced proud topaz eyes to meet steady silver, desperate to match his mild, expressionless demeanour. But she knew it was impossible. Every time he pushed bread her way or refilled her glass with sweet wine she tensed, wanting to throw it back at him. And he knew it, too, she realised as her eyes again rose valiantly and swept past dark, sardonic features on the way to glare at the fire.

When she was full and simply shook her head at him as he offered her more, he finally said, with absolute calm and reason, 'I think that it would be wise for your family to know of your whereabouts.'

'Leave us all be,' Emma responded with quiet civility, sensing an unspoken truce between them that she was willing to momentarily honour. 'You will cause us more grief by interfering. No one will thank you for broadcasting this matter, least of all my parents.'

There was a new, narrow-eyed intensity to his gaze. 'Have you been sent away? Banished from London?'

Emma averted her face, feeling it heat in indignation on comprehending his obtuse meaning. So he classed her morals as no better than those of the women he consorted with, did he? But his base imaginings might just serve her purpose, she realised, her refreshed mind back to investigating devious tactics.

Yes; why not comply? It would be sure to disgust and alienate such a hypocritical degenerate. If there was an infallible way to rid oneself of a gentleman's presence, it must be the hint of an approaching, illegitimate birth. Speculation as to the child's paternity was sure to be bandied about.

'It is a very delicate matter, sir, for a lady in my position...' Emma whispered. *And at least I am a lady!* she would have loved to raucously screech at him, but resisted and demurely lowered her face. 'And I do not wish to say more. I'm sure you understand...' she timidly concluded, pressing her lips tight to conceal a small, satisfied smile.

'But I wish you to say more for I do not understand,' he rejected with silky steel. 'Have your parents sent you away to avoid a scandal?'

She remained diffidently quiet yet was aware of his absolute stillness, his absolute attention. When the silence between them dragged interminably some of her smug confidence evaporated and her stomach's mellow satiety began to curdle.

'Are you with child?'

'I beg you will not press me on the matter, sir,' she pleaded shrilly, agitatedly, swivelling sideways on her chair. He hadn't leapt up and excused himself as she'd expected; moreover, he seemed content to simply sit and singe the top of her head with a quicksilver stare.

'What of your lover? Where is he?' he asked quite levelly, yet on shoving himself back from the table the chair almost tipped over.

She was aware of her body receiving a disturbingly thorough assessment. No doubt he did know of such things, she realised acidly. She'd seen him at the Fallow Buck with a child. Whether it was born of his wife or his mistress was anyone's guess. As Victoria had never mentioned Dickie—as she affectionately termed him—marrying, the child, she presumed, must be the offspring from some base union.

She and Victoria exchanged letters quite often. Via one of those, Emma had learned that this man had moved abroad a year or more ago to oversee his foreign estates. Such a shame he ever brought himself back! she viciously thought, squirming beneath his unrelenting observation.

'Is he married already or refusing to support you?'

'Please, do not ask for I...I really cannot say...'

Well, how lucky can you get? Richard sourly mused. You wanted her and now it looks as though not only can you have her but another man's bastard, too. For God's sake, leave now! he urged himself. You've done your best. You've fed her... offered to help. She doesn't want your aid. She's never liked you. Even at your mannerly best, she never liked you, he mocked himself, recalling how attentively civil he'd been to her three years previously in London when he and David Hardinge had been the bane of polite society. And there, of course, lay a prime reason why he was loath to abandon her: he owed it to the best friend he had ever had to protect her, for David's wife, Victoria, cherished this woman as a very dear friend.

In fact, he was quite surprised that she hadn't fled into Hertfordshire to seek support from Victoria rather than head this way where she seemed friendless and alone...unless... He twisted on his heel. Of course, you fool, he silently berated himself. If she's headed this way, that's because her lover lives locally. 'How long have you been in Bath?' he asked abruptly.

'Five days,' Emma answered honestly, yet looked warily at him.

So she'd been here five days and was starving and seeking employment, which meant that the bastard had no intention of taking on his responsibility. If he was already married the least he could do was settle her in her own establishment somewhere as his mistress.

Oh, no! Don't you dare give it a minute's pause! he inwardly raged. *A pregnant mistress?* In three months' time when her belly's swollen you'll be visiting Yvette and counting the cost of it all. *A mistress with a child?* You don't even like children! You like your nephew well enough, an inner voice argued back. He likes you too. Stephen says you're good with children. But they're family...they share your blood. This flyblow could be sired by a criminal...drunk...gambler. Should suit pretty well, then, echoed back drily as he recalled his duelling, his long nights spent heavy-eyed at card tables and numerous drunken brawls in his misspent youth.

Besides—he swivelled on a heel to look at her—at some time she's going to be this beautiful again...perhaps filled out a little too, he thought wryly as he discreetly surveyed delicately curving breasts and hips. 'You need someone to care for you,' he heard himself say. 'Even if you manage to get employment, you'll be put off as soon as your condition becomes apparent.'

Emma merely nodded, not knowing what else to do, for her stomach was in sickening cramps as she anticipated what would come next. But then, it had been niggling at the back of her mind since she'd stupidly threatened to cry rape to frighten him off. He'd looked at her from beneath his long, dusky lashes in a way he had three years ago...in a way he no doubt looked at all women who aroused his lust. And she knew she did that for some odd reason.

No other man had looked at her in that steady, intent way, as though the backs of his eyes were afire. Certainly not Matthew. Yet, even with so little experience of men, an innate sense warned her that throbbing, silent stare was a prelude to lechery. She slowly stood, quickly said, 'Thank you for your concern but I have made my own plans... If you will excuse me...'

They seemed to be pacing towards the door at the same time, at the same speed yet he reached it first from further away. A solid dark fist was planted casually against it and slitted silver eyes gleamed down at her. 'What plans?' he asked idly.

'Private plans,' she returned sweetly.

'Plans that include absconding from here as soon as I'm out of sight?'

'I have nothing further to say, sir,' she said with great dignity...yet alarmed, for he had a disturbing ability to read her mind. 'I can only ask you not to cause my family further distress by...by mentioning this to anyone at all. My parents are quite ill with worry.' And that was the truth, too, even if their anxiety stemmed from a different source entirely.

'You can't stay here; it's hardly fitting. Besides, as you and Mrs Keene insist, it is a respectable house,' he mentioned satirically. 'I'm sure you'll soon be asked to leave.'

'Mrs Keene need never know!' She realised immediately how naive that sounded. A pregnant woman was quite easily identifiable as she neared her time. 'I shall not be here for very long,' she quickly amended.

Richard looked meaningfully at the door. 'Oh, I'm sure a hint of it might already have reached Mrs Keene's ears.'

Emma glanced, horrified, at the door then actually caught a muffled shuffle of receding slippered feet.

'You need someone to care for you, Emma.'

She felt the soft words stir the hair at her brow, sensed the distance between them close and solidify with tension. She swallowed, trying to dredge up some clever snub, but nothing came. Nothing at all. Her volatile mind was unusually lethargic.

The fist planted by the side of her head slid down the panels on the door, dark knuckles brushing against fawn hair close to them. His long fingers uncurled slowly, moved a trailing tress back from her brow, then another with a mesmeric gentleness that would have rendered objection superfluous.

Her copper eyes were slowly raised, magnetised by eyes like tarnished silver stars. 'Let me care for you, Emma,' he said huskily before his moon-pale head dipped and his lips touched a feather-light caress to her brow.

Entranced, her body felt immoveable, her limbs heavy. Even her ivory lids felt weighted and drooped as warm, skimming kisses trailed her cool skin from temple to cheek.

Hit him! Push him away! resounded in her mind, but hollowly, as though from far, far away. And the tantalisingly soft caress was so soothing. Suddenly, it felt as though she'd been starved of human contact and this man's touch was as essential as the food she'd eaten.

A dark thumb traced her lower lip, a hand wound into thick tawny hair, tilting her head those necessary few inches. His mouth touched hers with infinite gentle persuasion, and Emma felt herself melting into it.

He knew it, too: unbelievably, her acquiescence seemed a mere kiss away. 'I'll care for you and the child,' he murmured confidently against her mouth. 'You'll want for nothing, I swear. I'll make lasting provision for you. Even if I marry at some time, you'll want for nothing.'

A glacier of icy feeling, bright and invigorating, seemed to meander from her pulsing lips to her rigid toes. As his mouth slid forcefully on hers and his hand spanned her jaw, manoeuvring it apart, she finally wrenched her head aside, simultaneously swinging small, clawed fingers up towards his face.

Swift reflexes had him ducking so the worst her nails did was glance off a bronzed cheek before her wrist was encircled by five tanned fingers and slammed back against the door beside her head. Her breathing was so fast and shallow, the cotton of her nightrobe chafed her soft breasts, tautening her nipples, but fiery feline eyes boldly held his as she cautiously primed her other hand for a like assault. This time he was prepared and those slender, curled fingers partnered the others on the opposite side of her head.

After a few moments straining her wrists against his easy imprisonment she cursed beneath her breath and flung herself back against the door. 'I do realise I deport myself unbecomingly with gentlemen,' she sweetly said through closed teeth. 'My mother tells me so all the time. I've omitted to thank you, haven't I, sir, for the offer of your kind protection? I do thank you, of course, but must, unfortunately, decline your generosity. My private plans are not negotiable—something I'm sure Madame Dubois will appreciate... Oh, and your future wife, whoever the poor fool may eventually be.'

She watched his eyes narrow, his jaw tighten but he laughed deep in his throat with a lack of amusement. 'It seems you've deported yourself extremely becomingly with one gentleman, sweet. Would that it had been me,' he said as his face lowered tormentingly towards hers. She fought against his captivity in earnest, but refused to look away from those savage silver eyes.

Her valour was her undoing. As she finally ceded and swung her head aside it was too late and his mouth slanted exactly over hers. The more she tried to shake her head free and avoid him, the more his mouth pursued and clung. With insulting ease and leisure, both her wrists were trapped in one large dark hand while his other spanned her jaw and stilled it.

No man had ever kissed her like this. Not one of the stolen kisses she had received following her debut nine years ago had made any lasting impression. On the few occasions Matthew had kissed her it was with an odd brevity, as though he was sorry for troubling her. She had never guessed kissing could be so disturbingly appealing that she knew the memory would brand itself on her mind to be remembered for ever. His mouth was warm and wooing, his tongue-tip lightly caressing the clamped line of her lips, tempting them to part. They did, curiosity subduing pride. His tongue tasted hers then traced the silk of her lower lip. Then, just as her breathing slowed and she felt that anodyne enchantment dooming her to whatever he wanted, it was over and he was wheeling away from her and into the room.

Strolling to the fender, he planted a booted foot against it. 'Good evening, Miss Worthington,' he said quite normally.

Emma put the back of a hand to her mouth. It clenched into a fist and angry knuckles scrubbed as though to remove his taint. He was actually now dismissing *her* from *his* presence! And the fact that part of her no longer wanted to go...wanted him back close to her...was unbearably humiliating. She fumed inwardly and then outwardly. 'When you leave this lodging house tonight you will pay for one meal...yours. I have already paid for my dinner this morning and you will pay nothing more for it.'

Richard watched her, amused, through a mesh of dark lashes. 'As you say,' he agreed solemnly, 'it is paid for.'

'And...and I am counting on the affection and friendship we both have for Viscount and Viscountess Courtenay to keep you from...from repeating any of this. You know Victoria would be deeply upset and anxious on my behalf if she came to hear of such gossip. I will tell her all in my own time. I hope I haven't overestimated your character in even that small respect. Whatever else I may believe you to be, I trust you are a loyal, true friend to them.'

'As you say,' he bit out, 'a loyal, true friend.' A brief pause preceded, 'In exchange for my promise I expect you to vow to stay here until some proper arrangements can be made for your future.'

'Goodnight, Mr Du Quesne,' Emma said shortly as she pulled open the parlour door and exited the room, with absolute aplomb.

She climbed the stairs sedately, chin high, yet on legs that felt weak and wobbly. On entering her room she lit the small candle by the bed, turned down the covers neatly with shaking hands and sat on the edge of the mattress. Her eyes squeezed shut, her mind jumbling with so many tumultous emotions that coherent thought was impossible. As she drooped sideways onto the bed, her hands covered her face and she felt hot tears wetting her palms. 'I hate him,' she whispered. 'I hate him...hate him...' she cried, muffling the sound with knuckles rammed against her sensitive, pulsing lips. How dared he treat her with such disrespect, such abominable familiarity, as though she were some...some shameless trollop like that Frenchwoman? She had been gently reared; a social equal to men such as he. Yet he had the gall to proposition her as though she'd emerged from some dockside tavern!

But you've made him believe you're a shameless trollop, a small inner voice justified. You've implied you've lost your virtue and your wits by getting with child, then impudently refusing his aid. He's been a rogue for years; you would have been a schoolgirl when he started philandering. It was sheer folly to imply you're a fallen woman. A man of his arrogance and experience probably believed you were inviting…begging his protection. No doubt he's now feeling pious for attempting to rescue a stupid strumpet from squalor.

He had offered lasting provision, and she believed he'd meant it. Out of the duty and affection she knew he felt for Viscount Courtenay, he would have honoured that promise. When his lust for her was expended and all she aroused was pity and disgust he would still have supported her financially.

That mortification was too much to bear. Emma rolled over onto her front and her small fists banged into the pillow in frustration and fury as she dried her face by scrubbing it against the linen. You could have been truthful. You could have explained you were here in Bath to marry an honourable man. Instead you've let three year old prejudices addle your wits. You've acted without due caution and brought all of this shambles down on your own head, you reckless idiot!

'Mrs Keene?'

The woman leapt up from her rocking-chair, sending it oscillating crazily. Her gin tot banged down onto the scrubbed surface of the scullery table which she careered into in her haste. 'Oh, your lordship, I didn't hear you come in. Is there somethin' else I can get you?' She bobbed, balancing on one foot, with an unobtrusive rub at her smarting knee.

'It was a good dinner,' Sir Richard Du Quesne said with an appreciative nod and a lazy indication that nothing further was required. 'I have it from Miss Worthington that she has already paid for her meal. What do I owe you for mine?'

Mrs Keene raised her mobcap to peer at him. The little hussy thought she'd paid a shilling for a crown special, did she? 'Why, nothin' o'course, sir,' she said humbly. 'It be a very great honour to have your noble self partake of me victuals and do return at any time to—'

'Thank you.' Richard cut off her fulsome invitation and gave her a smile. 'While Miss Worthington remains here, I should like her welfare scrupulously attended to. I imagine she forgets to eat at times...or to pay her way. I will settle any balance due on her account but would not want her to know that.'

'Ah, yes, sir; proud, studious little thing that she is.' Well, Mrs Keene mulled over shrewdly in her mind, he wants her looked after, an' no mistake. Jauntily she added, 'She fair forgets to come below for her meals when she's got her head in one of them books. Reads novels all the time, don't you know. 'Cept when her friend comes acallin' an' takes her for a drive.'

Richard pivoted slowly back towards the woman. 'Ah, yes...that must be...Mr Sullivan, her cousin and a good friend of mine. Dark hair...quite short and squat.'

'Oh, no, sir,' Mrs Keene said innocently, 'this be a different gentleman. Tall, he is...not so tall as you, though, with light brown hair. Sometimes he brings his children with him and they all ride in his little gig together. I believe I heard Miss Worthington call her friend Matthew,' she helpfully supplied with a sideways look. 'Not that it be none of my concern, o' course...or I tattle...'

'That's right, Mrs Keene, it is none of your concern, and I'd hate to learn you tattle...' Richard subtly warned.

Chapter Five

'So would you be likin' some mutton hotpot for your dinner this evenin', Miss Worthington?' Mrs Keene asked with a gap-toothed grin from the doorway.

This unexpected disturbance had Emma relinquishing Elizabeth Bennet's misfortunes, and focussing again on her own. Where was Matthew? Why had he not come calling? Clapping her novel shut with a sigh, she inclined forward to again peer along the street, hoping for a sign of his gig. Was he still vexed with her for attending that farcical interview yesterday? It was ironic—now she no longer wanted time to consider his proposal his absence was preventing her telling him so!

'Dumplin's are fresh made with a little herb 'n onion...' Mrs Keene's persuasive tone cut across her thoughts.

An awful inkling of the reason for her landlady's solicitude was followed by a flash of angry humiliation that seared Emma from head to toe. That disgusting lecher had, after all, last night paid for her dinner! If possible, she now hated him even more. *No, she didn't!* she scolded herself. He held no such power to disturb her. What he aroused was simple contempt. It was a decision, made in bed, that had soothed her inner turmoil enough to let her drift into an exhausted slumber as dawn approached. So had the comfort that her hateful reunion with Richard Du Quesne served a purpose: it made her appreciate more than ever the solid, upstanding qualities of a man such as Matthew Cavendish.

'Did Mr Du Quesne pay for my dinner yesterday?' Emma asked frostily.

'La...no, m'dear. You'd already paid me for yourn!'

A tad mollified, Emma, nevertheless, arrowed a suspicious amber glance at her landlady. 'Did he ask you to lie?'

Mrs Keene's crossed arms shivered, propped up her bosom, and a look of absolute affront preceded, 'O' course not! I, bein' the honest kind o' body I am, felt obliged t'inform *Sir Richard*—' she emphasised his aristocratic status by inclining forward '—that you'd squared with me earlier for your board.'

'A shilling was enough?' Emma asked, amazed. Obliquely she realised she had forgotten Victoria's postscript on a letter two years ago informing her that Sir John Du Quesne had died as a result of the grave illness that kept his heir from attending her baby daughter's christening. A proxy had taken on Richard's role of godfather while he remained at his father's bedside.

'Er...yes...yes, a shillin's right,' whistled through yellowing stumps.

'The mutton and dumplings tonight...that is also a shilling?'

'O' course...' was again ejected in a persuasive purr. If a poor widow could sell a crown special with all its juicy profit, a shilling-a-plate hot 'ordinary' could go hang. Why, the silver squire probably wouldn't quibble at a half-guinea a plate for this lucky young lady. She'd heard gossip that he was right generous to his women.

Emma rose from her chair by the window and approached the door. 'Excuse me, Mrs Keene.'

The landlady gathered her greedy thoughts, then her greasy skirts, and wobbled after Emma along the musty corridor. Emma halted at another door, knocked and, when summoned to enter, did so. She smiled at her fellow lodger, a young lady she guessed to be some years younger than herself. But, without consulting a mirror, she knew that this fair-haired, modestly dressed young woman had the same air of dejection and a haunted, hungry look.

Now, of course, *she* had recently been sated with delicious, nourishing food, and had drunk sweet, expensive wine—and at no extra cost, it seemed!

'Miss Jenner,' she greeted cheerfully, 'Mrs Keene is here to relay her shilling menus for tonight. Shall we listen and choose together?'

Emma was aware of Mrs Keene's head quivering in denial but ignored it. If the *silver squire*—she mockingly recalled his nickname—wanted to supplement her meagre meals with his...well...silver, she would let him. The thought of later sitting at the same table as this young lady, eating heartily while her fellow boarder picked over the unpalatable scraps that served as dinners night after night...the injustice of it set her small teeth ascrape. Either they both enjoyed mutton hotpot or neither of them did.

Mrs Keene was sure to charge him exorbitantly and that was so hugely gratifying she chuckled. It made her want to run into the street and invite every ragamuffin she laid eyes on into the house to dine courtesy of their generous local lord at a shilling a plate.

Felicity Jenner smiled back with shy friendliness and definite interest in what was being served up.

At Mrs Keene's slow backwards shuffle along the corridor, Emma called out, 'Oh, please don't disappear yet, Mrs Keene. Tonight is to be mutton hotpot with savoury dumplings or...what was the rest, Mrs Keene? Is it beef and roast vegetables, as yesterday? Saddle of lamb? Steak and oyster pie, perhaps? Such exceptional value is sure to tempt many customers into your eating room. Miss Jenner and I are both at a loose end. We can go into the street and drum you up some noon trade. Now what do you say to that?'

A burbled croak was all a horrified Mrs Keene was capable of emitting. Then, with a poisonous glare over a slumped shoulder, she was scurrying below.

Sir Richard Du Quesne looked at the list in front of him. A quill trailed the column of names, settled again by Matthew Drury and the nib tapped idly.

He looked up, at nothing in particular, then grunted a laugh. It couldn't be: the man was hardly tall and his hair was more red than brown...besides, to his knowledge he had no children. He glanced back at the listing of all the men he could bring to mind named Matthew, who seemed of about the right social status, lived locally and who in some shape or form fitted Mrs Keene's description. None seemed right.

If Emma Worthington's *friend* wasn't a figment of her land-lady's wily imagination, it seemed reasonable to assume he must be living somewhere hereabouts. Perhaps they'd travelled from London together. Perhaps, on learning of her condition, he'd bolted first and she'd followed him.

He pushed himself back from his desk with an irritated sigh, a tanned hand at the nape of his neck easing the tension beneath pale gilt hair. He was beginning to wish to God he'd never been at Yvette's when Emma had shown up. He'd not had a minute's peace since. Even that first glimpse of her at the Fallow Buck posting house—and he knew now with absolute certainty that it had been her—had left him unaccountably restless.

He wouldn't have been in South Parade at that time in the afternoon had he not succumbed to Yvette's erotic thanks for the bauble he'd bought for her during their shopping trip an hour earlier. The fact that he had been very actively employed with Yvette while Emma sat patiently awaiting an audience barely twenty yards away both humbled and harassed him.

The idea that the two women might ever have dealt 'companionably' together caused him to smile. Had he not been there, and Emma had been taken on, sparks would now be flying fit to burn his Palladian town house down. Miss Spitfire Worthington made Yvette...made most women...seem insipid. In fact, he acknowledged with a scowl, Miss Worthington was once again fascinating him too damned much, and continuing to justify his involvement in her welfare as simply duty to his friend, David, was self-deluding. His body was constantly reminding him just how interested he was on his own account.

He had become interested on his own account three years ago when David had been pursuing Victoria. Initially he had turned his attention to Emma to assist David and separate her from her friend. After one memorable meeting with Miss Worthington, when she'd stunned him as much with her beautiful golden eyes as with her memorable insults, he had been, for no sensible reason, smitten and planning his own courtship strategies. But she was having none of it. Every tentative friendly overture had resulted in a withering snub.

For an eligible bachelor hounded by tenacious debutantes and demi-reps alike, the novelty of unequivocal rejection had had him reinflating his crushed ego in a time-honoured way, thus fully meriting Emma's allusions to his turpitude.

She had made it clear she didn't like or trust him then; neither did she like or trust him now. And yet he just couldn't put her from his mind...or body. He'd kissed her now and that told him all he needed to know: she wasn't nearly as cold and indifferent as she wanted him to think. He'd experienced far more erotic kisses but nothing matched the satisfaction of her spontaneous surrender. It had both excited and gentled him, stirring something completely new: he *wanted* her to like him. He wanted her approval and respect because she had his...she had always had his. So he'd let her go.

When they'd first met, he had been struck by her beauty and wit. But her courage and honesty had captivated him too: she'd dared what no other woman ever had, even his mother. She'd flouted at his licentious lifestyle.

Three years on, she'd lost none of her spirit, which probably meant her pregnancy was the result of an ill-starred love-affair rather than ravishment. While that gave him a sense of quiet relief, it also agitated a burning resentment of this faceless man who had won her affection and esteem.

With an impatient curse at such singular sentimentality, he reached for the brandy decanter and the cigar box. One innocently alluring kiss...one clawed cheek for his noble self-restraint and eccentric generosity, and he was behaving like a languishing hero in a romantic novel. She was expecting another man's child, for God's sake! The sensible course of action was to keep her respectably lodged until this Matthew, if indeed he was her lover, could be found and persuaded to take her on.

He irritably jammed himself back in his chair just as Stephen entered his study with a companion. They were of approximately the same lofty height, yet the dark-haired man with his blond brother was of impressive muscular stature.

'Ross! I had no idea you were here. Where have you been hiding? Have you been in Bath long?' Richard greeted his friend and business associate recently arrived from Cornwall. In an instant he had risen from his desk and was striding towards him. The men shook hands and embraced warmly.

'Well, long enough for Stephen to introduce me to a rather fine claret and his very fine new addition to the family,' Ross

Trelawney said with a grin. 'The child's going to be a beauty like her mother.'

Noting his younger brother's wide grin and proud, puffed-up demeanour, Richard said drily, 'Have a cigar.'

Stephen took one; so did Ross on being offered the box.

Sauntering idly to the desk, Stephen frowned at the column of names on the paper. He picked it up, perusing it. 'What's this?'

'Just someone I was trying to bring to mind: a man named Matthew who lives locally—quite tall, I'm told, with light brown hair. He's probably reasonably well-connected and might have two children.'

'What's it all about? A woman? A lynching?' Stephen chortled.

Richard smiled at the fingers holding his smouldering cheroot. *'Touché...'* he murmured wryly to himself. 'Just some gossip I heard,' he said aloud. 'It's needling me that I can't recall the man. I'm sure I must know him.'

Stephen let the paper drift back to the leather-topped desk. 'We thought we'd go into town to Bellamy's, then perhaps on to the theatre...are you coming?' At his older brother's hesitation, Stephen slyly hinted, 'Or have you and the comely Yvette more exclusive plans for tonight?' A suggestive elbow nudged Ross's side. Stephen winked, slow and lewd, at the same time pouring himself a generous measure of brandy.

'You're not going,' Richard mentioned idly to his younger brother.

Stephen looked crestfallen, his jaw dropped and his untasted drink plonked onto the desk. 'Whaaat...?'

'You're not going. It's your wife's birthday this week. She's been left alone most evenings while you've been carousing in town. It's time you took her out. I'm sick of going into one room or another and seeing Amelia on the verge of tears and Mother clucking over her having a nervous attack.'

'Oh, Amelia's well enough,' Stephen dismissed cheerily. 'I'll take her to the opera on Saturday. I recall her being moody for a few months after Jake was born. It must be a female thing...a malaise that follows confinement. It makes her vexed and weepy.'

'Perhaps it's you that makes her vexed and weepy,' Richard coolly suggested.

'Am I missing something here?' Ross interjected, waving his cigar between them as he aimed perfect smoke rings at a scintillating chandelier.

'Stephen thinks he's in line for a little extra-marital entertainment. I expect he's hoping you'll show him the best places to find it later. He's bored, bless him.'

'Is that so...?' Ross said, with a thoughtful look at Stephen. 'And Amelia? Is she bored?' he asked.

'Of course not. Women don't get restless urges like men...like that...' Stephen blustered.

Richard and Ross exchanged looks of surprised enlightenment.

'Well, if she does get restless urges...like that,' Ross said with gentle gravity, 'be sure and let me know, won't you...?'

Stephen stalked off a way and stared out of the window. 'What is this? A conspiracy? Here I have under one roof, in the same goddamn room, no less, two of the most notorious Lotharios of my, or anyone else's, acquaintance. Do I get a little manly advice? Do I get a few tips on where the best muslin congregates? Oh, no! I get moralising and I get jokes...' His arm flung out, emphasising disappointment and disgust.

'Oh, I wasn't joking, Stephen,' Ross said.

Stephen stared at him as though he didn't fully understand, then he launched himself across the room, screaming, 'You filthy bastard...'

Ross adroitly sidestepped his flailing fists and put out his hands placatingly. When Stephen still swung savagely at him, a muscular arm gripped him restrictingly about the shoulders and held him close. 'Listen, Steve...' Ross soothed. 'Your wife's a very beautiful woman. I'm not blind or alone in noticing that. Once it's gossiped about that you're seeking diversion and neglecting her, she'll be approached. And there'll be plenty of eager young bucks ready to console her. Who would you rather it was...?'

Stephen wrenched himself free of Ross's comforting embrace and stalked, stiff-backed, towards the door. He glowered over his shoulder at the two tall men of strikingly dissimilar colouring. 'Enjoy yourselves...' he snarled before the door crashed shut.

Richard's grey eyes met Ross's green-flecked gaze over the rim of a brandy balloon. 'Yes, I know. We're a pair of rank hypocrites,' he muttered, before abruptly throwing the cognac down his throat. He smacked the glass back onto the desk.

'Thanks anyway. She's the best thing that ever happened to him. Unfortunately, she happened about ten years too soon. If he didn't love her I wouldn't bother. But, God knows, a love match is too rare and precious to be discarded lightly. If he takes a mistress things will never be the same between them. If she retaliates and takes a lover and he finds out...well, you just saw his reaction to the possibility. The reality might have him committing murder and I don't want my nephew and heir growing up in the shadow of some sordid scandal.'

Richard sighed and stared out of the window into a mellow autumn afternoon, his head angling so long fingers could massage the tension in his neck. 'I know it's been difficult for him...Amelia's been out of bounds for a while. The least I can do is throw a few obstacles in his way until she's recovered from the birth and he's retrieved his brain from his breeches.' Another hollow laugh choked out of him. 'The proof...I am a rank hypocrite,' he sourly observed then stuck the cigar in his mouth and drew deeply. His bronzed hands were braced at either side of the window and he watched an endless avenue of silver-leaved whitebeam shimmering in the light breeze.

'Sounds like that came out of experience and straight from the heart, Dickie,' Ross drawled with a small smile and a shrewd look. 'And I never imagined I'd be saying that to you. Is it anything to do with this Yvette?'

Richard snorted a laugh. 'Hardly,' he said to the blue sky.

'Who is she?'

'A talented whore, my friend. That's who she is. And yes...you're very welcome...'

The door slammed back against the wall, cutting off further conversation.

Richard pivoted on his heel to see Stephen posed regally in the opening. 'I am taking my wife and my mother to the Upper Assembly Rooms,' he announced in a crisp, martyred way. 'I shall endeavour not to stand around looking available, lest I receive unsolicited female attention. And it's Cavendish,' he gritted, before putting wood back in the aperture with a resounding crack.

'Cavendish?' Ross echoed, then shook his head and shrugged his total bemusement at all of it.

'Cavendish!' The name resounded like gunshot as Richard's

eyes flicked to the list on the desk. He swore beneath his breath then said with slow, measured vehemence, 'Good God! Why the hell didn't I think of him...?'

Emma frowned at the note then reread it, a simultaneous warm joy and chill suspicion assailing her as her fingers unconsciously comforted a burning cheek.

'Is everythin' all right, m'dear?' Mrs Keene asked, quite disturbed by her lodger's alternately receding and heightening colour.

'Oh, yes. Thank you. Thank you, Mrs Keene, for bringing this. Was it delivered a while ago?'

'No, miss. Just a few short minutes since. Sir Richard's man be waitin' below for a reply. What shall I tell him?'

'Tell him...tell him...' Oh, God, what was she to tell him? raced through her mind. She needed time to think what to tell him. 'Tell him to wait, please, Mrs Keene. I shall endeavour to pen a reply as quickly as I can.'

'I could give to him your spoken reply,' the woman slyly offered as she squinted sideways at the letter, wishing she could decipher a few words.

'That won't be necessary, thank you, Mrs Keene,' Emma said, with a flash of sooty-fringed topaz eyes.

The woman sniffed and flounced out. She flounced back again. 'If you be soon movin' out, I'll start reckonin' up your account, shall I?' she said, letting Emma know she could make a good enough guess as to a certain gentleman's intentions, written or otherwise.

'Yes, and please also reckon up what Sir Richard owes you.'

Mrs Keene slanted her a look. 'Just you remember, I never said nothin' to you about the silver squire bein' generous on your account.'

Realising that her landlady was quite seriously anxious, Emma reassured her. 'I shall have no qualms in letting Sir Richard know I guessed he offered to supplement my board. Include every extra cost on your bill and I shall willingly present it to him...' She added gleefully beneath her breath, 'And test his generosity.'

'Well, not that it be none o' my concern, o' course, miss, but you're too sharp. Mark my words, you'll end up cuttin' yourself bad.' A plump finger wagged warningly. She hesitated on the way to the door. 'Every cost?' she asked uncertainly.

Emma nodded, her eyes on the succinct note she had received from Richard Du Quesne conveying such startling yet welcome news:

I wish to inform you that I attend the arrival of our very dear mutual friends, Viscount and Viscountess Courtenay, at Silverdale. I imagine you would not wish Victoria to quit Bath before you have had the opportunity to meet with her and perhaps discuss certain pressing matters; thus I should be pleased to have you join us as house guest this weekend. My mother, the dowager Miriam Du Quesne, and my sister-in-law, Amelia, are currently in residence. We are also graced with the presence of my mother's sister who shows as little inclination to return home as do my closer kin. In short, Silverdale is at present overflowing with suitable chaperons for a virtuous single woman: you need not fret for your reputation.

Send word with my man, Gibbs, if you are to honour us with your presence and a carriage will collect you at six of the clock this evening.

Yours etc.

P.S. Should you decide not to attend, please indicate how you would wish me to respond if drawn into debate on how you go on. You seem adept at evading those questions; thus it might be in your best interest to deal personally with such enquiries for I can't promise to match your skill.

Emma folded the paper and closed her eyes. Even the sarcastic references to her reputation and her virtue and her dissembling could not dampen her happiness. Victoria was soon here in Bath! Perhaps already here. It had to be true! Why would he lie?

A few evenings ago he had quite tersely dismissed her from his company. He was hardly likely to bother plotting to lure her back into it. The tone of his invitation was hardly persuasive. It was as wearily dutiful as had been his offer of aid. She could imagine him, in private, heartily bemoaning her arrival in Bath, her embarrassing presence at his mistress's house. No doubt they laughed at her together.

Now he had done his best: offered her his protection and supplemented her keep with his money. What more could he have done? he would no doubt shrug and sigh sanctimoniously if pressed on the matter. As a shrewd opportunist he had attempted to discharge his duty and still exploit her predicament to some advantage. After all, it was costing him dear...even if he didn't yet know quite how much. Emma smiled to herself with a certain malicious satisfaction, thinking of Mrs Keene even now totting up his account.

The chance to see Victoria was too tempting an offer to turn down. If there was one person she knew she could confide in, it was Victoria. Victoria had three years ago been through hardships and heartbreak herself before finding such bliss with David Hardinge, Viscount Courtenay. She would understand, she would sympathise, she would not judge her.

And Emma felt now in desperate need of some advice. For she had still not seen or heard from Matthew. It had been several days since he had dropped her off at her interview. He had not called at Lower Place even to enquire whether she was now employed.

In the immediate aftermath of her skirmish with Richard Du Quesne, she had been determined to accept Matthew's proposal. As the days dragged on with no opportunity to tell him so, niggling doubts again set in. She knew he did not love her in the way she wanted; indeed, she was no longer sure she still loved *him* in the way she wanted. But...it was security of sorts and if it were to come to choosing between marriage to him or vile Mr Dashwood...or being housed and intermittently used by Richard Du Quesne when the fancy took him...she knew very definitely which shelter she preferred.

But now she was close to being able to share all her problems with someone she truly loved. And she did love Victoria as the sister she had yearned for but never had. Enduring Richard Du Quesne's company for a few days was a small price to pay for spending precious time with Victoria, perhaps even seeing darling Lucy, too.

She grabbed at her quill, drew a sheet of paper close and while dipping for ink mulled over her reply. Her first instinct was to

match his mordant tone, but...she would rise above it and be
civil, she decided; after all, she was accepting his hospitality,
however reluctantly it was bestowed.

Topaz eyes squinted up lazily through dusky lashes at a million
leaves fluttering like sinuous pearly wings in a cobwebby canopy.
The avenue of trees undulated into the distance like a discarded
silver necklace. Emma's tawny head swayed sideways on the
squabs and she stared out over verdant swards to wooded horizons, the first vibrant autumn tints tipping gold into the dense
foliage. Then, as the carriage rattled over planked boards, fording
a crystal-clear, rushing stream, it swung to the left and she saw
the house.

Shifting forward on the seat, she tilted her head for a better
view. Cream bathstone gleamed mellow honey in the setting sun,
a bank of high windows afire with low, slanting rays. A wistful
amber gaze meandered from majestic chimneys to raked gravel.
It was magnificent in every aspect: its grand size, the perfect
symmetry of its spare Palladian architecture, its central positioning with neatly manicured parkland sweeping gracefully away on
three sides. Somehow she had known Silverdale would be this
wonderful; ultimate confirmation elicited a small wry smile: the
injustice...the irony of it all! That such a degenerate should be
allowed to reside within such splendidly decorous walls.

The coach rumbled on, finally scrunching to a halt before an
imposing porticoed entrance. A footman opened the door for
Emma and politely assisted her to alight.

A smartly uniformed butler was sedately descending a flight
of flared stone steps. Halting by the carriage, he executed a stiff
bow. 'Simmons, at your service, Miss Worthington,' he formally
introduced himself. 'Sir Richard is expecting you. Please come
this way.'

Emma reached down for her carpet bag but Simmons shot her
an alarmed look. 'Gibbs will get that,' he reproved, with a
haughty glance at the hovering footman that sent his eyebrows
shifting in opposite directions.

Emma started to demur but, on noting Simmons's shocked
look, eyebrows jiggling, quickly dropped her bag to the driveway

gravel and smiled her thanks. 'When in Rome...' she muttered beneath her breath.

'Are Viscount and Viscountess Courtenay arrived?' she asked pleasantly on gathering her skirts in her fists and following Simmons's starchy black figure. As she climbed wide stone steps, a niggling anxiety returned to disturb her. She had fled London with very few clothes: she had quickly pounced on a few gowns with no thought other than they must be serviceable and versatile. She was sure to feel quite dowdy amid such grandeur. But then, she sighed, she wasn't here to parade in finery, simply to see her dear friend, and perhaps, with Victoria's fresh eye, discover a solution to her problems.

But then, logically, there were only two options and she was sure practical Victoria would soon point them out: she could return to London praying that Jarrett Dashwood had meanwhile taken himself off elsewhere in pursuit of a drudge to wed; alternatively she could finally contact her parents and inform them she was to marry Matthew Cavendish in Bath...assuming Matthew still desired her as a wife. There *was* a third possibility, or rather a probability: Victoria would insist on offering financial aid.

Viscount Courtenay would loan her father money—primarily because Victoria asked him to, but also because he was a very wealthy and very generous man. Emma's eyes squeezed in mortification. She wouldn't be able to bear the prospect of her wastrel father shamelessly accepting charity. She knew he would have no qualms in using another man's cash to pay his way at the card tables or the gin houses he frequented while he left a mountain of bills untouched on his desk.

Yet, as much as she despaired of her shallow parents, in her own way she loved and missed them too. It was some while since she'd decamped and now every passing hour increased her guilt and worry as to how they did.

With a sigh she allowed dresses to again monopolise her thoughts. No doubt, even in that inconsequential respect, dear Vicky would help out. They had before, on happier occasions, swapped gowns. Abruptly recalling that her query as to the Courtenays' arrival was still unanswered, she angled her face to Simmons. As they proceeded over the threshold into a spacious hallway she repeated, 'Are Viscount and Viscountess Courtenay yet arrived?'

'No.'

Emma stopped dead. Just one quietly spoken word yet she immediately recognised the voice. Momentarily blinded by the shadowy interior after such strong evening sunlight, she squinted in the direction of slow, approaching footfalls. She was obliquely aware of the great doors being closed behind her and that light now entered through a many-faceted window well set high in a domed ceiling. Sunbeams shafted into a central pool, gilding creamy marble flags between soaring marble pillars.

Sir Richard Du Quesne stepped through the dusty radiance, the top of his blond head momentarily incandescent, and then he was into the shadows again and closing with her.

Emma immediately raised her eyes to his, seeking to read something positive in his face despite his negative response.

She dipped a curtsey but refused to demurely lower her face. Instead it tilted a little to one side. Her chin came up, her full, soft mouth pursed aslant, proud and challenging. If he thought for one minute he had intimidated her with that proposition...with that kiss...he would find he was much mistaken. She had barely let it worry her. She had scarcely given it a second thought.

'How have you been?'

'Very well, thank you, sir. And you?' Emma politely returned.

'Do you care today how I do, Emma?' His expression was unreadable, his tone laden with irony.

Emma felt her colour rising as he alluded to her past discourtesies. 'No,' she retorted, impenitently, and her eyes slid away over stately furniture she could see looming against distant walls.

She could sense his sardonic amusement, his unwavering attention searing the side of her face as she studied her opulent surroundings. And suddenly she knew she couldn't possibly stay here, with him, longer than was absolutely necessary. 'I thank you very much for your invitation to spend the weekend here,' she stiltedly began, 'but I must decline your hospitality. I have simply come to speak to Victoria before I return to my lodgings. Is she soon due?'

'No.'

Emma's face jerked up to his dark, handsome features. 'No?' she breathed.

'No,' he repeated, his argentine eyes as cool as his tone.

'In your letter you wrote that...' She trailed into silence as her face pricked with an awful icy suspicion. 'You lied?' she whispered, unconsciously taking an unsteady step back.

'Yes.'

'Why?' she demanded, unable to keep a hint of panic from her tone.

'It's my turn,' he said.

Chapter Six

Emma took two faltering backward steps then swished about and made for the double doors. Her small hands lunged at heavy brass handles and frenziedly yanked, rattled. 'Open these doors! At once!' she hissed, lashing out at dense oak panels with a small clenched fist.

Approaching footsteps had her twisting about. Her head shook back, violently dislodging her bonnet to hang on unequal ribbons. One hand instinctively prevented it falling from tumbling, tawny hair; the other snaked behind to a cold metal knob and recommenced frantically jerking at it.

'Running away again, Emma? Where to this time?' Richard softly taunted.

'It's none of your concern!' Emma shrilled. Where was she going? Even if she had a destination, how on earth did she intend reaching it? She judged the city of Bath to be five miles distant from the estate of Silverdale. The nearest cottages she recalled passing must have been at least two miles away through that winding avenue of whispering silver-leaved trees.

She would walk back to Mrs Keene's lodging house, she intrepidly decided. But her fragile valour crumbled with the memory of her confrontation with this man in that parlour: she had brandished charges of molestation; he had disquietingly responded that she was a little early with such a complaint. Her reckless stupidity that evening dominated her thoughts. Why on earth had she used empty threats and insults? Or scratched his face? Or brazenly led him to believe she was with child?

'Is your mother here? Or your other female relatives? Or was that lies, too?' was quaveringly flung at him. Then, twisting about to face the massive doors, her small palms slid on brass fittings too huge for her grip. As betraying heat pricked the backs of her eyes her head bowed. As the first wet squeezed through her lashes, a small foot frustratedly kicked out at impenetrable oak.

'Come here, Emma...' Richard's voice was as thick and soothing as honey, all trace of humour gone.

She faced him at the soft command, her sculpted little chin immediately coming up and small teeth clamping into her wobbly bottom lip. Silver eyes narrowed on her proud white face, seeking contact with her fugitive eyes, but they were now riveted to one side of him.

Richard pivoted on a heel to see Ross Trelawney on the stairs, tossing and catching a coin single-handedly in slick rhythm as he descended. On seeing Richard he pocketed the sovereign and walked over, smiling.

A dilating amber gaze slid between two powerfully virile men of similar height but contrasting looks. Emma swallowed and stiffened against the door, her mouth too arid to again demand if ladies were present. But then she already knew the answer: Silverdale seemed shrouded in a solitude that scorned her panic. Only servants and these two men were within its stately walls.

Three years ago Richard Du Quesne had had a reputation as a profligate. The fact that he had taken himself off abroad for a while in no way indicated reform. When in London together, he and Dashwood might be colleagues who frequented the same sordid haunts. Drunken orgies...young, friendless women abused then discarded...she knew of the whispers, if not the perpetrators, and had dismissed it as salacious scandalmongering... Her desperation to see Victoria had made her negligent. Momentarily she had lost sight of the calibre of heartless rake she was dealing with.

You *encouraged* him to think you a fallen woman! reverberated through her, making her quake on the spot. Why *should* he now bother maintaining a sham of consideration or respect? This stranger with the dark hair and wickedly laughing eyes is probably a rogue in the same mould, too... The hysterical suppositions streamed together, converging into a maelstrom of plausible horror threatening to engulf her. She was aware of a hand reaching for her and instinctively shrank back against the door, slapping frantically at long bronzed fingers.

Dark hands fastened on her arms, restricting them to her sides as Richard jerked her against him. 'Listen to me,' he soothed, yet with such a razored edge of steel to his voice that she actually did so. 'This is a good friend of mine, who is presently a house guest...as you are.' A glance flicked at Ross. 'Ross Trelawney, meet Miss Emma Worthington. Emma is a close friend of the Courtenays. She's recently arrived from London and is to honour us with her presence at Silverdale for a while.'

Ross prised free one of Emma's small hands from Richard's restraint and raised it gallantly to his lips. 'I'm very pleased to meet you, Miss Worthington. No doubt we shall see a deal of each other in the next few days...if I'm allowed.' He slanted a canny glance at his friend and despairingly shook his head. 'Not you, too, Dickie... I'm off to Bath for an hour or so...' drifted back as he strolled away to collect his hat and gloves.

Emma strained ineffectively against Richard's imprisonment. 'I wish to return to Bath. May I beg a ride with you, please, sir?'

'No, you may not,' Richard bit out quietly.

Ross hesitated and said amiably, 'Dickie, you can't keep the lady here against her will.'

'I don't intend to,' Richard whiplashed back, his eyes like shards of ice.

Emma sensed the atmosphere leadening with tension and knew she was the cause of it. She could depart with this stranger she didn't know at all, or stay with this man she knew a little...and distrusted a lot. He had lied to her...tricked her.

But she had lied to him...tricked him.

Richard's eyes locked onto hers, warning, threatening... He was allowing her to choose yet she knew if she rejected him at some time she would pay.

A terrified exhilaration caught a ragged breath in her throat as she stressed for Ross, 'I should be most *grateful* for a ride to Bath, sir.' Long fingers reflexively bit into her arms and then they were gone.

Ross grimaced, gesturing himself innocent of influencing her decision with spread hands. Noting his friend's murderous expression, his dark head lolled back and he mouthed an expletive at the ceiling.

'She stays here with me,' Richard said very reasonably, very coolly as he slowly paced to confront Ross in the centre of the marble hallway.

Emma watched in awe, absently rubbing at lingering phantom pressure on her arms. Minutes ago she had believed herself in peril of degradation; now, for some inexplicable reason, she knew she was not...and never had been.

Ross Trelawney didn't want her to share his carriage into town; he wanted harmony with his friend. But his decency obliged him to offer whilst hoping she would decline. And she had been so quick to brand her champion a rogue! Guilt and chagrin made her complexion flush rosily, yet the few, required words of reparation refused to relinquish her throat.

Shunning Richard Du Quesne's company in favour of a stranger she had never met before was an insult to his character, his integrity and his hospitality. He was utterly enraged: she could see wrath in every harsh, rigid angle of his bronze face, in his light, purposeful step as he approached Ross. He wanted to punish her; instead he would fight his friend to soothe his ego.

'Richard...be sensible...' A disarming smile and conciliatory tone from Ross elicited no response other than a vague elevation of dark brows.

'The blue silk was preferable, Diane. You look like a complete fright in that...that... What is it, in any case? Is it a pink...a purple? A poor choice, indeed, with those fractured veins on your nose.' A cultured female voice penetrated solid wood, mingling with the scraping of footsteps on stone.

Abruptly the double doors swung inwards, forcing Emma to hasten away from them. Two liveried footmen took up position in the wide aperture and a party of chattering people trooped through the wedge of sunlight.

Emma gawped at the sight of two stylish middle-aged women picking and flicking at a red bonnet as they proceeded into the hallway. The shorter of the two rotated it in her hands to aid inspection. Behind came a young couple: the woman blonde and pretty and the man also fair and tall. A small boy slouched at the woman's side, attempting to wriggle his hand free of hers.

The more regal-countenanced of the matrons abruptly batted

away the hat as if bored with it. Her short companion smoothed the skewed crimson feathers then settled it atop her head.

'Ah, there you are Richard,' Miriam Du Quesne observed, spying her eldest son stationed in the centre of the sun-glossed marble flags. Her encompassing gaze took in his friend close by. 'Never say that you and Ross are about to bolt! I won't have it, you hear! Guests are due. The Petershams are to arrive at eight. Everyone is to sit down at nine. Now what is the time?'

Miriam gazed about and spied Emma hovering uncertainly in the shadows behind the door. She frowned, then comprehension widened her blue eyes. 'Oh, my dear... It's Miss Worthington, is it not?' A thin, pale hand flew in consternation to her delicately rouged mouth. 'I completely forgot you were to come earlier at six. Richard reminded me of it this morning, too. How awful of me not to be here to greet you!' She rushed to Emma and took her hands. 'I'm so sorry, my dear! We would have been back from shopping sooner but my sister, Diane, insisted on returning to the first ever shop we went into to purchase a Parisian hat...monstrosity,' she breathed at Emma with an expressive roll of her blue eyes.

'And then dear Jake—' a languid hand-flap indicated the young boy '—took a tumble and skinned his knee.' Miriam continued with her explanations. 'We were into the apothecary's sorting through the potions. Then on to the confectioner's to find a treat to cheer him up...and stop him howling.' Her lids fluttered, a tortured expression wrinkling her smooth, powdered features.

The young invalid trotted to his uncle and solemnly displayed his wound. With a final glare at Ross, Richard swung the boy into his arms, inspected the damage and gravely praised his bravery. Jake settled his small bright head against a powerful shoulder and sucked his thumb.

Emma looked at them together; the beautiful child she had believed to be his bastard son was obviously his nephew. Jumping so readily to a base conclusion was reprehensible and added to the remorse already choking her. She had misjudged so much! Even to thinking that he had lied about his female relatives being in residence.

'Now come along with me, Miss Wor...may I call you Emma?' Miriam asked. 'I feel as though I do know you. Every time dear Victoria is here she talks of you. We'll do proper introductions later, but for now…' Turning Emma by the arm, she wagged an elegant, indolent finger at people, listing, 'My younger son, Stephen, his dear wife Amelia and my sister, Diane, and sweet little Jake, my grandson.' She indicated the boy drowsing in his uncle's arms. 'Oh, stupid!' she chided herself. 'I, of course, am Richard's mama. You may call me Miriam.'

Emma moistened her lips, about to speak…say something, anything for her shock had receded enough for her to begin feeling uneasily dumb. But then she hadn't rallied quite enough intelligence to decide what to say…or do. And even if she had, slipping a word into her hostess's chatty monologue was not going to be easy. She drew a deep breath, managed a wavering smile and…

'The Courtenays are such a lovely couple. They visited me even when Dickie was abroad…oh, that's what they call him but then I expect you do, too, although I prefer Richard. And they brought that darling child especially to see me. Of course you are godmother to little Lucy and Richard is godfather, even though he missed the ceremony because of his beloved papa's ill health at that time. David, of course, is very fond of me. And I of him, rogue that he is…was, I should say. Such a change in a man I've never before witnessed! But then he *is* so in love…'

'I want to speak to you.' The clipped words sliced icily through Miriam's rambling discourse, making her cease, open-mouthed.

For a moment the hallway's occupants were united in silence. All eyes were riveted either on Richard's saturnine features or Emma's steadily heightening colour, for it became obvious from his relentless stare that he was addressing her rather than his gregarious mother.

'Now…' Richard purred into the crackling quiet as he set the child back onto the flags.

Ross exchanged an explicit, amused look with Stephen. With a hasty farewell, he was then through the door and on his way down the stone steps before Emma could launch even an appealing glance his way. With a perfunctory peck for his wife Stephen was soon after him in the hope of catching up with some gossip.

Diane and Amelia drifted away to the mirror, apparently accustomed to the brusque dictates of the master of the house, and assisted each other in positioning the *chapeau* to its best advantage.

Miriam shrugged stiffly. 'He has his moods...just humour him, my dear, or he'll storm off out and not be back in time for the Petershams. I expect he wants to talk privately to you of your mutual friends.' A weary sigh preceded, 'He can be so churlishly impatient at times...'

Emma felt like laughing hysterically and stating that unforgivably rude was her opinion, but there was no time. Her elbow was gripped in firm fingers and she was being propelled across the hallway at some speed. She tried to carelessly shake herself free. On glancing back, Miriam beamed a smile and flicked a hand in a dismissive, eloquent way. *Just go along with him,* Emma read in the languid signal, and some mouthed encouragement, before Miriam, too, was at the mirror and it was her turn with the scarlet headgear.

As soon as they had rounded the corner into a seemingly endless stretch of sumptuously carpeted corridor, Emma wrenched free and backed against the watered-silk wall.

Richard made no attempt to touch her again but a glimmering silver gaze scorched down at her. After an aggressive moment molten copper eyes finally flinched from his, and he pointed along the hallway. 'Second door along on the left-hand side. You can walk or I can carry you...'

She looked scornfully up at him, about to dare him to try and do so with his mother barely yards away, but something in the sardonic enquiring lift of one eyebrow told her he would do as he pleased in his own home. She'd already gleaned as much: his mother might demand his punctuality at dinner, but she guessed it was entirely at his own whim whether he even graced them with his presence.

She flung herself away from the wall, marched proudly to the appointed doorway and halted with her chin tilted. He opened the door, mocked her with a bow and indicated she should precede him in.

The spacious library soared upwards and outwards and for a moment held her quietly spellbound. She took a few paces within, her amber eyes clambering up library steps, sliding along polished shelves housing neatly ranged books within a mellow wood gallery then down the stairs on the opposite side of the room. She had never seen such a magnificent collection of books. It took her breath away and the fact didn't go unnoticed.

'Well, well,' Richard remarked drily, having allowed her a few moments of fascinated quiet. 'Had I known how a stocked library affects you, I would have had you brought into the house this way.' A bronzed finger flicked idly at large double doors that opened out onto a terrace.

Emma sensed her cheeks burn and her clinging gaze tore reluctantly from the tomes to study her feet. Then a cool, aloof gaze lifted to his dark face. 'I want to go home,' she stated.

'Home? You're ready to return to London?'

'No. I want to return to my lodgings.'

'You class that as home?' he asked quietly.

She turned away to hide her flushed confusion, for the fact that she subconsciously referred to such a lonely, soulless place as home was, indeed, disturbing. 'Temporarily...yes,' she murmured at some leather-bound spines.

He seemed about to speak then shoved his hands into his pockets and frowned at the ceiling. 'I'm sorry,' he said tightly. 'I shouldn't have misled you about David and Victoria being soon due. It wasn't actually a lie; I am expecting them in a fortnight. And I'm sorry I hadn't realised just how sincerely you despise me. I don't want to frighten you...quite the reverse.'

'I'm not frightened,' Emma choked fiercely but in a voice that was unevenly pitched.

'You were terrified,' Richard contradicted with a hollow laugh. 'If I'd known you seriously considered me capable of luring you here for some depraved purpose, I'd have arranged for my mother to collect and accompany you. But then I truly believed she would be about to greet you when you arrived. I apologise for that too.'

Emma sensed her own guilty regrets sharpen with his unexpected grace and honesty. She moistened her lips and raised topaz eyes to his face. He was watching her steadily, keeping his expression quite neutral.

'Why did you imply Victoria would be here?' she asked huskily, her disappointment keening in every word.

'Was there anything else I could have tempted you with? It was the only sure way of getting you here.'

'Why do you want me here?' she demanded in the same hoarse tone.

'I've told you...you need someone to care for you,' he returned impassively. 'You can't stay in that seedy hole, especially not in your delicate condition.'

Emma felt her face burn at the allusion to yet more of her deceit. It made her lash out defensively. 'And why should you worry about my accommodation? Why should you care at all? There's nothing in it for you...'

His eyes arrested hers as they attempted veering past. Her oblique reminder of spurning his proposition tautened the space between them.

Long, dusky lashes fringed low over silver eyes. 'Well, perhaps I'll let you entertain me in other ways. That acid tongue of yours for a start—maybe it sweetens when you sing.' A hand reached out so quickly she had no time for evasion. He raised slender, quivering fingers in his and looked at them. 'Perhaps these can set about an instrument more kindly than they do me.'

He abruptly released her and strolled to stare out into the garden. 'If you're going to fret over the cost of your keep here at Silverdale,' drifted back to her, 'just divert my mother's attention, and be a friend to Amelia; that'll repay me tenfold. They seem to have taken to you.'

'I think I shall like them, too,' Emma replied quietly, but her nervous thoughts were elsewhere. The mention of the cost of her keep reminded her she had in a pocket of her cloak two leaves of paper covered in Mrs Keene's sums. She was now loath to present him with that fraudulent account...and yet she had promised Mrs Keene she would.

She couldn't be sure how many of Lower Place's hungry residents had enjoyed fine dinners over four days courtesy of this man. She did know that in that time Mrs Keene had twice run out of meat and sitting space in her eating house. She also knew there was a grand total of ninety-five guineas at the bottom of a page followed by a flourishing signature.

'I...I have something for you.' She firmly withdrew the account with tremulous fingers and valiantly proffered it, watching with bated breath as his eyes leisurely descended first one, then the other page, without a flicker of expression.

'You have a good appetite, Emma, I see,' he eventually said.

'Over two hundred meals in four days. I'm not now sure I can afford to keep you here,' he solemnly added.

It was impossible to prevent the sudden rush of blood from staining her cheeks. 'I'm eating for two and get very hungry,' she returned flippantly, then floundered for she hated compounding her deceit. She hated feeling so wretchedly mean, too, after his chivalrous apology and offer of care and hospitality. 'I told you not to pay anything to Mrs Keene on my account. You insisted on interfering so you should take the consequences or...or Mrs Keene will sue you.'

'Will she?' he asked, with a flash of a white smile. 'How do you know?'

'I told her to. I told her how to go about it and that I would stand witness. I know how it's done.' Oh, she knew well enough! If there was one thing Emma had learned during twenty-seven years in her papa's wastrel company it was the process of being dunned.

He looked at the papers again and his smile transformed into a silent laugh. He had a team of the finest lawyers on retainer who would bury any such claim and counter-sue punitively if he let them...once they'd ceased guffawing.

'You will pay it, won't you?'

'What's it worth?'

He arrowed a sideways look at her and then frowned in regret. How many times had he heard that phrase? He'd responded spontaneously...as he always did on being presented with an outrageously extravagant bill by a woman he desired. And usually she was more than happy to suggest ways of repayment. Only this time, as he'd already been told, there was nothing in it for him. A brown hand flicked dismissively. 'My apologies. Just for a moment I forgot myself.' The papers were neatly folded and slipped into a pocket. 'Of course I'll settle it,' he graciously agreed, as though he'd never confused her with a mercenary harlot.

Emma burned in earnest, feeling more wretched than ever. Had she behaved in a way that a greedy, scheming mistress would? She believed he had, indeed, forgotten himself...and who she was. The money hadn't been spent on her own account! she wanted to shout. It had benefited people much worse off. She shouldn't have done it! Now she felt...

'I'm sorry,' she whispered. 'I shouldn't have done it. It was...it started as a joke. I just wanted Mrs Keene's other lodger to be treated as I was and then...there are many people who live in that area much hungrier than I have ever been and I was annoyed at you...'

She was unaware he had moved away from the window and approached her until a dark hand lifted into her line of vision. It drifted to her face, touching with just enough pressure to tilt it to his. 'Well, I'm not annoyed at you. I admire your philanthropy. I will pay it. But I don't want to hear any more of it. Now what's that worth?' he said huskily as grey eyes merged with amber. 'I'd say it must be worth at least...' He deliberately hesitated, looking thoughtful, then, as she flushed, concluded innocently, 'A truce?'

Her tongue-tip moistened her lower lip and she was aware of him unwaveringly watching its movement. Her soft lips immediately pressed together as though she could conceal them.

'I said a truce, Emma,' he said wryly, releasing her face with a trailing stroke of a finger. He extended a hand. 'Shake on it.'

After a momentary hesitation pale, slender fingers lightly curled about long bronzed ones. She gave him a wavering smile and, on doing so, realised it was the first time since their reunion in Bath that she had smiled at him with friendliness rather than sarcasm. Even three years ago in London she couldn't remember directing an amiable smile his way. Her fingers fluttered within his, endeavouring to tactfully withdraw, and finally he allowed it.

She backed away a few steps, hunting in her mind for some bland conversation as a prelude to escaping. 'The nickname Mrs Keene used...silver squire...is it because of how you look?' Emma blurted out chattily.

'How I look?' he echoed with a smile.

'Your blond hair and grey eyes...' She rattled off her observation so fast and quietly, she hoped he would dismiss it and change the subject, but his amusement increased.

As though savouring her revealingly intimate remark, he allowed a silent, lingering moment before teasing very gently, 'You've looked at me long enough to notice I have grey eyes? I'm amazed!'

Emma flushed in earnest, frowning through the window. All

she'd intended was a little civil dialogue. Why could she never
get anything right? As she was about to hurtle from the room
and devil take pleasantries, he came to her rescue.

'It's been used by locals for generations. I've always assumed
it grew out of the Du Quesne's involvement in silver mining in
Devon. And the house was named after the avenue of silver trees.
But, now you mention it, there has been a preponderance of
blond-haired, grey-eyed baronets in the family...several of us
with sterling qualities...'

She nodded quickly, hoping he would mock her no more on
the subject, wondering how she could escape to his mother and
thence, she hoped, to a chamber and rest. She felt drained and
in need of solitude and the opportunity to sleep for a while.

Recalling Miriam's preoccupation with dinnertime, she exploded quietly, 'I won't keep you. I expect you were going out
with your friend. Your mother will be upset should you return
late to dine with your guests.'

'I'm not going out,' he demurred, an air of latent amusement
still about him.

The thought of Ross Trelawney's gallantry made her dart a
look at Richard. Would they now avoid each other because of
the antagonism she had fired between them? She had almost
caused them to fight! The memory was simultaneously shameful
and oddly thrilling. Even in her youthful heyday, no man had
ever seemed desperate to retain the pleasure of her company. Of
course, Richard was simply minding his masculine pride by insisting she stay with him. She might distract him with her
gaucheness but she was sure the primary reason he kept her close
was onerous duty to David Hardinge.

A few days ago he had punished her with a kiss then dismissed
her as though she bored him. Today, she had nearly caused havoc
in his stately vestibule, fearing a dowdy spinster of twenty-seven
could incite him to act the lecher in his own home. Considering
the circumstances calmly now, and the fact of his pretty young
mistress housed in the neighbourhood, she knew her ridiculous
arrogance should have provoked hilarity; instead she cringed.
Aware that he was observing her pink-faced pensiveness, she
garbled out, 'I...I hope that you and Mr Trelawney will not be...
I didn't mean to cause you... That is, I should hate there to be
friction between you,' she finally settled on.

'Ross and I are used to a little...er...friction between us.'

Uncertain she had correctly understood the subliminal message, she ventured, 'You have fought Ross before?'

'Oh, yes,' he said with a grin.

'Over...over a woman?' she audaciously asked, but her inquisitiveness was too great for indelicacy to matter.

'Oh, no,' he said with a gentle smile.

Emma's wide glossy gaze was on him, thoughtfully assessing the lean angles of his handsome dark face. She recalled Victoria saying that David would have been killed abroad, in the war, but for this man fighting alongside him. David owed Dickie his life, Victoria had gravely told her.

Richard stared back, feeling the heat in his groin rage beneath her liquid golden gaze. His long lashes dropped low over his eyes. God, she was captivating, with those beautiful doe-eyes and fawn hair wisping untidily about her face. Her bonnet was still askew about her shoulders and he wanted to remove it and the drab cloak that obscured the slender lines of her body. But he knew if he touched her now he'd break the spell. She'd bolt, or lash out at him like some skittish little creature.

He inwardly groaned his frustration. The only way he could get her to relax, to look straight at him without wariness or disgust but with frank interest, was to discuss the various brawls he and Ross had participated in over the many years of their acquaintance.

'What did you fight over?' Emma asked almost brightly.

'What over?' Richard echoed huskily. 'Well...there was the time he cheated at cards. The time I did. The time he wagered on copper prices rising then reduced his mines' output to ensure they did. Then there was the time I did something similar with my mines and he was furious not to recognise the plot. There was the time he took my Highflyer out without asking and turned it over then brought it back...over several trips...' He hesitated, smiling at her engrossed attention. 'Do you want more instances?'

'Are there more?'

'Undoubtedly...if I care to set my mind to it.'

'Who wins these fights?'

'I think...at last count...it was about eight to five in my favour. One of those he claims against me I disallow, though, Emma,' he said with studied gravity. 'He waited until I was...er...a little inebriated before throwing the first punch. Very ungentlemanly. Besides, since I turned thirty and became a baronet a little more decorum is called for. We try to settle our differences with dignified discussion...initially,' he added on a slow smile.

She choked a little laugh, her eyes as warm and honeyed as cognac pools in her creamy complexion.

'Today, the fear of losing a truly unique woman to him, made me entirely disallow dignified discussion,' he admitted huskily.

Her smile fled. 'There's really no need to humour me.' She fiercely rebuffed his quiet compliment. 'I'm now quite composed. I'm also twenty-seven and no longer impressed by flattery. I apologise for causing a rift between you and your friend. And thank you for your hospitality which I should like to accept for a few days until I can implement my plans...my private plans,' she amended coolly. 'May I go now, please? I should very much like to freshen myself.' She walked quickly to the door yet hesitated by it, unsure if he would prevent her leaving.

Slow footfalls had her nervously removing her straggling bonnet and unsteady fingers winding the ribbons neatly into coils.

'Why do you keep reminding me how old you are, Emma? Do you think I forget? Do you think I'm likely to bother with flattery? Me?' he taunted. 'A callous lecher with money and sin enough to purchase sordid pleasure? Why, there's no need for me to notice you at all, is there?'

Emma flung herself about and glared up at him with sparking topaz eyes. 'Good. The less you notice me, the better I shall like it!' she choked.

He smiled but no humour warmed his icy eyes. 'Three years ago I brooded over what it was I did to make you dislike me so. I always treated you with respect and courtesy. Now I'm more inclined to think that was the problem. It wasn't anything I did, it was what I didn't do.' A hand moved towards her and she defensively recoiled. He watched her, his mouth slanting mockingly as his touch skimmed past to open the door.

'I'm older...wiser now, Emma—not nearly so easily affronted...or deterred. As for your private plans, you'll have the opportunity of sharing those with me later,' he softly stated. 'Wait here for a moment while I find my mother. She'll show you to your room,' he concluded, closing the door quietly behind him.

Emma stared at the wide mahogany panels, feeling absurd tears burning, stinging at her eyes, her throat at his infuriatingly calm authority. She marched to the nearest bookshelves, scrubbing a furious hand across her dewy eyes. Jerking a book from the shelf, she stamped to a chair, sat down and sightlessly turned pages while she did his bidding.

Chapter Seven

'*Merde! Merde! Merde!*'

Neither the butler nor the maid understood French but from Madame Dubois's raucous tone they knew the recently received note contained no welcome news for her but some most excellent tidings for them.

The elderly butler jigged, stiff-legged, on the hallway flags. The young maid looked less jovial and he was sympathetic: he could now disappear below stairs, and spread the word; she, poor thing, would no doubt take the brunt of *madame's* rancour for a few days more.

He shook his old head to himself. They rose from nothing to the heights and couldn't accept that eventually they would finish between the two. A very agreeable middle ground it was, too, by his reckoning.

The silver squire was renowned for his generosity: all departed, testing the coach's axles with trunks full of fine new clothes, decked with jewels. Their final, flouncing descent down the elegant steps of number three South Parade was often in a blinding flash.

None went willingly. The pattern was always the same. A brief note, a brief visit, a copious amount of weeping and pleading and within a day or so they were gone. Thankfully this foreign one had been here but a few months. The shortest stay of all that he could recall. That really made him smile as he made for the kitchens on his bowed legs.

* * *

Yvette Dubois screwed the note in her fist then raised it to her mouth and screamed at it. She immediately uncrumpled it and reread it but there was nothing ambiguous in the few lines. Pacing between window and table, she mulled over recent events while absently toying with a gold and ruby bracelet on her wrist, and malice and retribution slowly dried her tear-sparkling blue eyes.

Richard had bought the bracelet for her a few days ago and had seemed happy enough that afternoon to receive her amorous thanks for it...until he spied that drab woman cloaked in tan. The little mouse had run off without being interviewed and Richard had followed almost immediately. She must mean something to him. There was no other explanation for him staring at her, or later returning in the foulest mood imaginable, to demand to know where she lodged. Yvette's rosebud lips tightened indignantly as she recalled him impatiently repulsing all her erotic little tricks. Nothing would make him stay and he had not visited since.

A blonde ringlet was twirled about a plump finger, then yanked at in sheer peevishness. To be discarded for a woman prettier was insufferable...to be discarded for one so plain was *abominable*! An insult! In return she would insult him! Hurt him! Perhaps even win him back...she slyly calculated.

Yes...Richard might be very vexed if she played with that lascivious-eyed little brother of his. She could lure the panting cub tomorrow! On the occasions she had seen Stephen his limpet blue eyes had been so full of lewd imaginings, even when his pretty little wife was close by his side. Coyly, she had acknowledged his interest with just enough encouragement to sustain and whet his appetite. He might not be as handsome or as wealthy and influential as his big brother, but she was realist enough to accept that such a man as Sir Richard Du Quesne happened along but rarely. It made losing him so soon the more infuriating.

Since her sixteenth birthday, when her father had sold her to an elderly, wealthy merchant, Yvette had been pleasuring gentlemen. Far from being disgusted, she had relished her first lover's slow, sensual attention. He had taught her much: groomed her for the bedchamber and the drawing room, fashioning a quality courtesan his peers would envy. He'd tutored her in English, music, dancing, even imparted a little knowledge of cultural dis-

ciplines so she could act with refinement at supper before per-
forming bawdily at bedtime. Reluctantly he had passed her to his
son with his business when his health had failed and he had no
further use for sex or commerce other than as a spectator. His
lusty son had been happy to show off the savage energy he introduced to Yvette's repertoire, until his marriage and his heiress
wife's prohibition on all shenanigans had resulted in Yvette being
banished.

She had been keen for adventure, and a kindly ancient mariner
had agreed to bring her sailing to England with him. At Bristol
Yvette had seen Richard Du Quesne, just disembarked from foreign parts, and had been immediately smitten. For days she had
inveigled to hook him, finally coaxing her sea captain to engineer
an introduction. Still he'd been impervious to her overtures until
her sailor friend had endorsed her story that she had been one
family's hetaera for nine years and was not some sly jade. After
two nights of momentous passion that had rendered her French
lovers fumbling novices, she had managed to coax Richard to
take her with him to Bath.

She'd been certain he was as enamoured as she was, for no
indifferent man would make love in such a way. But within a
week she'd realised that he was unlike any man she had known:
Richard could be an attentive, expert lover one minute and a cool,
ruthless stranger the next. He might give her *incroyable* pleasure
for hours at night but he would never otherwise give her much
of his time at all and he would never at any time give her his
heart. So she had decided to settle for his child. Such an upstanding aristocrat would always make provision for his bastards and
thereby their mothers. Yet even that he'd denied her. The sheets
or her belly had received his seed; in the throes of passion, when
she was spent, he'd retained absolute control. The fact that she'd
believed he might not had seemed to amuse him.

And now...now she was to be returned to Bristol or France—
the decision was hers, he had written. Well, she had chosen. She
wanted a Du Quesne for a lot longer. He would be protective of
his brother...of his sister-in-law. She could read the signs that he
was paternalistic. She picked up his note from the table then
flicked it away with careless fingers. He would come to his
senses. The little brown mouse would soon loose her hold on
him when he discovered his brother was receiving the brand of

exotic passion at which she excelled. She flounced happily into a chair to write a letter of her own.

'May I come in?'

'Please do.'

'We didn't have a chance to talk earlier. I've just come to welcome you properly and see if there's anything you need.' Amelia grimaced guiltily. 'That scarlet bonnet really is the most hideous thing, and purchasing it made us so late back to Silverdale to welcome you.'

Emma smiled in acceptance of the oblique apology. She had been shown to this luxurious guest chamber by a servant toting her bag and a relentlessly gregarious Miriam. Having snoozed for a while in a comfortable armchair, lulled by a view of verdant landscape that stretched away as far as the eye could see, she now felt a little refreshed. She glanced at the tea-tray. She had left all virtually untouched: even those delicious little cakes had not tempted her to stay awake.

'Would you like me to find you a maid to assist you in your toilette?'

'No, but thank you, anyway. Miriam kindly offered earlier to send me her maid.' Emma indicated her few gowns draped over a chair. 'I'm travelling light and have nothing suitable for dining in distinguished company.'

'You are coming down to dinner, though?' Amelia queried with a frown.

'No. I shall eat here, if I may, and retire early. A headache too, I'm afraid...' It was the truth! It wasn't cowardice born out of a very great desire to avoid another confrontation with the master of Silverdale. Her head did feel heavy and she had no stylish gown with her.

Her tawny gaze lingered on Amelia, a stab of something akin to envy tightening her stomach, and that worried her for she had never coveted other ladies' looks or attire. Every drape and shimmer of cornflower satin highlighted Amelia's fair colouring and blue eyes and clung with an alluring elegance to her curvaceous figure.

Hastening towards the gowns on the chair, Amelia sorted through the dull, serviceable garments, tactfully silent until exclaiming, 'This is lovely!' She drew forth sheeny amber fabric. 'The colour is so unusual. It must suit you very well,' she said, swishing about and holding up the gown while glancing between it and Emma's autumn-gold hair and eyes. 'You have the most unique colouring, Emma...'

Emma felt her face heating. It was the second time today she had been termed unique. From this young lady she readily accepted the description was complimentary. Her eyes and hair were a strange colour; her mother had often told her so, with other disparaging remarks on the dismal lack of pink in her sallow complexion. It had always concluded with how stupidly obstinate she was in continuing to shun the rouge pot.

Richard Du Quesne said she was unique and she knew that meant he found her quaint. She was an engaging little oddity to divert him for a while. She might only have seen the one, but she knew she was nothing like the women he chose to consort with: far too thin, and plain, and dowdily dressed. Well, she'd no ambition to conform to his ideals, of that she was quite sure!

The memory of their skirmish in the library was shoved to the back of her mind then immediately retrieved with a malicious little smile. Their truce hadn't lasted long and she was glad. And if he thought for one moment he could bully her into disclosing her plans for the future...or details of her lover... *What lover?* Fingers were pressed to her mouth to contain a silent burst of laughter. She no longer felt guilty about deceiving him over that either. How dared he talk to her of his...*his sordid pleasure*, as though she were some lowlife trollop? He had no right to feel superior! No right to patronise her as though she were some insecure *ingénue* either. And how dared he insinuate she was craving his hateful attention?

But then, his conceit didn't surprise her: she knew men with such power and wealth who were continually fawned over considered themselves quite irresistible. Well, she found him utterly resistible and was perfectly capable of organising her own life, as he'd discover when she married Matthew. She was confident Matthew wanted her as his wife and as mother and tutor for Rachel and Toby. More for the latter than the former, she knew, but it no longer piqued her as sharply as once it had...

Forcing herself out of her wistfulness, she gave Amelia a smile. 'Unfortunately, that gown is badly creased, but it is a favourite...' It did suit her, too. She could clearly recall wearing it on the first ever occasion she and Richard had met—not that he was likely to remember any of it .

As she stroked the iridescent silk, her mind wandered to a soirée in London that she and Victoria had attended with her parents. She recalled their overbearing hostess, Petra Blair, and her blonde daughters preening and presiding in their hot, stuffy salon. The very welcome, very unexpected arrival of the *ton*'s most charismatic and eligible bachelors had caused a definite stir of excitement amongst the ladies present. Only she and Victoria had been dismayed by Richard and David's abrupt appearance. Discreetly they had whisked themselves off to the cool sanctuary of the Blairs' small conservatory to devise a plan to slip away home.

Emma smiled nostalgically: David had had no intention of letting Victoria escape him quite so easily that evening. In order to aid and abet his friend in his amatory pursuit, Richard had ambushed her...and she had insulted him...and thus the pattern of their very brief, very prickly relationship three years ago had been set.

'We can find Mrs Braithwaite; she'll arrange for your dress to be pressed,' drifted through to Emma's consciousness. 'Silverdale's housekeeper will make light work of these creases. She's also a marvel with her pills and potions. She'll find something for your headache.'

Amelia slipped an arm through Emma's and led her towards the door, crumpled amber silk draped over her other arm. 'You seem preoccupied, Emma. Have you troubles?' Amelia asked sympathetically.

'Well...a few, I suppose,' Emma admitted, with a nervous golden glance at the pretty woman. 'As everyone does, of course,' she dismissed lightly.

'Yes...' Amelia said on a sigh.

Emma looked keenly at Amelia; her attractive features seemed momentarily wan and drawn. A pang of guilt at her selfish introspection made her hastily say, 'I suppose you are anxious about your little son. Is his cut knee healing well?'

'Oh, yes,' Amelia reassured her, but with a melancholy smile. 'When married, one's children are sometimes the least of one's problems...' More cheerfully she added, 'Come...I daren't return downstairs with the news that you shall not be dining with us all. Richard already has a face like thunder.'

Emma felt the more determined to eat in her room with that news and was about to say so, but Amelia was already into the corridor and busily urging her along. 'We can call in at the nursery and see Alice.' With a throb of maternal pride, she explained, 'Alice is my beautiful little daughter. She is now four months old and really is the most darling thing. Stephen dotes on her, as he does his beloved Jake. Would you like to see the baby?'

'Oh, I'd love to,' Emma said simply. 'Thank you.'

His mother was matchmaking! Emma realised.

A surreptitious glance slid from beneath dusky lashes and slanted across glossed candlelit mahogany to where Miriam sat at the head of the table. She appeared at her elegant best in a lavender silk gown with her pale gold hair elegantly coiffured. Seated next to her was Squire Petersham. Opposite the squire was his wife, Susan, and seated between, at either side of the long grand dining table, was the rest of the Du Quesne family, Ross Trelawney and then the Petershams' daughter Veronica, positioned close to their host and opposite Emma who had been allocated a seat close to him too, much to her chagrin.

Aware of Veronica's dark scrutiny, Emma managed a small smile. It went unreturned. Veronica's attention was already sliding away to hover on the man seated at the head of the table, opposite his mother.

Emma had but briefly spoken to Veronica in the drawing room as polite introductions were made. Then Stephen Du Quesne had gallantly offered both his wife and Emma an arm and sedately led them into dinner. With barely two sentences having passed between Veronica Petersham and herself she knew she didn't care for this young lady. She judged her to be nineteen or twenty and she was certainly pretty. In fact she had similar colouring to her dear friend Victoria: her skin was pale, her hair and eyes dark, and her scarlet gown was a very effective foil for her colouring. But she had nothing like Victoria's ethereal beauty or sweetness of countenance or nature. Her features had a hard, sharp edge and her eyes, unless trained on the gentlemen, were cold and watchful.

Good! Emma thought maliciously. I hope his mother succeeds in pairing the two of them! They make an excellent couple! Very deserving of each other!

She avoided looking at the male of the prospective match although she knew she often came under his study, even if he had barely spoken to her. Perhaps he finds me ill turned out for such a grand banquet, Emma sourly mused. All the other ladies were richly bejewelled and had made elaborate toilettes. Her thick, glossy hair was simply twisted into a neat chignon and her amber silk gown was a plain empire-line style. Her only jewellery was a pair of modest silver and topaz eardrops.

Well, she didn't want to be at Silverdale! And a sandwich in her room would have suited her very well, she proudly thought. She glanced down at the delicious mixed viands on her plate. She had lost count of the number of courses served so far. Her hunger now sated, she simply tasted morsels from each dish from curiosity and politeness, leaving the majority of it untouched. Her thoughts turned uneasily to the residents of Lower Place she had so recently lived amongst, and what they would think of such sumptuous, endless fare. Or what her parents would think, for that matter. Their family meals at Rosemary House had dwindled to little more than reheated leftovers. The thought of her parents and how they did brought with it that stabbing cramp to twist at her insides. With each day now that passed the necessity to contact them, if only to let them know she was safe, tore at her conscience.

'Would you allow me to show you some of Silverdale's grounds tomorrow, Miss Worthington?' A low, well-modulated voice addressed her from the opposite side of the table, cutting into her guilty thoughts.

Through a gap in the bank of shimmering candelabra, Emma returned Ross Trelawney's smile. 'Thank you, sir. I should like that,' she quietly replied.

Laughing dark eyes strayed sideways to their host. Ross sipped from his crystal goblet then gestured his pleasure at her consent with it. 'Good. The Italian garden and gazebo are quite a pretty sight. Then the lake and summer house are well worth a visit. As are the knot garden and the maze, of course. We could take a picnic...' he suggested softly, intimately. Their conversation was exclusive, all the other diners seemingly engaged in their own cosy chats. Ross turned his dark head towards the blond man seated at the head of the table, smiling at a bubbling Veronica. 'Perhaps Richard might like to join us?' Ross whispered across the flickering candle-flame with an air of studied enquiry. 'Shall we ask him?' Without awaiting a reply he dismissed, 'No; we ought not to trouble him. Such a courteous chap would feel obliged to agree when he'd rather attend to business without distraction. I recall now he has much to do...'

Their host dropped his knife back to his plate with such a resounding clatter that it masked the curse ejected through his even white teeth. All conversation abruptly ceased and all eyes swivelled, startled, towards him. 'Why don't you and I take a stroll outside now, while I do have the time and don't feel courteous?' Richard bit out with an unwavering glimmering glare at Ross.

'Oh, not now, thanks, Dickie. I've not finished eating.' A smile of immense charm accompanied the remark, directed at the table as a whole.

'Later, then...I insist...' whipped back in a purr.

'Oh, well, if you're desperate for some air, of course I'll accompany you, old friend,' Ross agreed, all innocent affability. 'I must say, you look a little overheated,' he mentioned, with a concerned peer along the table at Richard's icy features.

'I should like a little air later,' Veronica trilled into the conversation, glancing at Richard through her lashes.

Ross shrugged easily. 'There you are...a far fairer companion. But I think, Miss Petersham, I shall challenge him for the pleasure of your company.' Ross treated the young lady on his left to a suave smile. 'You can tell me all about your visit to Lyme Regis last week. Was there seabathing?' He inclined close and Veronica dimpled and fluttered her lashes.

Emma sensed the side of her face prickling, burning. She slanted a glance sideways and her eyes clashed immediately with a threatening steely gaze. She stiffened indignantly. It wasn't her fault if his friend chose to tease him in company. Her chin tilted, prompting a twitch of amusement to soften his mouth, then he turned away as Stephen addressed him.

Emma also looked away...for all of a second or two, and then her eyes slid back. She might hate him but she couldn't deny he looked wonderfully handsome with his lengthy blond hair glinting silver in the candlelight.

Her appraisal dropped to a hand resting idly on the table. Lash-screened eyes travelled over long, well-shaped dark fingers to a cambric shirt-cuff. It ruffled starkly white against his tanned skin. Her covert observation took in a sleeve of charcoal superfine wool then a silver silk cravat set with a fiery diamond before reaching a shirt collar as razor-sharp as the bronze cheekbone above it. Tawny eyes again flitted to his hair, trailing lengthily over linen...then swerved to silver eyes to find them watching her. She spontaneously burned with heat and dropped her cutlery, much in the way he had done moments before. Cringing at the clatter, then again at the ensuing quiet, she managed a small apologetic smile for everyone.

Ross dropped her a discreet wink before resuming conversation with Veronica. A general chatter recommenced about the table. It was only her host's attention that stayed, making her squirm uncomfortably in her seat.

'And I think you look very nice, too,' she heard him eventually say, gently amused.

Emma felt her blush increase and was never more grateful for flickering candlelight mellowing her complexion. 'I thought we had established that I find flattery boring,' she rebuffed acidly, turning away.

'I thought we had established that I never bother using it.' His eyes skimmed the light swell of her petite breasts beneath her gown's square neckline. 'That dress always did suit you. The colour matches your eyes.'

Sheer astonishment that he should remember it made her face him again and her clamped lips involuntarily soften.

Reading her thoughts, he choked a laugh. 'Oh, I remember it all, Emma. Every meeting, every insult. You called me a novice that first evening. I'd still be interested to know exactly what experience you think I lack. I'm keen to prove myself proficient...' Richard watched her feline eyes sidle from his to ensure no one was listening then creep back to pounce.

'Perhaps a little discipline in restraint and moderation might benefit initially,' she hissed angrily, yet feeling guilty too at those three-year-old slanders and wishing that he had forgotten them all.

'I'm sure you'd make an excellent tutor in restraint and moderation, Emma. Finding out might be pleasurable enough.'

'Indeed,' Emma jibed softly. 'And you might become a model of propriety overnight!'

'Well, it might take several nights...unless *you're* very proficient at discipline,' he taunted huskily. He smiled at her blank-eyed concentration as she scrambled in her innocence for his meaning. As she guessed his intention to be ribald insult, her face tipped down and she glared at her plate.

'I also seem to recall you leading me to believe that you were practically betrothed.' He spared her blushing confusion and changed the subject. 'Your mother was soon expecting an offer for you, you said.'

'My mother was always soon expecting an offer for me,' she snapped in a low breath. 'She was ceaselessly optimistic of becoming some man's mother-in-law. It never mattered who he was.'

'I wish I'd known. Perhaps I might have obliged her.'

Emma stared at him with huge shining eyes. 'At times I very much hate you,' she whispered.

'Why? Because I tell you that with a little encouragement I might have offered for you three years ago?'

'That's a lie!' she choked while stabbing viciously at morsels of food on her plate. 'You had no real interest in me then!'

'And that lack of real interest forced me along to your birthday celebration, I suppose.'

'David forced you along. It was obvious he was only attending to pursue Victoria and obvious you came along to keep me well out of his way as usual.'

'David wasn't due to attend. He'd decided to change tactics with Victoria. He was going to play hard to get and stay away. I knew he'd never manage it, but then again I didn't expect him to turn up at close to midnight, either.'

'Why would you come on your own...for no reason?' Emma scoffed.

'I've no idea, Emma,' Richard said very drily. 'I'll own it certainly wasn't a habit of mine to attend young ladies' birthday tea parties.'

Emma stared, scanning his dark face for falsehood, for cunning. Was this how he set about trapping his prey? She had no experience of men but she suspected it was: flattery...a sham of liking and interest...offers of protection and financial help. She'd experienced all that now. He believed her so grateful and gullible, she'd yield like all the rest.

'You've lost your hearty appetite tonight, I see.' Richard cut smoothly into her frantic suppositions. His fingers toyed with silver cutlery and his eyes rested on her virtually untouched plate of food. 'And I've made a point of arranging for fifty courses...just to ensure you were adequately filled.'

Brilliant eyes shot to his face. 'You've not!' she whispered, horrified.

'Fifty dinners a night, wasn't it, by Mrs Keene's reckoning?'

Emma sent a flick of a glance about the table but everyone seemed happily engaged. 'Tell me that's a joke!' she squealed furiously, her glossy golden eyes shielded by thick inky lashes.

'It's a joke,' he said softly.

Emma looked up slowly, thankfully.

'Of course it's a joke. We're under truce at the moment... aren't we?'

She blinked and looked away.

'Aren't we, Emma?' he softly demanded. 'We shook on it, didn't we?'

Emma remained silent.

'Say yes, Emma, or I'll call in the remaining courses,' he said to the ceiling, with a husky laugh.

'Now you've monopolised Emma quite enough, Richard,' Miriam called, sliding a look at the matron seated on her left.

Susan Petersham had her gimlet eye resting on this unexpected rival to her daughter. Their eligible host seemed to be paying her unusual attention, even if she was nowhere near as modishly turned out as her own dear Veronica. Nowhere near as young either, she guessed, with a satisfied sniff. And that hair? Heavens, what sort of shade was it? Nowhere near as richly brunette as Veronica's elaborately teased tresses, that was obvious.

As though guessing her neighbour's shrewd imaginings, Miriam explained, 'Oh, Miss Worthington and Richard have very dear mutual friends: Viscount and Viscountess Courtenay, you know,' she informed, with an emphatic wag of her fair head. 'They are both godparents to the Courtenays' darling little girl and of course they have so much news to catch up with when they get together. It's a while since you saw Emma, is it not, Richard?'

'Indeed it is...too long,' he returned levelly.

Miriam widened her blue eyes and nodded meaningfully at Susan Petersham. 'Emma lives with her parents in Cheapside as a spin...single lady of educated pursuits. We had a wonderful chat together earlier. She has told me she loves to read. And so do I. Oh, yes, I love a romantic novel, as Emma does. We share a favourite author in Miss Austen, you know, and a favourite work in *Pride and Prejudice*. Anyway, Emma is visiting Bath and, of course, had to make a point of seeing Richard whilst here. They are such old friends...'

'Are your parents here with you, Miss Worthington?' Susan Petersham sliced through Miriam's speech.

'No, ma'am,' Emma ventured quietly. Heavens! What was she to say when asked whom she was with? It was highly irregular for a gentlewoman to be travelling alone...even one of advanced years. She had wondered why the Du Quesne family had so far made so little of it: the subject of her lone status had hardly been broached at all. After some silent debate she guessed it was because Richard had decreed no questions were to be asked. And she rather guessed that what Richard said was law at Silverdale.

'Not even your mother is accompanying you?' Susan Petersham interrogated.

'My mother is not well enough to travel at present, ma'am,' Emma returned quietly. And that was the truth! When she had quit Cheapside, her mother had been barely able to stir herself from bed in the mornings.

'Miss Worthington is in Bath specifically at my invitation. When the Courtenays visit, there shall be a happy reunion.' Richard cut into the conversation with such an air of icy finality that Susan Petersham nervously fiddled with her ringlets.

'Well...quite...' she was heard to murmur.

Into the ensuing silence came plaintively, 'I'd love to walk to the lake with the flares alight, Richard.' Amelia looked appealingly at her brother-in-law. 'Might we do that? It's always so romantic.'

'That's a good idea, Dickie,' Ross chipped in laughingly, and the atmosphere immediately lightened.

Stephen pulled a face. 'It's a bit chilly now, my dear,' he

moaned to his shining-eyed wife. 'Besides, gentlemen like a cigar and a tipple and a chat after dinner...'

'Go and ask Simmons to have them lit, so you can take your wife for a romantic stroll,' Richard directed firmly at his brother, with a nod at the door. As Stephen scowled, he returned him a smile, and continued looking at him until his brother moodily shrugged himself up from the table.

'I'd love to go, too,' Veronica announced, glancing coyly at Richard.

'Well, you shall, you shall,' Miriam said, exchanging a sly look with Susan Petersham. 'You wanted the air earlier, Richard. You must accompany Veronica,' Miriam decreed.

Ross shoved back his chair. 'I insist,' he said in a husky growl, 'that Miss Petersham allows me that privilege.'

Veronica visibly shivered beneath his intent dark gaze and rose, trance-like to stand close to him. They slowly strolled arm in arm from the table, Veronica's dark eyes widening on the piratical face smiling down at her.

Emma glanced at Richard to see a large, spanning hand in the process of soothing his brow. Beneath shielding fingers, he was laughing silently. He tipped back his head to smile at the wavering light on the ceiling.

'I expect you're going to say you'd rather jump in the lake than walk to it with me,' he remarked exclusively for her and with laughter still apparent in his tone.

'At last...something to admire about you, Sir Richard!' Emma gushed with mock wonderment. 'How marvellously perceptive you really are.' She dropped her napkin back to the table, ready to rise to her feet. She could finally escape to her room. Yet she felt ashamed of her insolence: he had so recently rescued her from the probing and prying of Susan Petersham.

The other diners were already away from the table, talking of fetching shawls and cloaks.

'Do come along, Richard, and you, my dear,' Miriam directed over her shoulder at them. 'I shall have Simmons fetch you one of my cloaks, Emma, and save you a trip to your chamber.' She was gone from the room before Emma had managed to draw in breath to offer up the excuses of fatigue and headaches.

* * *

'Well, is it romantic?'

Emma looked about at the shadowy swaying foliage. She gazed out over a sheet of rippling black silk patched with yellow, listening to the gentle lapping of water beneath the boarding she stood upon, the soporific rustling of a million leaves. Turning her head, she gazed back the way they had come. A pathway illuminated by parallel breeze-lengthened flares pointed up to the house, its honey aura enhanced by sconces aglow on its majestic walls. The hood of her cloak fell to her shoulders as she tipped back her head to marvel at a sky of velvet blue studded with glittering stars. Tepid wind stirred her hair, smoothed her face. She just couldn't lie. 'Yes,' she said simply. 'It is...'

Richard smiled and nodded, still staring out over the lake.

The other night-time strollers were some way off, keeping to the formal paths, whereas Richard had led her onto the landing stage where several small boats were moored for trips out to a large, densely wooded island. Emma squinted at what appeared no more than an immensely ragged floating boulder. Beneath her feet she glimpsed the hypnotic rocking of deep water.

'I imagine you had fine times here as a child,' she said pensively. 'Fishing and boating and swimming.'

'Very fine,' he agreed. 'David and I spent many summers without moving far from here. Sometimes it was days before we ventured back indoors, and then only for more supplies. We'd camp, shoot, sleep on that island.'

Emma gazed up at his shadowy profile fringed by strands of pale hair. It was so easy to imagine two small boys, one very dark, one very fair, grubby and dishevelled, with fishing lines, smelling of woodsmoke and sporting scraped knees. 'It must have been wonderful. I should have liked to be a boy...'

He choked a laugh and shot a look at her.

'Why is that funny?' she demanded haughtily.

'It's not...' he said wryly. 'Especially for a man who likes you as a girl.'

Emma disdainfully turned her head away but admitted soulfully, 'I should especially have liked a brother or sister. You were very fortunate. Even when David was not visiting you here, you had Stephen...a companion to play with.'

'David and I were inseparable...closer than kin. We were at school together or we were here at Silverdale or at his home,

Hawkesmere, together.' He paused. 'I feel quite guilty that I spent so little time with Stephen. But then he is seven years younger than me. When I was thirteen he was barely out of skirts. I'd never allow him into my camp. He used to throw a tantrum to get Mother to persuade me.'

'I should have liked to go away to school. I had a governess at home. A young ladies' academy or boarding-school might have been nice. Then I might have had a friend to spend the summer with...'

With great solemnity, he announced to her sweetly wistful profile, 'I'd have let you into my camp...you're only six years younger. If you'd known Victoria then, I expect David might have been happy to accommodate her too. Perfect... Fishing, shooting, swimming, boating...girls...'

'I was but seven or eight when you were thirteen!' she snapped icily. 'And Victoria was nine.'

'Old enough,' he said, with a white smile over the lake, then arrowed a look at her. 'I was able to cook over an open fire when I was eight. You'd have managed. Why else would we let two girls into our camp?'

Emma tutted disgust but to hide her smile flounced her face away and spied Miriam's pale head and a waving hand, some way off on the bank. 'I believe your mother wants you.'

She just caught his muttered curse. Aloud he said, 'Just ignore her...'

'You can be very rude to your mother, I've noticed,' she let him know.

'Don't nag, Emma,' he said with a smile in his voice. 'It's far too soon for that.'

'I think she's hoping you will take a turn about the walkways with Miss Petersham.' Emma vainly tried to suppress the malicious amusement honeying her tone. 'Or are you content to allow Ross to do that?'

Richard glanced down at her. 'I'm very content to let Ross do that...and he knows it. That's what good friends are for, Emma. He would have had access to my camp too, had I known him then.'

Emma allowed a small smile. 'Ross really is the most terrible flirt, isn't he? I imagine he is another accomplished

rogue...although a charming, likeable one,' she qualified, unaware how satisfyingly insulting it sounded.

'He comes from a very long line of accomplished Cornish
rogues. And, yes, he's a practised flirt. In comparison, I'll admit
to being a novice in pointless dalliance,' he said with biting irony.

'Well, you wanted to know earlier which qualities you lack,'
Emma taunted. 'Pay your addresses to Miss Petersham and polish
your flirting and charm.'

'That's what you think I should do, is it?'

'Indeed. You make an excellent couple.'

Richard looked over her head at nothing. 'If you're keen to
foist her onto me, I now know for certain how much you dislike
her.'

'Again, I can only marvel at your shrewd perception, sir. Oh,
please don't let me keep you from her,' she sweetly said, and
stepped back quickly along the planked boarding.

Richard grabbed at her and jerked her forward to teeter on her
toes. 'When I said you might prefer a dip in the lake to my
company, it was a joke, you know.'

Emma cautiously peeked over a shoulder to see inky water
undulating directly below. She could feel just the tips of her
shoes on solid wood. Her hands gripped frantically at muscular
forearms and she squeezed shut her eyes, wondering why he
didn't move backwards and take her with him. Her lids flicked
up to see moon-silver eyes on her face. 'Your mother is waiting,'
she desperately reminded him.

'I am waiting,' he returned softly.

'For what?' she squeaked.

'Lots of things: an apology...an explanation...another kiss...'

Her fingernails reflexively stabbed through the fine wool of his
sleeves into his arms, trying to gain purchase and pull herself
forward and away from danger. But he refused to help, holding
her rock-steady at arm's length.

'Let's start with your private plans,' he said. 'Why don't you
tell me about Cavendish?'

Emma's astonishment was so great, she almost relaxed her grip
and tottered backwards into the water.

She felt his support increase but watched an awful, sneering
smile twist his features. 'Good God, it really is him, isn't it?' he
ground out, at the same time swinging her easily about to gain

sure footing. He pushed her away from him as though disgusted. 'Matthew Cavendish?' he grated. He turned away and swore, then looked at her again as though he just didn't believe it.

'How did you find out?' Emma fumed. 'Who told you?'

'It's him, isn't it?' he repeated in amazement as though still hoping she'd deny it. 'Is the child his? Is it?' he hissed, completely ignoring her interrogation. When she remained silent he drawled in a stone-cold voice, 'He doesn't even know, does he? You've not told him, have you?'

'I've...I've said I won't talk of any of that,' she flared. 'It's nothing to do with you... It's none of your concern!'

A steely grip on her shoulders yanked her off the ground and slammed her against him, then shook her into silence. Her head swayed back, exposing an arc of slender throat, and she was staring up into vicious metallic eyes. 'Don't ever say that to me again, or I swear I'll live up to every sordid expectation you have of me. You'll discover just how unconcerned I can be.'

Emma opened her mouth to speak but something in his brutal gaze, in the pitiless line of his mouth, his rigid jaw, made her clamp it shut again.

Her heart fluttered like a caged bird against her ribs yet she couldn't think what it was she usually said or did to gentle him. He was utterly enraged; more angry than she'd ever known him. Yet she didn't understand why. He had somehow learned what had brought her to Bath: her relationship with Matthew. But surely that news would relieve him? At Mrs Keene's he had wanted to know whether her lover was prepared to support her.

'Take your filthy hands off me now, or my future husband will kill you,' she lashed with icy contempt. 'He'll kill you anyway when he hears of you insulting me with an offer to join your whores.'

'Will he, my dear?' was silkily queried. 'When will that be? Next time he's sober enough to stay on his feet? Had I known you'd already joined his whores, I'd have looked higher...Haymarket, perhaps.'

A small fist whipped out with an outraged gasp. 'Well, I'm sure you'd know where the cheapest harlots tarry,' she spat. 'The amount you've had you'd have lost this fine place to the brothels years ago.'

Long, harsh fingers anchored her flailing fist back to her side.

Without another word he made for the path, dragging her behind him. Once on solid ground, she was shoved away in the direction of the flickering flares. 'Get back to the house,' he directed coldly, imperiously, and with flint-eyed amusement watched her resentfully comply, before striding in the opposite direction.

Chapter Eight

'Richard looks so angry; have you quarrelled with him?' a shrill voice called from behind, making Emma stop and spin about. 'I've quarrelled with Stephen,' Amelia continued, then burst into tears.

Emma placed a comforting hand on Amelia's arm but her mind was in turmoil: she felt furious, so blazingly irate that for two pins she would have raced back down the firelit path to find Richard Du Quesne in the vain hope that this time her fist might surprise him and find its mark.

Had it been simply spite that had made him imply Matthew was a drunken womaniser? But why should a man such as Sir Richard, with power and wealth, stoop to vilify a man so far beneath his notice? She couldn't deny his shock and contempt had seemed genuine on learning that she was, indeed, involved with Matthew Cavendish. Neither could she deny that she'd already spotted signs of drunkenness about Matthew's haggard features, or that his housekeeper, Maisie, behaved in a decidedly familiar way with him. She had previously found plausible excuses: Matthew liked to relax with alcohol as most men did. His housekeeper was simply a little sluttish in her ways.

Amelia's soft weeping finally penetrated her chaotic thoughts. Slipping an arm through hers, she set a quicker pace along the path. 'Don't fret so, Amelia,' Emma kindly soothed. 'I'm sure you and Stephen will make up.'

Amelia shook her head, wiping her face with her fingertips

and sniffing loudly. 'We argued because he...he has another woman, I know it. And he didn't bother to deny it. He...he just said I was too possessive and should never question what company he keeps. He said I should be dutiful and modest as other wives are. He said he is entitled to have his freedom as other men do. Other men have mistresses...that's what he means.'

'Seven years between them, maybe...such similar brothers nonetheless,' Emma muttered. Aloud she reasoned, 'But he didn't actually say so?'

'Do...do you think perhaps I'm mistaken?' Amelia asked hopefully.

Emma bestowed an optimistic look on her while her heart sank. If Stephen even slightly resembled his older brother, his infidelities were probably more prolific than his poor wife could ever imagine.

'May I talk to you in your room for a while?' Amelia pleaded as they entered the house.

'Yes, of course,' Emma replied gently, yet feeling that she had no more advice to give. She sorely needed a confidante of her own and her thoughts immediately turned to Victoria. Oh, Vicky, she inwardly whispered, I so wish you were here for me.

The following morning at ten o'clock a note arrived summoning her to his study. It found the fire. So did the second bearing the same command and a veiled threat of retribution should she again ignore him. The third—stating that should she attempt to leave the house in his absence dire consequences would ensue— she kept and perused thoughtfully.

An hour later Emma was peeking down at the two riders on the circular gravel drive.

Richard, garbed in a long vented riding coat that reached down to his boots, swung athletically into the saddle of a golden stallion. Even to Emma's inexpert town eye, the animal looked to be such a sleek, graceful creature she unconsciously let go of the veiling curtain she was stationed behind to better her view of it. Ross was astride a chestnut horse that seemed quite wild. It restlessly pawed at the ground and flung up its head as though keen to be off. As she watched, the animal skittered sideways before being brought under control. Chill September air froze the animals' steamy breath and that of the riders as they shared some conversation which caused them both to laugh.

A fair head turned, angled. She screened herself with rust damask curtains just moments before he looked up at her window. As soon as the two riders were lost to sight along the shivering silver avenue, she grabbed a shawl and raced below.

She knew the directions of the stables and hurried along the shingle path to the coach house. A groom was chatting idly to one of the young serving girls and they sprang apart as Emma approached. The young maid dipped a curtsey at Emma then skipped over the dewy grass towards the kitchens.

'It's a fine day,' Emma greeted, looking about at the mist-wreathed landscape. 'I'm sorry, I don't know your name.'

'It's Martin, m'm,' he supplied while yanking at a lock of auburn hair flopping over a freckle-dusted brow.

'Well, Martin, I should like to take a little drive in the countryside. It's such a pleasant, fresh morning. Would you oblige me with a driver and conveyance, please?'

'Can't, m'm,' the young groom burst out, crimsoning with embarrassment.

'I shall take responsibility and speak to Sir Richard...' she coaxed, guessing what ailed him.

'Can't, m'm,' Martin repeated, his face screwing in remorse. 'Sir Richard said as you might ask and that I should tell 'im if you did and that I was to tell you that's what I must do.'

Emma strained a smile over gritted teeth. She spied another young stablehand watching, fascinated, from the coach-house doorway. 'If I ask that young man instead you need not be in trouble...'

'Master's told 'im 'n all. Master's told all of us in stables.'

Emma dredged up another stiff smile, before marching back to the house.

She found Amelia alone in the morning room stabbing listlessly at some embroidery. 'Might I speak to you?' Emma asked quietly.

Amelia let her sewing drop to her lap and she nodded. Her face was blotchy from crying and Emma directed her fury and hatred at both Du Quesne men.

'Amelia, I know you would like me to accompany you to the Assembly Rooms later and I know I have said I am reluctant to go, but I have been thinking...perhaps we ought to try and do each other a good turn. It seems we are both in need of a little kindness. If I promise to accompany you for an hour or two this evening...might I ask a favour in return?'

'Of course...anything, Emma,' Amelia said huskily.

'Would you please go to the coach house and ask for a conveyance to be brought round to the front door so you can go to Bath? And please don't mention that I am to accompany you.'

Amelia perked up. 'Is it some intrigue?' she breathed. 'Where are we really to go?'

'I'll tell you on the way,' Emma said with a satisfied smile.

'Are you in love with this man?' Amelia whispered as she leaned towards Emma, agog with curiosity.

Emma shrugged and smiled wistfully at her hand brushing lazily through leaves trailing against the landau's glossy coachwork. Now the early morning haze had lifted the sun was warm, early autumn tints singeing the overgrown hedgerows. She plucked at some blackberries as they passed a laden bramble, handed one to Amelia then popped the other into her mouth.

She unfastened her cloak and removed her bonnet. A fall of tawny hair tumbled free, honey and copper lights glinting in its sheeny thickness.

Martin was driving them and only occasionally turning to bestow on Emma a melancholy look as they bowled along the back lanes of rural Bath towards the village of Oakdene. Emma felt a little guilty: she hoped she had not caused this young man to fear reprimand, or, worse still, losing his position. But then, despite hating Richard Du Quesne, she imagined him to be a fair employer. Martin would surely not be punished for her deceit.

'It's why you're here in Bath, isn't it?' Amelia interrupted her reflection. 'You're here specifically to see your friend; not to see Richard, as he said at dinner yesterday. How romantic! You've travelled alone from London, risking all, to find your heart's desire,' she murmured theatrically. 'Richard knows, of course, and would try to help as you are such good friends.'

Emma's choke of sour laughter went unremarked upon. 'I wondered why Richard was so adamant that no one should quiz you about your being in Bath unaccompanied. What of your parents?' Amelia asked. 'Do they like this man? Do they object to him?'

'They probably hold no opinion, and only vaguely recall him from when he resided in London years ago. He has never been a wealthy man. My parents had every hope of me marrying well and thus easing their financial burdens, so he would be a disappointment in that respect.' Emma turned to gaze at the countryside, hoping Amelia would probe no more. She didn't want to fib.

She sighed and closed her eyes as a jumble of thoughts spilled into her mind. Let Matthew be an honourable man. Let him still want me. Let me be satisfied with my lot. Don't let Richard spoil it by maliciously interfering.

He was sure to be furious that she had disobeyed him and that she had involved Amelia in deceitfully obtaining a carriage. But he had forced her to it with his tyranny, she immediately justified.

'So it's you again.'

'Indeed it is,' Emma snapped, feeling indignant at Maisie's surlily amused expression. 'Is Mr Cavendish at home? I should like to converse with him.'

'Oh, he's home right enough. Whether you'll be able to converse with him...now that be a different matter,' she jibed darkly.

Emma glanced back at the landau to see Amelia and Martin diplomatically turn away their heads.

'Very top-notch now, ain't you? 'N all thanks to the silver squire, I'll be bound,' Maisie sneered, sheer envy coarsening her country brogue. 'Makes me wonder why you're here at all bothering with the likes of him.' Her brunette head jerked towards the cottage's interior.

'What do you know of the silver squire?' Emma demanded sharply, her tawny eyes scanning Maisie's sullen features.

'What's the likes of me likely to know of him?' Maisie snorted. ''Cept he's got money 'n influence aplenty. When he was here with Matthew, he scared him straight back into a bottle.'

'When was he here?' Emma gasped, completely overlooking Maisie's audacity in using her employer's given name and disclosing his chosen comfort.

'Earlier in the week. Then again this morning. Frightening, he were, both times, if quiet. Don't much raise his voice at all yet he were angry, right enough. Angry 'cos of you, I reckon. Wonder why that might be?'

Emma blanched and her heart started to hammer erratically. 'Tell Mr Cavendish I wish to speak to him,' she ordered in a shaking tone.

'Tell him yourself,' Maisie retorted carelessly, swishing away.

Emma hesitantly followed her towards the back of the cottage and entered a small kitchen. Maisie ignored her and continued supping tea, seated at a battered pine table.

'I don't want us to be enemies, Maisie,' Emma sighed. 'I'm sure you care well for Mr Cavendish...'

'You've got no idea just how well I cares for him, Miss Uppity. An' he don't want such as you to know,' she burst out bitterly. 'Just go away and leave us be. He's worse than ever since you came troublin' him...' After a gulp of tea, she blurted, 'He's upstairs a'bed.' A jerk of her head indicated the rickety stairs set at the back of the kitchen.

Gaining a creaking landing, Emma tried the first door she came to. It opened onto the children's chamber. Clothes and toys were strewn on the floor and bedding draped untidily from two roughhewn pine beds. She tried the other door and found him.

Matthew was sprawled, fully dressed, on the bed with his forearms flung up, framing his head. His eyes were closed and his breathing was stertorous.

The cloying smell of alcohol hit her with nauseating force as she proceeded into the room. As she tiptoed closer she noticed the flush on his features and sweat beading on his brow and top lip. Her heart hit her stomach, but mixed with grinding disappointment was pity and sorrow, for she knew even her treasured London memories of this man were doomed.

'Matthew...' she called softly. When there was no response she lightly shook his arm. A muttered blasphemy was ejected but he remained dozing. Emma shook him quite vigorously and then leaped back as he abruptly shot into a sitting position.

'What in damnation are you about, Maisie? You little bitch!' he rumbled. 'My head feels riven in two!' A massaging hand lowered from his brow and his lids were raised to reveal bloodshot eyes. He stared, unblinking, as though she were an apparition and twice his lips formed her name before it actually emerged. 'Emma?' he croaked. 'What in all that's holy are you doing here?'

'I've come to see you, Matthew,' she choked through the tears in her throat.

Matthew worked his way gingerly to the edge of the bed as though every movement pained him. Emma watched his hand hover over a glass with dregs of alcohol in it on the side table. His fingers clenched then withdrew, leaving it untouched.

He grunted a noise that could have been laughter. 'I never wanted you to see me like this, Emma,' he said hoarsely. 'I can control it,' he stated quite seriously, while red-rimmed eyes stared out of the small paint-peeling window to one side of him. 'It's just...since Sara died, it's been a solace of sorts. It helps me sleep...then when I'm asleep she comes back to me.'

Emma felt tears prick at her lids and quickly closed her stinging eyes.

Matthew turned his head to face her. His gaunt grey complexion split in a grin. 'So you're keeping quite exalted company with Sir Richard Du Quesne at Silverdale. He's been here twice, if I rightly recall it,' he mocked himself. 'For I was a little under the influence on both occasions. How do you know such as he, Emma?'

'We share very dear mutual friends,' Emma told him huskily. 'I was acquainted with him some years ago; but we have little liking for one another. He found out I was in lodgings and insisted I stay at Silverdale with his mother and sister-in-law.' She managed a weak smile. 'He deems Mrs Keene's lodgings an unseemly place for me to stay. Mostly he frets that our dear friends might find out and accuse him of neglecting me.'

Matthew swiped a tremulous hand about his stubbly jaw. 'I'm glad you dislike him as much as I. He can be...intimidating...'

'Oh, yes...' Emma endorsed bitterly. 'Very...'

'Despite his probing I told him nought, Emma. You must not trust him. That devil Dashwood and he are of the same breed...such as they stick together. Once he feels he has done his duty by you he may be glad for Dashwood to take you off his hands.'

Emma felt her heart and stomach squeeze at that for it so exactly confirmed her own fears.

'I thought maybe you'd guessed of my secrets when you with-

held your consent to our marriage. And I had no right to be
annoyed at that.' Matthew looked up at her sheepishly. 'I intended coming to Lower Place to talk to you but I've been too
bad in drink to get below stairs some days—' He broke off, a
palsied hand dragging through his matted hair. 'I would never
have told Sir Richard of our mutual affection, Emma. Such a
sophisticate would misconstrue: take the fact of your fleeing London and couple it with your visit to me and draw conclusions of
a base liaison. He was trying to prise as much from me, I'll
swear. I have done everything in my power to shield your reputation.'

'Thank you, Matthew,' Emma choked past the ache in her
throat, as the first tears trailed her cheek. 'Thank you very much
for that.'

She had falsely insinuated to Richard that she was no longer
chaste and because of that deceit this man's integrity had been
called into question. In return Matthew had done his utmost to
protect her, even whilst raddled by drink.

'Where are the children?' Emma asked in a bright, brittle
voice.

'At the vicarage. Maisie takes them there for their lessons.
They'll be home soon and glad to see you,' he said, but with
little conviction.

'I can't tarry, Matthew.' The relief in his face made the lump
in her throat thicken. 'I have a friend waiting in the carriage
outside. We are just out for a drive in the countryside and I
thought to call in...' she concluded in a ragged whisper.

Matthew nodded. 'I'm so sorry about...'

Emma rested a hand on his tangled hair. 'I'm so sorry too,
Matthew...'

'I'll show you out, shall I?' Maisie walked boldly to the closet
and drew forth a nightdress and deliberately placed it on the bed.
She then moved to the small dresser and picked up a comb and
began tidying her hair. Her eyes met Emma's in the mirror with
meaningful challenge.

But Emma already understood. With a last squeeze at Matthew's hand she murmured, 'Goodbye, Matthew,' and was
quickly out of the door and down the stairs.

'I shan't come here again,' Emma promised with apology un-
derlying the words.

Maisie smiled at her with something akin to wry humour. 'I can't say as I blame you. If I had such as the handsome silver squire looking out for me, I wouldn't be here either.'

Without another word, Emma turned and walked into the September sunshine.

Amelia had decided to journey on and join Miriam and Diane at the Petershams' for afternoon tea. She had attempted to persuade Emma to accompany her but the thought of spending time with those awful women while she felt so low was unimaginable. On alighting from the landau on the circular driveway it pulled away and disappeared along the avenue of whitebeam.

As Simmons opened the door to her, Emma tentatively enquired, fingers crossed in her pockets, 'Is Sir Richard home, to your knowledge?'

'To my knowledge, he is not, Miss Worthington,' he answered while his eyebrows tilted in opposite directions at the odd notion that something might yet occur at Silverdale that escaped his notice. 'Ah, now...' the butler began as he leaned sideways to peer past a mightily relieved Emma.

As she heard gravel spit and scrunch she spun about. She froze, determined not to flee, even as she glimpsed the sleek, champagne flanks of a large horse. She still held her ground when she saw the recently dismounted rider striding with long, purposeful paces towards the house.

She wasn't frightened, she impressed on herself as she watched him mount the stone steps two at a time with his riding coat flapping about long, muscular legs. Nevertheless she decided speeding across the hallway to the stairs might be a prudent move.

Sir Richard Du Quesne strode into the house, his blond hair glinting in the afternoon sunlight, his dark face thunderous. 'Have a groom brought round,' he flung at a stoical Simmons as he passed him without slowing his pace. His scouring gaze found Emma hovering by the bannisters. He continued walking with daunting deliberation and a satisfied smile curving the ruthless line of his mouth.

It was then Emma conceded that she was too shaken by the day's events for any further heroics. She *was* frightened and she no longer cared if he *did* know it. Turning on the bottom step, she launched herself upwards with a deep breath and her skirts gripped in shaking fists.

Before she'd managed three stairs she was jerked backwards into mid-air and against a hard, broad torso. She squirmed, attempting to twist about, but her arms were lashed to her sides with insolent ease by one arm encircling her body. He carried her as though she were a china doll...very carefully and very easily.

His study door was treated to no such attention: it was kicked inwards with such brute force that it crashed back against the wall, allowing them entry, then bounced back to seal itself.

Richard deposited Emma on the Persian rug and a hand nudged her forward away from him.

She swung about and immediately flew back at him.

He caught at first one then the other of her hands as they swung for his face and held her at arm's length. When she still kicked and fought, he took them behind her back, forcing her heart-stoppingly close.

So close, she could distinguish the clean sandalwood scent of him mingled with leather and a disturbing searing heat that seemed unnatural. Her wriggling immediately ceased. Her breathing was coming in short, sharp bursts and she gasped out, 'Let me go, this instant, or I shall scream.'

'Go ahead,' he said quietly while quicksilver eyes flowed over her and her soft body seemed to be melding to the hardness of his.

She strained at her imprisoned wrists, trying to force them out of his grip. 'I hate you...*I hate you*,' she raged against his chest.

The sadness that had been steadily strengthening since she'd first faced Jarret Dashwood in the drawing room of Rosemary House was no longer containable. Her melancholy meeting barely an hour before with Matthew had left tears betrayingly close to the surface and after the first jerking sob she was lost. She wrenched at her hands again and again, her head working this way and that in despair as she tried to free herself and conceal her wet face with thick, tawny hair. Finally submitting, she stilled, burying her face down against her shoulder.

He stepped back a few paces to the desk. Kicking his chair back from it, he spun her about abruptly then sat and pulled her down onto his lap. 'I think, Miss Worthington, it's quite likely you'll render me insane before too much longer,' was murmured huskily against her bent head. That wry observation seemed to increase her anguish, so he soothed, 'Hush, it's just a joke. I know you worry for my health.'

For what seemed an age they sat like that; the only noise disturbing the silence was Emma's weeping, the only movement a large dark hand smoothing against her face, her hair. As she quietened he searched his various pockets and eventually brought forth a handkerchief. Tilting her face up to his, he leisurely picked away damp fawn tresses stuck to her cheeks.

'Look at me,' he ordered, and she did. Luminous golden eyes fringed by clumps of wet black lashes glanced up at him. Richard closed his eyes, dropped his head forward and swore softly. 'Looking that appealing after crying gives you an unfair advantage, Emma.'

White linen moved gently across her face, removing salty wet, and she sat rigidly, a little sense and composure creeping back. He seemed momentarily mellowed by her angry tears and acting quickly would be wise. A tentative attempt to rise was thwarted. Immediately his eyes flicked to hers, narrowed and amused. 'Not yet,' he denied her, dropping the handkerchief to the floor. 'I really would be mad if I let you go without an explanation...or an apology. You've jeopardised Martin's livelihood and involved Amelia in your deceit.'

Emma made to twist her face away but a dark hand spanning her jaw arrested it. 'So tell me...was it worth it? Was he sober when you got there?'

Her lids drooped so that mercurial gaze couldn't mock her. But she felt drained of aggression and lies and so awfully guilty at the thought that he might, after all, put off the young grooms-man simply to punish her. She merely answered his question with a shake of her head. 'I apologise for disobeying you and borrow-ing a carriage. But if...if you put Martin off because of it I shall never forgive you, I swear I won't. Nor if you make trouble for Amelia. If you want to wreak your paltry revenge,' she flung at him, 'then do so with me.'

'Not a wise invitation, Emma,' Richard observed sarcastically. 'Never forget I'm that callous lecher you love to malign.'

As his hand moved away she turned her head to stare out of the window.

'You knew Cavendish in London, I take it?'

She nodded.

'Was he coherent enough when you got there? Have you told him now of the child?'

Emma stiffened in his arms, her heart thudding. Matthew's sweet defence of her virtue played over in her mind. She would show him the same respect and kindness and never allow this man an opportunity to vilify him once she had left the area. 'We were not lovers in that way,' she informed him coolly. 'But we like each other very much and Matthew had asked me to marry him. I came to Bath hoping he would again propose, and he did. I had no idea he drinks too much. But then the grief of losing his first wife has never left him. Alcohol helps him cope as, I suspect, does the company of his housekeeper. He is not a lax hedonist as some...' she darkly hinted. 'But he is a very sad man. I expect you know all of that,' she added bitterly. 'Matthew said you had visited and tried to make him admit to some base liaison between us.'

'Did he?' came back quietly. 'Well, which lax hedonist is responsible for a base liaison with you?'

'That's none of your con...'

A dark hand covered her mouth. 'I thought we had agreed you would never again say that to me.'

'I never agreed,' she snapped pettishly, jerking away from his touch.

Silver eyes clashed with sparking topaz. 'Don't bait me needlessly, Emma,' he gently warned. 'I could break that aggressive spirit of yours so easily.'

Emma felt icy fingers trail her spine. It was no idle threat. She had known as much for a long while. As long ago as her skirmishes with him in London. She slid on his lap, trying to get her feet flat to the floor to flee.

'Sit still,' he grated, hauling her backwards against his chest, and the rough command in the words petrified her.

A narrow mouth moved close to a delicately shaped ear. 'I shall ask you this just one final time; thereafter, I contact your parents and ask them for an answer...as I should have done days ago. Who is your lover?'

Emma stared out of the window, her mind racing. Again, Matthew's recent words came back to haunt her. 'You must not trust him... Once he feels he has done his duty by you he may be glad for Dashwood to take you off his hands...'

Richard's patience with her had expired and, in fairness, she couldn't wonder at it. She *had* been a nuisance and he would gladly rid himself of her. But if he relayed to her parents that she was pregnant... She dared not even contemplate what damage that would wreak on them. It would be best to bluff out this nightmare charade she had idiotically begun. Strive to be amenable for a day or so longer and then return to London and pray Dashwood had shown leniency in her absence. But which man was she to condemn? A character her lies could never harm was the only answer...

'You would not know him so it is pointless naming him. He lives in the north...in Derbyshire...and visits London at times.'

'Is he married?'

'No, but he is spoken for.'

'Have you told him of your condition?'

'There's no way I can do that.'

'You love him that much?'

'I've always held him in great affection.'

'What's his name?'

Emma took a deep breath and said quietly, 'William...'

At a raise of dark brows requiring the rest, she murmured, 'Fitz.'

'William Fitz?'

'I said you would not know him,' she uttered agitatedly. 'He lives in Derbyshire and would never move in the circles you do. He is an honourable man...quite shy in a way.'

'Very shy...' Richard said drily. 'Very honourable...' he muttered with increased cynicism.

'I have told you now,' she quavered. 'You have got what you wanted, for what good it will do you.'

After a pulsing silence, Richard said solemnly, 'What has happened to our truce, Emma? It's not yet a day since we made it yet still we snipe. I think we should reinforce it.' A dark hand flipped over, palm up, waiting.

Be amenable, she reminded herself. Humour him until you can devise a way out of this maze of deceit you've stupidly concocted. Long fingers immediately curled over the small hand she placed atop his.

'Perhaps some affection to seal it and help it last this time,' he suggested softly.

Emma's golden gaze flicked warily to his dark face. Oh, no! The humiliating memory of how easily he had subdued her with that last kiss...how she had hungered for more...the detached abruptness with which he'd released her...still needled mercilessly. She attempted to snatch back her hand and turn her burning face away.

But determined fingers laced into hers. 'Yesterday, by the lake, I wanted from you an explanation, an apology and a kiss. There's but one left for you to bestow. Come...I did save you from a watery fate,' he reminded her with humour in his voice. 'That alone must be worth a token of thanks...'

'I'd sooner be up to my neck in pond weed and kiss a frog!' she snapped, but her heart was pounding so much, the words were breathy.

'I think that's another lie, Emma,' he softly laughed, with a touch of cool lips to her hot cheek. 'I think, too, you'd not deem a casual kiss more important than Martin's acquittal of insubordination.'

She swung her face towards his, forgetting how close he was. Their lips were mere inches apart. 'That's blackmail!' she gasped, and tried to tilt away from him but a hand speared into her thick hair, holding her close.

'I know,' he said impenitently, a finger smoothing over her trembling lips. 'But then you expect no less of me, I'm sure.'

Fawn eyes were riveted on his narrow mouth as it approached and her head strained against the sturdy palm cupping her scalp.

His lips caressed over a cheekbone. 'You taste salty,' he whispered, and she watched his tongue slide over his lower lip, savouring her tears. That prompted an involuntary sweet smile, and as her lips softened and parted he immediately covered them with his.

Resisting his narcotic charm was impossible. She felt pliant as he tilted her face, made no objection as he manoeuvred her jaw until their mouths perfectly fused. His lips gentled at first then increased pressure, moulding her soft mouth beneath his as he sensed her entrancement.

GET FREE BOOKS and a FREE GIFT WHEN YOU PLAY THE...

Lucky 7

SLOT MACHINE GAME!

Just scratch off the silver box with a coin. Then check below to see the gifts you get!

YES! I have scratched off the silver box. Please send me the 2 free Harlequin Historicals® books and gift for which I qualify. I understand I am under no obligation to purchase any books, as explained on the back of this card.

349 HDL DFT4

246 HDL DFT3
(H-HB-OS-11/01)

NAME		(PLEASE PRINT CLEARLY)

ADDRESS

APT.#   CITY

STATE/ PROV.   ZIP/POSTAL CODE

7	7	7	**Worth TWO FREE BOOKS plus a BONUS Mystery Gift!**
cherries	cherries	cherries	**Worth TWO FREE BOOKS!**
clubs	clubs	clubs	**Worth ONE FREE BOOK!**
bell	bell	cherry	**TRY AGAIN!**

Visit us online at www.eHarlequin.com

DETACH AND MAIL CARD TODAY!

The Harlequin Reader Service® — Here's how it works:

Accepting your 2 free books and gift places you under no obligation to buy anything. You may keep the books and gift and return the shipping statement marked "cancel." If you do not cancel, about a month later we'll send you 6 additional novels and bill you just $4.05 each in the U.S., or $4.46 each in Canada, plus 25¢ shipping & handling per book and applicable taxes if any.* That's the complete price and — compared to cover prices of $4.99 each in the U.S. and $5.99 each in Canada — it's quite a bargain! You may cancel at any time, but if you choose to continue, every month we'll send you 6 more books, which you may either purchase at the discount price or return to us and cancel your subscription.

*Terms and prices subject to change without notice. Sales tax applicable in N.Y. Canadian residents will be charged applicable provincial taxes and GST.

If offer card is missing write to: Harlequin Reader Service, 3010 Walden Ave., P.O. Box 1867, Buffalo NY 14240-1867

BUSINESS REPLY MAIL

FIRST-CLASS MAIL   PERMIT NO. 717-003   BUFFALO, NY

POSTAGE WILL BE PAID BY ADDRESSEE

HARLEQUIN READER SERVICE
3010 WALDEN AVE
PO BOX 1867
BUFFALO NY 14240-9952

NO POSTAGE
NECESSARY
IF MAILED
IN THE
UNITED STATES

'Kiss me back!' The hoarse command was breathed against her skin and then he roughly showed her how and waited.

She copied what she could recall unstintingly, skimming her lips along his, touching her tongue to his lower lip, inserting it to touch the tip of his. With a low growl he crushed her closer, yet still her mouth hovered, parted, beneath his, tempting with light, inexpert touches, until he took back control, plundering the soft sweetness of her again with seductive skill.

Emma didn't hear the study door open. It was the abrupt removal of her source of drugging pleasure, the vehement curse of the man responsible for that ecstasy, that brought her jerking to her senses and then to her feet. Scarlet-faced, she glanced at Ross who had turned sideways and was grimacing his absolute remorse at the ceiling, hands linked behind his head.

'Emma...' Richard pleaded, but she was already backing towards the door. 'Emma!' Richard ground out imperiously, with a stabbing glare at Ross.

'Please don't go,' Emma addressed Ross in a shaking voice. But with a double-handed gesture of sheer apology he was closing the door quietly.

'Come here,' Richard demanded. 'We have things to discuss.'

'Leave me be...'

'To do what? Even if you decide to settle for your drunken swain, there's the matter of his concubine. A *ménage à trois* in a tumbledown cottage? I don't think it would suit you, Emma.'

'Neither does a Palladian town house and an allowance,' she forced through her bruised, pulsing lips, frightened that fresh tears were imminent and she would never control them.

'I'll think of something that does suit you.'

With her hand on the door knob she turned to glance at him. 'There is *nothing* you could think of that would suit me,' she managed disdainfully before closing the door.

Chapter Nine

'You seem a little happier this evening, Amelia.'

'Stephen has been so agreeable,' Amelia brightly disclosed. 'We chatted this afternoon for an age and although nothing was mentioned of those *suspicions* I told you of he seemed very attentive. He took Jake out on his pony...and spent time in the nursery with Alice and us all.'

Emma breathed a sigh of relief. 'Good...you were perhaps mistaken in your reasons for arguing by the lake, then.'

'I do hope so,' Amelia sighed. 'And I'm glad you managed to slip out and see your friend Matthew. It was very mean of Richard to deny you a carriage just because you had quarrelled. Unlike him, too. He is never usually petty when cross with someone.'

Amelia linked arms with Emma and they strolled away from the sets forming on the dance floor and towards some chairs ranged against the wall.

'Richard never accompanies you all to these dances?' Emma asked casually, yet praying that the answer would be in the negative. Her wanton behaviour in his study that afternoon was so fresh in her mind that her lips pulsed and her face flamed anew with the memory of it. It must have been the stress of the day that had caused her to act so, she consoled herself. There was no other explanation for acting like a mindless fool, obeying his every command.

'Heavens, no!' Amelia broke into Emma's pensiveness. 'You

would have more chance of spying him at one of Mrs Petersham's afternoon tea parties!'

'I'm sure Mrs Petersham and Veronica would be very happy to see him,' Emma returned a little sourly.

Amelia tinkled a laugh and flapped a hand. 'Oh, that is nothing. Miriam has no real wish for an alliance there. She simply hopes that by placing Veronica constantly in Richard's way he might surrender and finally pay his addresses to the woman he will eventually marry: a duke's daughter. As you are friends he will no doubt tell you himself of his intentions towards Lady Penelope—and her dowry, of course. Stephen says the settlement will bring Richard copper-mining rights in Devon that he is desperate to have.' She lowered her voice. 'Apparently there is a fortune to be unearthed on the Duke of Winstanley's land.' She smoothed her gloves, then continued. 'Naturally, it is no love match...although Penelope seems quite smitten. But Richard will not worry...he has his...*lady friends*.' She glanced at Emma from beneath her lashes. 'As you know him of old...in his London heyday...you know that he and David Hardinge were most terrible scoundrels. Richard is improved, but not cured of bachelor excesses. He and Ross are no doubt carousing about town as usual.' Amelia sighed. 'I think, at times, Stephen hankers after their permissive lifestyle...'

'I'm sure it's no more than an idle envy,' Emma reassured her friend, but her voice was thin and an odd chill seemed to seep through her veins. Richard, married? For some reason it had not occurred to her that a serious alliance might be brewing. Yet it should have: had he not mentioned it himself when propositioning her at Mrs Keene's? Words paraded mockingly through her mind...*I'll make lasting provision for you. Even if I marry at some time*... Three years ago he might have considered a modest spinster with little to recommend her, but now he had his birthright and family commitments. He would want a wife of status and dowry and an heir.

She deliberately shook off the melancholy, rubbing at her arms briskly. Brightly she resumed their conversation. 'I think that Ross perhaps envies your husband. He seems rather taken with you, Amelia. Stephen watches carefully when he pays you attention.'

'Ross is rather taken with every woman over fifteen and under fifty. He is the most prolific flirt I have ever met. But he is rather captivating…in a buccaneering sort of way.' She added mischievously, 'I'll admit I do encourage his interest…especially when Stephen is in the vicinity.' Amelia dipped her head quickly towards Emma's and shielded their faces with her fluttering fan. 'He is coming again!'

Emma peeked curiously about the fan. A soft groan escaped her lips. Since arriving at the Upper Assembly Room in Bath some half an hour ago, Emma had, for some reason, attracted the attention of a rather dashing young man she guessed to be about her own age. His dark eyes had fixed so unwaveringly on her that at first she had believed she must have a smudge on her face and had asked Amelia to check. Amelia had laughed and said he was staring because she looked most alluring in her amber silk gown with her sleek tawny hair and lovely eyes.

'I do believe he is soon to ask you to waltz,' Amelia squealed. 'He is rather good-looking, Emma. I wish he would ask me. Stephen might be utterly miffed!'

Spying Stephen's tall figure weaving through the crowd, a glass in each of his hands, Emma laughed. 'Well, let's hope our beau approaches you now, then, for never would there be a more opportune moment.'

'Your servant, ladies,' Stephen greeted them, proffering glasses of lemonade.

Amelia inclined towards her husband. 'Emma has an admirer, Stephen. He is sure to soon wangle an introduction.'

Stephen grinned. 'Well, he'd better make his move before Richard does. I have a feeling my brother is a little protective where Emma is concerned.'

'*Richard?*' Emma and Amelia chorused.

'An amazing sight, I have to own,' Stephen conceded, still grinning. 'But yes; he and Ross are just arrived and causing quite a stir among the ladies in the ante-room. Not least amongst our own kin. I believe dear Mama practically hit the floor when she spied her eldest son surrounded by muslin. It's the venue that's astonishing, of course, not the yards of petticoat…' Belatedly recalling to whom he spoke, he reddened a little and cleared his throat. 'Emma knows him well enough.' He pacified his pink-faced wife. 'Good Lord, she's not deaf to gossip, and she was in London three years ago, you know.' Distractingly, Stephen added, 'He should soon have fought his way through the throng, if only to assist Diane with the smelling salts. It is the least he can do after causing Mother to have an attack.'

Emma glanced nervously about and did indeed spot an unmistakable silver-blond head. He looked strikingly imposing dressed in elegant back tailcoat with such contrastingly fair hair. A press of colourful ladies and just a few gentlemen, she acidly noted, presently entrapped him. Although he was smiling and chatting his eyes were scanning the room. Emma deliberately looked away.

Aware of Amelia and Stephen's engrossed conversation, she diplomatically swivelled about on her chair, allowing them privacy, and unintentionally faced her admirer. Yes, please do come over and talk to me, she silently encouraged, with a coy smile. I should like to annoy him a little more before the day is out. Mostly I should hate him to think that kiss in his study affected me in the slightest. It means as little to me as it does to him.

The young man's features adopted a smouldering intentness which abruptly fixed, mask-like, making Emma choke a soft giggle. After a stiff bow, which seemed not for her, he was dashing in a different direction.

Emma turned slightly, eyes slowly climbing long legs encased in dove-grey material; a black sleeve was passed over on the way to glimpse a hard, dark profile. Steely eyes were fixed on the man's retreating figure. A tanned hand was braced casually on her chair-back and then he looked down at her.

Emma darted glances about the room, noting that many people were either staring at them quite openly or discreetly peeking at intervals. 'Don't look so...so...' she hissed in an underbreath. 'Just don't look like that; you're making people stare,' she resorted to muttering.

'How do I look? Annoyed to find you flirting quite outrageously with a man you're not even introduced to?'

'I was not flirting! Merely being friendly. And how dare you preach so sanctimoniously? I doubt you're formally introduced to any woman you consort with,' was spat out in a whisper.

He sat in the vacant chair next to her, looked at her and smiled. 'Very well. I concede. The women I used to consort with don't expect niceties, just nice things. Is that what you want to hear?'

Emma choked and shielded her heating face with a cool hand. 'Do you have to be so...so extremely vulgar?' she fumed.

'If you don't want to know, Emma, don't probe until I tell you.'

'I was not!'

'Yes, you were.'

She speared a glance at him to see he was still seriously amused. He slanted back an intimate look, dusky lashes screening his eyes as they targeted her still swollen ruby lips. Heat coursed through Emma and she shifted backwards on her seat.

'I want you to dance with me.'

'When? Why?' Emma asked nervously.

'Now. Because I want to,' he replied.

The orchestra played the opening bars to a waltz and, standing abruptly, he offered her his hand. Emma slipped white fingers onto lean, bronzed ones and allowed him to lead her away. Suddenly he diverted from the whirling couples on the dance floor so abruptly, it gave cause for blatant whisperings.

'I shall be but a minute...' he murmured apologetically, inclining close, on returning Emma to her chair. A thumb traced a lingering caress on her soft palm as he reluctantly relinquished it, and then he had turned away and was weaving swiftly through the throng.

Amelia looked at Emma and shrugged her bemusement. 'I see we've both been abandoned. Stephen has disappeared, too. They obviously have some men's gossip to catch up with.'

'Men's gossip?' interjected a familiar, laughing, voice. 'Do tell me more.' Ross seated himself next to them both with a raffish white smile.

Emma managed to greet him adequately although she blushed, recalling how mere hours ago she had been discovered by this man on his friend's lap looking for all the world like a wanton hussy. Ross seemed oblivious to any impropriety that might make her uneasy. In fact, despite his charming demeanour, he seemed unusually preoccupied himself as he chatted, yet kept watchful eyes on the entrance.

Richard's fingers closed vice-like about the woman's arm. Without slowing his pace he spun her about in the Assembly

Room doorway where she had boldly stationed herself, and pushed her in front of him as he made for the stairs that led below.

Once out in the cool evening air, and concealed at the side of the building from prying eyes, she was released with a small shove.

'I wasn't sure you would be 'ere, *chéri*,' Yvette Dubois purred at him. 'I didn't think such tame entertainment was what you liked.'

'Just listen,' Richard bit out. 'Go home. I'll come in an hour or so. You can then explain the reason for your impertinence. By the time I arrive, make sure you to have begun packing up to leave tomorrow afternoon. Make sure you to have chosen which side of the Channel you prefer...or I shall choose for you. Now get into that carriage.' His blond head jerked at a conveyance close by, a young maid's face visible at the window.

Yvette shivered beneath the stone-cold fury she could sense emanating from him. He terrified her when he was like this. But she forced a shrill laugh and jittery confidence, for she was determined to provoke his jealousy and win him back. 'Per'aps it is you who should listen, Sir Silver Squire,' she mocked. 'I am come 'ere to tell you that I 'ave done my choosing. This Bath suits me so ver' well. The *monsieur* I 'ave chosen to replace you suits me so ver' well, too.' Innocently, she asked, 'You did not think I am 'ere just to see you? My new lover is 'ere tonight...with his so *charmante* wife. She knows nothing of me, *naturellement*. As always I am so discreet...'

Blonde curls were twirled round a finger as she peeked slyly sideways at him. 'And I think you must forget your little visit to me later...unless...three people together excites you. Does it? Per'aps a new pleasure...something you never try before...' she throatily coaxed, pink tongue trailing her lower lip, a long fingernail trailing his black sleeve.

'How sweet,' he drawled, harsh boredom curling his lip. 'You think there's something I've never tried before. Unfortunately, my dear, there's nothing you can tempt me with...you've nothing I want.'

Yvette felt her temper firing, her vanity crushing. But she managed a Gallic shrug. 'I'm not so certain, Richard...I think per'aps

I 'ave in my power something you do want so ver' much... Ah...'
she purred contentedly. 'See, 'ere 'e comes now...'

Richard pivoted on a heel. Stephen was approaching, peering
about as though seeking someone.

Yvette chuckled huskily, with intense satisfaction. The astonishment on Richard's face was mingling with conflicting emotions of anguish and hopeless rage. They might fight over her,
Yvette happily mused. How *merveilleux* that would be! Two
handsome brothers fighting on the cobbles because of her, while
inside the polite people who shunned her presence at their gatherings wondered where the two dignified brothers could be.

As Stephen noticed his older brother, he approached uncertainly. 'What's going on?' he demanded nervously of Richard.
'She told me you'd finished with her.' A suspicious look was
arrowed at Yvette. 'And she was free to find someone else to...to
care for her.'

'And you think that should be you?' Richard asked, deadly
quiet. 'She contacted you, I take it? Suggested as much, then let
you know what delightful attention you'd get in return? Sampled
any of it yet?'

Stephen reddened and his eyes narrowed. 'You sound so
damned righteous it makes me sick. Don't lecture me! Never
once in your adult life have you been in a position to moralise!'

Richard put up dark hands in acceptance. *'Touché.'* he said
gravely. 'And I know you have. You put me to shame...I admit
it. You've been a good husband and father.' Richard paced away
then swung back to look at his brother. 'And now you think
you're due a little recreation. Who am I to deny you? But the
thing is, Stephen, I'm not sure how I feel about letting her
go...especially to you.' An uneasy laugh and rub at the bridge
of his nose preceded, 'Unfavourable comparisons might be made.
Besides, I've always been bad at sharing things with you...you
know that.'

'I shall see how Diane is faring with the smelling salts,' Emma
announced, feeling unaccountably uneasy. She left Ross and
Amelia innocently flirting as she wandered to the ante-room
where refreshments were set out. She spied Diane; seated next
to her was Miriam, feverishly fanning herself. And standing

nearby, conversing heatedly with them, were the Petershams. With a sigh and a steady smile, Emma approached.

Apart from a distracted welcome from the Du Quesne women she was virtually ignored. Soon she discovered why. Juicy gossip-mongering was in progress.

'Never say so!' she heard Miriam whisper at Susan Petersham. 'It cannot be true!'

Susan Petersham inclined forward. 'I have it straight from Mrs Jones who is just arrived from London. Dashwood is so enraged at the turn of events that it is likely the mother will still end in the Fleet. The daughter too if these investigators winkle her out. He is out for blood!'

'I feel so sorry for the girl's mother... What a terrible thing! To first lose a daughter then a husband!'

At the first mention of the name Dashwood, Emma had become petrified, straining to hear every snippet. Now she could hardly make out anything other than the pounding of blood in her ears. They were talking of her family, she was sure. And had mentioned that her mother had lost her husband! She grabbed behind her double-handed at the wall as she felt her legs weaken.

'Someone must know the family,' Miriam probed.

'Dashwood is so infuriated by being made to wear the jester's cap that he is keeping all close to his chest. The father is absconded too and one never knows what he might do to avoid the Fleet or pistols at dawn. It would be one or other and no mistake! The family's name will never survive the scandal. I imagine they are people of some station, but not of the first stare.' Mrs Petersham drew breath then hissed, 'I say it's disgraceful of the chit to leave her parents in such disarray! Thousands of pounds had changed hands, too, you know, with more to follow after the nuptials.'

'I have a little sympathy for the poor thing,' Miriam whispered with a shake of the head. 'I have heard such diabolical tales of that man as make a saint of the devil...'

Susan Petersham endorsingly wagged her head. 'I should not like to be in that chit's shoes when eventually she and Dashwood come face to face...'

Emma retraced a few steps from the gossiping women in the manner of a sleepwalker. She tottered woodenly about, obliquely aware that they had not noticed her withdrawal. She walked, not knowing where she headed, and twice bumped into people. Automatic apology was whispered through a throat that felt too tight for her even to breathe.

She found some stairs and quickly descended them, instinctively heading towards fresh air and comforting, obscuring darkness.

Richard's steady, sensual gaze had Yvette visibly drooping against the wall for support. 'So we disagree a little...' he murmured, eyes stripping her. 'I threaten to put her off. But the idea of my brother touching what's rightfully mine...'

Yvette swayed towards him. She clutched at his arm, grazing herself wantonly against him. ''E will never touch what's rightfully yours, Richard,' she fervently vowed. ''E is a boy compared to you! Three notes I send before 'e contacts me once. It is you I love. You won't regret keeping me, *chéri*. I will show you later just 'ow much you will not regret it, in every way you like,' she whispered, in so thick an accent the words were almost indistinct. 'I never wanted anyone else...only ever you. I like you to be jealous...I say it. I knew you would 'ate 'im to 'ave me.'

Richard backed her against the wall, arms stationed at either side of her, and bent his head. She immediately wound herself about him, jerking his face to hers and kissing him with a desperate ferocity, a little moan of pleasure and triumph breaking in her throat as his tongue filled her mouth.

Richard pulled open her cloak, exposing a thrusting cleavage, the skimpy muslin bodice cut so low, crescents of dark aureolas were visible. He lowered his face again. Before he'd touched her she was arching to meet him, eyes half-closed, sighing in anticipation.

'Still want her?' Richard asked idly as he pushed himself away from the wall and turned to face his brother.

Stephen's face was taut with mortification, white with rage. 'You bastard! You've tricked her into saying all that. She would have settled for me.'

'And that's what you want, is it?' Richard ground out in slow, measured tones of utter contempt. 'A whore who'll settle for you. You're my brother, goddammit! Look at her! I could take her back tomorrow...next week...next month.' He spun away from

Stephen in sheer disgust, ignoring Yvette's darkly furious face. 'That arrangement suits you, does it? Sharing her when the fancy takes me?'

Stephen stared stonily for a moment, then, with an enraged cry, he sprang forward, fists raised. Richard deflected the blow easily and pushed him away. 'You want her...you have her. I've never yet fought over a whore and I'm damned if I'll start now. She leaves for France tomorrow. You want her so damned much, bring her back at your own expense,' he sneered, before striding away.

Emma backed away in the shadows as she saw him approach. Although she felt rigid with shock and disgust, she knew to avoid him. What was best? Turn and run? Hide and hope he would pass? She shuffled backwards on weak legs, close to the brickwork, praying that the deep colour of her gown and the shadow cast by the wall gave her adequate protection.

As she retreated, all she'd witnessed...every revolting part... undulated before her eyes, whispered in her mind more woundingly than the matrons' gossip about her parents.

A silver-blond head dipping to kiss a woman was what she'd seen from afar and despite her cold dread she'd paced forward, mesmerised, out of sight. Then she'd recognised the woman's identity and seen Stephen, in the shadows, watching them.

'That arrangement suits you, does it? Sharing her when the fancy takes me?' she'd heard Richard suggest in a cold, careless tone. It had been enough to make her twist about, nausea churning her stomach, and immediately distance herself from the foul exchange. When she'd glanced back, she'd seen that Richard was moving away too, and it had sent her rushing to hug the wall for cover as she'd stepped back, for she was appalled she might appear a voyeur.

Emma froze. His pace was outstripping hers and she realised he would soon draw level. He was far more likely to notice her moving than stationary. Flattening herself motionless against the brickwork, she waited, barely breathing, for him to pass so she could flee. And she knew she would; at dawn she would quit Bath for London.

Snapping his head back, Richard spouted savage curses at the stars. His head whipped around to glance at the face of the little maid at the carriage window. She immediately dipped her bonnet and he looked away...and hesitated. He looked again. Then stopped. Pivoting on a heel towards the wall, he stood perfectly still and stared.

Emma moved first. She just couldn't endure the suspense any longer. She walked, head high, towards the entrance to the Assembly Rooms.

Richard proceeded too, at an angle, so he'd cut off her path within seconds. He braced his arm against the wall and she immediately tried to pass him, but he blocked her way with his body, forcing her back against the brick. 'Were you looking for me?'

Emma swallowed twice, desperate to act coolly, rationally. Still her throat wouldn't work so she shook her head and again made a move to pass him.

'Will you listen if I explain?' An odd hint of plea roughened the words.

'I needed some air,' exploded in a gulp. 'I came below for some air because I felt...I felt...' A tear trickling from the corner of an eye was smeared away without conscious thought.

A dark hand skimmed towards her face but she slapped it so swiftly and savagely, it spun up and away from her. It was controlled and on its way back so fast, she flinched, sure he would hit her, but his fist smashed into the brickwork above her head with such force that she felt the tremor at her back.

His moonlit head inclined a little. 'What did you hear...see?'

He asked it quite normally, she thought. In the way one would enquire after a diverting tableau. 'Enough,' she reported, striving for the same bland attitude. 'Enough revolting, loathsome...' She trembled into silence and stared past his shoulder at the starry night, her lower lip so tightly held by her teeth, she tasted coppery blood.

'Are you going to let me explain?'

'Why? I would not believe you if you told me the time of day. I would never listen to pathetic lies about why you share your mistress with your brother.'

A grunt of mirthless laughter met that and the sound shattered her fragile control. She lashed out at his face...and he let her. She hit him twice and each time he simply turned with the blow, making no attempt to stop her or protect himself. When she finally restrained her shaking fury and flung herself back against the wall, he looked at her.

'You *will* listen to me, Emma.'

'*You* will listen to *me*,' she quaveringly countered, a vestige of composure scraped together. 'Never think I came out here seeking you. I did not. I was not spying. When above stairs, I heard some...some gossip of people I know that upset me and I had to get away for a moment. I wish I had never seen you...her...or Stephen. Not because your disgusting debauchery has wounded me or surprised me, but Stephen's has. And Amelia already suspects that Stephen is unfaithful. She has spoken of it; asked my advice, and if she does so again, I shall not know what to say...' Her hoarse voice trailed into silence and she smeared away another tear before it left her lashes.

Richard inclined his head, sightlessly inspecting his torn and bleeding knuckles. Absently he turned the fist vertical, rested his forehead against it and swore with vehement abandon.

Aware of Stephen approaching, he abruptly pushed himself away from the wall and grabbed Emma's wrist. She twisted in his grip but his fingers brutalised just enough to make her cease straining. 'Let the others know we're on our way back to Silverdale,' Richard bit out without once looking at his brother as their paths traversed.

'Don't you dare manhandle me, you...you perverted bastard!' she spat.

'Don't make a scene, Emma. And don't, for God's sake, provoke me further.'

With a snap and an imperious flick of long fingers a carriage was soon drawing up close to them.

The journey to Silverdale passed in total silence. Emma watched the passing of pearly scenery as though branding it on her memory. She would see it a final time in dawnlight when she left for London and then no more. Once or twice she snatched a glance at Richard's profile to find him staring through the coach window in the same vacant-eyed, preoccupied fashion she imagined she had been.

When the avenue of ghostly whitebeam widened on to driveway shingle and the footman opened the coach door with an exceedingly wary glance at his master, Emma dismounted with the servant's help and an insulting tap at the dark hand that was extended towards her.

Richard followed her into the hallway. 'Go straight to bed, Emma. We'll talk of this in the morning,' he said with weary dignity.

She ignored him, but did, indeed, head immediately for the stairs without once deigning to look in his direction. Halfway up the sweeping staircase, the explosion of a door below slamming made her jump and grab at the bannister. She actually stopped dead for a few seconds to allow her heart rate to settle before continuing to her room.

Emma looked at the letters she had written: one for Amelia, one for Miriam and one for Diane. Each held virtually the same wording: that she was pleased to have known them and sorry to leave so abruptly, but pressing matters in London required her immediate return. She felt inordinately pleased that there was no hint of untruth in any of it. She raised her eyes from her writing table by the window and looked out over a pink-streaked dawn sky. She had not slept at all and felt quite light-headed with an odd mingling of fatigue and nervous energy.

If Martin refused to take her to the general coach office in Bath to catch the early London mail coach, she would walk. She judged she would still make it in time for seven-fifteen. She and Victoria had rambled for miles through Hertfordshire countryside at times, and her carpet bag would not be that much of a burden. She collected it now, and, with a deep breath and a closing of her tired eyes, knew she was ready to depart.

A light rap at the door had her welded to the spot, heart hammering. Who on earth would be up and about at this hour? It was far too early for one of the maids to rouse her.

The tapping came again, then a plaintive voice called, 'Emma? Are you awake? Please open the door if you can hear me.'

Emma turned the key at once and Amelia rushed in, her face white and her eyes red-rimmed. She, too, was fully clothed.

'Stephen didn't come home with me last night. He is still abroad. He has a woman; I know he has.'

Emma felt chill seep through her. 'You can't be sure, Amelia,' she whispered...hoping.

'Oh, I can. Look!' She thrust a vibrating piece of paper at Emma. 'I went through to his chamber to see if he had returned and found this under a book. He hadn't even bothered to properly conceal it!' she hysterically squealed.

Emma took the cloyingly scented note, her heart sinking as she immediately recognised the elegant script to be the same as that on the interview details she had received from Yvette Dubois. She scanned the invitation to meet then dine privately later that evening at South Parade. It was all couched in coy, suggestive terms and its purpose was indisputable.

As though just realising that Emma was not in nightclothes but actually cloaked and bonneted, Amelia cried softly, 'Are you leaving? Why?'

Emma nodded. 'I had written you a farewell note.' She turned her head indicatively towards the writing table but her eyes instinctively sought the brightening skies. 'There are urgent matters in London I must deal with. I'm so sorry, Amelia, but I must be going. If Martin refuses me a carriage, I shall need to walk to Bath.'

'I'm leaving too!' Amelia choked, too concerned with her own problems to ask further about Emma's. 'And I'm never coming back! He can keep as many cyprians as he pleases!'

Emma stared at her, aghast. 'Amelia, be sensible. You're a married woman. What of your beautiful children?'

Amelia's drawn face hardened intractably. 'He is a married man. Yet he conveniently forgets it! And my children will be well cared for. Miriam loves them. There are nursemaids, wet nurses, every conceivable help here at Silverdale.' She whispered brokenly, 'And their papa dotes on them...more than he does on me. They will be well cared for.' A bitter blue gaze was turned on Emma. 'I am leaving and if you will not let me travel with you, then I shall travel alone. I have a spinster aunt in London; we always deal well together. She won't tell of my whereabouts. Not even to her sister, my mama. For she is sure to rant and rail about duty and modesty—' She broke off and whirled about for the door. 'Well, I am done with duty and modesty!' she hissed. 'He pleaded with me to marry him, you know. A dozen times at least he must have proposed before I said he could approach my papa. I know how men are...even married men with their mistresses. But I believed we were different.' She added soulfully, 'It was a love match…is a love match…or so I thought…'

'Please consider what you are doing, Amelia,' Emma implored. 'You are being a little irrational. You might feel it impossible to abandon Jake and Alice in a few hours' time when you are calmer. It is a very great step to take: there may be no way back to your children.'

Amelia tossed her head and merely replied, 'Please wait, Emma; I should rather travel with you than alone. I'm sure you'd like a companion, too.'

Emma did wait, in the shadows in the spectral marble hallway, with thumping heart and dry mouth. All was eerily quiet until the sound of Amelia whisking down the stairs made her start.

Amelia, now cloaked and carrying a bag, grabbed at her hand and led her to a side door. 'At least you will not now have to walk to Bath, Emma,' she joked with muted hysteria. 'Martin will never refuse me a ride in the landau. We can take it directly to London. It will save time. If Stephen wants the vehicle back…he can blasted well search for it himself.'

Chapter Ten

The sound of the study door knocking back against the wall brought Richard's blond head up off his arms. As he pushed himself upright, a dark hand caught against the empty glass. He calmly righted it and slumped back in his chair to blink at the man by the door. 'What do you want?' he snapped irascibly.

'Amelia's left me,' Stephen croaked disbelievingly.

Richard drew a hand across his bleary eyes. 'Left you? What do you mean? How do you know?'

Stephen paced forward and let the note drift to the desk from his shaking fingers. 'The bed's not been slept in. She must have found this. It was lying on her pillow.' He choked an awful laugh. 'It's not the place I would have put it. She's run away. She's abandoned me and the children.'

Richard glanced over Yvette's note then flicked the perfumed paper away, grimacing in distaste. 'You've been out all night, I take it?'

'Yes, but…'

'He's been with me,' Ross chipped in from the doorway. 'We stayed at Bellamy's playing hazard and faro.'

'Why has she done it?' Stephen demanded, fingers dragging through his flaxen hair, tears glossing his blue eyes. 'Why?'

'Why?' Richard mimicked scornfully. 'She's done it so you'll follow her, you bloody fool. And you'd better make sure when you do catch up with her that your excuses and apologies are word-perfect.'

'I never did anything, I swear. You can ask that French trollop. All I did was write her a note and meet her outside the Assembly Rooms. I never touched her. I swear it!'

'They left at dawn, in the landau,' Ross interjected quietly.

'They?' Richard repeated, a slow realisation focussing his intoxicated grey vision. He was halfway towards the door in seconds. The stairs were taken two at a time, but he slowed as he noted Emma's chamber door was ajar. On entering, he approached the writing desk and glanced down at the three letters arranged neatly. So she'd intended fleeing alone, he realised with a taut smile. It would have been pointless leaving Amelia a note if she had planned for them to journey together, or had known Amelia also intended bolting.

He aimlessly wandered from window to bed, then back again, feeling bereft already, and on quitting the quiet, tidy chamber smashed his fist into the door in sheer frustration, breaking open the crusty wounds on his knuckles.

'Well, I'm getting myself some breakfast,' Ross said cheerfully as he glanced from a coldly exasperated man to one who looked on the point of blubbing.

'You have to come with me,' Stephen pleaded. 'I need an alibi. Amelia will never believe I was gambling after reading this!' He flapped Yvette's note.

A wry look softened Ross's piratical features as he indicated Richard with a hand and a meaningful elevation of ebony brows.

'Oh, no one believes me,' Richard snarled sarcastically. 'I'm a perverted bastard...'

Ross blew out his cheeks and looked quizzically at them both. 'Are you sure there really is some point to this being in love?'

Richard stared, scowled and stalked off. Stephen dropped his head into unsteady hands and ambled behind his brother towards the stables.

'*Derbyshire?*' Stephen cried in astonishment a few minutes later. 'For God's sake! Why there?'

'That's what I heard, Sir Richard,' Martin offered nervously. 'I'm sure I heard the lady with Mrs Du Quesne say about setting directly on the road to Derbyshire.'

Richard smiled grimly at the brightening horizon. 'No doubt she was aware you'd recount it to me,' he muttered. 'And I'd have reason enough to believe it plausible.' He mounted the palomino with swift agility. 'Let's try the London road,' he said, and was off in that direction.

'Horses could do wi' a drink 'n a rest,' the groom said. 'Fallow Buck be just up ahead, m'm. We can stop 'n you can take a drink too, if'n you fancy.'

'I should like a drink, Emma. It's getting quite warm now,' Amelia said.

'Are you sure you want to continue to London, Amelia?' Emma asked for the hundredth time. 'It is still early enough for you to change your mind. You could set about now and be back at Silverdale before you are properly missed.'

Amelia shook her head vigorously, setting blonde ringlets as-way. 'I hate him,' she informed Emma calmly, chin tilted. 'I utterly hate him...'

'But what of your children?' Emma gently reminded her. 'I don't mean to nag you, Amelia, and it's not that I don't want your company, but...'

Amelia leaned towards her and squeezed her hand. 'I know. You want what is best for me. But I truly would have run away whether or not you'd departed for London. Don't feel guilty that you set the idea in my head.'

'I sat here in exactly this spot by this window when I journeyed to Bath all those days ago,' Emma told Amelia soon after as they sipped tea and ate cake and gazed out through tiny-paned, leaded windows into the inner courtyard. 'It seems like eons since I left London.' She smiled at her companion. 'And, strange as it may seem, I saw your dear little Jake here, although of course at the time I didn't know him. He and his uncle were on the forecourt. I was waiting for the mail coach to leave and saw them moments before I boarded it.' At Amelia's quizzical look, she added, 'I only glimpsed Richard's profile and didn't recognise him. He looked...looks very different now. His tanned skin and sun-lightened hair make him appear quite a stranger.' She added quickly, 'Were you here too that morning, Amelia?'

Amelia shook her head. 'Richard and Stephen took Jake to the seaside for a few days. Miriam has friends at Lyme Regis whom she wanted to visit. I couldn't travel for I was still indisposed with my confinement.' She paused. 'Little Jake adores Richard;

he would make a good papa. I shall miss my Jakie,' she murmured with a throb to her voice. 'He is a good boy...'

With an anxious frown at Amelia's tear-bright eyes, Emma
tried again. 'You see, you are pining for the children already. I
think you should turn about and return home...'

'And I think that sounds like sensible advice, sweetheart,'
came huskily from behind them.

The two women exchanged startled glances before twisting
about on their chairs.

Stephen was standing directly behind, Richard was in the process of handing the landlord a sum of money for the small taproom's private use, and Ross was seating himself on a rickety
stool by the bar. Helping himself to a bottle and a glass, Ross
nonchalantly commenced making good use of both.

'I believe it is time we resumed our journey, Emma,' Amelia
said with icy deliberation. She stood and had managed two regal
steps towards the door before Stephen stepped in front of her.

'You're my wife and you're going nowhere at all but back
home with me,' her husband growled.

Ross winced and shook his head at his drink. Richard leaned
against the bar, helped himself to the bottle and poured while
slanting a flint-eyed gaze at Emma.

Emma stared through the taproom window. Her weary lids
dropped in sheer hopelessness. Why had it yet again all gone so
horribly wrong? If only she'd been selfish! If only she'd refused
Amelia's company and departed alone this morning from York
House coach office: she would have been well on her way home.

As it was, her only means of continuing to London would be
via a mail coach, if one stopped, sporting a vacant seat, to refresh
its passengers and horses. Failing that, she might be stranded at
a countryside inn or taken back to Bath by the detestable lecher
she was keen to escape. Perhaps Richard believed she had cajoled
Amelia into accompanying her by recounting what she'd witnessed outside the Assembly Rooms last night!

'Do you expect me to believe *that*?' sliced through Emma's
feverish thoughts in a savage hiss.

Stephen's coaxing response to his wife's outrage was also audible. 'Ross will tell you it's the truth! I *swear* I was with him...I
love you, Amelia...'

Feeling unbearably intrusive, Emma abruptly got to her feet

and made for the door. She kept her head high as she passed the two men at the bar, even managing eye contact and a quavering, 'Good morning.'

Ross gave her a lopsided smile. Richard looked so sardonically triumphant that it almost caused her to halt and wipe the smile from his face.

As she emerged into warm Indian summer sunshine, honey and copper glints flared in her fawn hair. She sped away towards the road and stared along it, willing a coach to appear right now...*this minute*.

There was nothing; all was pastoral and peaceful. It was a hauntingly glorious morning, she glumly realised. Dispiritedly she turned back to see a groom lead away the handsome stallion. Then its owner appeared in the tavern doorway and strolled towards her.

He stopped a little distance from her and stared along the dusty, rutted track in much the same way she had moments before. 'What are you looking for?'

'The mail coach,' she stiffly informed him, staring across hay-stacked fields.

'Ah,' he grunted in wry comprehension. 'Still intent on taking the scenic route to Derbyshire, then. Proceeding via London, are you?'

Emma flushed. She had forgotten about that little deceit.

Reading her thoughts exactly, he said softly, 'You see, I'm coming to know you well, Emma. If you want to outwit me, try telling the truth. I swear the surprise will kill me.'

'Indeed I shall, then, sir. The inducement is too great to ignore.'

He laughed at that and turned fully towards her, and as she looked properly at him she recognised the dissipation in his dark face. 'You're drunk,' she snapped.

'Not any more. I'm hung over,' he explained easily. 'And feeling much better now I've had a hair of the dog that bit me.' As though sensing her suspicions, he said softly, 'I was at home all night, drinking alone.'

'I really couldn't care less where you were or who you were with,' she dismissed with a shrill laugh.

'Well, persevering with my new wisdom that the truth is usually the opposite of what you say, I conclude you care very much.'

'That's not wisdom,' Emma shot back, startled, 'but conceit. And there's nothing new about it. I dare say it's been with you your life through.' She swished about to glare along the road.

'Well, enough of these pleasantries.' Richard laughed with an amount of contentment. 'It's time to be getting home. Between them, Stephen and Ross should have managed to persuade Amelia that her husband's not an adulterer but an idiot. There's been time enough for tears and making up.'

'Unfaithful in heart, unfaithful indeed,' Emma muttered.

'That makes you sound sweetly innocent, Emma,' Richard softly mocked. 'And I'd really like to think you were...rather than simply naive.' A searing silver look was levelled at her slender body from beneath low black lashes. 'It's got nothing to do with his heart. His heart has always been with Amelia. Stephen's only vice last night was gambling.'

'And his vice tonight? Or is it not yet his turn to visit South Parade?' she bitterly lashed out. 'Will Ross speak for him when it is? Will you? Will you both help him lie and cheat and deceive his wife?'

A dark hand spanned his brow, easing tension beneath a fall of sun-bleached hair. 'Are you now willing to let me explain about that?' he sighed.

'There is no point,' she whipped out haughtily. 'I still wouldn't believe you if you told me the time of day.' That jolted her thoughts to the morning passing. She peered again along the track for sight of the mail coach. 'I wonder how late it is? It surely cannot yet be noon,' she muttered to herself, with a squint at the sun.

'It's almost a quarter to eleven,' Richard informed her with studied gravity. 'Would you care to check my watch?'

As she glowered and blushed simultaneously, he said on a choke of a laugh, 'Come, I'll get the landau brought round.'

'I'm going to London,' Emma breathed at his back as he walked away.

'You're going to Silverdale,' he smoothly contradicted her without bothering to turn around.

'Don't give me your orders! I have to journey to London.'

'Why?'

'I want...need to see my parents.'

Richard turned towards her. 'Will they want to see you?'

'Yes, I'm sure they will now.'

He slowly retraced his steps. 'Well, come back to Bath today and I'll take you to London tomorrow. We have to return to Silverdale for a coach, in any case, and I have some business to conclude.'

'Thank you for your concern,' she said tightly, 'but I can board the mail coach. I wouldn't dream of imposing on you...'

'That means go to hell...'

'Indeed,' Emma said.

'I'll get the landau brought round; we'll discuss it all at Silverdale.'

'I'm not returning there.'

'This is foolishness, Emma,' Richard gritted with straining patience. 'I can't spirit you to London without transport. You can't be sure a mail coach with space will pull in here this week.' He stuffed his hands into the pockets of his long leather riding coat. 'Anyway, it makes no difference if the damned coach arrives empty and within the next five minutes—you're still not boarding it. You're not travelling to London alone.'

'I travelled from London alone!'

'Well, you're not travelling back in the same manner!' he suddenly roared. The grim exasperation in his face had Emma taking two hasty backward paces.

'Sorry.' He held out a hand, palm towards her, in placation and reassurance. As it moved to span his brow, massaging at his temples, she noticed the wounds crimsoning his knuckles.

'Is your hand sore?'

'Yes. I'll try and remember to use the other one next time you provoke me into sparring with a brick wall or a bedroom door.'

Their eyes met and held, silver engulfing amber as he walked back slowly towards her. 'I was peeved that you'd run without due thanks for my hospitality.' He ironically explained away the bedroom door incident. His fingers rose towards her face, then nimbly dodged the slap she aimed at them. 'That's very cruel, Emma,' he reproached her, with a pained look. 'You'll make me bleed again.'

Despite herself, she *felt* cruel, and ashamed. Seizing his damaged hand, she inspected rusty, crusty lacerations to make sure none had been caught. 'I'm sorry you hurt yourself,' she said quietly. 'You should ask Mrs Braithwaite for some salve. She has potions...' Becoming aware of his stillness and silence, she quickly released the injured digits.

Both dark hands curved about her upper arms, stubbornly drawing her close. 'You know, you can be incredibly sweet to me at times...when you forget you ought to hate me.'

'I was simply concerned that I had worsened your hurt,' she burst out, turning her face to study the ground as she sensed him getting ever closer.

'I love your concern. It's worth being hurt. That's the first time you've touched me with kindness.'

The sound of approaching footsteps and conversation had Richard blaspheming through closed teeth and Emma hastily breaking free.

She showed him a little sympathy and his damnable conceit made him think there was more to it! Just as it made him think she cared with whom he spent a drunken night...when of course she did not! It made no difference to her whether it was Ross and Stephen or a dozen French courtesans! She swallowed and made a conscious effort to unfurl her fingers and prevent her nails digging any deeper into her tender palms.

'Emma!' Amelia, face aglow with contentment, tripped daintily away from her husband. Drawing Emma aside for privacy, she whispered, 'Stephen has explained everything and Ross has said it is all true. And I do believe them.'

'Good...good,' Emma breathed. 'I am happy you are to return home.'

Amelia linked arms with Emma and urged her along the track. 'Come, let's take a little walk by the hedgerows and we can be as deliciously immodest as we like while I tell you all.' Amelia peered back over her shoulder at the men watching them. She sighed happily at her husband's smouldering-eyed semi-smile, flounced her blonde ringlets around and began, 'The note I showed you that I found in Stephen's chamber was sent by Richard's mistress! The shameless trollop was soliciting Stephen's protection because his brother had put her off. She actually attempted to peddle her vile services to my husband!' Amelia squeaked in outrage. 'For two pins I'd go to South Parade and scratch her evil eyes out. But I'd be too late: Richard is sending her back to France, thank heavens!'

Amelia narrowed her blue eyes. 'I saw her once or twice when she was at the theatre with Richard and she did slyly eye Stephen. The impudent hussy has got her comeuppance and will soon be gone. It was just so droll, Emma,' she confided breathily. 'Stephen was so desperate to convince me that this baggage is now out of favour, he revealed that his brother must already be coaching her understudy! The house of sin is apparently rarely vacant!' Hugging at Emma's arm, she squealed, 'Scandalous of us to talk so, isn't it? Miriam and my own dear mama would be utterly outraged by such indelicacy and have a wondrous fit of the vapours!'

Emma forced a brittle smile. 'Yes; but perhaps no more might be prudent. You should forget it for she is not worth further time or thoughts.'

So, Yvette Dubois was to be banished because Richard had someone in mind to replace her. Emma swallowed. She had an ominous feeling she knew who that might be! No wonder he was adamant she return to Bath with him. Though she doubted he had any intention of taking her to Silverdale. Her destination was likely to be a vacant Palladian town house in South Parade!

As they strolled on in September sunshine Emma's mind was in turmoil. She could return to Bath and choose between a temporary position as a gentleman's mistress or a lengthy labour as a drunkard's wife; or she could journey on to London and face Jarrett Dashwood and her mother's wrath. She thought of her pathetic, weak-willed papa and wondered in which direction he had absconded and whether Dashwood had yet tracked him there. Perhaps he had fled west, too, and was unknowingly close to her.

A tremor shivered through her as she recalled Susan Petersham's unwitting warning: 'I shouldn't like to be in that chit's shoes when eventually she and Dashwood come face to face...' And yet it seemed every passing moment proved, that for her parents' sake, and, yes, even her own, it would have been prudent to settle for the future he offered. The past several days had been a catalogue of her deceitfulness and trickery and the outcome was further jeopardy and harrowing self-disgust. Nought had been gained! Now she was scheming to return and right the mess her flight had caused. Her behaviour was reprehensible: utterly selfish and stupidly immature.

Dashwood had appearances to keep, she recalled her mother saying. Susan Petersham had implied something similar in that he was loath to name her family in this scandal or to reveal much of any of it. Even if it was for his own wounded pride's sake, she could only feel gratitude for the reprieve.

Her mother had been right all along: she was a fool to hanker after love when security was attainable. One couple of her acquaintance was blissfully happy and she coveted that for herself, ridiculously supposing *she* could live a romantic ideal. With hindsight, she saw she had allowed gossip to prejudice her views of Dashwood before she had passed five minutes in his company. Had she been pleasant to him he might, in turn, have been perfectly fair and civil.

Half an hour later, displaying maternal and wifely duty in abundance, Amelia was desperate to again be at Silverdale with her husband and children. Emma returned Amelia and Stephen a double-handed waving salute as the landau crunched over the Fallow Buck's forecourt and disappeared up the lane. Her amber gaze then slid sideways to the tall blond man standing close by. 'I shall do very well here,' she brightly told him. 'I was alone here once before and quite safe.'

'Yes, I recall seeing you here alone. I'm not likely to forget that morning. I've not had a moment's peace since,' Richard added ruefully.

Stunned that he had even noticed her hunching into her cloak and bonnet that misty morning, let alone remembered the drab sight she must have presented, she garbled, 'Thank you for your kind hospitality at Silverdale. I shall impress on Victoria just how attentive you were to my needs.'

'I'd like to return the compliment and impress on David just how attentive you were to my needs,' Richard rejoined smoothly. 'I shall have a carriage brought here from Silverdale and accompany you to London. *En route* you'll have a little more opportunity to redress the balance and be kind to me. It is time I checked on my London residence, in any case.'

Emma lowered fiery, tawny eyes. She was right! Be *kind* to him indeed! Once alone in a carriage with him, she would be seduced...tricked back to Bath and installed in that house as his mistress. Well, she wanted no more of his attentiveness! And he was certainly receiving none of hers!

Even should she be wrong, and he returned her to London, his presence would be hazardous: he might allow some of her stupid lies to leak out. Just the slightest rumour circulating that she was with child and Jarrett Dashwood was sure to believe himself duped into giving a bastard a name. The ensuing furore and ostracism would devastate her parents! What on earth had possessed her to contribute to the fallacy that she was ruined? Now the only way back was to admit she had intentionally misled him.

'I realise you have business concerns,' she burst out, trying a different tack. 'You will want to conclude those before quitting Bath. There is no point in us both returning to Silverdale whilst you do so. I shall wait here for you to return with a carriage.'

'There is only a minor concern,' Richard informed her, hard-pressed to keep laughter from his voice as he recognised her strategies. As soon as he was out of sight, she would be off in the opposite direction. 'Ross is to conclude that matter. It will be no hardship for him...' he added drily, recalling Ross's speculative look on being charged with ensuring Yvette Dubois was packed up and shipped out with her belongings and a banker's draft. Ross was certain to appease any tantrums with a little consideration of his own.

'Don't fret on my account, Emma,' Richard gently mocked. 'There is nothing else pressing. I shall not be terribly incommoded by accompanying you. However, a little show of gratitude for my pains would not go amiss...' He slanted her a smile then laughed at her narrow-eyed irritation.

'Come...pax,' he said softly. 'Our truce is still in force, you know. I'm determined to honour it a while yet.'

'Well, I am *not*,' she choked at his leather-coated back as he headed towards the tavern, with talk of feeling hungry. 'Our truce is over. *I* am ready to resume hostilities,' she impressed upon him, half running behind to keep up with his long stride.

'That's not an option following our truce, Emma.'

'Oh? What is, then?'

'Surrender.' He turned to face her so suddenly that she shoved her hands against his broad chest to prevent herself crashing into him. Topaz eyes flared beneath silver gleaming down at her. A nervous flick of a tongue moistened her dry lips and then she dodged past him and entered the tavern.

'Not like that!' Richard chided as the cards flew in all directions. A large hand swept the small baize-topped table, collecting them. He stacked them quickly, neatly cut the pack, shuffled them expertly then cupped a hand to square them.

Emma concentrated carefully, her sharp little chin resting on curled fingers. She held out a small hand, received the pack with a supercilious look and set about matching his mastery. Her thumbs seemed to stick to the card edges: instead of freeing them to neatly interleave they clumped down thickly without rhythm.

Dark fingers covered hers. 'Hold then lightly…let them flow.'

She watched their fingers flexing together and the cards did, indeed, mesh. With a confident smile, she cupped the pack in her hands and tried to adroitly flick them back as he had. They spattered across green baize. The few she still held were dropped onto the table with a wry grimace.

They had been playing piquet. The first occasion she had been dealt four sevens and he'd received four eights she had accepted it *might* be odd chance. She had resolved to shrewdly observe next time the cards were distributed. She'd noticed nothing up his sleeve or slipped from under the table…yet he'd then received four tens and she four nines. Sulkily, she had flounced back in her seat, snapping that he ought to have dealt himself the four knaves, he was such a Captain Sharp.

'That's fighting talk, Emma,' he had warned with a soft laugh, and next dealt her a hand devoid of royalty: a carte blanche.

Naively, she had been pleased, believing it might win, and was about to triumphantly display it…until he asked what he'd given her with an air of innocence and latent amusement that made the French term freeze on her lips. 'Nothing worth having,' she'd petulantly retorted, discarding the hand.

That had made him laugh outright and say softly, 'Very wise…I'm sure we'll manage better than that.' He'd proceeded to deal her four aces next time around. It was the first game she'd won and, gratified, she'd omitted to chide him for his chicanery.

He had taught her two card tricks; leaned across, empty-handed, and drawn forth the queen of hearts from behind one of her small ears, then idly erected a winding trail of barely touching dominoes. The last he'd flicked over and a sinuous line had gracefully bowed down. It was only when collapsed on the table she'd noticed it formed the shape of a heart. She had been entertained, impressed, too, until the heat of liquid-mercury eyes on her had cooled her humour. It was obviously his heart, she had acidly commented, as it was black.

Richard collected the scattered cards now and idly shuffled them, observing her sculpted, pensive countenance while she watched his nimble fingers.

'It's rude to stare,' she muttered at his hands.

'You're beautiful; why shouldn't I look at you?' he reasoned mildly.

Emma stabbed a fierce golden glance at him, sure he was jesting, but there was no hint of mockery in his face. But there was something else: it made her heartbeat check then start pumping erratically. 'My mother says I've faded as I've aged...I'm now quite near thirty,' she emphasised. 'I must admit when younger...much younger...my hair was darker...my eyes too, I'm sure.'

'Is that supposed to make me see you differently?' he asked gently. 'You looked exactly the same three years ago. You've not altered a bit. Your hair...your eyes are just as exquisite now as then. Don't you like it that I find you beautiful, Emma? Does it frighten you?'

She stood abruptly and wandered to the window and gazed out into the mellow afternoon. He was definitely attempting to seduce her, she realised, and she could feel some traitorous response to his flattery deep within her, ready and willing to succumb to his blandishments.

Matthew's compliments praised her kindness, her wit, her ability to tutor his children. No man had ever told her she was beautiful. This silver-tongued squire said it and made her believe it, too. But then, of all the men who had shown a modicum of interest in her since her debut, he was by far the most dangerously sophisticated. He was well versed in all aspects of seduction, she was sure, including pretty, contrived speeches. And it was simply stupid vanity that made her want to believe him sincere.

With a wistful sigh Emma gazed onto the courtyard, watching

a young ostler grooming a child's pony. She guessed the time must now be about four in the afternoon and there was still no sign of a mail coach pulling in.

Since the others had left for Silverdale, she and Richard had enjoyed a fine meal and animated discussion about the Courtenays and their cherished goddaughter, Lucy, and Richard's intention to soon bring about an overdue reunion with them now he was finally back home.

She had learned that Richard had spent most of the past two years, following his father's death, in the West Indies. He had no wish to keep the sugar plantations that his great-grandfather had bought more than a hundred years previously. Slave labour and all its barbarism was abhorrent to him, he had said, and besides, the abolitionists would eventually get their way and outlaw the practice. He had been content to live there for a time while he ousted the corrupt overseers and managers who had been left in charge. Then there was the lengthy process of selling on the vast acreage to a neighbour planter and issuing his workforce with manumissions which made them free men and women.

Emma had listened with awe, feeling quietly astounded by his humanity; disturbed, too, that he must, indeed, be acquainted with Dashwood. Dashwood had plantations in the Indies and a reputation as a very harsh master. She had practically had to bite her tongue to prevent her demanding whether all the foul gossip she had heard of her spurned fiancé was true. But she knew that any mention of Dashwood would arouse Richard's curiosity and suspicion and prompt an interrogation...and then all her tapestry of deceit would surely unravel. So she'd simply listened, engrossed, learning that Richard had no inclination or need to return abroad and was home at Silverdale to stay.

To an outsider they would have appeared what they were supposed to be: close cousins breaking their journey with refreshment, rest and absorbed conversation.

It had been Richard's idea to introduce them as kin. They were, after all, sharing a private dining room on the first floor and, as she was supposed to be a virtuous single lady, her reputation would suffer if it got out she had been closeted alone with a bachelor for some hours. It was a trifling deceit amongst so many, he had meaningfully said with a penetrating look, and would serve a purpose.

Emma picked up her novel from the window sill where earlier she had dropped it and idly flicked the pages over. She felt a prowling restlessness. She wanted to be gone from here. Wanted to be far from this man for he set such conflicting thoughts spinning in her mind. She wanted to hate him, yet she recognised feelings of immense respect that he had placed philanthropy above commercial gain. He had not brought it to her notice, but she knew he could have sold his slaves along with his acreage to his fellow planter.

Yet weighted against all that was his debauchery. She knew his history: he'd certainly been a scandalous rakehell for years. But he was no worse a rogue than David Hardinge had been, and Emma gladly admitted to being very fond of him. David was now a devoted husband and father. Perhaps Richard would be, too, when he married his duke's daughter. Despite Amelia dismissing his nuptials as no love match, he would surely reform enough to give his bride dignity and status and keep his paramours well out of sight.

Thoughts jumbled in her head...thoughts of when he'd kissed her and how it had made her feel—as though she would willingly join their numbers, remain in that entrancing, pleasurable limbo he sent her to and let him do what he would to her. That fearful, unwanted perception made her face flame and an involuntary 'No!' broke from between compressed lips.

Richard arrowed a look at her and then unwound himself from the chair he sat in and strolled towards her. Two dark hands braced either side of her, trapping her against the skewed black oak window frame. She felt hair stir at her nape as he bent towards her and said, 'Come, don't sulk. If I'd said you were ugly as sin you'd have a reason to be broody.'

That made her smile wanly at the autumn afternoon. A dark hand slid to cup her cheek, his thumb smoothing across a ridge of delicate high cheekbone. Her smile faded and she tried to twitch away from his touch.

Gently he turned her about and held her still. 'Look at me, Emma.'

Fawn eyes flicked to his, wary...suspicious.

'I want to explain about yesterday evening. Why I was with Stephen and Yvette Dubois outside the Assembly Rooms.'

Emma stared past his shoulder. 'There's no need. Amelia has

done so. You had decided to discard your mistress and she approached Stephen to replace you.' She made to sweep past but he wouldn't allow it.

'That doesn't explain why I appeared to be kissing her. In fact it makes the explanation seem false.'

'Appeared?' she snapped. 'Are you inclined to striking poses, then?'

'No. Just walls and doors, since you came back into my life.' Barely pausing, he continued, 'She was kissing me because she hoped I would be persuaded to take her back. It was a little unsuccessful seduction, nothing more. For my part, I went along with it because I wanted to convince Stephen he'd be a fool to jeopardise the love he and Amelia share for such a fickle, paltry liaison.'

'So noble of you to endure it all, sir, I'm sure,' Emma ground out caustically, and again vainly tried to pass him.

'Do you know why I didn't want to endure it?' At her careless show of ennui, he listed softly, 'Because I wanted to return above stairs to you. I wanted to dance with you...go home to Silverdale with you...kiss you... I want you.'

Emma sensed his lips closing with hers and jerked back.

'Don't do that, Emma. You know you love it when I kiss you,' was breathed huskily, warmly against her cheek.

'Don't you do it!' she whispered back hoarsely. 'Don't you dare! There's nothing you can say...no eloquent lies that will make me go to that house with you...' The rest was lost. This time she did put up a token resistance. As his mouth slanted warmly across hers she raised her hands, pushed at his shoulders, raised them further till her knuckles raked his face. Her nails *did* press against his lean cheeks, and she sensed his skin dipping beneath the pressure, but she couldn't do more.

And he realised it, too. His kiss was rewarding, gently courting. Her arms rose and for the first time she embraced him properly, slid quivering fingers into his beautiful pale hair, felt its silky glide against her skin.

Firm fingers skimmed her sides, drawing her close to his hardening body, massaging tantalisingly close to tautening breasts, and the moan tore from her, exploding softly into his mouth.

Richard pulled his hot mouth away across her cheek, nipped

at an ear, fanned steaming breath against her neck, making her twist her head, writhe her body to merge with his.

'Does he make you feel like this?' was rasped against her ear. 'Does he?'

'Who?' Emma whimpered as her throat arched temptingly towards him.

Tormenting kisses were trailed against the creamy column of her neck. 'Your Derbyshire lover. William Fitz,' he gritted out, his hands tightening on her hips, thrusting her close to his rigid groin. 'Tell me. Can he arouse you as I do…with just one kiss?'

Emma jerked back, looked up into grey eyes blackened by lust. 'Yes. Every time he kisses me,' she choked. 'Every single time. It's so much better than this…'

She attempted to squirm free, but a lean, dark hand wound into her thick, glossy hair, brought her face back to his. He fused their bodies, holding her unmoving. 'Thank you, Emma' he breathed with clean, raw satisfaction against her lips. 'That means he doesn't even compare.'

Chapter Eleven

If there was a perfect time to escape it was now: he would never suspect she might disappear while her only mode of transport was in full view in front of the tavern.

Wandering away from the pump where she had stationed herself, Emma broodily watched the passengers alight from the mail coach. To add insult to injury, there was one vacant seat that she could discern. She took another slow promenade about the whitewashed building, rays of late afternoon sun weaving gold into her reflectively bowed tawny head.

She tried to focus on the urgent need to travel but her mind recoiled time and again to fix on her humiliation above stairs minutes ago. Her complexion was still flushed with the memory of it, her lips puffed scarlet, her pupils so dilated her eyes resembled amber-ringed obsidian. Pearly lids shielded a mortified brilliance on recalling how he had unwound her tenacious arms from about his neck and gently put her from him. Not that he wanted to stop, he had softly sighed, but if he didn't they might finish being more than simply kissing cousins at this roadside tavern. And then, with a shattered little laugh, he had left her, saying that he needed some air to cool off.

By the time he returned, ten minutes or so later, Emma had salvaged a modicum of dignity and pride and with great aplomb informed him that she, too, needed to refresh herself, and immediately quit the room.

Out in the balmy autumn afternoon, she was soon grinding her teeth in vexation as the mail coach swayed to a halt. Of course, he would have noticed it too but was probably smugly confident she was now so in his thrall she would gladly surrender and go to South Parade. Well, he was vastly mistaken in imagining she would submit so feebly!

Be first to move; take the enemy by surprise! her papa had used to chortle when absconding from Rosemary House minutes before his creditors hammered at the door. That rhetoric had come good for some twenty years. When victory seemed unattainable, avoid the battle, was Frederick Worthington's hypothesis.

True to his word, her papa had again removed himself from the fray and disappeared and she would do likewise—perhaps in the process secure for her papa another twenty years' dun-shunning, she heroically fancied.

But how? Walking to London was hardly an option. Even if she possessed the courage and energy, she'd not manage more than a mile or two before Richard caught up with her. And bolting into woodland on foot would be idiotically reckless. She might be accosted by gypsies while getting hopelessly lost. She needed to keep close to the main road. She needed a ride, too.

Sensing eyes on her, she swung about and peered over a rough wood door into semi-darkness. A stable lad with a mop of curly flaxen hair peered back. A curry comb was in his hand and he had obviously been grooming the flanks of Richard's horse, silhouetted in the murk.

He looked to be little more than fourteen yet had a confident, cocky air. But he tugged a forelock politely at her. 'Yer cousin's 'orse be a fine animal, m'm,' he judged knowledgeably.

'Indeed,' Emma snarled in irritation. The lad looked abashed at her brusqueness, prompting a surge of remorse. 'He has quite wonderful colouring, don't you think?' she conversationally made amends. 'Just a few shades lighter than a new sovereign, I would judge.'

He nodded. 'And 'is tail and mane so near white. 'E's an Arab in part, I'll be bound. I should like t'ave rid such as 'e,' the boy wistfully said, patting a supple side with a reverent hand. ''Ave you rid 'im?'

Emma stared at the boy and then at the horse, her mind feverish in its machinations. 'Why, yes,' she fibbed. 'And a good

rid...ride he is too. It is the reason I am here...for a little exercise.
I am feeling a trifle restless while waiting for my cousin's transport to arrive.' Swallowing, she glanced uneasily back at the
tavern. Encouragingly, the upper window of their small private
chamber was not at all visible.

The stable boy was quizzically regarding the way she was
garbed. Hardly riding attire, she gleaned from his face.

'Oh, these will serve.' She carelessly twitched her plain brown
travelling skirts. 'Would you saddle him, please?' she charmingly
commanded.

'What's 'is name?' the boy asked, obediently unhooking the
saddle.

'Name?' Emma neared the animal and as it bobbed its head
around she noticed the ivory shape on its golden nose.

'Star,' she blurted with a smile. 'Leastways, that's what I call
him.'

Rather belatedly the boy asked cautiously, 'You sure yer
cousin knows, m'm, an' won't be objectin'?'

Emma bestowed on him her haughtiest look. 'Knows? Ob-
jecting?' she spouted, with a scornful little laugh.

''Ave to ask, m'm,' he apologised, his smooth cheeks redden-
ing. 'Master might be right mad if'n 'e don't know and do object.'

'Oh, but of course he will know of it...' Emma reassured him.
Eventually...whispered through her mind with frightening rever-
beration.

The lad nodded his head and heaved the saddle across the
animal's back. 'Can you ride wi'out side-saddle, miss?'

She hadn't thought of that. 'Oh, yes. It's no problem at all...'
In for a penny, in for a pound...scuttled deliriously through her
mind.

There seemed to be an inordinate amount of buckling and
tightening to be done and Emma felt some of her nervous exhilaration sapping. She bit at her tongue to stop herself scolding
him for sloth while congratulating her foresight in having donned
her cloak against an early evening chill before coming below.
She checked its pockets for her money pouch then glanced anxiously back at the courtyard. All seemed tranquil...almost too
quiet.

Aware the groom was finished with his task and eyeing her

expectantly, Emma surveyed the statuesque stallion with a wary eye, hoping she could recall all that David had taught her about riding.

She had owned a pony as a child when she and her parents had lived in Surrey. But as soon as her papa's gambling had become excessive their rural home had been lost and they'd lived permanently in Rosemary House, in Cheapside. Rumour had it that her papa had actually wagered the deeds to their modest country retreat on one throw of the dice. That had been when Emma was nine years old and she had not again mounted a horse until she'd visited Hertfordshire and stayed with the Courtenays at their opulent mansion.

Victoria wasn't an accomplished rider either so they had both been under David's expert tutelage and had had fine times trotting happily about together on gentle-natured beasts while improving their rusty skills. She imagined her friend would be an able horsewoman by now.

Emma looked fearfully at the palomino...anything less like those mild-mannered mares she could not conceive. With an inspiriting smile and her skirts bunched into her fists, Emma threw modesty and a shapely leg to one side. Once settled on the saddle, she decorously smoothed her clothing and gave gracious thanks, and a coin from the few left in her pouch, to the grinning young groom. He tugged his forelock, face aglow with admiration as he watched Emma proceed sedately, then at an easy canter into the distance.

He'd give her a while to sulk and feel ill-used and then go to find her, Richard decided with a wry smile. And when he did he might as well tell her. As he'd accepted it now himself, it was pointless not reassuring her that his intentions were entirely honourable. Yet he would rue the passing of these sparring sessions she manoeuvred them into...there was a definite sensual satisfaction in converting all that aggression to sweeter passion.

He sat in the armchair by the small fire, pulled the wine table close and rested his booted feet upon it while drawing deeply on his cheroot. Flickering logs held his attention as he acknowledged he was feeling undeniably content. Which was odd considering he'd obliquely acceded to another man's bastard, if male, being heir to Silverdale and all his vast estates and wealth. But then such madness was, he supposed, the price one paid for indulging in this bewitching torture that was love.

He could recall pitying David for succumbing to the ravages of that thankless emotion. Now here he was, three years on, gladly wallowing in it himself. He choked a laugh and blew a lazy blue haze at the ceiling as he wondered how she would react to his declaration. Astonishment...definitely, for he was still a heartless philanderer in her estimation. Suspicion...definitely; she would no doubt think he was lying to trick her back to his town house.

Reciprocation was what he wanted. He wanted her to look at him with those beautiful feral eyes, sheath her claws and melt sweetly against him, as he knew she could. But he wanted her to do it of her own volition, without him touching her. He wanted her, unreservedly, to love him back. Cynicism twisted his sensual lips. Which brought him neatly to a faceless man from Derbyshire and the uncertainties that plagued him.

Did she love this William Fitz? She didn't appear to be pining and seemed to have readily accepted that he was pledged elsewhere. Yet he knew she would never have indulged in a casual affair. It just wasn't her way. But it had been his way, for far longer than he cared to recall. That was why, in his heart, he knew her censure and distrust were justified.

His riotous past was wedged between them. He and David *had* been disreputable scoundrels for very many years. But watching David's father die from the pox had been a salutary lesson for them both. Time-served courtesans had never been of interest. Of greater attraction had been fresh young women, fallen on hard times, who were delighted to escape the penury of widowhood or the rigours of long hours toiling as seamstresses in favour of a position as pampered paramour until they were pensioned comfortably off. And they applied in droves. It had rarely been necessary to seek them out; both he and David were regularly propositioned by ambitious young women.

Yet since David's marriage and move to the countryside he had curbed his excesses and rarely kept more than one mistress at a time, rarely gambled, or drank to excess. In fact, yesterday evening was the first time in a long while that he'd imbibed too much to get to bed. Most of his fighting was now restricted to organised bouts at Gentleman Jackson's or the fencing academy.

He envied David: seeing him so serenely happy, so relaxed and content, with a wife he adored, had been one of the reasons he had opted to deal with his Jamaican interest himself rather than send an agent. Their friendship had been so intense he'd known he had to get away and allow the bond to loosen for both their sakes. And while overseeing the sale of his Jamaican estates he had often brooded on whether he wanted to return to such orgiastic excesses or whether David's marriage had neatly closed a youthful era for them both.

Relaxing some evenings beneath a heavy tropical moon, he'd reminisced about Emma too, yet dismissed sentiment and longing as being some contagious reaction to what David felt for Victoria. The idea that he and his best friend would neatly fall in love with the perfect harmony they did most other things was just too ludicrous. So he hadn't allowed himself to contact her again, discover whether she was now married, and his bruised pride had reminded him time and again that, in any case, she had never liked him.

Now he knew how stupid he'd been. Just one glimpse of a cloaked woman at a rural tavern and he'd been overwhelmed. His mind hadn't known it was her, but his heart had... instinctively. When he'd seen her waiting patiently in his hallway at South Parade, he'd known: fate had brought her to him. She had raised those extraordinarily beautiful eyes and her wild panic as she'd recognised him had aroused the strangest sensation: a welcome tranquillity.

After three restless months on English soil he felt truly home.

Wryly acknowledging that what couldn't be undone must be endured, he stood abruptly, wandered to the window and scoured the courtyard for sight of her. He smiled at the stationary coach. Perhaps she was ensconced within it, waiting for it to depart. A laugh throbbed in his throat. Hardly! With her temperament she would have attempted driving it off herself! It was as well one of the horses had pulled up lame.

He made to turn and his hand knocked against her novel, discarded on the window ledge. Collecting it idly, he carried it back to his seat. Sticking the cigar between his teeth, he flicked over pages and read: 'It is a truth universally acknowledged, that a single man in possession of a good fortune, must be in want of a wife...' He smiled past the cheroot...feeling mellow as he did, it seemed a reasonable enough assumption.

The knock at the door some time later had Richard dropping the book on the table. 'Well, I'll be damned!' he muttered, low and vehement, and shook his head in disbelief.

Stephen sauntered into the room, a grin livening his boyish features. 'What excellent service is this? What effusive thanks do I deserve?' he ribbed his older brother.

'What effusive thanks do *I* deserve?' Richard drily countered, reminding Stephen he was due a little gratitude for his part in recovering his wife and his senses for him.

Stephen had the grace to blush a little. 'Mmm...thanks for helping out with that. I've been a blasted fool of late, I admit it. But it's all finished now...' He shuffled uneasily, studying his nails.

'I'm glad to hear it. I'm sure Amelia is, too...'

'Not only does your carriage await, m'lud—' Stephen swiftly changed subject '—but I bear tidings.'

Richard raised dark brows as he lit a fresh cigar, waved the match about to extinguish it then flicked it towards the fire.

'Ross has attended to your business with his usual flair and speed. Yvette has set sail...apparently looking mightily content once your banker's draft was in her hot little hand...or perhaps it was something Ross put there that pleased her,' he drolly suggested. 'I can't now quite recall... Anyway, Ross sends word that he is to visit his brother, Luke, in Brighton and will see you in London in a few days.'

Stephen paused to help himself to a brandy from the decanter. 'Now the bad news...' He grimaced. 'Mother is fair prone with nervous fatigue. I've managed to persuade her that Amelia was missing due to an early morning drive to see Emma partway home and that Emma... Where is she, by the by?' he interjected, glancing about. 'And that Emma has important matters to deal with in London. Does that sound right?' he ventured.

Richard had risen while his brother was speaking and walked, frowning, to the window and looked down. The mail coach was still there, and his elegant carriage was close by. Of Emma there was still no sign.

'Not only has that vexed dear Mama,' drifted over to Richard, 'but I am bid to order you back by nine for dinner with the Duke and Duchess and Lady Penelope.' A taunting grin preceded, 'I'm sure you'll make that.'

A lewd suggestion as to how his Grace could amuse himself in his absence escaped Richard. But a stirring uneasiness was tightening his chest as he scoured the empty courtyard.

'Oh, and Mother's fretting she might have offended Emma, prompting her to quit Silverdale. Apparently in the Assembly Rooms last evening she and Diane and the Petershams were having a gossip about Dashwood. One moment Emma was with them then the next she had disappeared without a word.'

'Dashwood? What is it that foul bastard's about now?' Richard felt a knot of cold suspicion churn his stomach. He recalled Emma saying she had been upset by some talk of people she knew. He had wanted to believe her tears yesterday evening had sprung from jealousy at how she had come upon him with Yvette. Perhaps his arrogance had got the better of him...

'Dashwood has been made to look a monkey, by all accounts. He bought himself a genteel spinster to breed with. Money changed hands with a prospective impecunious father-in-law before the dowd of a bride had been informed of any of it. It was assumed she'd be so pleased to get off the shelf, she'd simply go along with it all. No more ado, she's shown more mettle and a clean pair of heels. Dashwood has investigators out on the hunt. The contract was signed and sealed and he's bent on revenge. The girl's father has now absconded, too, avoiding Dashwood's blood-letting, I imagine. What scandals we miss in this neck of the woods... Are you ailing? You look ghastly...' he tacked onto the end, splashing more fine cognac into his glass.

'I thought you might be out riding, actually,' Stephen added conversationally. 'I swear I saw Shah away in the distance as I turned in. What a coincidence! Two palominos in the neighbourhood!'

Richard stared, his lean cheeks ashen beneath bronze. He stood perfectly still for a moment then calmly walked to the fire, discarded the cigar butt and said, 'Have you brought along a ride back?'

At Stephen's nod of confirmation, he picked up his leather riding coat, threw it over a powerful shoulder and walked to the door. 'Thanks for getting back here so quickly. I'll be back in a week or so—or send word from London.'

Emma glanced behind at the fiery horizon, trusting that as long as she headed east and kept the road in sight she would be fine. Not that she was intending to ride *all* the way to London, she impressed upon herself, while jogging along. That was a futile expectation. What she would do was journey to the next posting house, leave Star in the landlord's care and charge him to get her note to Sir Richard Du Quesne. In it she would make her apologies for borrowing his horse and let him know where it was available for collection. Then she would buy a ride to London on the first conveyance heading that way able to accommodate her. By her increasingly optimistic calculations, she should be in London early in the morning. By this time tomorrow all her family's problems should be solved.

As the setting sun streaked the skyline a rich russet, she slanted a squinting gaze at a cluster of cottages and small farm buildings. She hoped soon a hostelry would come into view. It was rash for a lone rider to risk travelling at night. And this handsome steed would be enough temptation for a felon to accost a man. A woman would be easy pickings.

She patted at Star's head again and leaned forward to run a slender hand across the milky mark on his nose, while murmuring his name. He bobbed his head in acknowledgement. Perhaps she had correctly guessed his name for he indeed responded to it.

But he didn't seem to want to respond to her urgings to increase his pace. He ambled along and she refused to dig her heels into his flawless sides. Perhaps she had tired him...but then they had not galloped. She hadn't felt confident enough for that, and the covering trees and shrubbery they weaved through, in any case, made speed difficult. Perhaps he was hungry or thirsty, she mused as the horse slowed to a walk.

Emma tapped a creamy flank and made clicking noises with her tongue. After a few vain encouragements she huffed and sat still, deciding to allow him to crop for a while. Slackening her hold on the reins, she waited for him to dip towards sparse, coarse grass. He did no such thing, simply raised his head and curled his upper lip, scenting the air. He snorted and pawed at the ground then walked about in an aimless circle.

Perhaps he was above eating grass, Emma thought. Perhaps he was so used to feeding on sweet hay and oats in a stable he didn't know how to chew this thin, reedy stuff. He was altogether too indulged, she sniffily decided. Altogether his master's beast!

Warily eyeing the forest floor, she wondered if, once dismounted, she would be able to get back up. Trusting she would, she gathered her skirts in a hand, arced a bare leg nimbly over Star's head and slithered to hard earth. A controlling hand gripped the reins while she tore at grass stalks then offered them up on a flat palm.

Emma heard the sound properly this time, acknowledged it as significant, rather than again dismissing it as breeze-wafted pastoral melody. She peered nervously about. There were wild creatures in woods...foxes and deer and small, scurrying things. The eerie, high-pitched ululation was unidentifiable, but then all animal calls were uncommon to her urban ear.

Star acknowledged it: his ears pricked and he whinnied, bobbing his head excitedly. Perhaps he would take fright and bolt. She wound the reins round a hand and looked about for a boulder or tree stump she could stand on to aid clambering back astride him. Ready to discard her offering of grass and get moving, the stallion dipped its head and nuzzled her palm. She smiled at his gentle nibble, while smoothing his velvety nose. 'You were hungry...'

The hair at her nape prickled and icy needles assaulted her cheeks at the unmistakable slow clop of hooves. The approaching horse stilled and stamped and the rider remained silent...and she knew.

She had difficulty detaching her tongue from the roof of her mouth. It finally came free, allowing her to croak at Star's muzzle, 'I...I was just borrowing him...'

The ensuing quiet was shattered by a horse's soft snorting. That seemed to rouse Star. He nudged Emma firmly aside and trotted past, spinning her about and forcing her to run a few steps until she shook herself free.

Richard was sitting atop a grey mare, one leg bent and resting on the animal's neck as though he had happened upon an interesting spectacle and settled to watch it. In fact, he seemed so comfortable, so impassive, she was almost lulled into believing he wasn't angry.

'I *was* just borrowing him...' she emphasised in a quavering voice, her tilted chin wobbly. Her ragged murmur this time prompted some reaction. He swivelled, leaped down and abandoned the mare to Star's increasingly amorous attention.

Still he said nothing. He didn't need to; Emma could read wrath and retribution in every taut plane of his sardonic face, in every light, skimming pace that brought him purposefully closer. Swallowing jerkily, she stepped back clumsily, then spontaneously turned and fled.

She bolted into woodland, her skirts held high, away from the snatching briars. Thorns tore instead at her petticoats, her nude legs. She winced as sharp barbs nipped at her flesh. Still she swerved on, running and dodging the dense shrubbery that tweaked at her glossy fawn hair and loosened it to tumble in a tangle about her shoulders.

The blood was pounding so heavily in her ears, her sobbing breath hacking so sharply at her throat that she was conscious of nothing else. She expected any moment a grip on her shoulder...her neck, to jerk her about or push her to the root-heaving ground. She desperately wanted to know if he had given chase but turning to find out would lose her precious time.

The stitch in her side twisted relentlessly into torturing needle stabs until eventually she could endure no more. She plunged towards a large oak, almost fell against its rough, scabby bark and concealed herself.

She waited, her lungs pumping fit to burst, her rib-cage jerking so wildly she pressed trembling arms across it to forcibly restrain it. Unfastening her hampering cloak with clumsy fingers, she let it fall to the ground then scraped her back against wood to peer about the tree.

He was nowhere in sight and it was silent apart from muted forest sounds: rustling undergrowth and a crow cawing somewhere overhead. She closed her wide, fawn eyes. Perhaps he was glad enough to recover his horse and be finally rid of her. She couldn't blame him; he must be heartily rueing the day she'd ever appeared in Bath and caused havoc in his ordered life.

A sudden stinging sensation moistened her eyes and nose. She didn't want him to hate her. She didn't want him to think badly of her at all; but he would...and she deserved that. She had lied, abused his generosity, hit him on numerous occasions, stolen his horse...shown him no gratitude or respect...when in fact even her own papa had never provided for her so unstintingly...so uncomplainingly. She owed him so much. Yet some innate sense bade her escape him again rather than remain and explain.

She twisted her head sharply against bark, needing the spiteful abrasion against her scalp to drive out the weakness. He was a selfish lecher and she would do well to remember it! He had shown her such largess to protect his friendship with the Courtenays; she would do well to remember that, too, and forget any ideas that his kisses and flattery had been more than idle amusement as he'd sought to groom a quaint new paramour.

Slow minutes passed and finally, as her breathing and heart rate steadied, she swooped, gathering up her cloak, forcing her mind back to practicalities. She must travel urgently to London and her parents. In which direction were the farm buildings she had recently noticed? She might get assistance there. At the very least the locals would point her towards the nearest coaching inn.

She squinted up at the canopy of leaves overhead. The sun was gone and the evening was now drawing in. With a sigh and a shove away from the oak she ventured out from behind it.

'Why steal a horse when you can gallop like that...?' was drawled sarcastically from her left side.

Emma swirled towards him, stepped back in readiness...but a bronzed hand stretched out. 'Don't do it, Emma,' he gently warned. 'I swear, if you run or provoke me further... Come here,' he tacked onto the end without concluding the threat, long, autocratic fingers beckoning.

Emma moistened her lips, blinked her doe eyes before they veered around him, seeking escape routes. 'I didn't steal Star...just borrowed him. I intended to get word to you where I left him stabled, I promise.'

'Shah...'

'What?' Emma breathed.

'His name is Shah...'

'Well, I prefer Star.' Emma defiantly bristled.

Richard smiled and took an easy pace forward. When she remained unflustered by that he took another, all the while glancing idly about at his surroundings. 'For a woman in the early stages of a pregnancy you take remarkable risks with your health, haring about like that.'

'I am healthy…very healthy. I'm robust, my mother tells me…'

'Your mother says a lot I don't agree with.'

'Well, none of it is your con—!' Emma broke off as silver eyes streaked to hers and melded with them. 'I've never been frail,' she resorted to muttering.

'I imagine your lover might not approve of your hoydenish antics either. Tell me about him again. I believe I might know of him, after all.'

Emma flung him a scornful glance. 'And I tell you you do not!'

'He is betrothed, you say?'

A curt nod and pout laden with ennui answered him.

'To whom?'

'A respectable lady. Assuredly no one you would know!' was delivered in the same bored, impatient vein.

'Not a daughter, is she, of a certain Mr Bennet with four other girls to offload and a shrew of a matchmaking wife to contend with?'

Emma's tawny head flew about, glowing tiger eyes raking darkly ironic features.

'Very novel, Emma…' he said drily. 'But then I'll own Dashwood's no ideal personification of a raven-haired romantic hero. I can see why a fiction would prove preferable.'

Blood seeped from her complexion, ice shivered her spine, yet she met his gaze unflinchingly, trusting brashness might confuse him.

But his eyes and mouth narrowed at her reflexive reaction to mention of her spurned fiancé. 'If you lie to me again over this, Emma…' The vehement threat trailed into silence but she recognized ultimate retribution in his flinty eyes and a profound sadness in the thick timbre of his voice.

'Are you with child? Has Dashwood violated you? Or have you simply fled to avoid marrying him?'

Emma chewed at her trembling lower lip, wondering whether now to be honest; tell him everything: confess to deceit, cowardice, selfishness at having jeopardised her parents by reneging on a hateful marriage contract. But she didn't want him to know. She didn't want him to despise her for her disgusting failings.

'Tell me, dammit!' he thundered. 'Tell me if that bastard's touched you…whether you're carrying his spawn!'

'Mr Dashwood has not *violated* me. I might have been a little…startled by him initially…but not any more. I am travelling home to wed him. And that is all I shall explain. The rest is…*none of your concern*,' she whispered, quavering challenge mingling with the peace of ultimate defeat. 'Go away and leave me. Go and find your horse before he runs away.'

'Oh, he won't run for a while yet. He's being entertained…' he told her in a calm, quiet voice.

The air between them seemed to solidify, the evening birdsong and woodland hum to fade, leaving sheer silence. It was shattered with his ruthless need. 'I think it's high time I was…' he dulcetly stated, and started to approach so lightly it seemed he skimmed the peaty ground.

Her eyes were wrenched from his to dart glances left and right: an obstructing hazel thicket to one side and a tangle of bracken and bramble to the other. Beyond him a clearing. But that way lay easy capture… *Turn and run…turn and run* her reason whispered. *Escape him while you still can…*

Small, shaking hands spasmed on tree bark directly behind them, then, with an anguished cry, she hurtled instinctively forward, trusting destiny.

He sprang as she did, intercepting and catching her to him then driving her back against the ancient, sturdy oak. Wood and the granite pressure of his body kept her off the ground, breast against breast, thigh against hip, mouth welded to mouth with grinding, punishing force. Her head fell back into supporting, protective fingers pitilessly abraded against wood as she squirmed to liberate her face. She fought energetically, kicking and twisting, her pinioned hands bunching into futile fists, tirelessly seeking freedom to claw at him.

Long brown fingers speared into her thick tawny hair, winding just enough to make her cease straining and keep her face tilted to his.

He plundered her mouth with savage abandon, teeth and lips erotically barbaric in every nip, slide, stroke, his tongue thrusting with uncurbed lechery to explore sleek, moist velvet. A marauding hand hoisted her higher, parted her thighs so he could wedge between them, then coiled her calves about him. He pinned her like that—the full weight of his strong, muscular body inescapable, the iron of his erection pulsing raging heat at the heart of her vulnerable femininity.

Emma ground her head violently against his palm, trying to free her mouth, and each frantic evasion shredded his injured knuckles, and was countered with increased lust. Long fingers ripped free the buttons on her bodice, then leisurely peeled back first one then the other side to expose fragile ivory shoulders, the plump swell of small, firm breasts. His fingers worked at the laces on her chemisette and she gasped her outrage into his mouth, her head swinging in denial. Still he was relentless. A tormentingly slow disrobement followed, until she was naked to the waist, cooled by evening air, scorched by expertly teasing touches. The insolent, selfish assault on her mouth ceased and his face lowered.

Her head rolled to one side, air was gulped into her starved lungs, while her tongue gentled lips that felt excoriated. Then the first languid tasting at her breasts had her tensing, arching, whimpering like an animal in pain. Tantalising wetness traced puckering rosy skin with aching slowness, dried in the balmy breeze to be reapplied within moments. A flick of hot damp at a rigid nipple had her sobbing deep in her throat and fighting to work free a hand trapped between them, not now to hit but to hold. The torturous sensations were undeniable. She was defenceless against a barrage of carnal skill consummated over two decades. His tongue, teeth, lips at first one breast then the other taunted her with exquisite delirium and her slender back arched bowtight, begging for what she couldn't, wouldn't say.

He deliberately tempted back, lingering with butterfly brevity, drawing her leisurely to a peak of moaning pleasure. When finally he allowed her hands free they slid immediately into his soft hair, holding his cruel face against her exposed, swollen flesh. He rewarded her by giving her what she wanted, suckling deeper until some inner part of her seemed to detach and float in liquid ecstasy. His fingers plucked at the strings of her flimsy drawers, freed them so his fingers could smooth in long, hard strokes over her buttocks, her lissom thighs, slide torturously close to the dewy, petalled core of her before drifting away. She groaned and bucked against him, not knowing what she wanted but demanding it, sure it was his to give.

A gentle knuckle grazed artfully against the damp curls between her thighs, collecting the honey there, moistening the sensitive small bud blooming, before rotating, nudging a little way into her, repeating the action with slow, breathtaking rhythm.

Richard dipped his head, tipped her lolling face around with his so he could bring their mouths together, and his tongue leisurely mimicked the pleasure his fingers were giving her. A thumb circled slickly, making her writhe and whimper.

Calculatingly, he studied her flushed complexion, her mouth scarlet, sleek and parted, begging more attention, her eyes no more than fiery golden lustre beneath a net of jet lashes, and he realised he still wasn't absolutely sure. She responded like a woman already awakened to sensuality...yet she was overwhelmed, simply a recipient of whatever he next chose to give her. 'Shall I stop, Emma?' he roughly taunted her.

In response her lids squeezed in anguish and her head lolled further back but speech was impossible. The notion that he might finish enslaving her with this untasted delight simply left her breathless.

'Are you pregnant with Dashwood's child? Tell me!' he begged huskily.

Her lids flew wide and a wild fawn gaze was focussing on him...staring...and then she struggled.

Richard saw her concentration, her valiant attempt to fight free of the voluptuous web he'd spun, to gain some sort of control. He waited no more. His mouth meshed with hers, luring her back into the dark heart of desire. 'Hush. It makes no difference. I swear it makes no difference,' he breathed time and again against her febrile, fragrant skin until he sensed the tension he could feel in her was all for him. Her desire...her need was just for him.

'Tell me something else, Emma,' he whispered hoarsely. 'Tell me you want me as much as I want you...' As though to prompt her his mouth secured an erect nipple and laved it with such leisurely, loving attention, a sob rasped her throat and she instinctively thrust her pelvis into contact with his. He pressed her back against chafing bark, holding her still, lazy, teasing fingers trailing the sensitive, satiny skin of her inner thighs.

He raised his head, traced her pulsing, battered lips with a slow, soothing tongue, inserted it gently between her lips to taste hers before kissing her with pure, pitiless seduction.

'Tell me! Say you want me, Emma...please,' tore rawly from him.

'I do...' Emma wailed.

A shattered gasp of a laugh warmed her face. 'Save that for later, sweetheart. Say you want me like this...lie again. Just say it.'

'I want you like this,' burst out in a despairing whisper.

His eyes closed in peace...in gratitude...and he allowed the rampaging need to dominate and shake him. Coiling his arms about her fragile form, he turned them slowly about then sank, supporting her, to his knees before lowering her back onto her cloak, discarded on musky earth.

Chapter Twelve

It was the scent of woodsmoke that woke her.

Emma squinted through screening lashes at wavering yellow warmth. Forcing a leaden hand up, she touched soft material bunched beneath her cheek but couldn't rouse the energy to lift her tangled tawny head. She wondered how long she had slept; the dusk had deepened although, on flicking up drowsy eyes, patches of slate sky were still visible through branches overhead. A mournful soughing swaying the topmost foliage rippled shivers through her. She imagined it must be about seven of the clock and she had probably slept for an hour.

Agitated eyes flitted over murky undergrowth, seeking a tall, dark figure, a blond head, but beyond the fire's flickering orbit was mere shadow. Her naked limbs shifted position beneath his leather coat, causing the burn between her thighs to rage and ignite a flare in her wan face.

Despite sleeping she still felt enervated by the slow, insatiable intimacy to which she'd been subjected. Her whole being had been quaking, raw with sensitivity when, finally compassionate, he'd tipped her over the edge, allowing sapping spasms of ecstasy to spiral her towards a shattered peace.

And she knew that what most drove his need to torment her and seek such thorough satisfaction was nothing to do with any festering slights or swindles that had gone before. She recalled a stabbing pain that had made her shriek, instinctively squirm beneath him to free herself. Through waves of palliative excitement had throbbed painful vulnerability; she had realised why he'd stopped and sworn savagely at odoriferous earth: one deceit had certainly fooled him. Until that moment he had believed her no virgin.

Even though conscious of reprisal in his ensuing sensuality, she couldn't fight him again. She had been his to mould. Where he'd positioned her she had stayed, instructions he'd whispered she'd obeyed, mindlessly, absolutely, even though each was calculated...proven to notch her arousal to a new excruciating height. Nothing had mattered other than that the source of her punishing pleasure be sustained and she taste its ultimate explosive finish.

Exhausted, she had slept almost immediately, with their loins still in congress, with hard-muscled ribs still pressed to her breasts, long, ruthless fingers cradling her drooping head.

A slender shaking hand covered her eyes as though to blot out further mortifying memories. She rolled onto her stomach and jackknifed onto hands and knees, clutching his coat to her nudity, wondering apathetically when he had covered her with it, used his fine black jacket to cushion her head. She cast about on the ground for her clothes and tugged them close to her.

Dusty dark boots appeared at the edge of her vision and she scrabbled faster, hugging garments up against her as though he might snatch them away.

Richard crouched close by and Emma immediately sank back onto her heels.

A dark hand moved towards her grubby white face but she recoiled and it dropped away. It was back within moments, with the other. Grasping her by the shoulders, he pulled her closer. 'Look at me, Emma,' he requested hoarsely. When she refused to cease staring over a shoulder, he barked harshly, 'Look at me, dammit.'

Glass-bright topaz eyes sliced to him.

'I'm sorry,' broke gruffly from him. 'I didn't want it to be that way...'

'Yes, you did,' she countered, the bite in her voice blunted by an odd passivity. 'I know now. That's always what you intended. Even three years ago you wanted to shame me for insulting you.'

One dark hand released her, and his fingers pinched at the strain between his eyes. 'You're wrong, Emma...so wrong...'

'Go away so I can dress,' she begged in a brittle snap.

A travesty of a laugh preceded, 'Have you found something I've not seen?' Abruptly he stood, turning his back.

'I said go away!' she pleadingly screeched, wanting him out of sight so she could clean herself. She touched an inner thigh and her shaking hand came away stained. 'What have you done to me?' she whispered at her fingers as she stared aghast at the blood.

'You know what I've done to you, Emma,' he returned patiently. 'I've taken your maidenhead. And had you honestly told me it was still there to take…I wouldn't have…' His blond head fell back and a hand covered his eyes. 'Perhaps that's a lie…I don't know. But I swear it would have been different. I would have been different.'

He swung about to see her mesmerised by her hand. With careless savagery he ripped a strip of cambric from the bottom of his shirt, then again went down beside her. He slowly wiped her quivering fingers before pressing her back against her spread cloak. Unfolding leather from the curve of creamy hips, he carefully wiped her, holding her firm as she flinched from the intimacy of his methodical, impassive handling; he might attend to one of his injured animals so, she dully thought.

He walked to the fire and discarded the soiled rag and Emma used his absence to hastily commence pulling on her clothes. Her gaping bodice she managed to close with its one remaining button. She donned her cloak and was straightening it over her torn, crumpled dress with fussy precision when she started at the high-pitched whistle.

She watched him draw back his lips and signal again and realised blankly that he must have been following her and Star for some while earlier before locating them. Star…Shah had, of course, obeyed his master and refused to travel further when he'd heard his call. The noble creature, in his unwitting way, had betrayed her and that seemed to make her desolation complete.

As thudding hooves became audible and shrubbery was knocked aside, she blinked blurrily at stars intermittently visible through fluttering leaves. The two animals trotted obediently close and halted away from the fire.

She gasped hurriedly, huskily, 'I…I should be grateful if you would deliver me to the nearest posting house as it is now dark…'

Silver eyes glittered at her, his lean, angular face visibly tensing. 'Did you believe I might leave you here? Make you walk?' he suggested in a soft, liquid voice that dried her mouth. 'What villainy are you next expecting? That I'll act the heartless rake to the hilt and abandon you to all and sundry now I've had my wicked way? Is that what you think, Emma? Is it?' exploded in a strangled voice.

At her solemn silence, Richard strode to the fire and the toe of a boot savagely shovelled earth, smothering the flames. Eerie darkness shrouded them, prompting a hollow sob to swell, suffocate her. She stuffed a muffling fist to her mouth as it quaked her chest. All her aggression, her independence, her resourcefulness seemed to have been whipped from her at one and the same time and she felt utterly bereft...utterly alone...utterly useless.

He had threatened this, she forlornly recalled... 'Don't bait me needlessly' he had said. 'I can break that aggressive spirit of yours so easily...' And so he had and she had nothing left, not even the ability to hide from him his victory.

Shah's spectral shape approached through the gloom, the mare tied behind the stallion. Richard leaned down. 'Give me your arm.'

Praying for the courage to be defiant just once more, to manage flippantly telling him to go to hell, kept her unmoving...waiting. But it was hopeless. Suppressing her crying took all her energy, and left her dithering.

Dismounting, he closed the space between them. An unsteady dark hand lifted to a wet face, smoothed tentatively over cold, quivering cheeks. Abruptly she was pulled close, rocked comfortingly. 'Don't cry, Emma...' he groaned into her hair. 'It'll be sweeter next time, I promise. I'll love you tenderly... Please don't cry...'

And that was all she needed. Had he said again he was sorry or he had lost control, she might have accepted it. But not that...anything but mentioning that, for it was, she realised, all she craved hearing. He had coupled with her without once uttering a word other than to tutor her shame. No affection, no trifling endearment had passed his lips.

'You bastard...' she choked, wrenching free. 'Don't you dare ever touch me again or patronise me with your stupid lies...' The rest was lost in a gasp as firm fingers girdled a slender waist.

She was abruptly lifted and plonked atop Shah's back. Richard swung up behind her, wordlessly kicked Shah into action, then they were plunging through undergrowth towards the London road.

She was approaching home. Emma's eyes sought out the gates to Hyde Park as they passed in the splendid carriage. It was the first proper landmark she had recognised. From here she knew it would be but a few miles...a few minutes more until she alighted at Rosemary House and was confronted by her mother.

She swallowed her anxieties at the coming reunion and concentrated instead on her papa. Please let him be safe and well, whispered in her head as soulful amber eyes scanned a blue sky.

It was another beautiful autumn day, close to three in the afternoon, she guessed. They had made good time from the Fallow Buck posting house where they had overnighted.

On returning there yesterday evening, Emma had been allocated the same chamber as on her journey to Bath some eleven days earlier. Despite fretting she would never manage a wink of sleep, she had succumbed to sweet oblivion as soon as her aching head touched crisp, clean linen. A young maid, bearing a tray laden with food, had woken her about an hour later, then returned to fill a tub with warm, lavender-scented water for her to wash in.

Emma had not queried whence such consideration came for she already knew. Where Richard slept or ate she did not know...neither did she care, she told herself.

Feeling composed and refreshed after her meticulous bathing and drying on a spotless warm towel, she had attempted reading her book, but found that Elizabeth Bennet and Fitzwilliam Darcy no longer captivated as once they had and she'd wistfully pondered that loss, too.

She had once more snuggled into the white sheets and faced the window, staring at the moon, as she had on her outward journey. When last she'd wished upon it, she had thought of another man and felt optimistic about a future with Matthew. Now she'd stared at the silver sliver hating it, wishing it to be any other colour, as she'd flung herself onto her back and tears had dripped slowly from the corners of her eyes to soak her fawn hair. And time and again she'd told herself that she didn't love him; that the idea of it at all had only been prompted by his perfidious words, and that tomorrow, when back with her mother and all the mayhem that must ensue, things would seem so much better...

Emma sighed deeply and settled back from the window into sumptuous leather upholstery as the carriage slowed behind a press of vehicles ahead. A discreet glance was slanted sideways at the man she knew had watched her for practically the duration of the journey. For her part, she had endeavoured to avoid looking in his direction at all.

She could no longer meet those silver eyes without spontaneous colour staining her cheeks. No longer speak to him without stuttering or uttering stupid things. Once, stinging rebuffals and witty slights had slipped easily off her tongue; now she found basic dialogue difficult. Refusing or accepting food or drink when he asked if she was hungry or thirsty caused her to become tongue-tied. Replying that, yes, she was sleepy or, no, she needed no rest caused her to stammer. So she'd withdrawn from conversation. Withdrawn from him.

Huddled into her private world, only thoughts of her family's predicament had been allowed as she'd whiled away the journey with bouts of snoozing and sightless staring through the carriage window while he, sitting opposite, had made himself comfortable, propped in the corner, with his long legs raised and his booted feet stationed close to her hip.

Several times before they'd left the Fallow Buck posting house she had politely refused his coach, his escort to London. A public conveyance and her own company was adequate, she had insisted. When he'd continued calmly preparing for the journey and only brooding dark looks had met her quiet rejection of his aid, she'd eventually retreated to sip tea while he made arrangements for Shah to be returned to Silverdale in his absence.

First one then another highly polished top-boot withdrawing from the upholstery at her side dragged her thoughts back to the present.

Richard slid along the seat so that he sat directly across from her. Leaning forward, he rested forearms on knees, dark fingers loosely linked. 'You're nearly home.'

Emma nodded her knowledge of it facing the window, a frown puckering her brow.

'Are you going to talk to me before we finish our journey?'

'Yes, of course, if you want,' she politely replied to a passing curricle.

'I do want...' he said quietly. 'So look at me.'

Emma glanced at his dark face then at the seat then at the squabs, noting how very supple the hide was.

A heavy sigh preceded a dark hand spanning her face, holding it still so she couldn't avoid his eyes. 'Don't you think I'm due an explanation, Emma? Don't you think I deserve at least that courtesy?'

She sank back into the squabs, and his hand dropped to his knee.

'Yes, of course,' she repeated civilly while her fingers ceaselessly entwined. 'I hadn't bothered...expounded it all...for I believed you must have heard the gossip from your mother...or perhaps someone else has told you. But I was with her when she learned of the scandal in the Assembly Rooms...and it was very comprehensive so there's nothing to add to that...at all...' She finished the jumbled excuse for remaining silent about her family's disgrace.

'Nevertheless, I want you to tell me.'

So she did. Dispassionately, if disjointedly, she recounted to the passing pedestrians everything that had occurred to prompt her to flee to Matthew Cavendish in Bath.

When she had finished and sat with her lower lip caught between small white teeth, he said, 'And it was impossible to tell me that, honestly, days ago?'

'Yes,' she croaked, blinking.

'Why?'

Emma swung her head at the street scene. 'I don't know,' she whispered.

'Are you now planning to accept Dashwood?'

Sparkling fawn eyes met a heavy-lidded grey gaze. 'Yes.' She cleared her throat. 'Yes, I shall.'

Richard smiled tightly. 'Do you really think, Emma, I'll allow the possibility that a child of mine be reared by that vicious bastard?'

Emma's glossy topaz eyes widened in shock. Why had that

not yet occurred to her? Stupidly, it had never once entered her head that she might have conceived following their bitter-sweet passion. 'It won't be,' she stated, with a desperate, shaky confidence.

Richard twisted a smile. 'You can't be sure of that, Emma.'

'The marriage will soon take place. Thus Dashwood would never suspect a child was not his,' she reasoned fervently.

'If he thinks he's purchased a virgin he'll expect her to be intact on her wedding night,' Richard pointed out quietly. 'Discovering she's duped him would be sure to set him thinking…and counting, after he'd shown her the full force of his displeasure. You've not exactly protected your reputation by your antics. You've been unchaperoned a good deal of the time. Even now, travelling alone with me casts doubt on your virtue. It's likely he'll deem the contract void. And that would be the best possible outcome.'

'He will marry me! The contract is sealed and everything will be fine. My papa will come home. The debts will be cleared. All will be fine!' throbbed out in a raw voice. 'Dashwood won't ever know of…of us!'

'It won't ever matter if he does,' Richard countered mildly. 'For you're not marrying him.'

Before Emma had a chance to reply, a dark hand and a dark, mocking expression indicated that they had arrived.

'Miss Emma…!' the elderly butler said in a croaky voice while goggling his astonishment at his young mistress.

'Hello, Rawlings.' Emma managed a wavering smile. 'Have you been well? Is my mother yet downstairs?' she immediately pressed on. Although it was mid-afternoon it had been her mother's habit when overwrought to lie abed moping for the best part of the day. With such tribulations as she now had to contend with, Emma wondered if she ever at all emerged from her chamber.

Rawlings nodded but his old eyes were warily observing the distinguished blond man who had entered the hallway and stood just behind her. 'She's in the parlour, Miss Emma,' he intoned in a flat underbreath, as if someone living perpetually in an atmosphere replete with tragedy.

Before the onset of this catastrophe, Margaret Worthington would have been enraptured by the vision of such an eligible bachelor in her home, Emma hysterically realised. Now she couldn't predict how her mother would react. Turning to Richard, she coolly said, 'Please excuse me, sir; Rawlings will find you some refreshment while, first, I speak to her alone. But, of course, she will want to thank you, as I do, for your trouble in bringing me home.'

'My pleasure...' was returned immediately, in a soft drawl that brought her eyes swerving to his, her cheeks slowly staining scarlet. She twisted away and walked further into the cold, silent house.

'Mama...?'

Margaret Worthington's greying ringlets rose from the scrolled arm of the chaise longue. She gawped. Her mouth worked slackly a few times as she tried to gain purchase among the folds of her kerseymere gown and push herself upright on spindly arms. They were extended towards her daughter as silent tears rolled down her sunken, wan cheeks.

Emma flew across the few feet that separated them and, falling to her knees, hugged her mother's bony body to her. Sharp shoulder blades dug into her palms and self-disgust drenched her on recalling how well she had eaten recently while in Richard's care.

'Hush,' Emma soothed as her mother's frame shuddered and she sensed her own hot tears drip to her lips and seep salt into her mouth. 'Hush...all will be well now. I am come home and all will be well. Papa will be fine...you'll see...'

Mention of her husband spurred resentment to rescind welcome. Mrs Worthington uttered a shriek of rage fit to wake the dead. 'You insufferably selfish girl...' she berated, beating at Emma's arm with a puny fist.

'I know, Mama. I know I have been selfish and I am come home to apologise and make amends,' Emma choked, knuckling wet from her cheeks as she rose and backed away. 'I shall contact Mr Dashwood, apologise to him, too. The contract is signed; he must honour it and pay the debts when we marry.'

That caused another screech and a handkerchief to be stuffed between bloodless lips. 'Come back to make amends?' Margaret spluttered past lace. 'Now it is too late you would make amends? Why abscond in the first place if now it is amends you want?' she snarled.

'I went to Bath to find Matthew Cavendish and persuade him to marry me. I wanted to marry someone I could love.'

'Matthew Cavendish? That drunken sot? You love him?'

Emma gave a weary shake of the head. 'No...but I believed I did when I left here and I do respect him, drunkard or no. I had no knowledge of his weakness. It seems you knew more of him than I...'

'I know a drunkard,' Margaret snapped. 'Oh, yes, I can spot a drunkard. Do you think I cannot after having lived half a lifetime with such?'

Emma sighed. 'Then you cannot decry me, Mama, for seeking a man to respect in marriage, having lived so long yourself in want...'

'And such duty and disappointment is not for you? Just for me?'

'No...it is for me, too, Mama. I am come home. I have said I shall contact Mr Dashwood. I shall beg his forgiveness if need be. Papa will surely then come home too...'

'I wish I could say that would make me rejoice,' Margaret said bitterly. 'But for appearances' sake no doubt I shall. Yes, I shall be glad to see him alive...for if he is turned up dead and we are forced to put him to rest as paupers when once he could have had a decent burial...' She found her feet with surprising agility, then froze, mouth agape, eyes riveted past Emma.

Emma turned and stared at Sir Richard and the butler stationed in the open doorway. Rawlings cleared his throat and intoned, 'Sir Richard Du Quesne, m'm...' before withdrawing and closing the door.

Emma smeared the heel of a palm across her damp cheeks. She was horrified at what he must have overheard, but she introduced him composedly. 'Sir Richard has been kind enough to break his journey to Mayfair to deliver me home. I expect you must want to thank him, Mama.' Noting she looked on the point of swooning from shock and embarrassment, Emma slid her small fingers in readiness beneath one of her mother's jagged elbows.

Richard executed a bow then, face inscrutable, walked closer.

'Sir Richard...' Margaret finally whimpered out with a watery smile. 'What a great, great honour this is...'

Emma slowly closed her eyes and turned away. So, disaster

or no, it wouldn't prevent her mother fawning over this man, just as she had on the last occasion they had spoken, at her birthday celebration three years ago. Aware of her mother indeed thanking him profusely in a breathy, verbose way, in between plying offers of refreshment which were politely refused, Emma walked to the parlour window and gazed out sightlessly.

In her mind's eye she saw herself dressed in pastel apricot, velvet ribbon threaded into her hair...the belle of the ball on that particular occasion. Victoria had said she looked lovely and she'd even thought so herself, although she could recall her mother despairing over the unbecoming shade of orange she had chosen to wear.

The ridiculous expense of that ball had been borne in the hope she would finally net a husband. Even at twenty-four, the likelihood of her remaining an old maid was terrifying her mother, if not her liberal papa.

Richard Du Quesne had said he might then have been persuaded to offer for her with a little encouragement and she knew now that he meant it. He never lied. She might have had a husband to respect for three long years. In truth, there was never a man she respected more. Now it was too late, she realised it no longer mattered how many courtesans he'd kept, how many drunken brawls he'd participated in. She knew him now...knew intimately everything she needed to know. He was the most worthy man of her acquaintance. And even if he was not it wouldn't matter, because she loved him. And because of that she wanted him away from her in case she did or said something else that made him despise her even more than he must already. In all her life she'd never misled and mistreated anyone so often and so shamelessly.

Bitter regrets had her twisting about, interrupting huskily, 'Sir Richard will be wanting to get to his own home, Mama. It has been a long journey. I can tell you myself of how we came upon each other in Bath and so on...'

Richard's silver eyes rose from Margaret Worthington's thin, drawn features and met, mingled with melancholy amber.

'Thank you, once again, for your hospitality, sir, and for escorting me home. I'm sure you realise we have pressing matters...and must now bid you...bid you goodbye,' Emma quietly concluded.

'You must accompany Sir Richard to the door, Emma, as he has been so kind as to accompany you all the way home.' Margaret nodded meaningfully at her daughter, spots of excited colour in her cheeks.

Back in the cool hallway, Emma cast about in her numb mind for a little bland conversation to ease their parting. 'You...you will no doubt visit David and Victoria while close by. You must pass on my felicitations...'

He made no comment on that and Emma withdrew with a tiny farewell smile and backward steps.

'I meant what I said in the carriage, Emma,' splintered the solid silence. 'You're not marrying Dashwood. Don't contact him and don't defy me...you know how it affects me. I'll deal with Jarrett Dashwood. We've spent time in Jamaica together and understand each other very well.'

She so wanted someone she trusted to deny the terrifying gossip she'd heard of Jarrett Dashwood. Moistening her lips, she bravely asked, 'Is he as black as painted? A cruel and depraved man who ill-treated his plantation labour and...his women, too? I wondered whether you and he might be colleagues.'

'Similar perverted bastards, you mean?'

Emma coloured, winced, on recalling that particular insult outside the Assembly Rooms. 'No, I didn't mean that. I know you're not at all alike...'

Richard laughed mirthlessly. 'I'd like to think that's favourable on my account rather than his. Somehow I doubt it is.'

Before Emma could reassure him it was, he turned for the door, allowing idle words to flow back at her. 'Don't fret over any of it further...don't think of him. I'll deal with it.'

Margaret straightened her shawl about her scrawny neck and settled back into the sofa, wagging a bony finger. 'I will not have it that Sir Richard knows we are involved in a scandal. He has sent his card back already and visits us Wednesday. The *ton* will be dancing attendance on us once it gets out that we have Sir Richard's patronage. You must take a ride in Hyde Park with him and really crook some noses.'

Emma sighed. 'Papa's disappearance must have already stirred scurrilous whispers about us in London.'

'Oh, yes; but no one has proof,' Margaret smirked. 'For a while, I believe his cronies imagined he was in his cups and too foxed to rouse himself. Only his lawyer knows the truth and is luckily a loyal fellow. Petra and Daphne Blair cut me dead in Pall Mall, yesterday, while tattling behind their hands. Five minutes after *I* returned home, their calling card arrived. They were snooping to see if you were here! How I wish they would attend us this minute so you could verify the indisposition I gave you.' Margaret's thin lips puckered to a pleased pout. 'Sir Richard knows none of it. Do you think such an urbane aristocrat would associate with us had he an inkling of our woes?'

Emma closed her eyes in exasperation. Firmly she said, 'He does know, Mama. I told him.'

A shriek rent the air and Margaret flew to her feet. 'You have *what*? Oh...oh, this is the outside of *enough*! Dashwood and I have done our utmost to limit the scandal and you...you *broadcast* it?'

'You don't understand, Mama. Rumours are circulating in Bath, too. Sir Richard guessed of our involvement before I confirmed it. But he is an honourable man with no wish to gossipmonger or worsen our situation.'

Margaret eyed her daughter shrewdly, a little appeased. 'At one time, I recall he drew nothing but your censure. You were always so churlish, I was amazed he seemed so attentive to you...'

'It was all a long time ago, Mama,' Emma said, chilling miserably at such a wounding reminder. 'He is simply a kind gentleman who allowed me to travel home with him as he was to journey to Mayfair.'

'Pish...kind gentleman, indeed!' Margaret dropped back to the sofa. 'I am not blind. I can see how he looks at you...' she said slyly.

It was Emma's turn to fly to her feet. 'You are dreaming, Mama, and you know it,' she cried, walking distractedly about the room. 'The facts are thus: I am contracted to wed Jarrett Dashwood; Papa is absconded to avoid his duns and Dashwood's revenge; the house is cold and dark for we have no candles or fuel; there is scarce a morsel to eat; there are but three servants left now...and you imply it might all turn right because of how Sir Richard *looks* at me! Well, before you say anything very silly, please listen: I have it from his sister-in-law that he is to wed a duke's daughter. It is an alliance that will bring valuable mining rights in Devon which he is keen to have.'

Margaret looked crestfallen. 'A duke's daughter? Oh, well, I own that's hard to contest.' She glumly twirled her wedding band about on a bony finger and huffed a sigh. 'Leastways, we might be able to get some credit at the merchants, when it is known we are his friends...'

Emma shook her head at her mother in mild despair before approaching the window to gaze at the busy street scene. She didn't want to defy Richard's wishes but she knew she must contact Jarrett Dashwood. He was another gentleman she had treated badly. Her prejudices had been lively there too! She had no proof he would be a bad husband. Richard had not confirmed her fears about his evil ways. He had said he would deal with it, but what would he do? Dissuade Dashwood's suit because he wasn't sure whether *he* had impregnated her and he was unwilling to allow another man the rearing of his child? She had heard of instances of wealthy men being paternalistic towards their bastards, even when the child's mother no longer held their interest.

'Dashwood stipulated a woman of unimpeachable character.' Margaret cut astutely into her daughter's reflections. 'You have been negligent with your reputation and that won't mend.' She looked speculative. 'Perhaps Sir Richard might plead your case as you were chaperoned for a while by his mother.'

'I won't hear any more of Sir Richard, Mama!' Emma burst out, and swept to the door. 'He has his family around him at Silverdale and will soon be back there. We must sort out our own problems. I shall endeavour to start on it by writing to Mr Dashwood and you had best pray for a favourable reply.'

Chapter Thirteen

The young clerk craned his thin neck to peer over the top of a mountain of ledgers teetering on a wormy desk. His weak, adolescent jaw dropped. Such impressively imposing gentlemen never gave patronage to Critchley & Critchley. Quality fallen on hard times and middle-class merchants unable to afford more prestigious law firms to act on their behalf were the best they could hope for.

'The nature of your business, sir...if I might be so bold as to enquire?' he ventured in an unbroken squeak.

'Inform Donald Critchley that Sir Richard Du Quesne is here on a matter concerning a client of his: a Mr Worthington.'

Richard noted the youth's Adam's apple jiggle inside his loose collar and his artless eyes blink and swivel agitatedly. No doubt he imagined he was another creditor come to lay his account before Frederick's man of business.

The lad scurried away to another door and disappeared. A moment later both the apprentice and Donald Critchley were gaping at him.

'Sir Richard!' Critchley croaked, flustered by the astonishing appearance of one of the *haut ton's* fabled millionaires. 'Please do come into my office. Please do excuse the jumble.' He grabbed a bundle of papers from a chair. Dropping them to the floor, he dusted the seat with a sweaty palm before nervously extending it.

Richard graciously accepted a woolly handshake and a cracked leather seat.

'Some refreshment for Sir Richard—hurry... There is some port...'

'Nothing, thank you,' Richard cut over the man's panic. 'I have little time and this matter will soon be dealt with.'

Such appalling confidence had Donald flinching and frowning. A discreet look worked from the top of a gleaming head to expensively shod feet. Extreme power and wealth seemed to exude from this man like a bright white light that accentuated every crumbling corner of his littered office.

He cursed inwardly; Frederick had assured him he had provided a comprehensive listing of all his creditors. But then his friend was an arrant coward and apt to conveniently forget to mention one of such renown.

Donald knew of Sir Richard's business acumen and that of his friend Viscount Courtenay. Both men were engaged in commercial ventures jointly and severally that had made them very rich indeed. Both men shared the services of the finest firm of litigators. He blanched. In his mind's eye he saw a lifetime's endeavour snatched away...crippling lawsuits...

He should have refused to act for his spendthrift friend years ago. But Frederick had that hangdog way of looking at one with his mournful, bloodshot eyes that had the most hard-hearted of men softening, believing his lies and promises. Unfortunately, it took only one creditor to lose patience and sue for the others to panic and pitch in too. This battered old desk had fair groaned beneath the weight of Worthington's promissory notes.

'Where is Frederick Worthington?' Richard genially interrogated.

'Er...I...er...I have no idea, Sir Richard,' Donald Critchley mumbled while his face ruddied and beads of sweat decorated his bushy eyebrows.

Richard grimaced in regret. 'Pity; I'd like to have contacted him. I'm aware he is embarrassed for funds at present and would welcome a contribution.'

Critchley's weary eyes popped wide, his drooping features lifted. 'You mean...you owe *him* an amount?' he spluttered in disbelief.

'I am lately returned from abroad and prepared to allocate

funds to those with a stockholding in the plantation I sold.' Silver eyes steadily met those of the goggling, slack-jawed lawyer.

'I have no recollection of this. I am sure I must have certification, unless Frederick has kept it himself...' He leafed frantically through papers on his desk as though he might miraculously turn up the non-existent document.

'I should be able to provide certification...' Richard informed him idly.

'And...and how much would Mr Worthington receive from this investment?'

'How much do his debts total?' Richard rebuffed the question with one of his own.

Again the lawyer looked disconcerted. 'That is...er... confidential, Sir Richard... I'm sure you must...er...understand my delicate...er...my professional...'

'How much?' Richard insisted dulcetly.

'A little more than eighteen thousand pounds...or thereabouts.'

'What a happy coincidence. I believe his allocation should total that...or thereabouts,' Richard said drily. Taking a card from his pocket, he flicked it across the desk. 'So if by some fortuity you do see Worthington,' he added, with a cynical smile, 'give him that and tell him to contact me urgently, lest I soon recover my wits.'

At any other time the redolence of tobacco and alcohol and cheap musky perfume that clung to male clothes long after the woman was dislodged might have stirred a pleasant reminiscing. As it was, Richard simply stood on the threshold of the Palm House gambling den, his silver eyes sorting methodically through a seething mass of humanity and a haze of smoke to find a face.

He paced slowly forward, aware of astonished greetings as gentlemen looked up from baize and saw him. A few actually pushed back chairs, dropped their hands in order to come and shake his and chummily clap him on the back.

'Dickie!'

Richard pivoted on a heel at the bellow to spy Charles Mainwaring moving through the smog with Paul Wainwright hot on his heels. They shoved determinedly through the throng, and so pleased was Paul to see him, he actually proffered his newly replenished brandy balloon.

'Well, look what the cat dragged in,' Charles chortled affectionately. 'Courtenay with you?' he asked, glancing about. 'What's arranged for tonight, then? Something heavenly, I'll warrant,' he sighed enviously, dropping a wink at Wainwright. 'It's been deadly dull, don't you know, since Courtenay got himself leg-shackled and you took off abroad.' He ceased moaning to swig his cognac.

Richard strolled forward, still scanning tables, chatting amiably to his two old friends trailing in his wake. A languid hand was raised now and then in acknowledgement as acquaintances called out to him.

'*Is* Courtenay here?' Wainwright demanded, peering searchingly about.

'Not as far as I'm aware,' Richard replied, drawing on his cheroot then sipping from his glass.

'We'll have to go *en masse* to Hertfordshire. Abduct him if needs be,' Paul chuckled. 'It'll be like old times. We'll persuade him he can still function well enough without that pretty little wife of his.'

Richard laughed past the cheroot clamped at one corner of his mouth. 'You can try...until he persuades you you can still function well enough without your teeth.'

'You are staying, though, aren't you?' Wainwright wrinkled his beaky nose, shoving a hand through his springy dark hair. 'You *have* lined up a few pretty petticoats for later...and a few spare?' At Richard's preoccupied searching look past him, he queried, 'Well, what *are* you doing in this neck of the woods?'

Wasting time, by the look of things...ran responsively, self-mockingly through Richard's mind. Jarrett Dashwood wasn't here...neither had he been at any of the other seedy haunts he frequented with the thuggish little entourage he paid to accompany him. As did most friendless bullies, he liked to appear popular and to ensure that he had ample backing should a scuffle erupt. Mr Dashwood was in London, though, so he had been informed by a pinch-faced servant when he'd called at his home, and his message would be relayed as soon as possible.

Idly emptying the glass Wainwright had magnanimously relinquished, he returned it with a smile. 'Can't stop now...' He grimaced in mild apology and left them both squinting sorrowfully through smoke after him.

Back in his carriage and heading west towards Mayfair, he suddenly leaned forward and rapped out instructions for the driver to turn about and proceed east to Cheapside. Leaning his blond head back wearily into the cushioned squabs, he closed his eyes. He'd not seen Emma for three days—not since she'd politely dismissed him from Rosemary House—and it felt like three months…three damned years.

The longing was debilitating… Just to look at her would be enough: drown in her brandy eyes, watch the animation in her small expressive features as he said something that interested her, or she laughed at him, slapped at him, tossed insults at him. No, looking wouldn't be enough, he mocked himself. The yearning clenched his fingers as he fantasised about them plunging deep into a luxuriant mass of tawny hair.

A hand shot up and instead tugged irritably through his own lengthy locks as he tried to divert his mind from memories of her slender, supple body writhing beneath his, his fingers, his mouth teasing her scented, silky skin.

He swore viciously at the emerging crescent moon, wishing to God she'd wed some worthy young buck a year or so ago. That way he'd still be in blissful ignorance of this hellish emotion. No, he wouldn't, he again reasoned with infuriating efficiency. They had mutual friends: at some point their paths would have crossed. He would have seen her again and realised… And it would have been worse than this…so much worse. So he continued to curse less volubly at the night as the handsome matched greys pulling his splendid carriage made a cracking good pace through quiet streets towards Rosemary House.

Emma glanced, frowning, away from Dashwood's terse, uncompromising instructions to meet him later as she heard the vehicle in the street below. She twitched the curtain to see who alighted. Her stomach somersaulted and her heart thumped crazily as a street lamp pooled a mercury sheen on his hair.

After a dazed moment, there followed a few frantic seconds when she actually twirled about on the spot, crumpling Dashwood's letter in her fingers while scouring her mind for truthful excuses to avoid seeing him.

Deceitfulness drew its humbling, just rewards as she had learned to her cost, and she wanted no more of those. Truth was all she would now deal in. If she went downstairs, Richard was sure to ask if she had contacted Dashwood and she would not lie. Thus he would know she had deliberately gone against his wishes and have further reason to despise her...and she desperately didn't want that.

She stilled her agitated dance and forced her mind to work. She did have an honest reason to give to her mother why she must stay in her room even if it no longer seriously confined her. It was an indisposition that would release Richard from caring whether or not she contacted, or even married, her spurned fiancé. There was no longer any need for him to fret over a child of his being reared by Jarrett Dashwood.

The very evening of her return to Rosemary House a familiar cramping in her abdomen had heralded the start of her menses. She had not conceived. The initial draining relief had been replaced by a sense of dreadful loss that had had her weeping and her mother anxiously pressing a hot brick to her aching stomach, while muttering about the cursed regularity of women's trials.

'How kind of you to call, Sir Richard,' Margaret beamed at him. 'I trust you are not here to tell us you will be unable to take tea tomorrow?'

Richard smiled. 'No. I was just passing and thought to call in and see how you do.' He prowled the room's perimeter, stuffed his hands in his pockets and looked at the door. 'Is your daughter at home?'

'Oh, yes, sir,' Margaret confirmed, settling comfortably into the sofa. 'But she is ailing.' She coloured a little in embarrassment despite having no intention of imparting the nature of the malaise. Besides, the excuse she would use was perfectally valid. 'She frets so much over her papa, it has fair set her head athumping.' She flicked a glance at Richard from beneath her sparse lashes. 'Emma has said she confided to you our very great troubles.'

Richard approached and looked down at the small woman huddled into an array of shawls to ward off the chill of the fireless room. 'Yes, she has told me, and I find it hard to believe that any parents would insist their daughter marry someone so repulsive that she was forced to flee from home.'

Margaret flushed scarlet. 'Well, of course, had there been another way,' she gruffly murmured. 'Had Emma striven to attract a husband in her prime—that is to say...a gentleman of her own choosing...' Bony fingers clasped together on her lap. 'Naturally we only ever wanted what was best for her...'

'Naturally, I should very much like to think so,' Richard mellifluously concurred.

'Mr Dashwood offered us all a settled future free of debt. But now it is all gone awry. As parents we have been further scandalised by our own flesh and blood when all we intended was to give our dear girl security. The longer Frederick is away, the more I fret he might be tempted to take his own life to avoid further opprobrium.'

'Well, proof, then, madam, that every cloud has a silver lining,' Richard drawled. 'Should he do the decent thing, I shall be spared a task.'

Margaret simpered up stupidly at a stern, handsome face, while, vacant-eyed, her mind struggled on.

Richard executed a curt bow. 'My regards to your daughter for a speedy recovery,' was bitten out over his shoulder as he strode to the door, oblivious to the woman abruptly flopping back into the cushions in a swoon.

'You have a visitor, Sir Richard,' Thomas Webb informed his master as Richard discarded his gloves and silver-topped cane onto the stately Heppelwhite table in the flagged hallway of his Mayfair mansion.

Richard appeared not to have heard as he savagely flung off his coat and left it where it landed.

He was still seething that she had refused to see him. He knew Emma well enough: a headache would never lay her low. This was the girl who could uncomplainingly exist for days with little to eat; who could fight like a vixen, dash through undergrowth like a fawn, who had the courage to purloin a horse she couldn't even ride properly. It was the woman who would lash out at him

with her tongue and her fists even as she trembled imagining
how he might retaliate. A headache would never have prevented
her coming downstairs. She had chosen not to see him. She was
punishing him for seducing her. And what rankled most was that
he knew he deserved it. Aware that his butler had spoken, he
frowned at him.

'You have a visitor, sir,' Thomas Webb repeated with a cir-
cumspect peer at his master's tense, tic-ridden jawline. 'I have
shown him into your study. He refused to offer up his name but
says you are expecting him.'

Richard paced along the wide, spacious hallway, aglitter with
chandeliers and crystal wall sconces, and as he walked he suddenly recalled how dark and dismal it had seemed at Rosemary
House. He threw back his head with a curse. It had slipped his
mind that the Worthingtons probably had little or no credit available to them at the merchants'. Now he'd have to go back and
see the accursed woman again to ensure they weren't about to
starve or freeze.

He irritably shoved open his study door, hoping viciously that
Dashwood was within for he was never likely to more enjoy
dealing with him.

He slowed his pace into the room as the stumpy, balding man
twisted away from the fire where he had been warming himself.
He hadn't changed in the three years since last he'd clapped eyes
on him, Richard realised. He still resembled a glassy-eyed little
weasel.

Richard glared at Frederick Worthington and then ignored him.
He strode to his desk, selected a cheroot, stuck it in his mouth,
lit it, poured himself a brandy, then sent his chair skidding back
with a jab of a foot, and dropped into it. He drew deeply on his
cigar, raised his booted feet to the edge of his desk, crossed them
at the ankles and then gave Frederick his attention.

'Sit down.'

Frederick shambled a few steps closer. 'I heard you wanted to
see me about a matter of business.' Sandy lashes shielded pale,
wary eyes. His unexpected benefactor's barely restrained temper
was making him exceedingly apprehensive.

'*Sit down,*' Richard growled with such mean ferocity that Frederick scuttled to the desk and bounced into the chair opposite.

Richard withdrew his cigar and studied its glowing tip. 'I've

just been to see your wife and daughter... Well, I saw your wife,
not your daughter.'

Frederick gawped at him nervously. He gulped a breath. 'Ah,
yes. My daughter is away from home visiting...er...no...she
might be indisposed...'

'That's what I heard,' Richard said with a dry laugh as he
watched a smoke ring drift towards the ceiling. 'She says she's
indisposed but I think she's lying and won't see me.'

Frederick goggled at him anxiously, wondering if he was a
madman and all the talk of thousands of pounds available to clear
his debts was merely a fantasy. Well, in truth he knew it was.
This man owed him nothing and they both knew that. But, unless
he'd been afflicted by a recent full moon, Sir Richard Du Quesne
wasn't a lunatic. Far from it. He was an accredited businessman
and very influential...very affluent. So there had to be some point
to all this. And now that he had mentioned his daughter it jogged
his memory that Margaret had once imagined this fellow held a
certain interest in Emma. Not that Frederick could recall any such
attention, but then he rarely noticed anything other than the
amount of spending cash in his pocket, or the time of the day,
and whether it merited him wending his way towards Brook's or
White's.

Richard removed his feet from his desk and sat back in his
chair, stubbing out his cigar while he watched his grinding fingers with frowning thoughtfulness. 'There's just one reason why
I'm contemplating clearing your debts and saving your miserable
hide from gaol. She's the same reason I shall no doubt swallow
a burning desire to kill you or even maim you a little for neglecting her so appallingly. She's also the reason I shall be persuaded to provide for you and your lady wife till you shuffle off
this mortal coil in your own sweet time rather than mine. In
short,' he said through lips strained thin against his teeth, 'whatever I do, I do for Emma, and you had best make very sure you
show her daily gratitude for it, in the manner of a fond papa, and
never allow her to know that this conversation took place.' Flint
eyes suddenly speared the man to his seat. 'Is that quite clear?'
he asked softly.

Frederick wobbled his jowls up and down in assent, his pale
eyes blinking ceaselessly. He licked dry lips. 'May I...?' He
looked forlornly at Richard's brandy decanter. It was shoved

across the desk at him together with a glass. Once Frederick had poured with an unsteady hand, sunk the tot and wiped his wet mouth with the backs of hairy fingers, he said with a foxy look, 'You're not jesting? You really will pay my debts?'

At Richard's sardonic, silent agreement, Frederick laughed and poured himself another. 'That's damned amazing,' he chortled. 'Who'd have thought it? My little Emma's got two blades after her now! Astonishing, I tell you...'

'I'll tell you what's astonishing,' Richard sneered, standing up and tersely indicating that Frederick follow. 'The fact that a jewel was got from such base metal. Oh, I'll tell you something else, too; Dashwood doesn't count.' He then offered quite cordially, 'Come, I'll have the carriage brought round and we can reunite you with your family. Perhaps your daughter will feel happy enough to see me this time.'

Emma walked confidently forward, but kept on the perimeter of the crowds of people posing in their finery. Strains of a serenade could be heard and people were increasing their pace towards the gaily lit boxes and the orchestra podium situated towards the centre of Vauxhall Gardens. The groves and grottoes, waterfalls and pavilions that comprised these pleasure gardens drew visitors from all social classes, but tonight it was a special concert to mark thirty years since Mozart's demise that made available these delights on this Indian summer evening.

Promenading young ladies, laughingly at ease with their beaus or their parents, only served to emphasise to Emma just how terrifyingly foolhardy was her solitary excursion.

Despite Jarrett Dashwood's specific instructions that their tryst should be confidential and that she must see him alone, she had decided at the last moment to follow her own instinct, and persuade her mother to accompany her.

In the event it had proved impossible. By seven-thirty that evening, when her firm decision was made, her mother had been snoring in the cold parlour on the chaise longue, covered with a blanket. A Madeira decanter was on the table at her side with little left in it: apparently her father's comfort was, in his absence, consoling her mother. When the clock had chimed eight, and Margaret Worthington had refused to relinquish her comfortable oblivion, even with Emma's pleading and shaking, Emma had retrieved her cloak from the hallway and slipped quietly from the house to hail a hackney cab.

She was unsure whether to be glad or perturbed that Jarrett Dashwood had settled on such a public place for them to meet. On the one hand she felt some reassurance that there were so many people around; on the other, she knew that it was scandalously unseemly for her to be there unaccompanied, and she was terrified that someone she knew might spot her.

Rallying her courage, she again drew her cloak tighter about her and allowed the hood to conceal more of her face. With a heavy sigh she conceded that most of the past two weeks had seen her behaving in a most scandalous and unseemly manner. No doubt Jarrett Dashwood was keen to drive home that point by summoning her here alone. As she had been prepared to risk all by escaping him unchaperoned, he was sure to gain quite deliberate satisfaction from making her return to apologise in the same manner.

She had gleaned from his curt, explicit note that he was extremely angry yet extremely eager for a meeting. That had seemed to her exactly the reaction she should expect and it had reassured her. He was certain to be voluble in his censure, yet he obviously deemed the agreement still viable.

With her face lowered and sunk in depressing thoughts, she didn't see the dandy until he grabbed at her arm and addressed her lewdly, enveloping her in alcoholic fumes. Emma reflexively wrenched herself free, aware of his male companions jeering and laughing at his bold antics. She understood why he looked angry at her rejection: lone women frequenting these dimly lit walkways were usually happy to attract such attention.

A shaking hand went up to retrieve her hood, which had been knocked back in the struggle. Concealing her frightened pallor, she quickly turned away and had taken two paces when she heard, 'Miss Worthington?' It was what she had dreaded: a familiar voice addressing her.

Ross Trelawney walked away from a group of stylish people. He was frowning at her and Emma read frank surprise in his dark features as she looked fully at him and confirmed his suspicions. Ross glanced from her to the young buck who was now glowering with increased indignation on seeing another man had successfully arrested her progress.

'Mr Trelawney...how are you?' Emma greeted with a smile, forcing lightness to her voice. 'I...I had no idea you were in London.'

'I am only lately arrived from Brighton where I was visiting my brother and sister-in-law,' Ross informed her with a gleaming smile but his dark eyes narrowed thoughtfully. He took her arm, manoeuvring her out of a crush. 'Is Richard with you?' he asked without preamble. 'I called at his town house earlier and learned he was abroad.'

'Why...no,' Emma quickly said. 'I am...I am just on my way to meet...an acquaintance. I had best be off, too. I am already late...' She gave an apologetic little smile and bobbed in readiness to go. She knew she had to go quickly for, in truth, she was so pleased to see Ross she might, in her feeble state of mind, be persuaded to stay safely with him. She had always liked him, right from the start when he had been prepared to act as her champion without having known her more than a few minutes.

Ross caught at her arm, charming smile still in evidence. 'You must allow me to accompany you to your friend. Who are you to meet? Perhaps I might be acquainted, too.' His shrewd, penetrating gaze forced nervous topaz eyes to swerve away.

Ross knew that this was an independent young lady. Apparently untrammelled by etiquette, she was not averse to travelling alone or keeping her own company. Nevertheless, she was tense with anxiety and her arm quivered beneath his light restraint. Something was amiss. Richard obviously had no idea the woman he loved was walking the grounds of Vauxhall Gardens, frightened and unchaperoned. How he would react to knowing she had just been mistaken for a soliciting harlot by a drunken cub roistering with his chums, Ross didn't want to contemplate.

His brooding was interrupted by a gloved hand gliding over his arm. 'We're waiting for you, Ross,' the dark-haired woman said, but her sharp black glance was on Emma's profile. 'Lord Grantham is to convey us to his supper box.'

It was the distraction Emma needed; with a murmured farewell, she slipped her arm free and was almost running along the path that led away from the concert area and towards the southerly grove.

* * *

'Ah, there you are, my dear! I had almost given up hope of you putting in an appearance and that would have made me so much angrier...'

Emma felt her arm gripped and she was whirled about, by a man who had emerged from the shadows. He urged her along a narrow path which terminated in a small clearing with a bench. Jarrett Dashwood released her, crossed his arms over his considerable chest, and eyed her contentedly through heavy lids.

Emma's attention, however, was immediately drawn to the seat. Slumped on it was an unidentifiable male figure and, standing at either side, were two huge, burly men. She took an unsteady pace forward, her breath wedged dizzingly in her throat, as she tried to discern what was familiar about the hunched body barely illuminated by the globe lamps twinkling, with incongruous prettiness, in wavering tree branches.

'You said we were to meet privately,' she hoarsely snapped at Dashwood. 'I am courageous enough to come alone yet you bring accomplices.'

Olive eyes glittered like wet pebbles. 'They aren't accomplices, my dear. The two standing are my employees, the one sitting is in fact a friend of yours, I believe. So, there you are. You are not alone. I am a thoughtful soul who has brought along for you an accomplice. I thought it might be nice to reunite you tonight, while you explain to me what it is about him you find so appealing.'

Emma's fearful gaze lurched to the slouching figure on the bench and she slowly approached on wobbly legs, her chest afire with dread. Gently raising the lolling head, she looked into Matthew Cavendish's battered features, blood trailing from nose and lip. A shaking hand touched his cold cheek, and he roused enough to moan her name. The strong smell of liquor enveloped her, for once giving her a surge of comfort, for his insensibility was probably due as much to that as the beating he had sustained.

She felt rage smouldering, reigniting her courage. Straightening, she turned proudly towards the thick-set, raven-haired man who was watching her so malevolently. 'How did you find him? Why have you brought him here?'

'My investigators found him, my dear, and...persuaded him to accompany them to London. As to why he is here...I have just told you. An explanation is, I believe, due as to why my costly, chaste fiancée should see fit to abscond to a drunken pauper.'

'Is there some point to any of this, Mr Dashwood? Have you come here to discuss our marriage contract, or just to prove to me that every appalling whisper I have ever heard of you is in fact justified?'

A grin split his swarthy coutenance. 'Why, both, my dear. How astute you are.' He paced closer to her while a hand went to an inside pocket and with a flourish he withdrew a document. 'To wit...the marriage document,' he leered at her. 'Which stipulates my intention to wed a virtuous spinster.' He sighed. 'Alas, you no longer fit the bill.' Very slowly, very deliberately he also withdrew an elegant silver box, struck a match from it, and brought the two together. When the contract was burning well his fingers opened and he allowed it to drop to the ground.

'There...one matter promptly dealt with. But the loss of my two thousand pounds, and that of my credibility, still remains,' he ruefully jibed. 'And I must own the money to be of less moment. You have made of me a veritable pantaloon in this farce.' He marched away from her, hands clasped behind his broad back, then came again close, and as he raised fiendish dark eyes to her face Emma realised he was, in fact, insane with bitter fury. 'So I have decided that you must atone. You must be punished...'

The blow made Emma gasp, burst coloured lights behind her eyes as she stumbled back a few steps and steadied herself against the hedge. A shaking hand went to her split mouth, pressing at warm blood. But she valiantly raised her head and glared her loathing. 'You are an evil madman and you will pay dearly for this.'

Jarett Dashwood nodded with satanic enjoyment. 'I could sense spirit the first time we met. I knew there was fire beneath the ice. Well, I'll extinguish it...eventually.' He confided in a fervent whisper, 'You know, when every pleasure has been taken so often it has palled, there can be a most exquisite sport in pain. I'll teach you that...' he vowed excitedly, as one promising a gift. 'As you absconded for eleven days you should doubly make amends. Twenty days you will this time disappear while I discipline you...for lessons should never be rushed.'

'You obviously rushed yours, Dashwood,' came Ross's scoff-

ing drawl as he burst into view. 'Twice eleven is twenty-two...'
he sneered as his fist smashed efficiently against the side of the
man's head, sending him reeling.

Ross grabbed at Emma's arm and shoved her behind him while
facing the two thugs who had suddenly sprung from inanimate,
disinterested statues into sinister life at his unexpected appearance.

'Get him, you fools,' Dashwood shrieked while a hand
clutched at his gaping cheek. 'Where's that dolt Watts? Can't he
keep a watch? Is it too much to expect him to keep his infernal
eyes open?'

Ross swung about at the unwitting warning of unseen danger
but his desperation to protect Emma rather than himself was his
downfall. As he pushed her away from the looming figure behind,
a club caught him behind an ear and he collapsed to the ground.

Emma dropped immediately to her knees, cradling Ross's dark
head in her lap, her frantic fingers soothing his brow.

'Get up, you little whore,' Dashwood screamed, while his fingers trembled incessantly over his wound. 'Get up so I can finish
the bastard off.'

Emma frantically shook her head, arching her upper body into
a protective shell about Ross.

'So that's how it is!' Dashwood barked. 'Not only do you dally
with a drunkard but with a marauding Cornishman, too. Oh, I
know of the Trelawneys. You have a knack of entertaining dangerous men, my dear...this footling toper excepted, of course. I'll
own that, had not Trelawney been surprised, we might have been
a little in trouble. He is a renowned pugilist and swordsman.
Rather like his good friend...your cousin.'

Dashwood balefully circled her, jabbing a foot towards Ross
and chortling as she guarded him, taking kicks on her slender
arms. 'You overnighted with your *cousin* at the Fallow Buck, did
you not, my dear? My investigators revealed that too. How you
ever managed to whore your way to Sir Richard Du Quesne's
precious attention is beyond me. And who would have thought
it? He even gallantly dumped you back on your own doorstep
when he'd done. I really must find time to thank him for running
my errands.'

Emma's head spontaneously bowed at that, and he saw it and
scoffed, 'I trust you're not anticipating further gallantry from that

quarter? A knight in shining armour? *A silver squire?*' He laughed loudly, looking about at his henchmen who obediently joined in. 'I should tell you, my dear, Du Quesne is not renowned for returning to lightskirts he discards.'

Despite an outward show of nonchalance, there was a shrillness to his spite. Inwardly he cursed that the little bitch had managed to secure Du Quesne's notice, even for a short while. He was a menacing, unpredictable man. In Jamaica they had been bitter enemies. Du Quesne's coddling of his labour disgusted him. Slaves were there to toil or quench a man's lust and uppity ones needed to be made an example of to bring the others into line. What was most astonishing was that Du Quesne had managed to get a ridiculous yield from his workforce and his crop with such leniency. Any other planter on such a run of luck would surely have stayed, milked all resources dry... Not him. Once the fraudster overseers had been ejected, and the business was in fine order, he had sold the estate for a phenomenal price to his neighbour and, most startlingly of all, disbanded his workforce with manumissions and cash!

Closer to home he was a man with a quite deadly reputation. Not only had he and Courtenay brawled their way through many a long night and stood to tell the tale—and repeat the exercise— but his war record was exemplary.

It was a little-known fact, and one that Du Quesne refused to speak of, that Courtenay owed him his life. Suicidal missions had for some reason seemed to lure the young David Hardinge, prompting many to whisper he had lost his wits. The fact that he survived to inherit his viscountcy at all was credited to Du Quesne's valour and vigilance finally bringing them both home.

As soon as he'd learned from the detectives he'd hired that Emma Worthington had spent time alone with Du Quesne he'd been enraged. The man was too dangerous to meddle with, yet he'd known the little spinster would never return intact. There was no such thing as an unwilling woman where Du Quesne was concerned. He'd had her, then dumped her, he just knew it, and his irritation made him prod at Emma again with his boot.

Ross grabbed at the foot, twisting and shoving, sending him off balance and crashing onto his back. Dragging himself to his feet with Emma's assistance, Ross deftly sidestepped Watts, who had clubbed him, and rammed him head-first into the hedge.

Retrieving the man's dropped club and testing its weight in his hand, he commanded in a concussed slur, 'Go, Emma. Go home this minute!'

'I can't leave you! You're injured. There are too many of them. You'll be killed!'

Ross grunted a laugh then winced as it pained him. 'I'll be killed if you don't go,' he muttered hoarsely. 'Believe me, I'd rather face this motley crew than Richard if he discovers I let you stay. Go now!' roared out of him with such vehement authority that without further thought she turned and fled.

Chapter Fourteen

Handicapped by burning tears that trailed to sting her torn mouth, she ran clumsily, every step pounding her skull, rattling her teeth in their sockets until the ache in her face from the blow Dashwood had delivered was a throbbing agony.

The dim pathways seemed endless, maze-like, and it was only the strengthening serenade that guided her towards the exit to the gardens. *Eine Kleine Nachtmusik* wafted delicately, the globe lamps overhead seeming to sway in perfect, incongruous tempo as the tepid breeze caught them.

Moments ago, Emma had accosted a couple strolling the deserted pathways to pour out that a man was in peril and needed help. They had peered through the dusk at her dishevelled appearance and bloodied face with a mix of doubt and contempt. Barely listening to her garbled pleas, they were soon hurrying away, probably having decided she was a footpad's decoy.

Trying to enlist the aid of an elderly gentleman sauntering jauntily had also been fruitless. He'd obviously suspected she was away from the concert and seeking less cultured diversion in the shrubbery as he was. Freedom was gained thanks to the staggering amount of alcohol he'd imbibed.

Reaching the exit to the grounds at last, Emma sped to the roadside, and began scouring the gloom for a charley on his beat or someone disposed to help. A hackney passed, and too late her befuddled brain told her to hail it.

She spun about at the kerb, trembling violently, searching for another as she instinctively wrapped herself into her cloak for warmth and protection from prying eyes.

'What in God's name are you about, Emma?' The despairing words accompanied a grip on her arm swinging her about.

The relief was overwhelming. A shuddering sob exploded as she fell against him, clutched hungrily at him, leaned her cheek against his shoulder. His familiar height and breadth, the hint of sandalwood, the tenor of his dear voice combined to ensure she would have recognised him had she been truly sightless rather than simply blinded by prickling brine. 'They'll kill Ross. You must quickly help him, Richard, or they'll kill him...' she cried out.

Dark hands secured her slippery face, tilting it immediately up to his. About to interrogate her, questions died on his lips, his eyes freezing on her injured mouth, the blemish beneath her eye.

Emma felt his hands start to vibrate against her skin, sensed him try to gentle their reflexive clenching. Through tear-spiky black lashes she watched his despair: a soundless mouthing of her name, lids slowly screening glaring, dilating pupils. Within a moment he was again examining her with fanatical intensity. A thumb brushed, feather-light, across her swollen purple lip, collecting the blood there.

'Dashwood did this?'

'He's with Ross,' Emma forced through chattering teeth, answering him obliquely. 'Ross sent me away. He has been clubbed but he's again conscious and poor Matthew has been beaten too! It's all my fault, Richard!' she choked. 'If it weren't for my foolishness none of this would have happened. It's *me* he wants to punish, yet Ross has sent me away, and now he'll be killed!'

'Hush...' Richard soothed, pulling her close, his fingers spearing up through tangled, tawny hair to cradle her scalp, his lips ceaselessly caressing her. Then, without warning, he suddenly bellowed, 'Wainwright!'

Through straggly locks, Emma spied a man run from the other side of the road to greet Richard with a jovial, 'Dammit, Dickie, you've started on the muslin early. It's not yet ten...'

'I have a favour to ask, Paul.' Richard cut sharply across his friend's ribald observation. 'I want you to take Miss Worthington home to Rosemary House, Cheapside, without delay.'

Paul Wainwright blinked at Emma's ashen, damaged face and

then at Richard. 'Of course...why, of course...' he murmured, grimacing apology for his inappropriate jest while a hand pressed down his coarse dark curls. But he asked for no explanation. Richard's forbidding, rigid countenance tacitly conveyed urgency and gravity and suppressed a natural inquisitiveness.

'Take my carriage...' Richard dictated, indicating the sleek conveyance close by. The door was still open from when he had alighted, on seeing her, before the vehicle had properly stopped. 'And Paul...you're on pain of death on this,' was quietly emphasised. He gently prised away Emma's clinging hands, touched his lips to them, and handed her over to his friend. With a last, lingering look at her forlorn face, Richard was running towards the gardens. 'Take her straight home and see her delivered safely within to her parents!' was yelled back at Wainwright.

'I think I know you,' Ross said, squinting through double vision at Richard. He had sustained another glancing blow to the head and yet remained on his feet thanks to doggedness and cunning learned over two decades of every conceivable form of combat. The club swung viciously in front of him, keeping the thugs at bay, while he spoke to his friend.

'You do know me,' Richard reassured him as he paced steadily closer.

'Dickie, how nice to see you,' Dashwood greeted, yet he spontaneously backed away at the blond man's purposeful stalking.

The thugs were ignored as though they were of no real threat; Richard's only focus was the swarthy-countenanced man his eyes had targeted like silver bullets.

'I was saying to Miss Worthington just a short while since,' Dashwood drawled, 'I really must thank you for returning her to me. Unsullied would have been preferable, but not to quibble...' The sarcasm was smooth but the frantic fingers that were not fidgeting incessantly at his bleeding face were urgently beckoning forward his bodyguards.

They had ceased aiming blows at Ross to gawp at the nonchalant newcomer. This swell had made Dashwood increasingly uneasy. If he fought like the Cornish fiend they had trouble. Even concussed, Trelawney battled with awesome instinct, feinting and dodging, using his fists, feet, the club with a natural skill.

One of the brutes gathered what little wit he had, decided to earn his fee, and surged forward, fists ready. With spare savagery he was hit once in the face. As his legs wobbled, a knee jerked into his groin, then, as he sank, found his chin, before he found the ground. Richard tipped him disdainfully off the end of a polished boot where he sprawled, stunned, before looking enquiringly at his colleague. Eyes swivelled in a square skull as the henchman nervously sought his master's instruction. Dashwood managed a thin smile and put up a hand for him to wait.

Watts, who had been hanging limply in the hedge where Ross had left him, started to stir, squirming to free his shoulders. Ross idly shoved him further into the bush with a booted foot. 'Ah, now I recall,' he said, with a grin at Richard, as he battled with waves of amnesia. 'Was it Devil's Cove in eleven? A consignment of tea and geneva? You must be Revenue.'

'No,' Richard said easily, 'but I am here to exact payment.'

'Don't be a fool, Dickie,' Dashwood whined, understanding exactly what was meant and why. 'I have every right to be angry with the little trollop. She deserves more chastisement than she got. She and her conniving parents have fleeced me. What's it to you, in any case? It's my credibility at stake, my two thousand pounds, my fiancée...'

'She's mine,' Richard contradicted him coolly. 'She's always been mine...'

Dashwood peered speculatively at him from beneath heavy lids. 'Well, have her, then. I'll never take the little slut to wife now you're done with her.' He shrugged and coaxed chummily, 'Come, we can both make use of her. We oughtn't let petty rivalry worry us unduly. It's nothing to me if you still bed her. In some ways, we're very much alike, you and I...'

'We're nothing alike and if you say it again I'll kill you just for that.'

'A skinny chit with cat's eyes isn't worth this, Du Quesne! We'll call it quits. Take Trelawney and this worthless sot she's in love with and go.'

Richard turned to Ross. 'Are you ready to go?'

Ross deliberately lowered the club. 'Whenever you are.'

Ross felt in the inside pocket of Matthew Cavendish's coat and eventually located what he sought. He drew out the pewter flask and up-ended it, allowing a stream of whisky to fill his mouth. He swilled it round, wincing as it seared raw flesh. Anointing himself with a little of the liquor, he swore and shook himself as it found the contusion behind his ear.

'God, don't waste it,' Richard growled, and relieved him of the flask. He took a swig then lowered Matthew Cavendish from his shoulder to the ground, one hand keeping him upright.

The flask was waved at the carriage and it immediately pulled forward. 'Thank God Wainwright was about here tonight,' he sighed to himself.

Paul Wainwright jumped from the carriage and grinned at the three men, two swaying on their feet, their marked faces, their torn clothes, indisputable evidence of a vicious brawl. The other man was seemingly unconscious and reeking of alcohol. Before he could utter a jovial word a bloodied hand grabbed him by the lapels.

'Is Miss Worthington safely home?'

Paul nodded. 'Delivered to her mother and safely within Rose-mary House, Dickie.' He chuckled and nodded to himself with intense satisfaction. 'I knew it... I just *knew* it. It *is* going to be like old times, isn't it?' With a flourish he ushered them forward, waving away the groom so he could hold the door himself for them as a sign of respect. 'Come on, gentlemen...get in. How many of them, Dickie? Five? Six? Weapons?'

'Shut up,' Richard directed mildly as he loaded Matthew Cavendish into his carriage, ignored the censorious gawping of his driver and groom, and got in himself. Ross clambered in after him and, as one, they fell back into the squabs, exhausted.

'I'm getting too old for this, Dickie,' Ross eventually said, flexing his strained shoulders. 'You know, I barely saw that first blow coming. It took me out for a while and left Emma at that bastard's mercy. He might have hurt her again.'

'Shut up, dammit!' Richard gritted as his blond head fell forward into massaging hands. He dropped one away and studied the bloody mess opened up across his knuckles again. Then he gazed sightlessly out into the gloaming for a while. Eventually he said quietly, 'Thanks, Ross. I owe you so much...I don't know how I can ever repay you... I daren't think what might have happened if you hadn't found Emma when you did... I just can't talk about it...' At his comrade's silence he turned his head. Ross was propped in the corner, arms crossed over his chest, head lolling, sound asleep, oblivious to his gruff gratitude. Richard smiled wryly, glancing at the carriage's other occupants: Wainwright, still grinning and shaking his head happily to himself as his imagination entertained him; Matthew Cavendish snoring quite peacefully. He turned back to brood, alone, at the night.

'But she's abed, Sir Richard!' Margaret Worthington exclaimed agitatedly. 'Even if I wanted to wake her, which I do not, it would prove impossible. I dosed her with laudanum to ease her hurt and get her a good night's sleep.'

Richard looked from Frederick Worthington to his wife and then slowly nodded. 'Yes...good...she needs to sleep,' he echoed while in his mind he raged, *Well, let me go to her. I must see her. I need her.*

Having delivered Ross, Matthew and Wainwright to his Mayfair town house, he had immediately journeyed on to Cheapside. The fact that Emma was now in peaceful oblivion was comforting, yet he desperately wanted to be close to her again, lie down beside her, take her in his arms and hold her lest another danger menace her before the dawn.

Frederick Worthington shuffled on the spot, a shaking hand wiping about his bristly chin. He blinked at Sir Richard's haggard profile, for the first time in the twenty-seven years of his daughter's life, tearfully distraught on her account.

Earlier that evening, when Sir Richard had brought him home to be reunited with his family he'd been feeling exceedingly content. Having woken his wife from her tipsy snooze, to be simultaneously nagged and hugged, he'd found that within five minutes all the gladness was gone.

Emma was missing. She *had* written to Dashwood, Margaret had nervously replied to Sir Richard's abrupt enquiry as to whether the two had been in contact, and a reply from Dashwood *had* been received. The fact that Emma had made no attempt to conceal Dashwood's letter, and it was easily located on her writing desk, had made the reason for her unexpected absence from home that evening ominously apparent. The time of eight-thirty and the venue of the south grove at Vauxhall Gardens was all

Sir Richard had waited to learn before hurtling from Rosemary House.

Frederick glanced again at Sir Richard's dishevelled appearance: his fine tail-coat torn and dirty, his boots scuffed and dusty. Blood was caked thickly on his knuckles and was just visible on his temple, beneath a fall of fair hair. And the damage told its own story: Sir Richard had fought Dashwood and emerged victorious.

Frederick knew himself for an abject coward and he knew this man for an intrepid warrior. Sir Richard's military record alone was proof of his prowess; his youthful hellraising added another shocking dimension to his skill. Never before had he felt so thankful for anything or anyone. He prayed to God the deed was already done as he choked, 'I shall kill Dashwood for this. He has abused my little Emma!'

Richard swung back to face him, lips tight against his teeth. 'What the hell did you think he intended doing over the next twenty or more years? You're not deaf. You've heard talk. Yet you were prepared to sell a beautiful, spirited woman into what would have been a life of unremitting misery.' He stepped close to the man and glared, livid-faced, down at him. 'The worst of it is, she would have eventually welcomed a split lip over other atrocities.'

Frederick dropped his face to his hands, grazed his palms with his stubbly countenance. 'Does the bastard still live?'

'Yes...just...'

'I'll get Dashwood his two thousand pounds in pennies and feed him each coin. I'll swing from a gibbet myself to see him buried!' Frederick's shrieking voice caused Margaret to flee to an armchair and huddle into it.

'Dashwood is no longer a problem,' Richard bit out, but calmingly. 'And he has obligingly destroyed the marriage contract himself. Do likewise with your document.'

Margaret fidgeted in the chair, wringing her hands. 'Still Emma must be married,' she gabbled hysterically. 'Dashwood would never again dare meddle with her if she were wed. Frederick, we must find our daughter a husband.'

'Perhaps you'd best leave that to me, too...' Richard drawled witheringly, and with a curt bow he was gone.

* * *

'I don't believe Sir Richard would have said that, Mama,' Emma quavered.

'Well, of course he said it! Am I a liar? Is that what you mean?' her mother demanded. 'You may ask your papa.' She flicked a finger at Frederick who was pacing the room, head bowed, lost in his own thoughts.

'Sir Richard said quite clearly that he would assist us in finding for you a husband. And it must be done. You need the protection only a husband can give you. Dashwood obviously has no fear of your father.' A whip of a glance scorned her husband. 'But he will perhaps not harass a man's wife.'

Margaret inspected her daughter's white face, a shading of blue beneath her transluscent skin, extending from cheekbone to jaw, branding her with Dashwood's malice. 'Come closer to the fire; you look cold.' Margaret anxiously patted the seat beside her as her daughter's pallor increased.

Emma obediently took her place by the hearth and stared, sightlessly, into the blaze. Richard would never cold-bloodedly conspire in marrying her off! She wouldn't believe it! He had held her tenderly by Vauxhall Gardens; his concern for her injury had been palpable. Every soothing, gentle touch at her bruised face had shown he cared... But now he had offered his services as marriage broker? He would see her wed for convenience?

'Sir Richard has promised us lasting provision,' Frederick suddenly mumbled. 'Why would the man do that if he were intending finding for us a son-in-law? I don't understand it. He said he would do all for our Emma. He must mean to marry...'

'He is to marry a duke's daughter,' Margaret hissed into his speech with an emphatic, silencing nod. 'Emma has that news from his own relations!'

Emma's soulful golden eyes raised to her drop-jawed father and suddenly *she* understood. She understood very well. Richard's concern, his generosity to her parents were born out of the desire he felt for her. He had shown her so very explicitly how ardently he wanted her. That lust was still unassuaged. He still intended her as his paramour despite her defying him ever again to touch him. The interdict was empty bravado, and they both knew it. But, thinking sensibly of it now, he would never have installed her in that town house so close to his home. She had been introduced to his mother, his other relations. She had met his neighbours. They shared mutual friends and similar social standing. To flout convention and decency and house a genteel spinster locally for such an obvious purpose would never have been his intention. More discretion was called for to prevent embarrassing those he cared about.

If Richard found for her a puppet husband it need not interfere with his plans at all. She would gain acceptability and status through marriage, and he would gain a mistress and copper-mining rights when he wed his heiress. Heaven only knew that such alliances were forged time and again throughout polite society: marriages brokered for money and pedigree that allowed men freedom to seek diversion elsewhere. It gave him access to any children of their union, too. If he appointed their nominal father, it would set his mind at rest that they would remain well cared for should he later distance himself.

'He must be lying about lasting provision! He has tricked me from hiding and will never settle my duns. I shall still face the Fleet.'

'No, Papa,' Emma reassured him huskily. 'He does not lie. If he has said he will discharge your debts and provide for you, then he will. He had already offered me lasting provision...weeks ago when first we met in Bath.' Emma felt blood seeping into her cold complexion as her parents' eyes swivelled to her.

'Why would he do that?' Frederick asked, frowning.

'Why do you think, you fool?' Margaret snapped. She looked at her daughter and moistened her lips. 'And how did you respond to that, Emma?'

'I said, no,' Emma flung back immediately.

Margaret straightened the lap of her gown, smoothed it. 'If an agreeable gentleman could be found who would marry you and welcome Sir Richard's discreet...arrangement,' she stated matter-of-factly, with a shrewd peer at her daughter's flushing complexion, 'what would you say then?'

Emma sprang to her feet, whirled to face her mother, and then found no rebuke could be forced past the throb of anger and sorrow in her throat. 'I don't know what to say anymore,' she finally whispered back at them, before quitting the parlour to seek the peace of her chamber.

* * *

'There is a gentleman below to see you, Miss Emma,' Polly informed her softly, with a peek about her bedroom door.

Emma raised her head away from the pillow to blink at her mother's maid. Since her parents had quit the house for an afternoon stroll, in the hope of being confused with any other happy and harmonious couple, Emma had been fitfully snoozing fully clothed on top of her bed's counterpane.

Her heart leaped to her mouth at this unexpected visitor. Had Richard finally come? It was two days since the fracas at Vauxhall Gardens. She had not seen him since he had sent her home with his friend, although she knew he had returned to see her that night while she slept.

'Who is it, Polly?'

'A Mr Trelawney, Miss Emma.' The young girl chuckled saucily. 'A very handsome, charming gentleman, Miss Emma.'

'Oh, yes...' Emma agreed wryly, with an indulgent look as Polly coloured to her hair-roots for having so boldly voiced her opinion. It wasn't the gentleman she was hoping for, Emma realised. Nonetheless, her spirits lifted as she swung her legs to the floor then tidied her thick glossy hair and her crumpled gown.

'Mr Trelawney, how nice to see you,' she greeted a few minutes later. 'I am so glad you are come so I can thank you for the great service you did me.'

Ross took her hands as they were extended and raised them to his lips. 'Think nothing of it, Miss Worthington,' he said affably. More gravely he continued, 'My only regret is that I didn't happen upon you a few moments sooner and save you this.' A dark finger just touched the fading bruising on her cheek. 'Now we're well acquainted, perhaps we should be a little less formal. I'd like it if you called me Ross.'

'Thank you, Ross. Please call me Emma,' Emma agreed, with a little dip of her burnished tawny head. She anxiously looked him over. He seemed virtually unscathed apart from a light swelling beneath one eye. 'Are you recovered? You took such a nasty blow...'

Ross raised fingers to press at the back of his skull as though testing his fitness himself. 'I'm fine,' he said, with a laugh. 'My mother says I must have stone for bone, judging from the amount of times I've limped home and frightened her witless, then been up bright and early demanding breakfast.'

'Your poor mama...' Emma murmured, not wholly in jest.

Ross grimaced his chagrin. 'You are looking very fine, if I might say so. Are you feeling better?'

'I am much better...much wiser too.' A bashful look accompanied, 'I must own to behaving with idiotic recklessness over the past weeks. I feel very ashamed at having put your life at risk because of it.'

'I've risked my life lots of times, Emma,' she was gently reassured. 'And for far less worthy reasons.'

'Thank you for your chivalry, sir,' Emma said. Then, to ease the solemnity, she asked, 'May I get you some tea? Or a little wine? I believe we have some cognac now our deliveries have been made...'

'No...nothing, thank you.' Ross soothed her agitated need to supply him with refreshment. 'I have just come to bid you farewell...until we again meet. And I'm certain we will. I am journeying west. I shall take your friend, Matthew, home to Bath now he is recuperated— Oh, I am bid to convey his warmest regards— After that, I promised to call in again on my brother, Luke, and his family at Brighton; then on home to Cornwall.'

'Please return my good wishes to Matthew and say I shall soon write to him.' He was another gentleman who was owed apologies, Emma sorrowfully realised. He had been abducted and ill-treated simply because she had unwittingly drawn him into Dashwood's web of malice and revenge.

'Are you wondering where Richard is?' Ross shrewdly interpreted her melancholy mien.

Emma flushed and forced a vague smile at his unexpectedly direct question. 'Yes...no...' she flustered. 'That is...I'm aware he is a businessman and has things he must do. He is no doubt occupied...'

'Yes, he is. He's away from London for a few days but he will shortly be back. I know he intends coming to see you as soon as he is able.' Ross knew very well that his friend couldn't return from finishing matters with Dashwood soon enough. He also knew that not finishing the blackguard off permanently would prove a constant trial for Richard.

When Ross had taken his leave Emma felt oddly restless as though already missing his company. She returned, sighing, to her room and paced it aimlessly. Her head dropped despairingly back and she frowned at a blurry, fragmented ceiling, wishing that this awful feeling that she no longer controlled her life would go away.

Only a month ago she had been so confident and decisive. Any problem was logically scrutinised for a fitting solution. Now she felt incapable of analysing the gains and losses of being paired off with a stranger so the man she loved could dally with her. Yet in her soul whispered the truth: the gentlemen might remain blasé, but she was no sophisticate; it would finish for her in heartache. So her conscious thoughts simply skimmed the surface of it all, while she wished for someone she trusted to tell her what to do...to help her balance what she could reasonably expect with what she yearned for. And there was only one such confidante.

With a sigh she found her carpet bag and the few things she wanted to take with her and then sat at her writing desk to try and find words to explain to her parents why she must again be gone for a while.

An unsteady brown hand rasped over a shady, angular jaw. 'Something must have prompted her to leave today. What was it this time?'

Margaret shrugged. 'Who is to know, Sir Richard?' was sighed out in a martyred tone. 'It seems each time I tender sensible advice she sulks or runs away. I am done with trying to help...'

'That sounds very sensible,' Richard concurred exceedingly softly. 'What wise counsel were you offering?'

Margaret looked warily at his hard, sardonic face. 'Why, I simply promoted what you endorsed yourself, sir. You said you would assist in finding for her a respectable husband, did you not?'

A metallic glare was turned on her and then his eyes closed and he smothered a groaning blasphemy. With a defeated sigh and weary shake of his head he made for the door, Margaret close to his heels.

'My maid tells me a Mr Trelawney visited while I was out. Perhaps she has gone with him. He might be the person she alludes to in her note.'

'No, he is not.' Richard felt his insides twisting. Emma's distress and confusion had been apparent in each neatly scripted word in her note yet her mother didn't even know her well enough to realise that 'seeking advice from a good friend' meant she was travelling into Hertfordshire.

'What will you do, Sir Richard? Will you search for her? If you find her, what will you say?'

Richard barked a laugh. 'I've no idea, Mrs Worthington. What would Mr Darcy say, do you think?' he savagely mocked himself. 'Would that I knew.'

'Mr Darcy? He of the novel she reads, you mean? Of what importance is he?'

'None, I hope...' Richard said.

She decided against purchasing a drink in the tavern. The mail coach driver had said it would be but a short wait for the large bay to be reshod and then they would be back on the road to Hertford. They had been travelling for four hours and had so far made very good time. Emma hoped to reach her destination a little after seven this evening. To occupy herself she walked towards the stables, reminiscing on the last time she had peered over a stall and caught sight of Star's golden flanks gleaming in the shadows. She ambled the ramshackle building idly observing horses being groomed or munching at their feed. She gained the last stall, about to glance in, but her attention was diverted to a racing curricle just turning in in a spray of gravelly dust...and then she flew backwards, heart pumping.

She must be mistaken, she impressed upon herself as she steadied her breathing. Just because she'd momentarily glimpsed a flash of very blond hair and an expensive equipage, it didn't mean... She surreptitiously peeked about the side of the stables again. The dusty curricle was by the tavern entrance; only the tiger was with it; the driver was nowhere to be seen. He had gone within, Emma realised, expelling some breath, and she was being ridiculous. And then he came without and she stared at him.

His impressive height and broad shoulders, the elegant cut of his dark clothes, the pearly sheen on his long hair as he abruptly swung his head to say something to someone standing behind tightened a knot of bitter-sweet melancholy. And she was suddenly aware she had travelled into Hertfordshire for no real reason.

She needed no advice. As she indulged in hungrily watching him, unseen, she knew there was only one sensible conclusion to be drawn: for once he touched her again she would want him for ever. She would want that tender loving he had promised her, would want it until she died. She would want him there in the mornings, to talk of his family, to talk of their family...of their children and how they did with their lessons...how tall they were getting. She would want him to proudly listen to their daughter sing or play the piano. She would want to see him soothe their son's scraped knees as she had seen him tend to his nephew... She would want it all and have none of it. Perhaps not even keep him very long at all. And when that time came she might shatter into pieces and beg and weep, then watch him from shadows as he and a duke's daughter reared heirs.

Earlier that day Ross had told her that Richard was away from London for a while and foolishly she had given little thought to where. Naturally, he would visit his close friend, Viscount Courtenay, as soon as he was able. He was probably now returning to London having spent time with Victoria and David. And in her haste to escape him and seek her dear friend's counsel she had unwittingly followed him to the very same place. A hand covered her face and she laughed, shook with soundless hysteria at the awful farce of it.

'If you loiter about the stables someone might take you for a horse thief.'

'If you loiter about lone women someone might take you for a philanderer.' She composed her features, abruptly dropping her hands from her face, and looked up at him, wishing she'd been aware of his approach.

He gave her a slow, devastating smile. 'Well, we both know we're reformed characters, Emma...so what matter what anyone else thinks?'

Emma busied herself tidying her hair, straightening her cloak. 'What an odd coincidence,' she brightly remarked. 'I am just on my way to see Victoria. I expect you must be just returning from visiting David. I intended to write you a brief note thanking you for all your assistance with...Dashwood...and my papa and...Matthew. I expect I still shall once I am home. But for now, thank you very much, sir. And it was nice to see Ross earlier, before he left for Cornwall... Oh, and now I must go, too...the coach is about to leave, I see.' She made to sweep past him but he took a step sideways so she careered into him.

'Damn the coach! If you once more travel alone on public conveyances...!'

Emma backed away. 'I have to go!' she cried with the anger of desperation.

'Very well, go! Go away! I give up!' He flung his hands into the air in sheer exasperation as he spun away from her. Turning back almost immediately, he withdrew from his pocket a silver clip of bank notes. Taking a hand, he placed the cash on her palm then closed her fingers over it. 'Take some money for incidentals. Go and visit Victoria then go home. I've not recently seen David but I know he will insist on you being accompanied back to Cheapside. I promise I won't trouble you while you stay with them...I won't trouble you ever again.'

With that he abruptly left her and strode towards the tavern.

Stunned, Emma watched his broad, black-jacketed back for a moment and then rushed after him. 'I can't possibly...I can't accept your money. It's not...not right...'

'No one but us will know,' he replied coolly without slowing his pace. 'You're under no obligation; treat it as a loan, if you prefer. Go. I swear I will never trouble you again.'

Emma looked glassily at the notes in her hand then at the door closing as Richard entered the tavern. The coachman was waving and beckoning, indicating that they were ready to leave. She dithered on the spot, swinging her gaze between the tavern and the vehicle. The horses stamped restlessly and she saw one of the coach passengers poke her head through the window to glare in irritation at her.

Emma shook her head at the driver and he carelessly shrugged his caped shoulders and shouted something to the groom.

Emma watched her carpet bag hit the ground.

Chapter Fifteen

The savoury aroma inside the tavern reminded Emma of Mrs Keene's boarding-house 'specials' and that prompted a less pleasant memory: her mean abuse of Richard's generosity under the prim guise of altruism. She squirmed anew with remorse, his cash suddenly singeing her hand. It was hastily shoved into her cloak pocket as she peeked into a room. Two dour-faced peasants swivelled their heads, aiming clay pipes at her. She withdrew and moved on, the scent of more mellow tobacco leading her to a small sitting-room and drawing her hesitantly within.

He was sitting close to the hearth, his blond head turned towards the fire. One hand had dropped over the chair arm and between long fingers a smoke-curling cigar was slanted at the floor. His other hand propped a bronzed jaw. She sensed he was aware of her presence but chose to dismiss it.

'I...I thought you must be travelling back from visiting David...but you said you've not seen him.' Emma ventured a little conciliatory conversation.

Richard's hand rose from the oak boards and he drew on the cheroot until it glowed red but he didn't turn his head.

'Please don't ignore me. I want you to talk to me...' she said, voice quavering, hating trying so hard to make him look at her.

'Are you going to reciprocate and talk to me?' he asked levelly, watching the flickering flames. 'Or are you going to ignore questions you don't like?'

'Why are you here?' she asked, immediately avoiding answering him.

An acknowledging smile twisted his lips. 'You know why, Emma,' he mildly reproved. 'The first time we met in Bath, you fled. You've not stopped running since and I've not stopped chasing you from place to place.' He drew deeply on the cigar again then pitched it towards the grate. 'But no more.'

Oddly disturbed by that gruff, determined vow, she bristled defensively. '*I* never wanted you to follow me. I didn't expect to see you at Mrs Keene's or at the Fallow Buck...or even at Vauxhall Gardens. I certainly never expected to see you here.'

Richard laughed wryly at the ceiling. 'Of course you did. That note you left made more sense to me than your mother. But, as I said, I'm no longer playing games. I give up. I'm a thirty-three-year-old baronet with, I hope, a certain dignity and status to uphold. And you're an intelligent woman of advanced years, as you're wont to constantly remind me. It's time to act with a little more maturity.' A hand was extended sideways; his long fingers beckoned.

Emma slowly approached. She withdrew the silver note clip from her pocket and placed the money lightly on his palm.

Richard looked at it, and then at her. 'Thank you, Emma,' he said with studied politeness. He pocketed it, then determinedly drew her down to kneel by his chair. 'Let's reminisce,' he urged in a voice as thick and sweet as honey. 'I believe you omitted to mention the most vital stage of the chase. By my recollection, I followed you to the Fallow Buck...then you stole my horse and I trailed you to Abbey Wood where you ran away again...'

'How...how did you know I was travelling into Hertfordshire?' Emma hastily gabbled into his disturbingly comprehensive recollection.

'Your mother showed me the note you'd written. What about your future worries you?'

Emma blinked, seeking some way to prevaricate, and she was aware of him watching her, expecting her to do just that. So she settled on candour. 'My parents told me you would assist in finding me a husband to provide security and so on,' she stiffly explained. 'I must thank you for your trouble in that, too. I know it to be a very sensible course of action. Just as I have come to realise it was foolish wanting to seek advice from Victoria. At my age, I should be able to decide my own future...and now I have.'

Glossy amber eyes rose to his impassive dark face. He was waiting for her to elaborate, so, with a brisk lightness, she did. 'I have always been independent, and keen to travel. I have seen little of anywhere outside London. It is time I broadened my horizons,' she informed him, with a small, firm smile. 'I should like to visit some of the north of England. I have read of moors and rugged landscape which is spectacular...quite wild. So I shall, after all, be travelling to Derbyshire via London...taking the scenic route, I believe you said. And, of course, as I am judged to be a lady of educated pursuits, I will manage to earn a living of some sort, while I do a little exploring...' Her voice wobbled but her little smile was unwavering.

'That's what you think you should do, is it?' Richard said quietly. 'Tell me, what do you think I should do? Just let you go?'

A golden gaze bathed his unshaven jaw, his long-lashed, low-lidded eyes, silver barely discernible. He looked very tired and drawn. A pang of inexorable affection made her fingers tremble; they wanted to graze over his skin, touch the wound just visible beneath a fringe of silky silver hair: she wanted to soothe him. Then she realised what must be worrying him.

Drawing on her new, constrained maturity, she quickly explained, 'Oh, you need not fret that I... I am certain now that I...I am not with child. I wanted to let you know that I would never have met with Dashwood had the possibility still existed,' she finished, with a warm blush.

'I wish the possibility did still exist.'

There was such husky sincerity in the statement that she shot a searching glance his way. Why had he said that? Because she would be unbruised had she still been unsure of her condition?

'You've not answered me, Emma. What is there for me if you go away?' Desire harshened his face, burned coal in his eyes. Long fingers stirred in her hair, moved to caress her neck.

Oh, he wanted her still! But what loss was he rueing? she indignantly wondered. A mistress he'd not quite done with? Would that lust endure once he found another young courtesan to occupy his town house? Or would he then be happy enough for her to play the loyal wife to the husband he allocated?

'What is there for you, sir?' she echoed, with ungovernable shrill bitterness. 'I hear there is a duke's daughter and copper-mining rights and a small fortune to add to what you already have. I trust that is an acceptably adult understanding of your prospects...' She snapped back her tawny head, and sparking feline eyes raked his face.

Richard stared at her then tipped back his head and barked a laugh. 'Thank God for that! You're jealous,' he muttered in obvious relief. 'For a moment I really believed you intended going to Derbyshire to search for Darcy and Pemberley.'

He abruptly stood up, lifting her with him. 'It seems to me, Miss Worthington, we might fare better if we ignore gossip. Who told you about a duke's daughter? Amelia?'

Emma nodded, confused by his mild amusement.

'I never seriously considered marrying her, Emma, even for that copper lode,' he softly reassured her. 'How could I? I don't love her. Now David and Stephen have set this damnable precedent of love matches...immature as it may seem...it's all that will do. I know that's all you want.'

She swallowed painfully, her eyes magnetised by his, her mind in limbo...waiting.

A dark finger reached out, touched her face gently. 'That's why I'm hoping you'll accept the husband I've found for you, for he really does love you so much. And he's sure, when you've forgiven him for that callous seduction, you'll tell him that you love him, too.'

Emma forced herself back from him. 'Don't say that...it's not true...it's cruel...' she choked. The palm of a small hand cupped her swimming eyes.

A silence, solid with tension, finally fissured as he said coolly, 'I could have told you ages ago. From the moment I saw you sitting in the hallway at South Parade, I knew I'd never again let you go. Do you know why I said nothing? I was frightened you'd spurn me like this. I knew you'd think me an unprincipled liar plotting to lure you into my decadent clutches...just for a short while, of course, until I found someone new and ejected you into the gutter. That's accurate, isn't it?'

Emma turned sideways, arms crossed over her middle, head back as she fought for composure.

'Come, admit it. It's how you read my character three years

ago and how you see me now. I'm a selfish rake, so how could I possibly love you...or any woman? The truth is, Emma, I can't love any woman...just you, it seems. And the truth is, I've treated all those women to consideration and generosity if not to much time or affection. And the truth is, if I could change all of it, boast a history of dignified abstinence in the wilds of Derbyshire, I would do it for you. But I can't. And I won't lie. I regret some of my past; that's all I can say. You're my future. I love you. And I know you love me.'

'How do you know?' whispered out of her.

'You could have run the other way,' he said, with a quirk of a smile. 'But you didn't. You ran at me because you trusted me...because you loved me.'

Their eyes locked timelessly, then, because she knew it was all truth, because he never lied, the tears finally spilled and her joy frothed into an explosive sob that squeezed tight her eyes.

Richard approached her slowly, stopped inches away. 'Say you love me or I won't hold you,' he threatened softly.

She leaned into him, crying.

'Say it!' erupted in a pleading growl.

'I love you...' she wailed, and was lifted off the ground and crushed to a broad, muscular torso. Fair and tawny hair mingled as he bent close, soothing her, whilst spinning them slowly about in sheer thankful happiness.

'We were reminiscing...where were we?' he said as she quietened and clung to him. 'Ah, yes, Abbey Wood where you ran away again and I caught you...and proved to us both, without a shadow of a doubt, that you were absolutely right. I am a novice.'

Emma's limpid golden eyes lifted to smoky grey, identifying pain behind his rueful humour. She shook her head. 'I didn't think that, Richard. I didn't think that at all.'

'I did,' he said huskily. 'The one time in my life when I needed it to be right and it all went so wrong. The one time, too, I merited being slapped but you were too anguished to do it and that terrified me. I thought I'd cowed you. The shame wasn't yours, sweetheart. It was mine. I swear I'll never again hurt you...'

'You didn't hurt me much,' Emma whispered, shielding her pink face with a hard shoulder. 'Not in the way you mean... It was a different hurt...more in my heart. And I don't blame you:

I'd made you think I was unchaste and I wanted you...I said so...'

'I never gave you a chance to deny me. I only asked for consent when positive the seduction was done.' He sighed in remorse. 'I was furious with you, Emma,' he rawly admitted. 'When Stephen told me of the gossip circulating that evening in the Assembly Rooms, I knew it referred to you: you'd absconded from London and Dashwood, and I knew him for a sadistic fornicator. It all seemed to fall so logically into place. I was sure he must have violated you. And the galling thought of perhaps rearing his male child as my heir was racking me as I tracked Shah... Yet by the time I caught up with you I had become reconciled even to that: I loved you and would marry you no matter what. Then you seemed to defend him, which made me angrier... When I discovered you'd deceived me all along about being any man's lover...that I'd agonised needlessly over rearing any man's bastard as my own...I was too mad with relief and frustration to know what I was doing. It was impossible to decide whether to reward or punish you. So I veered between the two, I suppose, like a demented fool.' He laughed against her soft, thick hair. 'I told you you'd render me insane, Miss Worthington. And so it proved.'

'That's how it seemed, Richard,' Emma whispered with bashful wonderment. 'Exactly like that. As though you were both rewarding and punishing me. It was really quite...'

'Tell me, Emma, please. I need to know.'

'It was really quite...thrilling...unique, perhaps, for I've nothing to compare...' She glanced at him, horrified by what they were discussing, and her face flamed. 'I must be a terrible wanton to speak so...'

Long fingers threaded into her amber hair. 'No, you're not. Not yet...but with all that passion in you I'm optimistic...' As a small fist thumped his arm he grunted a laugh. 'It was thrilling and unique and unbearably erotic...just like you. But I swear it will be sweeter next time.'

Richard studied her beatific face, watched curiosity and shyness flit across her beautifully expressive features. He touched his mouth to the small, healing cut on her lower lip. 'Say you'll marry me—Emma, please. Put me out of my misery. I don't want to resort to blackmail and threaten your father with the Fleet.'

'That's not blackmail, sir, it's almost an inducement.' She sighed. 'I can't believe any sensible man would want my parents as his in-laws...'

'But I'm not sensible, sweetheart. I'm completely mad about you.'

She snuggled against him. 'I suppose I'll marry you, then,' she teased. 'Might we journey on the little way further to David and Victoria and let them be the first to know?'

At his smiling agreement, she queried brightly, 'If I'd boarded the coach would you have followed? Or had you really decided to give up?'

'I never expected you to leave. I was quite confident you'd never accept my money. Failing that, gentleman that I am, I would have given you a ten-minute head start.'

Dusky-fringed topaz eyes narrowed at him. 'You're very crafty...'

A smile impenitently acknowledged it. 'Are you grateful I don't give up?'

Emma nodded, blushing as his eyes became sultry.

'Show me,' he whispered huskily against her full, soft lips.

And with diligent inexpertise she did exactly that.

Shining amber and ebony tresses fluttered and tangled as Emma and Victoria whirled about joyfully then warmly embraced. Victoria spun Emma about again. Coming to a breathless halt, she blurted, 'Oh, it's so wonderful to see you, Em. Why did you not write and say you were coming? This is such a wonderful surprise! Oh, I just can't believe it. David!' she abruptly called. She peered past Emma along the Italian marble and mahogany hallway of her opulent home at the blond man smiling indulgently at them. 'And Dickie is with you! Why? How intriguing...David...*David*!' she squealed excitedly.

'What is it, Vicky?' A man's fond, firm baritone was heard as a door opened. David Hardinge, Viscount Courtenay emerged into the hallway in his shirt-sleeves, a black Labrador at each heel, looking for all the world like a contented country gentleman.

'Emma is here,' his lovely wife squeaked, with a double-handed indication. 'And Dickie, too!'

David stared, frowning, then a slow grin spread over his handsome features and he paced into the hallway. He stooped to embrace and kiss Emma on both cheeks then carried on walking.

He circled Richard, looking him up and down, then blue eyes targeted his friend's face. 'You look like a heathen with that ungodly colour. I told you you'd stay there too long. You should have come back last year, when you said you would.'

'Hello, David, it's good to see you, too,' Richard returned drily. He extended a hand as David did, gripped and embraced him in perfect unison, felt no embarrassment at the surge of emotion that tightened his chest, blocked his throat, clamped shut his eyes, for he was aware that David felt it equally. When finally they broke apart, David slid a hand to his shoulder, shook him with profound affection and croaked, 'It's been too long, Dickie. You're a bastard! You promised you'd be back last year.'

'I'm back now,' Richard said. 'I'm back for good.'

David smiled in understanding. 'I told you she liked you. I told you that three years ago.'

'I remember; I just wish you'd told me how much,' Richard laughed, as his grey eyes strayed past to linger lovingly on Emma.

'Ah, but that was for you to find out, my friend,' David said softly. 'Bit of a battle, was it?' he asked, with an elevation of his dark brows indicating he'd noticed the wound on Richard's head and his general air of fatigue. 'Come, let's find somewhere comfortable to sit and something ancient and alcoholic with which to celebrate. You can tell me all about it while the girls gossip. You're going to be a godfather again...' David added brightly.

Richard looked at him, then at Victoria, and he shook his head emotionally. 'That's marvellous!'

Richard lifted his feet to rest them on the small table close to David's. They were seated outdoors on the flare-lit, flagged terrace that ran the length of the southerly wing overlooking magnificent formal gardens that marched off into shadows. He sank back in the comfortable chair, threw back his pale head and studied the night sky.

The breathtaking beauty of it struck him anew as he pondered the many times that he and this man had sat beneath it together: in amicable contentment, as they did now, when no words were necessary; in appalling anguish as they had on battlefields a decade and more ago, when no words were possible. Then there were the numerous occasions between those polar instances when wenching, drinking, brawling in their youth. He lifted his glass to his lips, drew on his cheroot, then asked David, 'What are you thinking?'

There was a pause before David replied, 'I'm thinking if it wasn't for you I'd have nothing. No life... I owe everything I've got to you...'

A dark hand came out and comfortingly gripped his friend's forearm resting on the chair beside him. 'It was a long time ago and I would have expected the same from you...you know that.' With sublime disparity he added, 'Besides, you taught me about investing in stocks and shares.'

After a little undisturbed drinking and smoking, David asked, 'What are *you* thinking?'

Richard turned his head and smiled crookedly. 'I'm thinking, if I'm perfectly honest, you drove me to such distraction with your antics, I came close to killing you myself on occasion.'

'What are you really thinking?' David asked mildly.

'I'm thinking I've never felt so bloody done up.'

'I remember that...' David said with a huge grin. 'Courting can be hellish hard work.'

Richard smiled at the stars. 'I'm also thinking you must have a few interconnecting chambers in this damned great place of yours.'

'Victoria allocates guest rooms, Dickie,' his friend solemnly teased. 'Nothing to do with me which room you get.'

'Make it to do with you,' Richard mock-threatened, 'or I might remind you you owe me everything.'

'You sound desperate...'

Richard sat forward abruptly and shoved vibrating fingers under his friend's face. 'Look at that!'

David obligingly inspected his friend's shaking hand. 'Nasty graze,' he observed. 'I hope Dashwood's looking a worse mess.'

'Dashwood's looking a corpse; and that's what he should be...' was gritted out in response.

'No,' David said gently. 'Trelawney was right. I wouldn't have let you kill him either. If you had, it would have ruined everything. It would have tainted your future with Emma. You've done the right thing.'

Closely watching Richard's rigid profile, David asked quietly, 'You're happy enough, though?'

Richard stared into his glass, stared at a velvet blue, diamantéd horizon. 'Happier than I've ever been. It's like finally finding peace...it's hard to explain...'

David nodded. 'I know,' he said huskily. 'That's exactly it. And in a moment that peace will take us inside. We'll retire before midnight, whereas once we'd have set out about now and returned watching the dawn come up, trailing empty bottles.'

Richard sank back into his chair, shaking with cathartic hilarity that bordered on hysteria, and the infectious sound soon had David guffawing too. The tension of the past torturous, hectic weeks finally released, Richard gasped, wiping at his eyes, 'Perhaps it's just our age, Davey...we're not getting any younger.'

David shook his head, smiling nostalgically. 'We had some good times,' he stressed slowly. 'Some damn good times...'

'Yes...' Richard agreed, with a far-away smile. 'Definitely plenty to tell the grandchildren...'

'Well...grandsons, perhaps....' David corrected him with a wry grimace.

And with that they shoved back their chairs and strolled into the grand house, two black dogs padding after them.

'And then what happened?' Victoria whispered, agog, her eyes fixed on her friend's lightly bruised face as Emma came close to concluding her narrative of the action that had buffeted her between heartache and heaven over the past weeks.

'My papa says that Dashwood still lives but has been dealt with. I've not had a chance to ask Richard exactly how. On the way here we barely spoke two words...' She shot an expressive glance at Victoria. 'It's possible to drive a curricle and pair one-handed, you know; or get the tiger to take the reins.'

'I do know,' Victoria said, with a shrewd little smile. 'It's amazing how very ingenious an amorous man can be. Oh, no, that he's ever had any practice whatsoever, you understand, in kissing and cuddling while keeping a straight path on the road,' was added ironically.

Emma gave a little laughing scowl. 'They are so very alike, aren't they?'

'Indeed; that's why you have nothing to fret over. They do reform, you know. David is perfect in every way: a wonderful husband and a doting papa.'

As the last pitcher of steaming water filled the porcelain tub, Victoria dismissed the servants then helped her friend disrobe.

Emma sank into the luxury of warm, perfumed water, sighing as it lapped at her weary body. 'But I'm so glad Richard did not kill Dashwood,' she murmured sleepily. 'It would have over-shadowed all this bliss.'

Victoria rhythmically soaped Emma's creamy, slender back with scented soap. 'Well, I'm sure Richard has taught him a good lesson! David says Dickie can be a vicious fighter. The vile man will never again dare bother you.'

As Emma dipped her head, Victoria gently poured a stream of warm water over her long, amber hair. She leaned forward and whispered, 'You sly thing! Why did you never let on that you liked Dickie? You never had a good word for him. You always said you thought him a disgraceful libertine.'

Emma shook back dripping tan tresses, making Victoria squeal as the droplets scattered over her face and gown. 'And so he is!' Emma endorsed fiercely. Then she sighed, 'But I love him any-way. I expect I'd love him even if he didn't reform...and that's quite worrying.'

'He *is* a fine gentleman, Emma,' Victoria quietly reassured her. 'I love him myself for he brought David home from the war alive when he wanted to die on foreign soil. I've never made much of it to you before because you seemed to hold Dickie in such disfavour. Besides, Dickie never willingly speaks of it and it's almost like breaking a confidence. He is not one to brag so I shall tell you what sort of heroic man your future husband is. When I wed my first husband—in David's absence abroad, and in ignorance of him still loving and wanting to marry me—David was so mad with grief he returned to the battlefields. He delib-erately sought out peril and Richard followed, shielding him until he could bring them both back safely...to a heroes' welcome. I owe Dickie so much—all my happiness—and I'm so glad my best friend is to have him. I couldn't wish for more. You make such an excellent couple and I'm so happy for you I feel I could burst.'

Emma closed hot, wet eyes. 'I'm not surprised at his courage,' she gasped. 'I know he is a worthy man. In truth, he always attracted me far too much. I understand that now. But I never believed he would sincerely notice me and I couldn't bear being just another conquest. I feel…felt so vulnerable when with him. So I would never allow him close. I think part of me always knew, once we touched, he could shatter all my defences and make me do anything he asked.'

Victoria put a hand to her dewy eyes. Laughing and sniffing, she said, 'Neither of us must say anything else likely to make the other blub.' Briskly she added, 'Now let me tell you happy news: David is to again be a papa.'

Emma touched Victoria's arm with a damp hand. 'I'm so pleased for you, Vicky. I'm so pleased for me, too. Despite everything, it has all turned out so right for us both.'

'Begging pardon, your ladyship,' one of the young maids meekly interrupted. 'His lordship wants to speak to you downstairs,' she informed Victoria with a deferential little bob.

'David probably wants to show Lucy to her godfather. If she is awake I shall bring her in to you, too, before you retire.'

With a huge, warm towel draping her slender curves, Emma dismissed the young maid with a smile and murmur of thanks. She sat on the high feather mattress dabbing at her damp hair and body. She shook out the nightclothes Vicky had found for her, thinking of Richard, and the need to see him once more before she slept had her sinking slowly backwards onto the bed, eyes closed. She turned onto her side, peeping through drowsy lids at a star-studded night. Nestling her head into the pillow, she smiled softly, privately, realising she had never felt more languidly tranquil.

As she heard the door click, she murmured, 'Is Richard yet retired, Vicky? I'd really like to wish him goodnight.'

'Good. He really wants to let you do so,' came back softly.

Emma shot upright on the bed, damp towel clutched tightly. She moistened her lips as he walked slowly into the candlelit room. He had never before seemed so tall, so blond, so hand-some...or so devastatingly predatory.

'Richard...I...I just wanted to say goodnight and...'

As he passed the tub he dipped his hand into the water, testing it.

'Good, it's still warm.'

Emma stared at him as he began to loosen his cravat then dropped it to the floor. His jacket soon followed and she realised what he intended. 'Richard...!' she squealed in a gulp. 'I don't think you should. You shouldn't be here! It's not seemly... You can't! The servants might gossip. David and Victoria might be embarrassed...'

Naked to the waist, he reached her and stooped to lightly brush his brandy-scented mouth over hers. 'Hush. I just want to hold you, that's all. I want to sleep with you in my arms. As far as the servants are concerned, we're married; it's only a few days before the event. And don't fret over David,' he added with a crooked smile. 'Nothing embarrasses him.'

Within a moment more he was blithely lowering his awe-somely powerful physique into the tub, with a long exhalation of sheer ease.

Emma watched him with a mingling of horror and fascination. She knew he had been naked in the woods when he'd made love to her—in retrospect she had wondered how on earth he had managed to shed even his shirt when she couldn't clearly recall him releasing her long enough to undo one button—but she had seen little of him, her eyes had been closed so much. Now, as he began soaping himself, she let the towels clutched to her drop, and hastily pulled the embroidered lawn nightgown over her head. Once decently attired, she approached the tub and sank down behind him.

Richard continued bathing, almost as though he was unaware of her proximity, so, retrieving the soap from the dish, she lath-ered an expanse of tanned torso, her fingertips exploring little dips and nicks here and there on his back. She noticed the large muscles in his broad shoulders flex as she began her ministra-tions.

'Do you like it when I touch you like this?' she asked curi-ously.

His silver head dipped at the water and he smiled. 'I love it when you touch me in any way, Emma.'

Emma dropped the soap to the dish and ran two slippery palms up the smooth, firm contours at either side of his spine. Large hands covered her fingers as they strayed playfully over his shoulders to splay on the satin-sheathed steel of his chest.

Emma frowned at the nasty lacerations across four knuckles. 'Your poor hand,' she sighed sorrowfully. 'It will never heal.'

He sank back into the tub and ebony-pupilled grey eyes caressed her. 'That's nothing, sweetheart. I've had far worse injuries than that.' He took her hand resting on the side of the bath and ran it over a faint, proud scar on a forearm. 'A piece of a Frenchman's bayonet is in there somewhere.' Raising her fingers, he pressed them to the base of his skull and she sensed the dip. 'A bullet in the Peninsular...'

He continued teaching her about his body via the wounds he'd sustained over the years. Finally, he slid her hand below the water and to his hip and moved her small fingers over a ragged cicatrice. She looked enquiringly at him. 'Another shrapnel wound?' she guessed.

'A broken bottle. I rolled on it while brawling in Cheapside. Close to your home as I recall. About fifteen years ago. The dolt of a physician who stitched it was more drunk than me. It never knitted properly.'

'I was twelve then. You were fighting outside my home when I was twelve...' Emma murmured.

'Shall I show you how much I want you, Emma?' he softly asked as his slate gaze roved over lambent amber eyes, the fluffy halo of damp fawn hair lightly curling and framing her pointed, pixie face.

At her almost imperceptible nod, she felt his fingers mesh with hers underwater, then he moved her hand so the back of it slowly skimmed the silky fever of erect manhood on its way back to the surface. She watched his reaction with awe. His eyes closed, his breathing ceased for that infinite moment and the planes of his lean, handsome face seemed equally stiff.

'Is this what a mistress does?' she whispered. 'Washes you and...touches you? I am your mistress now, aren't I?'

Eyes still closed, one side of his sensual mouth relaxed into a smile. 'You're my fiancée now. And I can't recall,' he mentioned with convenient amnesia, 'any mistress helping me bathe.'

Raising their clasped fingers, he kissed the back of her wet hand before letting it go and abruptly standing up. Emma averted her eyes hurriedly and handed him a towel. As he dried himself she wandered back to the bed and perched upon it, watching from beneath lowered lids...and thinking...thinking.

'It...it might be best if you return to your own chamber, Richard, now you have bathed... Please...'

He tucked a towel about his waist and proceeded to dry his hair as though he'd not heard her.

'There are still some things we should talk of before we again... That is...'

'What things?' flew out from beneath the towel over his head.

'I don't believe...I find it hard to believe that you truly love me,' she whispered raggedly.

As the towel was whipped from his hair and hurled towards a chair, Emma sprang to her feet, then sank back to shift uneasily on the mattress again.

'Why is that?' he enquired, dead calm.

'I've...I've treated you so badly,' she croaked. 'I've lied constantly, been deceitful, hit you and insulted you. I even swindled your money for those dinners at Mrs Keene's. Why would someone as worthy and generous as you love a person as mean as me?' she cried in anguish. 'And I'm not young or pretty...'

With a curse he crossed the room in two strides, so fast, she shot backwards to the centre of the enormous bed. With tender obstinacy, he pulled her to the edge. Lifting her, he carried her towards the pier-glass then spun her about to face it. A muscular brown arm banded her tight to his hard, hot body, her toes barely touching the floor, her nightdress askew and displaying the perfection of one long, lissom leg. 'What do you see?' he demanded.

When she tried to avoid looking at her reflection, a hand went to her face, tilting it up. 'Look, Emma,' he instructed hoarsely. 'Tell me what you see.'

Hesitantly she looked into the glass. Wide, dusky-fringed oval eyes stared back at her with the liquid profundity of precious stones. Her hair crumpled over the snowy cambric of her nightgown like amber satin and her complexion was tinged with a peachy blush.

Richard's hand framed her jaw, his thumb following the curve of her full lower lip. 'I'll tell you what I see, shall I? I see a woman who three years ago fascinated me because she, alone, shunned my company. She hinted that I was a shameless hedonist and she wanted nothing to do with me. And I knew then that she was special to me. Not just because she had the courage to tell me the truth but because she was beautiful. Not conventionally pretty, but uniquely beautiful. When I saw you dressed like this at Mrs Keene's boarding house that first evening in Bath, and you threatened to accuse me of rape, it was dangerously close to prophecy, Emma. I thought I'd never seen anything quite so tempting in my life. That's how you affect me. I've been fighting to keep my hands off you most of the time. Not touching you has been a constant ordeal. And you've known that. Deep down, in here...' he slid a possessive hand over a breast to rest on the quivering ribs beneath it '...you've known that very well. That's why you've insulted me and hit me and been deceitful; it's the only defence you've had and I've never once blamed you for using it.'

Emma's eyes rose to his in the glass and clung, adored him. 'I see a lovely, lucky woman and the wonderful man she loves...her Silver Squire.'

He smiled and dipped his head to rest a bronze cheek atop her tawny hair. She twisted immediately to face him, sliding her arms up around him and hugging him close, closer still as though she would fuse their bodies.

'I love you. Don't ever say again that I don't or that you're undeserving, or plain. Whatever rubbish your mother's drummed into you over your looks, is just that. Utter rubbish! You're the most beautiful thing I've ever seen,' he vowed huskily as he swung her up in his arms and carried her to the bed.

Chapter Sixteen

'What were you and Richard talking about?' Viscountess Courtenay asked her husband as he lounged, naked to the waist, on the edge of the bed, watching her brush her glossy jet hair.

'Business ventures we're contemplating, our misspent youth, women...that we love...' he tacked on with a teasing smile as he saw her eyes narrow and glide to his reflection in the dressing-table glass. 'And how inquisitive they become at entirely the wrong time. Your hair looks perfect, sweetheart. Come to bed,' he ordered huskily. When she still gazed dreamily into space he added, 'Oh, Dickie also told me that Wainwright and Mainwaring are coming to Hertfordshire to kidnap me and take me back to Mayfair and a life of vice.'

'Don't tell stories, David! I'm not prying...I'm just interested in your reunion with your best friend.'

'I never lie to you, Vicky,' he reminded her, with a smile.

Victoria rose from her stool, contentedly aware, as always, of her husband's deceptively sleepy blue gaze on her. 'Perhaps you manipulate the truth a little. I think they make an excellent couple.' She happily reverted to her original train of thought. 'I've never said so, because I thought Emma truly disliked him, and thus it would never be, but I've always hoped they would fall in love. I'm so happy tonight.'

'Me too. I'll be happier still when you come here.'

In obeisance, she gracefully swayed up the three steps to their decadently large four-poster. David lithely came upright; his hands shot out, were placed firmly on her hips, and directed her between his spaced feet. Her idle fingers combed through lengthy strands of dark hair while she smiled serenely into space. 'I could tell three years ago that Dickie was interested in getting to know her better. But then I couldn't be sure what was designed, so I said nothing to Emma. After all,' she remarked archly, 'the most honourable intentions sometimes, confusingly, masquerade as lechery...so *I've* found...so Emma, *also*, has found...' She squealed as a warm hand deftly breached her diaphanous nightgown. It ran possessively up a smooth, shapely leg on its way to cup and caress a pert derrière.

'But we're alike in other ways, too,' David purred. 'So you need not fret your friend might be seduced by my friend beneath our roof, then abandoned.'

'Richard does love her so very much, doesn't he? Oh...the deed is already done,' Victoria insouciantly added, with a flick of a slender white hand.

'Yes, he loves her utterly, and... Has he, indeed?' David grunted an approving, male laugh. 'He didn't tell me that.'

Victoria sighed with pleasure, her eyes drowsy, as a tender mouth steamed kisses against her lace-covered midriff and reverent fingers stroked her baby-rounded abdomen. 'Tell me what he did say,' she persevered.

'He wants to give her everything she's never had: beautiful clothes, fabulous jewels, whatever her heart desires.' Her doting husband truthfully indulged her curiosity.

Victoria smiled contentedly down at him. 'He *is* so like you. And Emma *is* like me. All she wants is Richard. She'd take him as a pauper.'

'I know. So does he. But it won't stop him wanting to give her the sun...the moon...the stars...'

Victoria placed her hands on her husband's broad, naked shoulders. They slid over his cool, solid flesh, then she pushed him down onto the bed and flopped on top of him. 'Oh, that's impossible, David!' she giggled as she enveloped him in silky, rose-scented skin and hair. 'You already gave those to me...'

'Will your mother be disappointed?'
'Disappointed? Why should she be?'

'I imagine she hoped you'd marry well,' Emma quietly mentioned. 'A duke's daughter would have been preferable to...' The rest was muffled by his body as he urged her closer, dropped a kiss on a crown of burnished coppery-gold hair resting against his shoulder.

'She's a little like your own dear mama in one respect: she's keen to see me wed; to whom matters little. She's seen David reform and, damn him,' he chuckled, 'ever since he renounced bachelorhood, I've been treated to veiled lectures on the redeeming effect of a good woman.'

At Emma's solemn silence he reassured her, 'She'll be delighted with her new daughter-in-law. She's often said how much she likes you. She realised straight away I cherished you but imagined it was a platonic love. Amelia let slip to her that you were in Bath because of a romantic attachment. Had she not, it would by now have occurred to my mother to put you in my way.'

'Do you really think so?' Emma asked doubtfully.

'Oh, yes,' he said drily. 'She said you'd make someone an excellent wife and that your beau would be a fool not to propose. She also said that with a little embellishment you'd be stunning.'

'What did you say?' Emma asked, unsure if she was pleased or mortified.

'I said I was confident you would soon be wed, and that it was pointless primping perfection.'

In thanks for the compliment, Emma languorously grazed her cheek against the masculine skin beneath it. 'I think our mothers mingling will result in a volatile reception. Might we wed quietly, Richard...and soon, and present them all with a *fait accompli*? Please?'

'Oh, yes,' he agreed, with a grunting laugh. 'Very quietly and very, very soon. Before we journey back to London or Silverdale. Perhaps in the chapel at Hartfield...as David and Vicky did. It would take but a few days to arrange, if you don't mind wearing a gown purchased locally. Vicky can attend you and David act as my groomsman.'

Emma closed her eyes, sighed her quiet rapture. 'I'm so happy, Richard.'

'Good,' he said huskily. 'Then I am, too.'

'Truly?'

'Truly.'

She shifted against him, her legs nudging his, almost accidentally. They had been lying wrapped together for so many long, blissful minutes while they talked, yet he'd made no attempt to kiss her properly or touch her. Had he meant what he said about simply wanting to hold her? Sleep with her in his arms? Part of her wanted that to be true...wanted to admire his noble restraint...and part of her wanted to demand he kiss her into insensibility. Now acknowledged, the longing niggled, making her fidget.

'Richard?'

'Mmm?'

'I'd like it if you kissed me goodnight.'

'I can't do that, sweetheart. Go to sleep.'

Stung into silence for a moment, she then gasped, 'Why not?' anxiously wondering whether she was ignorant of a physical reason preventing it.

'I can't lie in bed with you and kiss you...then stop. Just holding you so close is torture. You know how much I want you, Emma...I showed you,' he reminded her huskily.

After a throbbing quiet, Emma ventured demurely, 'Will you still cuddle me till I sleep?'

'You could have given my hard predicament a little more sympathetic thought, sweet.'

His low, velvety reproof, thick with need, made a delicious shiver ripple through her. And she *was* giving it thought...too much. She could scent rich earth, balmy night air; hear woodland musically sighing, while guttural noises rasped her throat. She could sense soft lips, hard fingers flowing over her, branding, tantalising... 'What have you done with Dashwood?' she distractingly burst out, reflexively clinging to him as her heart hammered with stimulation.

Mistaking her agitation for fright, strong arms and legs bound her to him, as though he would calm and protect her by merging their flesh. 'Don't worry about him, sweetheart. He's finished with.'

'But what have you done with him?'

'Sent him back to Jamaica. I'm sure there'll be a welcoming committee: newly freed slaves with memories of their own or their kins' dealings with him over two decades. They'll be anxious for a quick reunion.'

Thick sable lashes brushed up. She stared at the unaltered rhythmic rising and falling of bronze skin beneath her cheek, his warmth wafting a light herb scent of the water they had both bathed in. 'Will they kill him?'

'First chance they get.'

She pushed back from him and looked down into silver eyes, smoky in the muted glow of the candlelit chamber. He raised a hand, threaded it into her long amber hair, savouring the sensation of it streaming through the forks of his fingers. Smoothing it away from her face, he anchored its sheeny weight by winding it about a broad palm so her delicate, elfin features were revealed. 'Does that worry you? That people he has tormented and abused for years might finally settle scores?'

'I don't think so,' Emma whispered. 'I know now he is a very evil man. Had he managed to abduct me, he would have shown me no mercy...'

'Hush. Don't speak of it,' Richard groaned, drawing her down into the security of his arms. 'I can't bear to think of it. You asked me to verify his devilry and I stupidly said nothing. And it wasn't simply to avoid frightening you. If I'm truthful, resentment played a part. I was sure you believed me equally despicable. I should have told you that no gossip did justice to his depravity. It might have stopped you meeting him. Arrogantly, I trusted forbidding it would be adequate.'

'Don't blame yourself, Richard!' Emma cried, distraught on seeing his eyes glaze. 'I might not have heeded your warning, in any case: I so wanted to atone for my escapades that I acted with little sense or caution.' After a short pause, she quizzed, 'But how did you persuade him to go?'

'I gave him a choice: a little sojourn abroad while he licked his wounds and pondered the error of his ways or a magistrate and all the attendant ignominy of a prosecution for having Cavendish kidnapped and beaten, and for assaulting and plotting to abduct my fiancée. Once he'd obligingly burned that marriage contract he had no hard proof of being defrauded or that you were ever betrothed. He has always deluded himself he has some reputation and standing. He hates ridicule and would want none of this broadcast.

'His henchmen are probably gone to ground but with a little incentive they'd betray Dashwood and he knows it. He also knows my capacity for retribution is enduring and far outstrips his. That worries him the most: that I'll hound him to the grave. When I told him I intended soon marrying you, he was very keen to put distance between us.'

'I feel terribly guilty that Matthew was embroiled in this...'

'I'll make it up to him. Financially, he and his family will never want.'

Emma looked at his taut jaw, his eyes fixed on the pleated damask canopy above. As she wriggled closer, her silky tawny hair trailed his torso; tender lips touched a lean, brown cheek. 'I never really loved him, Richard. But he was a good friend. There's never been anyone else in all my life I've liked in that way. Except you, of course. But then that's so different...so much more...' She watched the tension in his face relax as she struggled to voice her devotion to him. 'Even three years ago you set my heart racing,' she shyly confided. 'Although I would have died rather than let you know, of course. I was sure you would never really be interested in me...and it hurt.'

'How interested did you want me to be, sweetheart?' he laughed. 'I almost proposed. David realised...probably before I did myself...that I'd fallen in love at first sight. I was captivated by everything about you: your looks, your wit...everything about you. What I should have done,' he said, with a thoughtful smile, 'was drag you over to your mother at that tedious soirée and offer for you there and then. I'm sure I would have got her approval.'

'*Approval?*' Emma choked. 'Oh, I *daren't* think! She might have dropped to the floor and kissed your feet...she *still* might!' she cried in genuine dread.

'If I'd asked you to marry me three years ago, would you have accepted?'

'Oh, yes; I would never have let you go. Had you reconsidered when sober, I would have sued you for breach of promise. I would have hounded *you*...chased *you* from place to place.'

'Sounds like heaven... If only I'd known...' he growled ruefully. 'So, in fact, Cavendish didn't figure too seriously even then,' he mused with an amount of masculine satisfaction.

'It was always just an infatuation. Have you never been enamoured, Richard?'

'I'm totally enamoured now.'

'You know I mean when you were younger.'

'In my impressionable youth I suppose I was regularly besotted with pretty opera dancers or opera singers...or their like...'

'How do you know you didn't love them all?' Emma asked, a trifle waspishly now she'd prised the revelation from him.

'Because it happened so regularly, sweetheart,' he said, with a wry laugh. 'After six months or so with a blonde I'd fancy a brunette, or they'd feel inclined towards someone richer, or someone offering commitment. It was all just a trade of basic needs. By the time I reached my late twenties it would never have occurred to me to still fool myself over motives.'

As Emma started to withdraw, his hands curved about the tops of her arms. He slid her on top of him, locking her slender, satiny legs under the hair-roughened, brawny length of his. 'Do you know what makes it all so insignificant, Emma?' he asked gently. 'In your dignified innocence you're more erotic than any of them...all of them.'

Emma dipped her face, then lambent doe eyes rose, met his, hoping to learn more.

'If I had no money at all, you'd stay. You love me touching you. You respond because you can't help it. You respond even when you'd rather not...and never because there might be clothes or cash or trinkets in it for you. You haven't the artifice to deny me until the price is right. Do you know how wonderful that makes me feel? How powerful? The money I gave you at the tavern kept you with me. But not as a bribe or as a payment. I knew you'd stay long enough to return it. With any other woman I've wanted they'd stay long enough to spend it. If I was dispossessed tomorrow I know I'd still have you in my bed, loving me. There's never been anyone else I could trust to stay in those circumstances. But, in truth, I've avoided those who might. I've chosen to keep company with venal women. I've never felt guilty about putting any off or refusing to fight to lure back any tempted away. I'd die for you. Give you everything I have. That's how powerful you are.'

Emma whispered his name, traced feather-light fingers over

his hard, angular jaw. She relaxed down onto him, nestling her head into the cosy cleft on his shoulder.

'What happens in the end?'

'What?' she whispered, frowning against his face.

'I didn't finish the novel. Does Darcy marry Elizabeth? I imagine so.'

She giggled, with sheer silly joy, her body bumping against his, causing the proof of his noble restraint to burn, like a hot, hard log, into her belly. 'Of course! He's an honourable gentleman who acknowledges the error of his arrogant ways. He kindly pays debts incurred by a wastrel relation of Elizabeth's and wins her love and respect.'

'Sounds like a fantasy…'

She recognised the wry laughter in his voice. 'That's why I liked it so. I liked fantasising that one day I would happily marry such a worthy man.'

From the edge of an eye, she watched the corners of his mouth lift, his long, lush lashes fall. He rolled over slowly, holding her close until she was turned completely onto her back. Idly he braced himself over her.

A trusting golden gaze merged with silver gleaming down at her as a knuckle brushed slowly, rhythmically against her cheek. 'Do you fantasise a lot?' he asked, something in his honeyed, husky tone sending those thrilling tremors hurtling through her again.

'I…I used to daydream about the characters in novels…pretend them real. I used to like to go elsewhere in my head,' she self-consciously revealed.

'Well, next time you go…every time…take me with you?' The request was accompanied by an appealing smile. 'Shall we now fantasise that you're happily to marry a worthy man?'

Pearly lids veiled topaz eyes and a sultry smile curved her soft mouth. 'I thought you were too mature to still play games.'

'Oh, some games improve with maturity.'

'Who sets the rules?' she asked in a tiny, breathy voice.

'You do.'

'Always?'

'Always.'

'But…my rules are that I'd only happily marry a worthy man

I adore, a man who will give me sweet, tender loving, for so I've been promised.'

'And so it shall be...I solemnly swear...until you want more.'

At her quick, startled look, a soundless laugh preceded gentle reassurance. 'You'll know when... Shall I tell you my favourite fantasy?' he offered casually. He could see a confusion of innocent curiosity and suspicion in her beautifully limpid eyes, but, after an indecisive moment, she nodded. 'On each wedding anniversary I should like it if you stole Shah and fled to the woods...'

'Will you be angry when you chase me?' she asked with sweet solemnity.

'Only if you want me to be... You make the rules.'

Emma slid a small hand up into fine ivory hair, gently touched the wound beneath his fringe, grazed the backs of her fingers along the stubble on his shady jaw, feeling utterly at peace in her love and trust and loyalty.

'Whatever happened to my wicked silver squire?' she teased.

'Whatever happened to my fiery wildcat?'

She drew his head down slowly until their mouths nearly touched, wanting to prove her adoration his way. 'Take me back now to find them, Richard...'

* * * * *

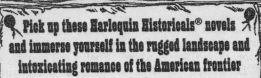

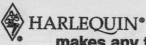

Travel to the British Isles
and behold the romance and
adventure within the pages of these
Harlequin Historicals® novels

ON SALE JANUARY 2002

MY LADY'S TRUST
by **Julia Justiss**
(Regency England, 1812)
A society lady fakes her own death and discovers
true love with an eligible earl!

DRAGON'S DOWER
by **Catherine Archer**
(Medieval England, 1200)
Book #1 of *The Brotherhood of the Dragon* series
By the king's decree a brave knight must marry
the daughter of his fiercest foe....

ON SALE FEBRUARY 2002

HIS LADY FAIR
by **Margo Maguire**
(Medieval England, 1429)
A world-weary spy becomes embroiled in intrigue—
and forbidden passion!

 Harlequin Historicals®
Historical Romantic Adventure!

HHMED22

If you enjoyed what you just read,
then we've got an offer you can't resist!

Take 2
bestselling novels FREE!
Plus get a FREE surprise gift!

Clip this page and mail it to The Best of the Best™

IN U.S.A.	IN CANADA
3010 Walden Ave.	P.O. Box 609
P.O. Box 1867	Fort Erie, Ontario
Buffalo, N.Y. 14240-1867	L2A 5X3

YES! Please send me 2 free Best of the Best™ novels and my free surprise gift. After receiving them, if I don't wish to receive anymore, I can return the shipping statement marked cancel. If I don't cancel, I will receive 4 brand-new novels every month, before they're available in stores! In the U.S.A., bill me at the bargain price of $4.24 plus 25¢ shipping and handling per book and applicable sales tax, if any*. In Canada, bill me at the bargain price of $4.74 plus 25¢ shipping and handling per book and applicable taxes**. That's the complete price and a savings of over 15% off the cover prices—what a great deal! I understand that accepting the 2 free books and gift places me under no obligation ever to buy any books. I can always return a shipment and cancel at any time. Even if I never buy another book from The Best of the Best™, the 2 free books and gift are mine to keep forever.

185 MEN DFNG
385 MEN DFNH

Name	(PLEASE PRINT)	
Address	Apt.#	
City	State/Prov.	Zip/Postal Code

* Terms and prices subject to change without notice. Sales tax applicable in N.Y.
** Canadian residents will be charged applicable provincial taxes and GST.
All orders subject to approval. Offer limited to one per household and not valid to current Best of the Best™ subscribers.
® are registered trademarks of Harlequin Enterprises Limited.

BOB01   ©1998 Harlequin Enterprises Limited

*Together for the first time
in one Collector's Edition!*

New York Times bestselling authors

Barbara Delinsky

Catherine Coulter

Linda Howard

Forever Yours

**A special trade-size volume containing three
complete novels that showcase the passion,
imagination and stunning power that these
talented authors are famous for.**

Coming to your favorite retail outlet in December 2001.

HARLEQUIN®
Makes any time special ®

Visit us at www.eHarlequin.com   PHFY